CHAINS

CHAINS

LESSER NOVELS AND STORIES BY

THEODORE DREISER

New York

BONI & LIVERIGHT

1927

c. S.

Printed in the United States of America

FOREWORD

The inevitabilities of our fate are: Love and hope, fear and death, interwoven with our lacks, inhibitions, jealousies and greeds.

c.1

CONTENTS

CHAINS

I

SANCTUARY

I

PRIMARILY, there were the conditions under which she was brought to fifteen years of age: the crowded, scummy tenements; the narrow green-painted halls with their dim gas-jets, making the entrance look more like that of a morgue than a dwelling-place; the dirty halls and rooms with their green or blue or brown walls painted to save the cost of paper; the bare wooden floors, long since saturated with every type of grease and filth from oleomargarine and suet leaked from cheap fats or meats, to beer and whiskey and tobacco-juice. A little occasional scrubbing by some would-be hygienic tenant was presumed to keep or make clean some of the chambers and halls.

And then the streets outside—any of the streets by which she had ever been surrounded—block upon block of other red, bare, commonplace tenements crowded to the doors with human life, the space before them sped over by noisy, gassy trucks and vehicles of all kinds. And stifling in summer, dusty and icy in winter; decorated on occasion by stray cats and dogs, pawing in ashcans, watched over by lordly policemen, and always running with people, people, people—who made their living heaven only knows how, existing in such a manner as their surroundings suggested.

In this atmosphere were always longshoremen, wagon-drivers, sweepers of floors, washers of dishes, waiters, janitors, workers in laundries, factories—mostly in indifferent or decadent or despairing conditions. And all of these people existed, in so far as she ever knew, upon that mysterious, evanescent and fluctuating something known as the weekly wage.

Always about her there had been drunkenness, fighting, complaining, sickness or death; the police coming in, and arresting one and another; the gas man, the rent man, the furniture man, hammering at doors for their due—and not getting it—in due time the undertaker also arriving amid a great clamor, as though lives were the most precious things imaginable.

It is entirely conceivable that in viewing or in meditating upon an atmosphere such as this, one might conclude that no good could come out of it. What! a dung-heap grow a flower? Exactly, and often, a flower—but not to grow to any glorious maturity probably. Nevertheless a flower of the spirit at least might have its beginnings there. And if it shrank or withered in the miasmatic atmosphere—well, conceivably, that might be normal, although in reality all flowers thus embedded in infancy do not so wither. There are flowers and flowers.

Viewing Madeleine Kinsella at the ages of five, seven, eleven and thirteen even, it might have been conceded that she was a flower of sorts—admittedly not a brave, lustrous one of the orchid or gardenia persuasion, but a flower nevertheless. Her charm was simpler, more retiring, less vivid than is usually accorded the compliment of beauty. She was never rosy, never colorful in the high sense, never daring or aggressive. Always, from her infancy on, she seemed to herself and others to be slipping about the corners and out-of-the-way places of life, avoiding it, staring at it with wide, lamblike eyes, wondering at things, often fearfully.

Her face, always delicately oval and pale, was not of the force which attracted. Her eyes, a milkish blue-gray with a suggestion of black in the iris, her hair black, her hands long-fingered and slim, were not of a type which would appeal to the raw youth of her world. Unconsciously, and ever, her slender, longish body sank into graceful poses. Beside the hard, garish, colorful, strident types of her neighborhoods—the girls whom the boys liked—she was not fascinating, and yet, contemplated at odd moments as she grew, she was appealing enough—at times beautiful.

What most affected her youth and her life was the internal condition of her family, the poverty and general worthlessness of her parents. They were as poor as their poorest neighbors, and quarrelsome, unhappy and mean-spirited into the bargain. Her father came dimly into her understanding at somewhere near her seventh or eighth year as an undersized, contentious and drunken and wordy man, always more or less out of a job, irritated with her mother and her sister and brother, and always, as her mother seemed to think, a little the worse for drink.

"You're a liar! You're a liar! You're a liar! You're a liar!"—how well she remembered this sing-song echoing reiteration of his, in whatever basement or hole they were living at the time! "You're a liar! I never did it! You're a liar! I wasn't there!"

Her mother, often partially intoxicated or morose because of her own ills, was only too willing to rejoin in kind. Her elder sister and brother, much more agreeable in their way and as much put upon as herself, were always coming in or running out somewhere and staying while the storm lasted; while she, shy and always a little frightened, seemed to look upon it all as unavoidable, possibly even essential. The world was always so stern, so mysterious, so non-understandable to Madeleine.

Again it might be, and often was, "Here, you, you brat, go an' get me a can o' beer! Gwan, now!" which she did quickly and fearfully enough, running to the nearest wretched corner saloon with the "can" or "growler," her slim little fingers closed tightly over the five-cent piece or dime entrusted to her, her eyes taking in the wonders and joys of the street even as she ran. She was so small at the time that her little arms were unable to reach quite the level of the bar, and she had to accept the aid of the bartender or some drinker. Then she would patiently wait while one of them teased her as to her size or until the beer was handed down.

Once, and once only, three "bad boys," knowing what she was going for and how wretched and shabby was her father, not able to revenge himself on any one outside his family, had seized her en route, forced open her hand and run away with the dime, leaving her to return fearsomely to her father, rubbing her eyes, and to be struck and abused soundly and told to fight—"Blank-blank you, what the hell are you good for if you can't do that?"

Only the vile language and the defensive soberness of her mother at the time saved her from a worse fate. As for the boys who had stolen the money, they only received curses and awful imprecations, which harmed no one.

Wretched variations of this same existence were endured by the other two members of the family, her brother Frank and her sister Tina.

The former was a slim and nervous youth, given to fits of savage temper like his father and not to be ordered and controlled exactly as his father would have him. At times, as Madeleine recalled, he appeared terribly resentful of the conditions that surrounded him and cursed and swore and even threatened to leave; at other times he was placid enough, at least not inclined to share the dreadful scenes which no one could avoid where her father was.

At the age of twelve or thirteen he secured work in a box-factory somewhere and for a while brought his wages home. But often there was no breakfast or dinner for him, and when his father and mother were deep in their cups or quarreling things were so generally neglected that even where home ties were strong no one of any worldly experience could have endured them, and he ran away.

His mother was always complaining of "the lumbago"

and of not being able to get up, even when he and Tina were working and bringing home a portion of their weekly wage or all of it. If she did, it was only to hover over the wretched cookstove and brew herself a little tea and complain as before.

Madeleine had early, in her ignorant and fearsome way, tried to help, but she did not always know how and her mother was either too ill or too disgruntled with life to permit her to assist, had she been able.

As it had been with Frank so it was with Tina, only it came sooner.

When Madeleine was only five Tina was a grown girl of ten, with yellow hair and a pretty, often smiling face, and was already working somewhere—in a candy store— for a dollar and a half a week. Later, when Madeleine was eight and Tina thirteen, the latter had graduated to a button-works and was earning three.

There was something rather admirable and yet disturbing connected dimly with Tina in Madeleine's mind, an atmosphere of rebelliousness and courage which she had never possessed and which she could not have described, lacking as she did a mind that registered the facts of life clearly. She only saw Tina, pretty and strong, coming and going from her ninth to her thirteenth year, refusing to go for beer at her father's order and being cursed for it, even struck at or thrown at by him, sometimes by her mother, and often standing at the foot of the stairs after work hours or on a Sunday afternoon or evening, looking at the crowded street or walking up and down with other girls and boys, when her mother wanted her to be doing things in the house—sweeping, washing dishes, making beds— dreary, gray tasks all.

"Fixin' your hair again! Fixin' your hair again! Fixin' your hair again!" she could hear her father screaming whenever she paused before the one cracked mirror to arrange her hair. "Always in front of that blank-blank mirror fixin' her hair! If you don't get away from in front of it

I'll throw you an' the mirror in the street! What the hell
are you always fixin' your hair for? Say? What're you
always fixin' your hair for? Say! What? What're you
always fixin' your hair for?"

But Tina was never cast down apparently, only silent.
At times she sang and walked with an air. She dressed herself as attractively as possible, as if with the few things she
had she was attempting to cast off the burden of the life by
which she was surrounded. Always she was hiding things
away from the others, never wanting them to touch anything
of hers. And how she had hated her father as she grew,
in bitter moments calling him a "sot" and a "fool."

Tina had never been very obedient, refusing to go to
church or to do much of anything about the house. Whenever her father and mother were drinking or fighting she
would slip away and stay with some girl in the neighborhood that she knew. And in spite of all this squalor and
misery and the fact that they moved often and the food was
bad, Tina, once she was twelve or thirteen, always seemed
able to achieve an agreeable appearance.

Madeleine often remembered her in a plaid skirt she had
got somewhere, which looked beautiful on her, and a little
gilt pin which she wore at her neck. And she had a way
of doing her yellow hair high on her head, which had stuck
in Madeleine's mind perhaps because of her father's rude
comments on it.

II

It is not surprising that Madeleine came to her twelfth
and thirteenth years without any real understanding of the
great world about her and without any definite knowledge
or skill. Her drunken mother was now more or less dependent upon her, her father having died of pneumonia and
her brother and sister having disappeared to do for themselves.

Aside from petty beginners' tasks in shops or stores, or

assisting her mother at washing or cleaning, there was little that she could do at first. Mrs. Kinsella, actually compelled by the need for rent or food or fuel after a time, would get occasional work in a laundry or kitchen or at scrubbing or window-cleaning, but not for long. The pleasure of drink would soon rob her of that.

At these tasks Madeleine helped until she secured work in a candy factory in her thirteenth year at the wage of three-thirty a week. But even with this little money paid in regularly there was no assurance that her mother would add sufficient to it to provide either food or warmth. Betimes, and when Madeleine was working, her mother cheered her all too obvious sorrows with the bottle, and at nights or week-ends rewarded Madeleine with a gabble which was all the more painful because no material comfort came with it.

The child actually went hungry at times. Usually, after a few drinks, her mother would begin to weep and recite her past ills: a process which reduced her timorous and very sympathetic daughter to complete misery. In sheer desperation the child sought for some new way in her own mind. A reduction in the working-force of the candy factory, putting her back in the ranks of the work-seekers once more, and a neighbor perceiving her wretched state and suggesting that some extra helpers were wanted in a department store at Christmastime, she applied there, but so wretched were her clothes by now that she was not even considered.

Then a man who had a restaurant in a nearby street gave her mother and Madeleine positions as dishwashers, but he was compelled to discharge her mother, although he wished to retain Madeleine. From this last, however, because of the frightening attentions of the cook, she had to flee, and without obtaining a part of the small pittance which was due her. Again, and because in times past she had aided her mother to clean in one place and another, she was able to get a place as servant in a family.

Those who know anything of the life of a domestic know

how thoroughly unsatisfactory it is—the leanness, the lack
of hope. As a domestic, wherever she was—and she obtained no superior places for the time being—she had only
the kitchen for her chief chamber or a cubby-hole under the
roof. Here, unless she was working elsewhere in the house
or chose to visit her mother occasionally, she was expected
to remain. Pots and pans and scrubbing and cleaning and
bed-making were her world. If any one aside from her
mother ever wanted to see her (which was rare) he or she
could only come into the kitchen, an ugly and by day
inconvenient realm.

She had, as she soon came to see, no privileges whatsoever. In the morning she was expected to be up before
any one else, possibly after working late the night before.
Breakfast had to be served for others before she herself
could eat—what was left. Then came the sweeping and
cleaning. In one place which she obtained in her fifteenth
year the husband annoyed her so, when his wife was not
looking, that she had to leave; in another it was the son.
By now she was becoming more attractive, although by no
means beautiful or daring.

But wherever she was and whatever she was doing, she
could not help thinking of her mother and Tina and Frank
and her father, and of the grim necessities and errors and
vices which had seemed to dominate them. Neither her
brother nor her sister did she ever see again. Her mother,
she felt (and this was due to a sensitiveness and a sympathy
which she could not possibly overcome), she would have
with her for the rest of her days unless, like the others,
she chose to run away.

Daily her mother was growing more inadequate and less
given to restraint or consideration. As "bad" as she was,
Madeleine could not help thinking what a "hard" time she
had had. From whatever places she obtained work in these
days (and it was not often any more) she was soon discharged, and then she would come inquiring after Made-

leine, asking to be permitted to see her. Naturally, her shabby dress and shawl and rag of a hat, as well as her wastrel appearance, were an affront to any well-ordered household. Once in her presence, whenever Madeleine was permitted to see her, she would begin either a cozening or a lachrymose account of her great needs.

"It's out o' oil I am, me dear," or "Wurra, I have no wood" or "bread" or "meat"—never drink. "Ye won't let yer pore old mother go cold or hungry, now, will ye? That's the good girl now. Fifty cents now, if ye have it, me darlin', or a quarter, an' I'll not be troublin' ye soon again. Even a dime, if ye can spare me no more. God'll reward ye. I'll have work o' me own to-morra. That's the good girl now—ye won't let me go away without anything."

Oscillating between shame and sympathy, her daughter would take from the little she had and give it to her, tremulous for fear the disturbing figure would prove her undoing. Then the old woman would go out, lurching sometimes in her cups, and disappear, while an observant fellow servant was probably seeing and reporting to the mistress, who, of course, did not want her to come there and so told the girl, or, more practical still, discharged her.

Thus from her fourteenth to her sixteenth year she was shunted from house to house and from shop to shop, always in the vain hope that this time her mother might let her alone.

And at the very same time, life, sweetened by the harmonies of youth in the blood, was calling—that exterior life which promised everything because so far it had given nothing. The little simple things of existence, the very ordinary necessities of clothing and ornament, with which the heart of youth and the inherent pride of appearance are gratified, had a value entirely disproportionate to their worth. Yes, already she had turned the age wherein the chemic harmonies in youth begin to sing, thought to thought, color to color, dream to dream. She was being touched by the promise of life itself.

And then, as was natural, love in the guise of youth, a rather sophisticated gallant somewhat above the world in which she was moving, appeared and paid his all but worthless court to her. He was physically charming, the son of a grocer of some means in the vicinity in which she was working, a handsome youth with pink cheeks and light hair and blue eyes, and vanity enough for ten. Because she was shy and pretty he became passingly interested in her.

"Oh, I saw you cleaning the windows yesterday," this with a radiant, winning smile; or "You must live down toward Blake Street. I see you going down that way once in a while."

Madeleine acknowledged rather shamefacedly that it was true. That so dashing a boy should be interested in her was too marvelous.

In the evenings, or at any time, it was easy for a youth of his skill and *savoir-faire* to pick her out of the bobbing stream of humanity in which she occasionally did errands or visited her mother in her shabby room, and to suggest that he be permitted to call upon her. Or, failing that, because of her mother's shabby quarters and her mother herself, that the following Sunday would be ideal for an outing to one of those tawdry, noisy beaches to which he liked to go with other boys and girls in a car.

A single trip to Wonderland, a single visit to one of its halls where music sounded to the splash of the waves and where he did his best to teach her to dance, a single meal in one of its gaudy, noisy restaurants, a taste of its whirly pleasures, and a new color and fillip were given to hope, a new and seemingly realizable dream of happiness implanted in her young mind. The world was happier than she had thought, or could be made so; not all people fought and screamed at each other. There were such things as tenderness, soft words, sweet words.

But the way of so sophisticated a youth with a maid was brief and direct. His mind was of that order which finds in the freshness of womankind a mere passing delight, something to be deflowered and then put aside. He was a part of a group that secured its happiness in rifling youth, the youth of those whose lives were so dull and bleak that a few words of kindness, a little change of scene, the mere proximity of experience and force such as they had never known, were pay ample for anything which they might give or do.

And of these Madeleine was one.

Never having had anything in her own life, the mere thought of a man so vigorous and handsome, one with knowledge enough to show her more of life than she had ever dreamed of, to take her to places of color and light, to assure her that she was fitted for better things even though they were not immediately forthcoming, was sufficient to cause her to place faith where it was least worthy of being placed. To win his way there was even talk of marriage later on, that love should be generous and have faith—and then—

III

Plain-clothesman Amundsen, patrolling hawk-like the region of Fourteenth and K streets, not so far from Blake, where Madeleine had lived for a time, was becoming interested in and slightly suspicious of a new face.

For several days at odd hours, he had seen a girl half-slinking, half-brazening her way through a region the very atmosphere of which was blemishing to virtue. To be sure, he had not yet seen her speak to any one; nor was there that in her glance or manner which caused him to feel that she might.

Still—with the assurance of his authority and his past skill in trapping many he followed discreetly, seeing where she went, how she lingered for awhile nervously, then returned as she had come. She was very young, not more than seventeen.

He adjusted his tie and collar and decided to attempt his skill.

"Excuse me, Miss. Out for a little stroll? So am I. Mind my walking along with you a little way? Wouldn't like to come and have a drink, would you? I work in an automobile place over here in Grey Street, and I'm just off for the afternoon. Live here in the neighborhood?"

Madeleine surveyed this stranger with troubled eyes. Since the day her youthful lover had deserted her, and after facing every conceivable type of ill, but never being willing to confess or fall back upon her drunken, dreaming mother for aid, she had tested every device. The necessities and expenses incident to a prospective, and to her degrading state, as well as the continued care of her mother, had compelled her, as she had finally seen it, to come to this —for a time anyhow. A street girl, finding her wandering and crying, had taken her in hand and shown her, after aiding her for weeks, how to make her way.

Her burden that she feared so much was artificially if ruthlessly and criminally disposed of. Then she was shown the way of the streets until she could gain a new foothold in life; only, as she had since learned, it was difficult for her to accommodate herself to this fell traffic. She was not of it spiritually. She really did not intend to continue in it; it was just a temporary makeshift, born of fear and a dumb despair.

But neither Detective Amundsen nor the law was ready to believe that. To the former she seemed as worthless as any—one of those curious, uncared-for flowers never understood by the dull.

In a nearby café she had listened to his inquiries, the fact that he had a room in a nearby hotel, or could secure one. Contemning a fate which drove her to such favors, and fully resolved to leave it soon, to make something better of her life in the future, she went with him.

Then came the scarring realization that he was an officer of the law, a cynical, contemptuous hawk smirking over her tears and her explanations. It was absolutely nothing to him that she was so young and could scarcely have been as hardened as he pretended. She was compelled to walk through the streets with him to the nearest police station, while he nodded to or stopped to explain to passing brothers of the cloth the nature of his latest conquest.

There was the registering of her under the false name that she chose, rather than be exposed under her true one, before a brusque and staring sergeant in shirtsleeves; a cell with a wooden bench, the first she had ever known; a matron who searched her; then a ride somewhere in a closed vehicle, and the usual swift and confusing arraignment before a judge whose glance was seemingly so cold that it was frightening.

"Nellie Fitzpatrick; Officer Amundsen, Eighth Precinct."

The friend who had taught her the ways of the streets had warned her that if caught and arrested it might mean months of incarceration in some institution, the processes or corrective meaning of which she did not quite comprehend. All that she had grasped fully was that it meant a severance from her freedom, the few little things, pitiful as they were, that she could call her own. And now here she was, in the clutches of the law, and with no one to defend her.

The testimony of the officer was as it had been in hundreds of cases before this; he had been walking his beat and she had accosted him, as usual.

There being no legal alternative, the magistrate had held her for sentence, pending investigation, and the investigation proving, as it only could, that her life would be better were some corrective measures applied to it, she was sent away. She had never had any training worthy the name.

Her mother was an irresponsible inebriate. A few months in some institution where she could be taught some trade or craft would be best.

And so it was that for a period of a year she was turned over to the care of the Sisterhood of the Good Shepherd.

IV

The gray and bony walls of that institution starkly dominated one of the barest and most unprepossessing regions of the city. Its northern façade fronted a stone-yard, beyond which were the rocks of the racing Sound and a lighthouse. To the east, rocks and the river, a gray expanse in winter picked over by gulls, mourned over by the horns of endless craft. To the south, bare coal-yards, wagon-yards, tenements.

Twice weekly, sentenced delinquents of various ages— the "children," of whom Madeleine was one; the "girls," ranging from eighteen to thirty; the "women," ranging from thirty to fifty; and the old people, ranging from fifty until the last years of life—were brought here in an all but air-tight cage, boxed like a great circus van, and with only small barred air-holes at the top. Inside the van were bare, hard benches, one against either wall. A representative of the probation and control system of the city, a gaunt female of many years, sat within; also an officer of such prodigious proportions that the mere sight of him might well raise the inquiry of why so much unnecessary luggage. For amusement in dull hours he smoothed his broad mouth with the back of his red, hairy hand, and dreamed of bygone days.

The institution itself was operated by a Mother Superior and thirty nuns, all of the order mentioned, all expert in their separate ways in cooking, housekeeping, laundering, buying, lace-making, teaching, and a half dozen other practical or applied arts.

Within the institution were separate wings or sections for

each of the four groups before mentioned, sections in which each had its separate working, eating, sleeping and playing rooms. Only one thing was shared in common: the daily, and often twice or thrice daily, religious ceremonies in the great chapel, a lofty, magi-decorated and be-altared and be-candled chamber, whose tall, thin spire surmounted with a cross might easily be seen from many of the chambers in which the different groups worked. There were masses in the mornings, vespers and late prayers in the afternoons, often late prayers at night or on holidays, when additional services of one kind and another were held. To the religious-minded these were of course consoling. To the contrary-minded they became at times a strain.

Always, and over all the work and all the routine relaxations or pleasures of the institution, there hung the grim insistence of the law, its executive arm, upon order, seemliness, and, if not penance, at least a servility of mind which was the equivalent thereof. Let the voices of the nuns be never so soft, their footfalls light, their manners courteous, their ways gentle, persuasive, sympathetic, their mood tender; back of it all lay the shadow of the force which could forthwith return any or all to the rough hands of the police, the stern and not-to-be-evaded dictum of the courts.

This, much more than any look of disappointment or displeasure, if such were ever necessary, spoke to these delinquents or victims, whatever their mood, and quieted them in their most rebellious hours. Try as they would, they could not but remember that it was the law that had placed them here and now detained them. That there reigned here peace, order, sweetness and harmony, was well enough, comforting in cases, yet and always the life here had obviously a two-fold base: one the power of the law itself, the other the gentle, appealing, beautiful suasion of the nuns.

But to so inexperienced and as yet unreasoning a child as Madeleine all of this savored at this time of but one thing:

the sharp, crude, inconsiderate and uninquiring forces of law or life, which seemed never to stop and inquire how or why, but only to order how, and that without mercy. Like some frightened animal faced by a terrifying enemy, she had thus far been able to think only of some darksome corner into which she might slip and hide, a secret place so inconspicuous and minute that the great savage world without would not trouble or care to follow.

And well enough the majority of the Sisterhood, especially those in immediate authority over her, understood the probable direction and ramifications of her present thoughts.

They knew her mood, for had they not during years past dealt with many such? And stern as was the law, they were not unmindful of her welfare. So long as she was willing and obedient there was but one thing more: that somehow her troubled or resentful or congealed and probably cruelly injured mind should be wooed from its blind belief in the essential injustice of life, to be made to feel, as they themselves were ready to believe, that all paths were not closed, all forces not essentially dark or evil.

For them there was hope of sorts for all, a way out, and many—even she—might find ways and means of facing life, better possibly than any she had ever known.

V

Sister St. Agnes, for instance, who controlled the spotlessly clean but barnlike and bleak room in which were a hundred machines for the sewing of shirtwaists, was a creature of none too fortunate a history herself.

Returning at the age of eighteen and at the death of her father from a convent in which she had been placed by him in order to escape the atmosphere of a home which he himself had found unsatisfactory, she had found a fashionable mother leading a life of which she could scarcely conceive, let alone accept. The taint, the subterfuge, the self-indulgent waste, had as soon sickened her as had the streets Madeleine.

Disappointed, she felt herself after a time incapable of enduring it and had fled, seeking first to make her way in a world which offered only meagre wages and a barren life to those incapable of enduring its rugged and often shameless devices; later, again wearied of her own trials, she had returned to the convent in which she had been trained and asked to be schooled for service there. Finding the life too simple for a nature grown more rugged, she had asked to be, and had been, transferred to the House of the Good Shepherd, finding there for the first time, in this institution, duties and opportunities which somehow matched her ideals.

And by the same token the Mother Superior of this same institution, Mother St. Bertha, who often came through and inquired into the story of each one, was of a history and of an order of mind which was not unlike that of Sister St. Agnes, only it had even more of genuine pathos and suffering in it. The daughter of a shoe manufacturer, she had seen her father fail, her mother die of consumption, a favorite brother drink and carouse until he finally fell under the blight of disease and died. The subsequent death of her father, to whom she had devoted her years, and the failing of her own dreams of a personal love, had saddened her, and she sought out and was admitted to this order in the hope that she, too, might still make especial use of a life that promised all too little in the world outside.

Her great comfort was in having some one or something to love, the satisfaction of feeling that lives which otherwise might have come to nothing had by some service of hers been lifted to a better state. And in that thought she worked here daily, going about among those incarcerated in different quarters, seeing to it that their tasks were not too severe, their comforts and hopes, where hope still remained, in nowise betrayed.

But to Madeleine at first the solemn habits of the nuns, as well as the gray gingham apron she had to don, the grayer woolen dress, the severe manner in which she had to dress her hair, her very plain shoes, the fact that she had to rise at six-thirty, attend mass and then breakfast at eight, work from eight-thirty to twelve-thirty, and again from one-thirty to four; lunch regularly at twelve-thirty and sup at six, attend a form of prayer service at four-thirty, play at simple games with her new companions between five and six and again between seven and nine, and then promptly retire to a huge sleeping-ward set with small white iron beds in long rows, and lit, after the retiring bell had sounded, by small oil cups or candles burning faintly before various images, all smacked of penance, the more disturbing because it was strange, a form of personal control which she had not sought and could not at once accept.

Nor could she help thinking that some severer form of punishment was yet to be meted out to her, or might ensue by reason of one unavoidable error or another. Life had always been so with her. But, once here a time, things proved not so bad.

The large workroom with its hundred machines and its tall windows, which afforded a stark view of the coal-pockets to the south, and the river with its boats and gulls, proved not unpleasing. The clean, bright windows, polished floors and walls—washed and cleaned by the inmates themselves, the nuns not disdaining to do their share—and the habits of the Sisters, their white-fringed hoods, black robes and clinking beads and their silent tread and low speech, impressed her greatly.

The fact that there was no severe reproof for any failure to comprehend at first, but only slow and patient explanations of simple things, not difficult in themselves to do; that aside from the routine duties, the marching in line with hands crossed over breast and head up, as well as genuflections at mass, prayers before and after meals, at rising and on retiring and at the peal of the Angelus, morning, noon and night, there was no real oppression, finally caused her to like it.

The girls who were here with her, shy or silent or cold or indifferent at first, and each with her world of past experiences, contacts and relationships locked in her heart, were still, placed as they were elbow to elbow at work, at meals, at prayer, at retiring, incapable of not achieving some kind of remote fellowship which eventually led to speech and confidences.

Thus the young girl who sat next at her right in the sewing-room—Viola Patters by name, a brave, blonde, cheerful little thing—although she had endured much that might be called ill-fortune, was still intensely interested in life.

By degrees and as they worked the two reached an understanding. Viola confessed that her father, who was a non-union painter by trade, had always worked well enough when he could get work, but that he managed badly and could not always get it. Her mother was sickly and they were very poor and there were many children.

Viola had first worked in a box-factory, where she had been able to earn only three dollars or less at piece work— "pasting corners," as she described it—and once she had been sworn at and even thrown away from a table at which she had been working because she didn't do it right, and then she quit. Then her father in turn swearing at her for her "uppishness," she had got work in a five-and-ten-cent store, where she had received three dollars a week and a commission of one per cent on her sales, which were not sufficient to yield more than a dollar more. Then she had secured a better place in a department store at five dollars a week, and there it was that she had come by the handsome boy who had caused her so much trouble.

He was a taxi-driver, who always had a car at his disposal when he worked, only it was very seldom that he cared to work. Although he married her swiftly enough and took her away from her family, still he had not supported her very well, and shortly after they were married he was arrested and accused with two others of stealing a machine and selling it, and after months and months of jail life he had been sentenced to three years in the penitentiary.

In the meantime he had called upon her to aid him, pressed her to raise sums of which she had never previously dreamed—and by ways of which she had never previously dreamed—was pleaded with, all but ordered—and still she loved him. And then in executing the "how" of it she had been picked up by the police and sent here, as had Madeleine, only she never told, not even to Madeleine, what the police had never discovered—that at the suggestion of her first love she had included robbery among her arts.

"But I don't care," she had whispered finally as they worked. "He was good to me, anyhow, when he had work. He was crazy about me, and he liked to go places and dance and eat and see shows when he had money, and he always took me. Gee, the times we've had! And if he wants me to stick to him when he gets out, I will. He ain't half as bad as some. Gee, you oughta hear some of the girls talk!"

And so it was finally that Madeleine was induced to tell her story.

There were other girls here who, once this bond of sympathy was struck, were keen enough to tell their tales— sad, unfortunate, harried lives all—and somehow the mere telling of them restored to Madeleine some of her earlier faint confidence or interest in life. It was "bad," but it was vivid. For in spite of their unfortunate beginnings, the slime in which primarily and without any willing of their own they had been embedded and from which nearly all were seeking to crawl upwards, and bravely enough, they had heart for and faith in life.

In all cases, apparently, love was their star as well as their bane. They thought chiefly of the joy that might be

had in joining their lives with some man or being out in
the free world, working again possibly, at least in touch
in some feeble way with the beauty and gayety of life, as
beauty and gayety manifested themselves to them.

And so by degrees, the crash of her own original hopes
echoing less and less loudly in the distance, the pain of
her great shame and rude awakening passed farther and
farther from her. The smoothness and regularity of this
austere life, indifferent as it seemed at times, consoled her
by its very security and remoteness from the world. It
was lean and spare, to be sure, but it offered safety and
rest to the mind and heart. Now, rising in her dim, silent
ward of a morning, repeating her instructed prayers, marching in silence to chapel, to breakfast, to work, hearing only
the soft hum of the machines, marching again to chapel,
playing each day, but not too noisily, and finally retiring
in the same ordered and silent way to her tiny bed, she was
soothed and healed.

And yet, or perhaps because of this, she could not help
thinking of the clangor and crash of the world without. It
had been grim and painful to her, but in its rude, brutal way
it had been alive. The lighted streets at night! The cars!
That dancing pavilion in which once she had been taught
to dance by the great blue sea! The vanished touches of
her faithless lover's hands—his kisses—brief, so soon over!
Where was he now in the great strange world outside?
With whom? What was she like? And would he tire of
her as quickly? Treat her as badly? Where was Tina?
Frank? Her mother? What had happened to her mother?
Not a word had she heard.

To Sister St. Agnes, after a time, sensing her to be generous, faithful, patient, she had confided all concerning
herself and her mother, crying on her shoulder, and the
Sister had promised to learn what she could. But the investigation proving that her mother had been sent to the work-
house, she deemed it best to say nothing for the present.
Madeleine would find her quickly enough on returning to

the world. Why cloud the new budding life with so shameful a memory?

VI

And then once more, in due time, and with the memory of these things clinging fast to her, she was sent forth into the world, not quite as poorly-armed as before, perhaps, but still with the limited equipment which her own innate disposition and comprehension compelled.

After many serious and presumably wise injunctions as to the snares and pitfalls of this world, and accompanied by a black-habited nun, who took her direct to one of those moral and religious families whose strict adherence to the tenets of this particular faith was held to provide an ideal example, she was left to her own devices and the type of work she had previously followed, the nuns themselves being hard put to it to discover anything above the most menial forms of employment for their various charges. Theirs was a type of schooling and training which did not rise above a theory of morality requiring not so much skill as faith and blind obedience.

And again, here, as in the institution itself, the idea of a faith, a religion, a benign power above that of man and seeking his welfare, surrounded her as the very air itself or as an aura, although she personally was by no means ready to accept it, never having given it serious thought.

Everywhere here, as in the institution itself, were little images or colored pictures of saints, their brows circled by stars or crowns, their hands holding sceptres or lilies, their bodies arrayed in graceful and soothing robes of white, blue, pink and gold. Their faces were serene, their eyes benignly contemplative, yet to Madeleine they were still images only, pretty and graceful, even comforting, but at so great variance to life as she knew it as to be little more than pretty pictures.

In the great church which they attended, and to which

they persuaded her to accompany them, were more of these same candle-lit pictures of saints, images and altars starred with candles, many or few, at which she was wont to stare in wonder and awe. The vestments of the priest and the acolytes, the white-and-gold and red-and-gold of the chasuble and the stole and the cope, the gold and silver crosses, chalices and winecups, overawed her inexperienced and somewhat impressionable mind without convincing it of the immanence of superior forces whose significance or import she could in nowise guess. God, God, God—she heard of Him and the passion and death of the self-sacrificing Lord Jesus.

And here, as there, the silence, the order, the cleanliness and regularity, as well as simplicity, were the things which most invested her reason and offered the greatest contrasts to her old life.

She had not known or sensed the significance of these things before. Now, day by day, like the dripping of water, the ticking of time, they made an impression, however slight. Routine, routine, routine, and the habit and order and color of a vast and autocratic religion, made their lasting impression upon her.

And yet, in spite of an occasional supervisory visit on the part of one or other of the nuns of the probation department, she was not only permitted but compelled to work out her life as best she might, and upon such wages as she could command or devise. For all the prayers and the good-will of the nuns, life was as insistent and driving as ever. It did not appear to be so involved with religion. In spite of the admonitions of the church, the family for whom she was working saw little more in its religious obligation than that she should be housed and fed according to her material merits. If she wished to better herself, as she soon very clearly saw she must, she would have to develop a skill which she did not now have and which, once developed, would make her of small use here. At the same time, if the months spent in the institution had conveyed to her the reasonableness of making something better of her life than hitherto she had been able to do, the world, pleasure, hope, clanged as insistently and as wooingly as ever before.

But how? How? was the great problem. Hers was no resourceful, valiant soul, capable of making its own interesting way alone. Think as she would, and try, love, and love only, the admiration and ministering care of some capable and affectionate man was the only thing that seemed likely to solve for her the various earthly difficulties which beset her.

But even as to this, how, in what saving or perfect way, was love to come to her? She had made one mistake which in the development of any honest relationship with another would have to be confessed. And how would it be then? Would love, admiration, forgive? Love, love, love, and the peace and comfort of that happy routine home life which she imagined she saw operative in the lives of others—how it glimmered afar, like a star!

And again there was her mother.

It was not long after she had come from the institution that sheer loneliness, as well as a sense of daughterly responsibility and pity, had urged her to look up her mother, in order that she might restore to herself some little trace of a home, however wretched it might be. She had no one, as she proceeded to argue. At least in her own lonely life her mother provided, or would, an ear and a voice, sympathetic if begging, a place to go.

She had learned on returning to their last living-place on one of her afternoons off, that her mother had been sent away to the "Island," but had come back and since had been sent to the city poor-farm. This last inquiry led eventually to her mother's discovery of her and of her fixing herself upon her once more as a dependent, until her death somewhat over a year later.

But in the meantime, and after all, life continued to call

and call and to drive her on, for she was still full of the hope and fever of youth.

Once, before leaving the institution in which they had worked together, Viola Patters had said to her in one of those bursts of confidence based on attraction:

"Once you're outa here an' I am, too, I'd like to see you again, only there ain't no use your writin' me here, for I don't believe they'd give it to me. I don't believe they'd want us to run together. I don't believe they like me as well as they do you. But you write me, wherever you are, care of —," and here she gave a definite address—"an' I'll get it when I get out."

She assured Madeleine that she would probably be able to get a good place, once she was free of the control of the Sisters, and then she might be able to do something for her.

Often during these dark new days she thought of this, and being hard-pressed for diverting interests in her life she finally wrote her, receiving in due time a request to come and see her.

But, as it proved, Viola was no avenue of improvement for her in her new mood. She was, as Madeleine soon discovered, part of a small group which was making its way along a path which she had promised herself henceforth to avoid. Viola was more comfortably placed in quarters of her own than Madeleine had ever been, but the method by which she was forwarding her life she could not as readily accept.

Yet her own life, move about as she might and did after a time from one small position to another, in store or factory, in the hope of bettering herself, held nothing either. Day by day as she worked she sensed all the more clearly that the meagre tasks at which she toiled could bring her nothing of permanent value. Her mother was dead now, and she more alone than ever. During a period of several years, in which she worked and dreamed, leading a thin, underpaid life, her mind was ever on love and what it might do for her—the pressure of a seeking hand, the sanctuary of an enveloping heart.

And then, for the second time in her brief life, love came, or seemed to—at least in her own heart if nowhere else.

She had by now, and through her own efforts, attained to a clerkship in one of the great stores at the salary of seven dollars a week, on which she was trying to live. And then, behold, one day among her customers one of those suave and artful masters of the art of living by one's wits, with a fortune of looks, to whom womanhood is a thing to be taken by an upward curl of a pair of mustachios, the vain placement of ringed locks, spotless and conspicuous linen, and clothes and shoes of a newness and lustre all but disturbing to a very work-a-day world. His manners and glances were of a winsomeness which only the feminine heart—and that unschooled in the valuelessness of veneer—fully appreciates.

Yes, the sheer grace of the seeking male, his shallow and heartless courtesy, the lustre of his eye and skin, a certain something of shabby-grand manner, such as she had never known in the particularly narrow world in which she moved, was sufficient to arrest and fix her interest.

He leaned over and examined the stationery and pencils which she sold, commenting on prices, the routine of her work, smiled archly and suggested by his manner entire that she was one in whom he could be deeply interested. At the same time a certain animal magnetism, of the workings of which she was no more conscious than might be any stick or stone, took her in its tow.

Here was one out of many, a handsome beau, who was interested in her and her little life. The oiled and curled hair became the crown of a god; the mustachios and the sharp, cruel nose harmonies of exquisite beauty. Even the muscular, prehensile hands were rhythmic, musical in their movements. She had time only to sense the wonder of his perfect self before he went away. But it was to return another day, with an even more familiar and insinuating grace.

He was interested in her, as he frankly said the next time, and she must be his friend. At lunch-time one day he was waiting to take her to a better restaurant than she would ever have dreamed of entering; on another day it was to dinner that she accompanied him.

According to him, she was beautiful, wonderful. Her flower-like life was being wasted on so rude a task. She should marry him, and then her difficulties would be solved. He was one who, when fortune was with him, so he said, made much, much money. He might even take her from the city at times to see strange places and interesting scenes.

As for her own stunted life, from most of the details of which she forbore, he seemed in nowise interested. It was not due to any lack on her part in the past that her life had been so ill. . . .

Love, love, love. . . . The old story. In a final burst of admiration and love for his generosity she told him of her one great error, which caused him a few moments of solemn cogitation and was then dismissed as nothing of importance, a pathetic, childish mistake. Then there followed one of those swift and seemingly unguarded unions, a commonplace of the tangled self-preserving underworld of poverty. A clergyman was found whose moral assurances seemed to make the union ideal. Then a room in a commonplace boarding-house, and the newer and better life which eventually was to realize all was begun.

VII

To those familiar with the brazen and relentless methods of a certain type of hawk of the underworld, which picks fledglings from the nest and springlings from the fields and finds life itself only a hunting-ground in which those mentally or physically weaker than itself may be enslaved, this description will seem neither strained nor inadequate.

Fagins of sex, creatures who change their women as they would their coats, they make an easy if reprehensible bed of their lives, and such of their victims as have known them well testify that for a while at least in their care or custody they were not unhappy.

So it was with Madeleine and her lover. With amused and laughing tolerance toward her natural if witless efforts to build up a home atmosphere about their presumably joint lives, to build for a future in which they should jointly share, he saw in them only something trivial or ridiculous, whereas to her it was as though the heavens had opened and she was surveying a new world. For in his love and care there was to be peace. Latterly, if not now—for already he complained of conditions which made it impossible for him to work—the results of their several labors were to be pooled in order to prepare for that something better which would soon be achieved—a home, an ideally happy state somewhere. Even children were in her mind.

The mere fact that he shortly complained of other temporary reverses which made it necessary for him and her to keep close watch over their resources, and that for the time being, until he "could arrange his affairs," she must find some employment which would pay much better than her old one, gave her no shock.

Indeed, it was an indescribable joy for her to do for her love, for love had come, that great solvent of all other earthly difficulties, that leveler of all but insurmountable barriers. Even now love was to make her life flower at last. There was an end to loneliness and the oppressive indifference of the great sea of life.

But, as in the first instance, so now the awakening was swift and disconcerting. Realizing the abject adoration in which she held his surface charms and that his thin, tricky soul was the beginning and the end of things for her, it was all the easier to assure her, and soon insist, that the easiest and swiftest way of making money, of which she was unfortunately aware, must be resorted to, for a great necessity had come upon him. The usual tale of a threatening disaster, a sudden loss at cards which might end in imprisonment for him and their enforced separation, was enough.

Swiftly he filled her ears with tales of rescues by women of many of his men friends similarly circumstanced, of the "fools" and "marks" that filled the thoroughfares to be captured and preyed upon by women. Why hesitate? Consider the meagre, beggarly wages she had previously earned, the nothingness of her life before. Why jeopardize their future now? Why be foolish, dull? Plainly it was nothing to love, as he saw it. Should it be so much to her? In this wise she was persuaded.

But now it was not the shame and the fear of arrest that troubled her, but the injury which love had done and was doing to her, that cut and burned and seared and scarred.

Love, as she now began dimly to realize once more, should not be so. More than anything else, if love was what she had always dreamed, should it not protect and save and keep her for itself? And now see. Love was sending her out again to loiter in doorways and before windows and to "make eyes."

It was this that turned like a wheel in her brain and heart. For in spite of the roughness of her emotional experiences thus far, she had faith to believe that love should not be so, should not do so.

Those features which to this hour, and long after, like those features of her first love, seemed so worship-worth, those eyes that had seemed to beam on her with love, the lips that had smiled so graciously and kissed hers, the hands and arms that had petted and held her, should not be part of the compulsion that sent her here.

No, love should be better than that. He himself had told her so at first—that she was worth more than all else to him—and now see!

And then one night, fully a year and a half later, the climax. Being particularly irritated by some money losses and the need of enduring her at all, even though she might still prove of some value as a slave, he turned on her with a savage fury.

"What, only . . . ! Get to hell outa here! What do you think I am—a sucker? And let go my arm. Don't come that stuff on me. I'm sick of it. Don't hang on my arm, I tell yah! I'm tired, damned tired! Get out! Go on—beat it, an' don't come back, see? I'm through—through—yuh hear me? I mean what I say. I'm through, once an' fer all. Beat it, an' fer good. Don't come back. I've said that before, but this time it *goes!* Go on, now quick— Scat!—an' don't ever let me see yah around here any more, yah hear?—yah damned piece o' mush, yah!"

He pushed her away, throwing open the door as he did so, and, finding her still pleading and clinging, threw her out with such force that she cut her left eye and the back of her left hand against the jamb of the door.

There was a cry of "Fred! Fred! Please! Please!"—and then the door was slammed and she was left leaning disconsolately and brokenly against the stair-rail outside.

And now, as before, the cruelty and inscrutability of life weighed on her, only now, less than before, had she hope wherewith to buoy herself. It was all so dark, so hopeless. Often in this hour she thought of the swift, icy waters of the river, glistening under a winter moon, and then again of the peace and quiet of the House of the Good Shepherd, its shielding remoteness from life, the only true home or sanctuary she had ever known. And so, brooding and repressing occasional sobs, she made her way toward it, down the long streets, thinking of the pathetically debasing love-life that was now over—the dream of love that never, never could be again, for her.

VIII

The stark red walls of the institution stood as before, only dim and gray and cold under a frosty winter moon. It was three of a chill, cold morning. She had come a long way, drooping, brooding, half-freezing and crying. More than once on the way the hopelessness of her life and her dreams had given her pause, causing her to turn again with renewed determination toward the river—only the vivid and reassuring picture she had retained of this same grim and homely place, its restricted peace and quiet, the sympathy of Sister St. Agnes and Mother St. Bertha, had carried her on.

En route she speculated as to whether they would receive her now, so objectionable and grim was her tale. And yet she could not resist continuing toward it, so reassuring was its memory, only to find it silent, not a single light burning. But, after all, there was one, at a side door—not the great cold gate by which she had first been admitted but another to one side, to her an all but unknown entrance; and to it after some brooding hesitation she made her way, ringing a bell and being admitted by a drowsy nun, who ushered her into the warmth and quiet of the inner hallway. Once in she mechanically followed to the bronze grille which, as prison bars, obstructed the way, and here on one of the two plain chairs placed before a small aperture she now sank wearily and looked through.

Her cut eye was hurting her and her bruised hands. On the somewhat faded jacket and crumpled hat, pulled on indifferently because she was too hurt to think or care, there was some blown snow. And when the Sister Secretary in charge of the room after midnight, hearing footsteps, came to the grille, she looked up wanly, her little red, rough hands crossed on her lap.

"Mother," she said beseechingly, "may I come in?"

Then remembering that only Mother St. Bertha could admit her, added wearily:

"Is Mother St. Bertha here? I was here before. She will know me."

The Sister Secretary surveyed her curiously, sensing more of the endless misery that was ever here, but seeing that she was sick or in despair hastened to call her superior, whose rule it was that all such requests for admission should be referred to her. There was no stir in the room in her absence. Presently pattened feet were heard, and the face of Mother St. Bertha, wrinkled and a-weary, appeared at the square opening.

"What is it, my child?" she asked curiously if softly, wondering at the crumpled presence at this hour.

"Mother," began Madeleine tremulously, looking up and recognizing her, "don't you remember me? It is Madeleine. I was here four years ago. I was in the girls' ward. I worked in the sewing-room."

She was so beaten by life, the perpetual endings to her never more than tremulous hopes, that even now and here she expected little more than an indifference which would send her away again.

"Why, yes, of course I remember you, my child. But what is it that brings you now, dear? Your eye is cut, and your hand."

"Yes, mother, but please don't ask—just now. Oh, please let me come in! I am so tired! I've had such a hard time!"

"Of course, my child," said the Mother, moving to the door and opening it. "You may come in. But what has happened, child? How is it that your cheek is cut, and your hands?"

"Mother," pleaded Madeleine wearily, "must I answer now? I am so unhappy! Can't I just have my old dress and my bed for to-night—that little bed under the lamp?"

"Why, yes, dear, you may have them, of course," said the nun, tactfully sensing a great grief. "And you need not talk now. I think I know how it is. Come with me."

She led the way along bare, dimly lit corridors and up cold solid iron stairs, echoing to the feet, until once more, as in the old days, the severe but spotless room in which were the baths and the hampers for soiled clothes was reached.

"Now, my child," she said, "you may undress and bathe. I will get something for your eye."

And so here at last, once more, Madeleine put aside the pathetic if showy finery that for a time had adorned and shamed her: a twilled skirt she had only recently bought in the pale hope of interesting *him,* the commonplace little hat for which she had paid ten dollars, the striped shirtwaist, once a pleasure to her in the hope that it would please *him*.

In a kind of dumbness of despair she took off her shoes and stockings and, as the Mother left, entered the warm, clean bath which had been provided. She stifled a sob as she did so, and others as she bathed. Then she stepped out and dried her body and covered it with the clean, simple slip of white which had been laid on a chair, brushing her hair and touching her eye, until the Mother Sister returned with an unguent wherewith to dress it.

Then she was led along other silent passages, once dreary enough but now healing in their sense of peace and rest, and so into the great room set with row upon row of simple white iron beds, covered with their snowy linen and illuminated only by the minute red lamps or the small candles burning before their idealistic images here and there, beneath which so many like herself were sleeping. Over the bed which she had once occupied, and which by chance was then vacant, burned the one little lamp which she recognized as of old—her lamp, as she had always thought of it—a thin and flickering flame, before an image of the Virgin. At sight of it she repressed a sob.

"You see, my child," said the Mother Superior poetically, "it must have been waiting for you. Anyhow it is empty. Perhaps it may have known you were coming."

She spoke softly so that the long rows of sleepers might not be disturbed, then proceeded to turn down the coverlets.

"Oh, Mother," Madeleine suddenly whispered softly as she stood by the bed, "won't you let me stay always? I never want to go out any more. I have had such a hard time. I will work so hard for you if you will let me stay!"

The experienced Sister looked at her curiously. Never before had she heard such a plea.

"Why, yes, my child," she said. "If you wish to stay I'm sure it can be arranged. It is not as we usually do, but you are not the only one who has gone out in the past and come back to us. I am sure God and the Blessed Virgin will hear your prayer for whatever is right. But now go to bed and sleep. You need rest. I can see that. And to-morrow, or any time, or never, as you choose, you may tell me what has happened."

She urged her very gently to enter and then tucked the covers about her, laying finally a cool, wrinkled hand on her forehead. For answer Madeleine seized and put it to her lips, holding it so.

"Oh, Mother," she sobbed as the Sister bent over her, "don't ever make me go out in the world again, will you? You won't, will you? I'm so tired! I'm so tired!"

"No dear, no," soothed the Sister, "not unless you wish it. And now rest. You need never go out in the world again unless you wish."

And withdrawing the hand from the kissing lips, she tiptoed silently from the room.

II

THE HAND

I

DAVIDSON could distinctly remember that it was between two and three years after the grisly event in the Monte Orte range—the sickening and yet deserved end of Mersereau, his quondam partner and fellow adventurer—that anything to be identified with Mersereau's malice toward him, and with Mersereau's probable present existence in the spirit world, had appeared in his life.

He and Mersereau had worked long together as prospectors, investors, developers of property. It was only after they had struck it rich in the Klondike that Davidson had grown so much more apt and shrewd in all commercial and financial matters, whereas Mersereau had seemed to stand still—not to rise to the splendid opportunities which then opened to him. Why, in some of those later deals it had not been possible for Davidson even to introduce his old partner to some of the moneyed men he had to deal with. Yet Mersereau had insisted, as his right, if you please, on being "in on" everything—everything!

Take that wonderful Monte Orte property, the cause of all the subsequent horror. He, Davidson—not Mersereau —had discovered or heard of the mine, and had carried it along, with old Besmer as a tool or decoy—Besmer being the ostensible factor—until it was all ready for him to take over and sell or develop. Then it was that Mersereau, having been for so long his partner, demanded a full half— a third, at least—on the ground that they had once agreed to work together in all these things.

Think of it! And Mersereau growing duller and less useful and more disagreeable day by day, and year by year! Indeed, toward the last he had threatened to expose the trick by which jointly, seven years before, they had possessed themselves of the Skyute Pass Mine; to drive Davidson out of public and financial life, to have him arrested and tried—along with himself, of course. Think of that!

But he had fixed him—yes, he had, damn him! He had trailed Mersereau that night to old Besmer's cabin on the Monte Orte, when Besmer was away. Mersereau had gone there with the intention of stealing the diagram of the new field, and had secured it, true enough. A thief he was, damn him. Yet, just as he was making safely away, as he thought, he, Davidson, had struck him cleanly over the ear with that heavy rail-bolt fastened to the end of a walnut stick, and the first blow had done for him.

Lord, how the bone above Mersereau's ear had sounded when it cracked! And how bloody one side of that bolt was! Mersereau hadn't had time to do anything before he was helpless. He hadn't died instantly, though, but had turned over and faced him, Davidson, with that savage, scowling face of his and those blazing, animal eyes.

Lying half propped up on his left elbow, Mersereau had reached out toward him with that big, rough, bony right hand of his—the right with which he always boasted of having done so much damage on this, that, and the other occasion—had glared at him as much as to say:

"Oh, if I could only reach you just for a moment before I go!"

Then it was that he, Davidson, had lifted the club again. Horrified as he was, and yet determined that he must save his own life, he had finished the task, dragging the body back to an old fissure behind the cabin and covering it with branches, a great pile of pine fronds, and as many as one hundred and fifty boulders, great and small, and had left his victim. It was a sickening job and a sickening sight, but it had to be.

Then, having finished, he had slipped dismally away, like a jackal, thinking of that hand in the moonlight, held up so savagely, and that look. Nothing might have come of that either, if he hadn't been inclined to brood on it so much, on the fierceness of it.

No, nothing had happened. A year had passed, and if anything had been going to turn up it surely would have by then. He, Davidson, had gone first to New York, later to Chicago, to dispose of the Monte Orte claim. Then, after two years, he had returned here to Mississippi, where he was enjoying comparative peace. He was looking after some sugar property which had once belonged to him, and which he was now able to reclaim and put in charge of his sister as a home against a rainy day. He had no other.

But that body back there! That hand uplifted in the moonlight—to clutch him if it could! Those eyes.

II—JUNE, 1905

Take that first year, for instance, when he had returned to Gatchard in Mississippi, whence both he and Mersereau had originally issued. After looking after his own property he had gone out to a tumble-down estate of his uncle's in Issaqueena County—a leaky old slope-roofed house where, in a bedroom on the top floor, he had had his first experience with the significance or reality of the hand.

Yes, that was where first he had really seen it pictured in that curious, unbelievable way; only who would believe that it was Mersereau's hand? They would say it was an accident, chance, rain dropping down. But the hand had appeared on the ceiling of that room just as sure as any-thing, after a heavy rain-storm—it was almost a cyclone—when every chink in the old roof had seemed to leak water.

During the night, after he had climbed to the room by way of those dismal stairs with their great landing and small glass oil-lamp he carried, and had sunk to rest, or tried to, in the heavy, wide, damp bed, thinking, as he always did those days, of the Monte Orte and Mersereau, the storm had come up. As he had listened to the wind moaning outside he had heard first the scratch, scratch, scratch, of some limb, no doubt, against the wall—sounding, or so it seemed in his feverish unrest, like some one penning an indictment against him with a worn, rusty pen.

And then, the storm growing worse, and in a fit of irritation and self-contempt at his own nervousness, he had gone to the window, but just as lightning struck a branch of the tree nearest the window and so very near him, too— as though some one, something, was seeking to strike him— (Mersereau?) and as though he had been lured by that scratching. God! He had retreated, feeling that it was meant for him.

But that big, knotted hand painted on the ceiling by the dripping water during the night! There it was, right over him when he awoke, outlined or painted as if with wet, gray whitewash against the wretched but normally pale-blue of the ceiling when dry. There it was—a big, open hand just like Mersereau's as he had held it up that night—huge, knotted, rough, the fingers extended as if tense and clutching. And, if you will believe it, near it was something that looked like a pen—an old, long-handled pen—to match that scratch, scratch, scratch!

"Huldah," he had inquired of the old black mammy who entered in the morning to bring him fresh water and throw open the shutters, "what does that look like to you up there —that patch on the ceiling where the rain came through?"

He wanted to reassure himself as to the character of the thing he saw—that it might not be a creation of his own feverish imagination, accentuated by the dismal character of this place.

"'Pears t' me mo' like a big han' 'an anythin' else, Marse Davi'son," commented Huldah, pausing and staring upward. "Mo' like a big fist, kinda. Dat air's a new drip come las' night, I reckon. Dis here ole place ain' gonna hang togethah much longah, less'n some repairin' be done mighty quick now. Yassir, dat air's a new drop, sho's yo' bo'n, en it come on'y las' night. I hain't never seed dat befo'."

And then he had inquired, thinking of the fierceness of the storm:

"Huldah, do you have many such storms up this way?"

"Good gracious, Marse Davi'son, we hain't seed no sech blow en—en come three years now. I hain't seed no sech lightnin' en I doan' know when."

Wasn't that strange, that it should all come on the night, of all nights, when he was there? And no such other storm in three years!

Huldah stared idly, always ready to go slow and rest, if possible, whereas he had turned irritably. To be annoyed by ideas such as this! To always be thinking of that Monte Orte affair! Why couldn't he forget it? Wasn't it Mersereau's own fault? He never would have killed the man if he hadn't been forced to it.

And to be haunted in this way, making mountains out of mole-hills, as he thought then! It must be his own miserable fancy—and yet Mersereau had looked so threateningly at him. That glance had boded something; it was too terrible not to.

Davidson might not want to think of it, but how could he stop? Mersereau might not be able to hurt him any more, at least not on this earth; but still, couldn't he? Didn't the appearance of this hand seem to indicate that he might? He was dead, of course. His body, his skeleton, was under that pile of rocks and stones, some of them as big as wash-tubs. Why worry over that, and after two years? And still—

That hand on the ceiling!

III—DECEMBER, 1905

Then, again, take that matter of meeting Pringle in Gatchard just at that time, within the same week. It was due to Davidson's sister. She had invited Mr. and Mrs. Pringle in to meet him one evening, without telling him that they were spiritualists and might discuss spiritualism.

Clairvoyance, Pringle called it, or seeing what can't be seen with material eyes, and clairaudience, or hearing what can't be heard with material ears, as well as materialization, or ghosts, and table-rapping, and the like. Table-rapping —that damned tap-tapping that he had been hearing ever since!

It was Pringle's fault, really. Pringle had persisted in talking. He, Davidson, wouldn't have listened, except that he somehow became fascinated by what Pringle said concerning what he had heard and seen in his time. Mersereau must have been at the bottom of that, too.

At any rate, after he had listened, he was sorry, for Pringle had had time to fill his mind full of those awful facts or ideas which had since harassed him so much—all that stuff about drunkards, degenerates, and weak people generally being followed about by vile, evil spirits and used to effect those spirits' purposes or desires in this world. Horrible!

Wasn't it terrible? Pringle—big, mushy, creature that he was, sickly and stagnant like a springless pool—insisted that he had even seen clouds of these spirits about drunkards, degenerates, and the like, in street-cars, on trains, and about vile corners at night. Once, he said, he had seen just one evil spirit—think of that!—following a certain man all the time, at his left elbow—a dark, evil, red-eyed thing, until finally the man had been killed in a quarrel.

Pringle described their shapes, these spirits, as varied. They were small, dark, irregular clouds, with red or green spots somewhere for eyes, changing in form and becoming longish or round like a jellyfish, or even like a misshapen cat or dog. They could take any form at will—even that of a man.

Once, Pringle declared, he had seen as many as fifty about a drunkard who was staggering down a street, all of them trying to urge him into the nearest saloon, so that they might re-experience in some vague way the sensation of drunkenness, which at some time or other they themselves, having been drunkards in life, had enjoyed!

It would be the same with a drug fiend, or indeed with any one of weak or evil habits. They gathered about such an one like flies, their red or green eyes glowing—attempting to get something from them, perhaps, if nothing more than a little sense of their old earth-life.

The whole thing was so terrible and disturbing at the time, particularly that idea of men being persuaded or influenced to murder, that he, Davidson, could stand it no longer, and got up and left. But in his room upstairs he meditated on it, standing before his mirror. Suddenly— would he ever forget it—as he was taking off his collar and tie, he had heard that queer tap, tap, tap, right on his dressing-table or under it, and for the first time, which Pringle said, ghosts made when table-rapping in answer to a call, or to give warning of their presence.

Then something said to him, almost as clearly as if he heard it:

"This is me, Mersereau, come back at last to get you! Pringle was just an excuse of mine to let you know I was coming, and so was that hand in that old house, in Issa-queena County. It was mine! I will be with you from now on. Don't think I will ever leave you!"

It had frightened and made him half sick, so wrought up was he. For the first time he felt cold chills run up and down his spine—the creeps. He felt as if some one were standing over him—Mersereau, of course—only he could not see or hear a thing, just that faint tap at first, growing louder a little later, and quite angry when he tried to ignore it.

People did live, then, after they were dead, especially evil people—people stronger than you, perhaps. They had

the power to come back, to haunt, to annoy you if they
didn't like anything you had done to them. No doubt
Mersereau was following him in the hope of revenge, there
in the spirit world, just outside this one, close at his heels,
like that evil spirit attending the other man whom Pringle
had described.

IV—FEBRUARY, 1906

Take that case of the hand impressed on the soft dough
and plaster of Paris, described in an article that he had
picked up in the dentist's office out there in Pasadena—
Mersereau's very hand, so far as he could judge. How
about that for a coincidence, picking up the magazine with
that disturbing article about psychic materialization in
Italy, and later in Berne, Switzerland, where the scientists
were gathered to investigate that sort of thing? And just
when he was trying to rid himself finally of the notion that
any such thing could be!

According to that magazine article, some old crone over
in Italy—spiritualist, or witch, or something—had got together a crowd of experimentalists or professors in an
abandoned house on an almost deserted island off the coast
of Sardinia. There they had conducted experiments with
spirits, which they called materialization, getting the impression of the fingers of a hand, or of a whole hand and
arm, or of a face, on a plate of glass covered with soot, the
plate being locked in a small safe on the center of a table
about which they sat!

He, Davidson, couldn't understand, of course, how it was
done, but done it was. There in that magazine were half a
dozen pictures, reproductions of photographs of a hand, an
arm and a face—or a part of one, anyhow. And if they
looked like anything, they looked exactly like Mersereau's!
Hadn't Pringle, there in Gatchard, Miss., stated spirits could
move anywhere, over long distances, with the speed of light.
And would it be any trick for Mersereau to appear there at

Sardinia, and then engineer this magazine into his presence, here in Los Angeles? Would it? It would not. Spirits were free and powerful *over there,* perhaps.

There was not the least doubt that these hands, these partial impressions of a face, were those of Mersereau. Those big knuckles! That long, heavy, humped nose and big jaw! Whose else could they be?—they were Mersereau's, intended, when they were made over there in Italy, for him, Davidson, to see later here in Los Angeles. Yes, they were! And looking at that sinister face reproduced in the magazine, it seemed to say, with Mersereau's old coarse sneer:

"You see? You can't escape me! I'm showing you how much alive I am over here, just as I was on earth. And I'll get you yet, even if I have to go farther than Italy to do it!"

It was amazing, the shock he took from that. It wasn't just that alone, but the persistence and repetition of this hand business. What could it mean? Was it really Mersereau's hand? As for the face, it wasn't all there—just the jaw, mouth, cheek, left temple, and a part of the nose and eye; but it was Mersereau's, all right. He had gone clear over there into Italy somewhere, in a lone house on an island, to get this message of his undying hate back to him. Or was it just spirits, evil spirits, bent on annoying him because he was nervous and sensitive now?

V—October, 1906

Even new crowded hotels and new buildings weren't the protection he had at first hoped and thought they would be. Even there you weren't safe—not from a man like Mersereau. Take that incident there in Los Angeles, and again in Seattle, only two months ago now, when Mersereau was able to make that dreadful explosive or crashing sound, as if one had burst a huge paper bag full of air, or upset a china-closet full of glass and broken everything, when as a matter of fact nothing at all had happened. It had frightened him horribly the first two or three times, believing as he did that something fearful had happened. Finding that it was nothing—or Mersereau—he was becoming used to it now; but other people, unfortunately, were not.

He would be—as he had been that first time—sitting in his room perfectly still and trying to amuse himself, or not to think, when suddenly there would be that awful crash. It was astounding! Other people heard it, of course. They had in Los Angeles. A maid and a porter had come running the first time to inquire, and he had had to protest that he had heard nothing. They couldn't believe it at first, and had gone to other rooms to look. When it happened the second time, the management had protested, thinking it was a joke he was playing; and to avoid the risk of exposure he had left.

After that he could not keep a valet or nurse about him for long. Servants wouldn't stay, and managers of hotels wouldn't let him remain when such things went on. Yet he couldn't live in a house or apartment alone, for there the noises and atmospheric conditions would be worse than ever.

VI—June, 1907

Take that last old house he had been in—but never would be in again!—at Anne Haven. There he actually visualized the hand—a thing as big as a washtub at first, something like smoke or shadow in a black room moving about over the bed and everywhere. Then, as he lay there, gazing at it spellbound, it condensed slowly, and he began to feel it. It was now a hand of normal size—there was no doubt of it in the world—going over him softly, without force, as a ghostly hand must, having no real physical strength, but all the time with a strange, electric, secretive something about it, as if

it were not quite sure of itself, and not quite sure that he
was really there.

The hand, or so it seemed—God!—moved right up to his
neck and began to feel over that as he lay there. Then it
was that he guessed just what it was that Mersereau was
after.

It was just like a hand, the fingers and thumb made into
a circle and pressed down over his throat, only it moved over
him gently at first, because it really couldn't do anything yet,
not having the material strength. But the intention! The
sense of cruel, savage determination that went with it!

And yet, if one went to a nerve specialist or doctor about
all this, as he did afterward, what did the doctor say?
He had tried to describe how he was breaking down under
the strain, how he could not eat or sleep on account of all
these constant tappings and noises; but the moment he even
began to hint at his experiences, especially the hand or the
noises, the doctor exclaimed:

"Why, this is plain delusion! You're nervously run down,
that's all that ails you—on the verge of pernicious anemia, I
should say. You'll have to watch yourself as to this illusion
about spirits. Get it out of your mind. There's nothing
to it!"

Wasn't that just like one of these nerve specialists, bound
up in their little ideas of what they knew or saw, or thought
they saw?

VII—November, 1907

And now take this very latest development at Battle Creek
recently where he had gone trying to recuperate on the diet
there. Hadn't Mersereau, implacable demon that he was,
developed this latest trick of making his food taste queer to
him—unpalatable, or with an odd odor?

He, Davidson, knew it was Mersereau, for he felt him
beside him at the table whenever he sat down. Besides, he
seemed to hear something—clairaudience was what they

called it, he understood—he was beginning to develop that, too, now! It was Mersereau, of course, saying in a voice which was more like a memory of a voice than anything real —the voice of some one you could remember as having spoken in a certain way, say, ten years or more ago:

"I've fixed it so you can't eat any more, you—"

There followed a long list of vile expletives, enough in itself to sicken one.

Thereafter, in spite of anything he could do to make himself think to the contrary, knowing that the food was all right, really, Davidson found it to have an odor or a taste which disgusted him, and which he could not overcome, try as he would. The management assured him that it was all right, as he knew it was—for others. He saw them eating it. But he couldn't—had to get up and leave, and the little he could get down he couldn't retain, or it wasn't enough for him to live on. God, he would die, this way! Starve, as he surely was doing by degrees now.

And Mersereau always seeming to be standing by. Why, if it weren't for fresh fruit on the stands at times, and just plain, fresh-baked bread in bakers' windows, which he could buy and eat quickly, he might not be able to live at all. It was getting to that pass!

VIII—AUGUST, 1908

That wasn't the worst, either, bad as all that was. The worst was the fact that under the strain of all this he was slowly but surely breaking down, and that in the end Mersereau might really succeed in driving him out of life here —to do what, if anything, to him there? What? It was such an evil pack by which he was surrounded, now, those who lived just on the other side and hung about the earth, vile, debauched creatures, as Pringle had described them, and as Davidson had come to know for himself, fearing them and their ways so much, and really seeing them at times.

Since he had come to be so weak and sensitive, he could see them for himself—vile things that they were, swimming before his gaze in the dark whenever he chanced to let himself be in the dark, which was not often—friends of Mersereau, no doubt, and inclined to help him just for the evil of it.

For this long time now Davidson had taken to sleeping with the light on, wherever he was, only tying a handkerchief over his eyes to keep out some of the glare. Even then he could see them—queer, misshapen things, for all the world like wavy, stringy jellyfish or coils of thick, yellowish-black smoke, moving about, changing in form at times, yet always looking dirty or vile, somehow, and with those queer, dim, reddish or greenish glows for eyes. It was sickening!

IX—October, 1908

Having accomplished so much, Mersereau would by no means be content to let him go. Davidson knew that! He could talk to him occasionally now, or at least could hear him and answer back, if he chose, when he was alone and quite certain that no one was listening.

Mersereau was always saying, when Davidson would listen to him at all—which he wouldn't often—that he would get him yet, that he would make him pay, or charging him with fraud and murder.

"I'll choke you yet!" The words seemed to float in from somewhere, as if he were remembering that at some time Mersereau had said just that in his angry, savage tone—not as if he heard it; and yet he was hearing it of course.

"I'll choke you yet! You can't escape! You may think you'll die a natural death, but you won't, and that's why I'm poisoning your food to weaken you. You can't escape! I'll get you, sick or well, when you can't help yourself, when you're sleeping. I'll choke you, just as you hit me with that club. That's why you're always seeing and feeling this hand

*of mine! I'm not alone. I've nearly had you many a time
already, only you have managed to wriggle out so far, jumping up, but some day you won't be able to—see? Then—"*

The voice seemed to die away at times, even in the middle
of a sentence, but at the other times—often, often—he could
hear it completing the full thought. Sometimes he would
turn on the thing and exclaim:

"Oh, go to the devil!" or, "Let me alone!" or, "Shut
up!" Even in a closed room and all alone, such remarks
seemed strange to him, addressed to a ghost; but he couldn't
resist at times, annoyed as he was. Only he took good care
not to talk if any one was about.

It was getting so that there was no real place for him
outside of an asylum, for often he would get up screaming at
night—he had to, so sharp was the clutch on his throat—
and then always, wherever he was, a servant would come
in and want to know what was the matter. He would have
to say that it was a nightmare—only the management always
requested him to leave after the second or third time, say, or
after an explosion or two. It was horrible!

He might as well apply to a private asylum or sanatorium
now, having all the money he had, and explain that he had
delusions—delusions! Imagine!—and ask to be taken care
of. In a place like that they wouldn't be disturbed by his
jumping up and screaming at night, feeling that he was
being choked, as he was, or by his leaving the table because
he couldn't eat the food, or by his talking back to Mersereau, should they chance to hear him, or by the noises
when they occurred.

They could assign him a special nurse and a special room,
if he wished—only he didn't wish to be too much alone.
They could put him in charge of some one who would understand all these things, or to whom he could explain. He
couldn't expect ordinary people, or hotels catering to ordinary
people, to put up with him any more. Mersereau and his
friends made too much trouble.

He must go and hunt up a good place somewhere where they understood such things, or at least tolerated them, and explain, and then it would all pass for the hallucinations of a crazy man,—though, as a matter of fact, he wasn't crazy at all. It was all too real, only the average or so-called normal person couldn't see or hear as he could—hadn't experienced what he had.

X—December, 1908

"The trouble is, doctor, that Mr. Davidson is suffering from the delusion that he is pursued by evil spirits. He was not committed here by any court, but came of his own accord about four months ago, and we let him wander about here at will. But he seems to be growing worse, as time goes on.

"One of his worst delusions, doctor, is that there is one spirit in particular who is trying to choke him to death. Dr. Major, our superintendent, says he has incipient tuberculosis of the throat, with occasional spasmodic contractions. There are small lumps or calluses here and there as though caused by outside pressure and yet our nurse assures us that there is no such outside irritation. He won't believe that; but whenever he tries to sleep, especially in the middle of the night, he will jump up and come running out into the hall, insisting that one of these spirits, which he insists are after him, is trying to choke him to death. He really seems to believe it, for he comes out coughing and choking and feeling at his neck as if some one has been trying to strangle him. He always explains the whole matter to me as being the work of evil spirits, and asks me to not pay any attention to him unless he calls for help or rings his call-bell; and so I never think anything more of it now unless he does.

"Another of his ideas is that these same spirits do something to his food—put poison in it, or give it a bad odor or taste, so that he can't eat it. When he does find anything he can eat, he grabs it and almost swallows it whole, before, as he says, the spirits have time to do anything to it. Once, he says, he weighed more than two hundred pounds, but now he only weighs one hundred and twenty. His case is exceedingly strange and pathetic, doctor!

"Dr. Major insists that it is purely a delusion, that so far as being choked is concerned, it is the incipient tuberculosis, and that his stomach trouble comes from the same thing; but by association of ideas, or delusion, he thinks some one is trying to choke him and poison his food, when it isn't so at all. Dr. Major says that he can't imagine what could have started it. He is always trying to talk to Mr. Davidson about it, but whenever he begins to ask him questions, Mr. Davidson refuses to talk, and gets up and leaves.

"One of the peculiar things about his idea of being choked, doctor, is that when he is merely dozing he always wakes up in time, and has the power to throw it off. He claims that the strength of these spirits is not equal to his own when he is awake, or even dozing, but when he's asleep their strength is greater and that then they may injure him. Sometimes, when he has had a fright like this, he will come out in the hall and down to my desk there at the lower end, and ask if he mayn't sit there by me. He says it calms him. I always tell him yes, but it won't be five minutes before he'll get up and leave again, saying that he's being annoyed, or that he won't be able to contain himself if he stays any longer, because of the remarks being made over his shoulder or in his ear.

"Often he'll say: 'Did you hear that, Miss Liggett? It's astonishing, the low, vile things that man can say at times!' When I say, 'No, I didn't hear,' he always says, 'I'm so glad!' "

"No one has ever tried to relieve him of this by hypnotism, I suppose?"

"Not that I know of, doctor. Dr. Major may have tried it. I have only been here three months."

"Tuberculosis is certainly the cause of the throat trouble, as Dr. Major says, and as for the stomach trouble, that comes from the same thing—natural enough under the circumstances. We may have to resort to hypnotism a little later. I'll see. In the meantime you'd better caution all who come in touch with him never to sympathize, or even to seem to believe in anything he imagines is being done to him. It will merely encourage him in his notions. And get him to take his medicine regularly; it won't cure, but it will help. Dr. Major has asked me to give especial attention to his case, and I want the conditions as near right as possible."

"Yes, sir."

XI—JANUARY, 1909

The trouble with these doctors was that they really knew nothing of anything save what was on the surface, the little they had learned at a medical college or in practise—chiefly how certain drugs, tried by their predecessors in certain cases, were known to act. They had no imagination whatever, even when you tried to tell them.

Take that latest young person who was coming here now in his good clothes and with his car, fairly bursting with his knowledge of what he called psychiatrics, looking into Davidson's eyes so hard and smoothing his temples and throat—massage, he called it—saying that he had incipient tuberculosis of the throat and stomach trouble, and utterly disregarding the things which he, Davidson, could personally see and hear! Imagine the fellow trying to persuade him, at this late date, that all that was wrong with him was tuberculosis, that he didn't see Mersereau standing right beside him at times, bending over him, holding up that hand and telling him how he intended to kill him yet—that it was all an illusion!

Imagine saying that Mersereau couldn't actually seize him by the throat when he was asleep, or nearly so, when Davidson himself, looking at his throat in the mirror, could see the actual finger prints,—Mersereau's,—for a moment or so afterward. At any rate, his throat was red and sore from being clutched, as Mersereau of late was able to clutch him! And that was the cause of these lumps. And to say, as they had said at first, that he himself was making them by rubbing and feeling his throat, and that it was tuberculosis!

Wasn't it enough to make one want to quit the place? If it weren't for Miss Liggett and Miss Koehler, his private nurse, and their devoted care, he would. That Miss Koehler was worth her weight in gold, learning his ways as she had, being so uniformly kind, and bearing with his difficulties so genially. He would leave her something in his will.

To leave this place and go elsewhere, though, unless he could take her along, would be folly. And anyway, where else would he go? Here at least were other people, patients like himself, who could understand and could sympathize with him,—people who weren't convinced as were these doctors that all that he complained of was mere delusion. Imagine! Old Rankin, the lawyer, for instance, who had suffered untold persecution from one living person and another, mostly politicians, was convinced that his, Davidson's, troubles were genuine, and liked to hear about them, just as did Miss Koehler. These two did not insist, as the doctors did, that he had slow tuberculosis of the throat, and could live a long time and overcome his troubles if he would. They were merely companionable at such times as Mersereau would give him enough peace to be sociable.

The only real trouble, though, was that he was growing so weak from lack of sleep and food—his inability to eat the food which his enemy bewitched and to sleep at night on account of the choking—that he couldn't last much longer. This new physician whom Dr. Major had called into consultation in regard to his case was insisting that along with his throat trouble he was suffering from acute anemia, due to long undernourishment, and that only a solution of strychnin injected into the veins would help him. But as to Mersereau poisoning his food—not a word would he hear. Besides, now that he was practically bedridden, not able to jump up as freely as before, he was subject to a veritable storm of bedevilment at the hands of Mersereau. Not only could he see—especially toward evening, and in the very early hours of the morning—Mersereau hovering about him like a black shadow, a great, bulky shadow—yet like him in outline, but he could feel his enemy's hand moving over him.

Worse, behind or about him he often saw a veritable cloud of evil creatures, companions or tools of Mersereau's, who were there to help him and who kept swimming about like fish in dark waters, and seemed to eye the procedure with satisfaction.

When food was brought to him, early or late, and in whatever form, Mersereau and they were there, close at hand, as thick as flies, passing over and through it in an evident attempt to spoil it before he could eat it. Just to see them doing it was enough to poison it for him. Besides, he could hear their voices urging Mersereau to do it.

"That's right—poison it!"

"He can't last much longer!"

"Soon he'll be weak enough so that when you grip him he will really die!"

It was thus that they actually talked—he could hear them.

He also heard vile phrases addressed to him by Mersereau, the iterated and reiterated words "murderer" and "swindler" and "cheat," there in the middle of the night. Often, although the light was still on, he saw as many as seven dark figures, very much like Mersereau's, although different, gathered close about him,—like men in consultation—evil men. Some of them sat upon his bed, and it seemed as if they were about to help Mersereau to finish him, adding their hands to his.

Behind them again was a complete circle of all those evil, swimming things with green and red eyes, always watching —helping, probably. He had actually felt the pressure of the hand to grow stronger of late, when they were all there. Only, just before he felt he was going to faint, and because he could not spring up any more, he invariably screamed or gasped a choking gasp and held his finger on the button which would bring Miss Koehler. Then she would come, lift him up, and fix his pillows. She also always assured him that it was only the inflammation of his throat, and rubbed it with alcohol, and gave him a few drops of something internally to ease it.

After all this time, and in spite of anything he could tell

them, they still believed, or pretended to believe, that he was suffering from tuberculosis, and that all the rest of this was delusion, a phase of insanity!

And Mersereau's skeleton still out there on the Monte Orte!

And Mersereau's plan, with the help of others, of course, was to choke him to death, there was no doubt of that now; and yet they would believe after he was gone that he had died of tuberculosis of the throat. Think of that.

XII—MIDNIGHT OF FEBRUARY 10, 1909

THE GHOST OF MERSEREAU (*bending over David-son*): "Softly! Softly! He's quite asleep! He didn't think we could get him—that I could! But this time,—yes. Miss Koehler is asleep at the end of the hall and Miss Liggett can't come, can't hear. He's too weak now. He can scarcely move or groan. Strengthen my hand, will you! I will grip him so tight this time that he won't get away! His cries won't help him this time! He can't cry as he once did! Now! Now!"

A CLOUD OF EVIL SPIRITS (*swimming about*): "Right! Right! Good! Good! Now! Ah!"

DAVIDSON (*waking, choking, screaming, and feebly strik-ing out*): "Help! Help! H-e-l-p! Miss—Miss—H—e—l—p!"

MISS LIGGETT (*dozing heavily in her chair*): "Everything is still. No one restless. I can sleep." (*Her head nods.*)

THE CLOUD OF EVIL SPIRITS: "Good! Good! Good! His soul at last! Here it comes! He couldn't escape this time! Ah! Good! Good! Now!"

MERSEREAU (*to Davidson*): "You murderer! At last! At last!"

XIII—3 A.M. OF FEBRUARY 17, 1909

MISS KOEHLER (*at the bedside, distressed and pale*): "He must have died some time between one and two, doctor. I left him at one o'clock, comfortable as I could make him. He said he was feeling as well as could be expected. He's been very weak during the last few days, taking only a little gruel. Between half past one and two I thought I heard a noise, and came to see. He was lying just as you see here, except that his hands were up to his throat, as if it were hurting or choking him. I put them down for fear they would stiffen that way. In trying to call one of the other nurses just now, I found that the bell was out of order, although I know it was all right when I left, because he always made me try it. So he may have tried to ring."

DR. MAJOR (*turning the head and examining the throat*): "It looks as if he had clutched at his throat rather tightly this time, I must say. Here is the mark of his thumb on this side and of his four fingers on the other. Rather deep for the little strength he had. Odd that he should have imagined that some one else was trying to choke him, when he was always pressing at his own neck! Throat tuberculosis is very painful at times. That would explain the desire to clutch at his throat."

MISS LIGGETT: "He was always believing that an evil spirit was trying to choke him, doctor."

DR. MAJOR: "Yes, I know—association of ideas. Dr. Scain and I agree as to that. He had a bad case of chronic tuberculosis of the throat, with accompanying malnutrition, due to the effect of the throat on the stomach; and his notion about evil spirits pursuing him and trying to choke him was simply due to an innate tendency on the part of the subconscious mind to join things together—any notion, say, with any pain. If he had had a diseased leg, he would have imagined that evil spirits were attempting to saw it off, or something like that. In the same way the condition of his throat affected his stomach, and he imagined that the spirits were doing something to his food. Make out a certificate showing acute tuberculosis of the esophagus as the cause, with delusions of persecution as his mental condition. While I am here we may as well look in on Mr. Baff."

III

CHAINS

AS Garrison left his last business conference in K——,
where the tall buildings, and the amazing crowds always seemed such a commentary on the power and force and
wealth of America and the world, and was on his way to the
railway station to take a train for G——, his home city, his
thoughts turned with peculiar emphasis and hope, if not
actual pleasure—and yet it was a pleasure, of a sad, distressed kind—to Idelle. Where was she now? What was
she doing at this particular moment. It was after four of a
gray November afternoon, just the time, as he well knew,
winter or summer, when she so much preferred to be glowing at an afternoon reception, a "thé dansant," or a hotel
grill where there was dancing, and always, as he well knew,
in company with those vivid young "sports" or pleasure
lovers of the town who were always following her. Idelle,
to do her no injustice, had about her that something, even
after three years of marriage, that drew them, some of the
worst or best—mainly the worst, he thought at times—of
those who made his home city, the great far-flung G——,
interesting and in the forefront socially and in every other
way.

What a girl! What a history! And how strange that
he should have been attracted to her at all, he with his
forty-eight years, his superior (oh, very much!) social position, his conservative friends and equally conservative manners. Idelle was so different, so hoyden, almost coarse, in
her ways at times, actually gross and vulgar (derived from
her French tanner father, no doubt, not her sweet, retiring

64

Polish mother), and yet how attractive, too, in so many ways, with that rich russet-brown-gold hair of hers, her brown-black eyes, almost pupil-less, the iris and pupil being of the same color, and that trig, vigorous figure, always tailored in the smartest way! She was a paragon—to him at least—or had been to begin with.

How tingling and dusty these streets of K—— were, so vital always! How sharply the taxis of this mid-Western city turned corners!

But what a period he had endured since he had married her, three years before! What tortures, what despairs! If only he could make over Idelle to suit him! But what a wonderful thing that destroying something called beauty was, especially to one, like himself, who found life tiresome in so many ways—something to possess, a showpiece against the certain inroads of time, something wherewith to arouse envy in other persons.

At last they were reaching the station!

She did not deserve that he should love her. It was the most unfortunate thing for him that he did, but how could he help it now? How overcome it? How punish her for her misdeeds to him without punishing himself more? Love was such an inscrutable thing; so often one lavished it where it was not even wanted. God, he could testify to that! He was a fine example, really. She cared about as much for him as she did for the lamp-post on the corner, or an old discarded pair of shoes. And yet— He was never tired of looking at her, for one thing, of thinking of her ways, her moods, her secrets. She had not done and was not doing as she should—it was impossible, he was beginning to suspect, for her so to do—and still—

He must stop and send her a telegram before the train left!

What a pleasure it was, indeed, anywhere and at all times, to have her hanging on his arm, to walk into a restaurant or drawing-room and to know that of all those present none had a more attractive wife than he, not one. For all Idelle's commonplace birth and lack of position to begin with, she was the smartest, the best dressed, the most alluring, by far—at least, he thought so—of all the set in which he had placed her. Those eyes! That hair! That graceful figure, always so smartly arrayed! To be sure, she was a little young for him. Their figures side by side were somewhat incongruous—he with his dignity and years and almost military bearing, as so many told him, she with that air of extreme youthfulness and lure which always brought so many of the younger set to her side wherever they happened to be. Only there was the other galling thought: That she did not wholly belong to him and never had. She was too interested in other men, and always had been. Her youth, that wretched past of hers, had been little more than a lurid streak of bad, even evil—yes, evil—conduct. She had, to tell the truth, been a vile girl, sensuous, selfish, inconsiderate, unrepentant, and was still, and yet he had married her in spite of all that, knowing it, really. Only at first he had not known quite all.

"Yes, all three of these! And wait till I get my sleeper ticket!"

No wonder people had talked, though. He had heard it —that she had married him for his money, position, that he was too old, that it was a scandal, etc. Well, maybe it was. But he had been fond of her—terribly so—and she of him, or seemingly, at first. Yes, she must have been—her manner, her enthusiasm, if temporary, for him! Those happy, happy first days they spent together! Her quiet assumption of the rôle of hostess in Sicard Avenue at first, her manner of receiving and living up to her duties! It was wonderful, so promising. Yes, there was no doubt of it; she

must have cared for him a little at first. Her brain, too, required a man of his years to understand—some phases of her moods and ideas, and as for him—well, he was as crazy about her then as now—more so, if anything—or was he? Wasn't she just as wonderful to him now as she had been then? Truly. Yes, love or infatuation of this kind was a terrible thing, so impossible to overcome.

"Car three, section seven!"

Would he ever forget the night he had first seen her being carried into the Insull General on that canvas ambulance stretcher, her temple bruised, one arm broken and internal injuries for which she had to be operated on at once—a torn diaphragm, for one thing—and of how she had instantly fascinated him? Her hair was loose and had fallen over one shoulder, her hands limp. Those hands! That picture! He had been visiting his old friend Dr. Dorsey and had wondered who she was, how she came to be in such a dreadful accident and thought her so beautiful. Think of how her beauty might have been marred, only it wasn't, thank goodness!

His telegram should be delivered in one hour, at most— that would reach her in time!

Then and there he had decided that he must know her if she did not die, that perhaps she might like him as he did her, on the instant; had actually suffered tortures for fear she would not! Think of that! Love at first sight for him—and for one who had since caused him so much suffering—and in her condition, torn and bruised and near to death! It was wonderful, wasn't it?

How stuffy these trains were when one first entered them —coal smoky!

And that operation! What a solemn thing it was, really,

with only himself, the doctor and three nurses in the empty operating room that night. Dorsey was so tall, so solemn, but always so courageous. He had asked if he might not be present, although he did not know her, and because there were no relatives about to bar him from the room, no one to look after her or to tell who she was, the accident having occurred after midnight in the suburbs, he had been allowed by Dorsey to come in.

"Yes, put them down here!"

He had pulled on a white slip over his business suit, and clean white cotton gloves on his hands, and had then been allowed to come into the observation gallery while Dorsey, assisted by the hospital staff, had operated. He saw her cut open—the blood—heard her groan heavily under ether! And all the time wondering who she was. Her history. And pitying her, too! Fearing she might not come to! How the memory of her pretty shrewd face, hidden under bandages and a gas cone, had haunted him!

The train on this other track, its windows all polished, its dining-car tables set and its lamps already glowing!

That was another of those fool dreams of his—of love and happiness, that had tortured him so of late. From the first, almost without quite knowing it, he had been bewitched, stricken with this fever, and could not possibly think of her dying. And afterward, with her broken arm set and her torn diaphragm mended, he had followed her into the private room which he had ordered and had charged to himself (Dorsey must have thought it queer!) and then had waited so restlessly at his club until the next morning, when, standing beside her bed, he had said: "You don't know me, but my name is Garrison— Upham Brainerd Garrison. Perhaps you know of our family here in G——, the Willard Garrisons. I saw you

brought in last night. I want to be of service to you if
I may, to notify your friends, and be of any other use that
I can. May I?"

How well he remembered saying that, formulating it
all beforehand, and then being so delighted when she accepted his services with a peculiar, quizzical smile—that
odd, evasive glance of hers!

*Men struck car wheels this way, no doubt, in order to
see that they were not broken, liable to fly to pieces when
the train was running fast and so destroy the lives of all!*

And then she had given him her address—her mother's,
rather, to whom he went at once, bringing her back with
him. And so glad he was to know that there was only her
mother, no husband or— And the flowers he had sent. And
the fruit. And the gifts generally, everything he thought
she might like! And then that queer friendship with Idelle
afterwards, his quickly realized dream of bliss when she had
let him call on her daily, not telling him anything of herself,
of course, evading him rather, and letting him think what he
would, but tolerating him! Yes, she had played her game
fair enough, no doubt, only he was so eager to believe that
everything was going to be perfect with them—smooth,
easy, lasting, bliss always. What a fool of love he really was!

*What a disgusting fat woman coming in with all her
bags! Would this train never start?*

At that time—how sharply it had all burned itself into
his memory!—he had found her living as a young widow
with her baby daughter at her mother's, only she wasn't a
widow really. It was all make-believe. Already she had
proved a riant scoffer at the conventions, a wastrel, only
then he did not know that. Where he thought he was
making an impression on a fairly unsophisticated girl, or
at least one not roughly used by the world, in reality he
was merely a new sensation to her, an incident, a con-

venience, something to lift her out of a mood or a dilemma in which she found herself. Although he did not know it then, one of two quarreling men had just attempted to kill her via that automobile accident and she had been wishing peace, escape from her own thoughts and the attentions of her two ardent wooers, for the time being, at the time he met her. But apart from these, even, there were others, or had been before them, a long line apparently of almost disgusting—but no, he could not say quite that—creatures with whom she had been—well, why say it? And he had fancied for the moment that he was the big event in her life—or might be! He!

But even so, what difference did all that make either, if only she would love him now? What would he care who or what she was, or what she had done before, if only she really cared for him as much as he cared for her—or half as much—or even a minute portion! But Idelle could never care for any one really, or at least not for him, or him alone, anyway. She was too restless, too fond of variety in life. Had she not, since the first six or seven months in which she had known and married him, little more than tolerated him? She did not really need to care for anybody; they all cared for her, sought her.

At last they were going!

Too many men of station and means—younger than himself, as rich or richer, far more clever and fascinating in every way than he would ever be (or she would think so because she really liked a gayer, smarter type than he had ever been or ever could be now)—vied with him for her interest, and had with each other before ever he came on the scene. She was, in her queer way, a child of fortune, a genius of passion and desire, really. Life would use her well for some time yet, whatever she did to him or any other person, or whatever he sought to do to her in revenge, if he ever did, because she was interesting and desirable. Why attempt to deny that? She was far too attractive yet, too clever, too errant, too indifferent, too spiritually free, to be neglected by any one yet, let alone by such seeking, avid, pleasure lovers as always followed her. And because she wouldn't allow him to interfere (that was the basis on which she had agreed to marry him, her personal freedom) she had always been able to go and do and be what she chose, nearly, just as she was going and doing now.

These wide yards and that ruck of shabby yellow-and-black houses, begrimed and dirty externally, and internally no doubt, with souls in them nearly as drab, perhaps. How much better it was to be rich like himself and Idelle; only she valued her station so lightly!

Always, wherever he went these days, and his affairs prevented him from being with her very much, she was in his mind—what she was doing, where she was going, with whom she might be now—ah, the sickening thought, with whom she might be now, and where—with that young waster Keene, possibly, with his millions, his shooting preserve and his yacht; or Browne, equally young and still in evidence, though deserted by her to marry him, Garrison; or Coulstone, with whom Idelle had had that highly offensive affair in Pittsburgh five years before, when she was only eighteen. Eighteen! The wonder year! He, too, was here in G—— now after all these years, this same Coulstone, and after Idelle had left him once! Yes, he was hanging about her again, wanting her to come back and marry him, although each of them had remarried!

That flock of crows flying across that distant field!

Of course, Idelle laughed at it, or pretended to. She pretended to be faithful to him, to tell him all this was un-avoidable gossip, the aftermath of a disturbing past, before ever she saw him. But could he believe her? Was she not really planning so to do—leave him and return to Coulstone, this time legally? How could he tell? But think of the vagaries of human nature and character, the conniving and persuasive power of a man of wealth like Coulstone. He had left his great business in Pittsburgh to come here to G—— in order to be near her and annoy him (Garrison) really—not her, perhaps—with his pleas and crazy fascination and adoration when she was now safely and apparently happily married! Think of the strangeness, the shame, the peculiarity of Idelle's earlier life! And she still insisted that this sort of thing was worth while! All his own station and wealth and adoration were not enough—because he could not be eight or ten people at once, no doubt. But why should he worry? Why not let her go? To the devil with her, anyhow! She merely pretended to love him in her idle, wanton spirit, because she could—well, because she could play at youth and love!

Barkersburg—a place of 30,000, and the train not stopping! The sun, breaking through for just one peep at this gray day, under those trees!

The trouble with his life, as Garrison now saw it, was that throughout it for the last twenty years, and before that even, in spite of his youth and money, he had been craving the favor of just such a young, gay, vigorous, attractive creature as Idelle or Jessica—she of his earlier years—and not realizing it, until he met Idelle, his desire. And this, of course, had placed him at a disadvantage in dealing with women like them. Years before—all of fourteen now, think of it!—there had been that affair between himself and Jessica, daughter of the rich and fashionable Balloghs, of Lexington, which had ended so disastrously for him. He had been out there on Colonel Ledgebrook's estate attending to some property which belonged to his father when she had crossed his path at the colonel's house, that great estate in Bourbon County. Then, for the first time really, he had realized the delight of having a truly beautiful girl interested in him, and him alone, of being really attracted to him—for a little while. It was wonderful.

The smothered clang of that crossing bell!

But also what a failure! How painful to hark back to that, and yet how could he avoid it? Although it had seemed to end so favorably—he having been able to win and marry her—still in reality it had ended most disastrously, she having eventually left him as she did. Jessica, too, was like Idelle in so many ways, as young, as gay, nearly as forceful, not as pretty, and not with Idelle's brains. You had to admit that in connection with Idelle. She had more brains, force, self-reliance, intuition, than most women he knew anything about, young or old.

But to return to Jessica. At first she seemed to think he was wonderful, a man of the world, clever, witty, a lover of light, frivolous, foolish things, such as dancing, drinking, talking idle nonsense, which he was not at all. Yes, that was where he had always failed, apparently, and always would. He had no flair, and clever women craved that.

That flock of pigeons on that barn roof!

At bottom really he had always been slow, romantic, philosophic, meditative, while trying in the main to appear something else, whereas these other men, those who were so successful with women at least, were hard and gay and quick and thoughtless, or so he thought. They said and did things more by instinct than he ever could, were successful—well, just because they were what they were. You couldn't do those things by just trying to. And gay, pretty, fascinating women, such as Idelle or Jessica, the really worthwhile ones, seemed to realize this instinctively and to like that kind and no other. When they found a sober and reflective man like himself, or one even inclined to be, they drew away from him. Yes, they did; not consciously always, but just instinctively. They wanted only men who tingled and sparkled and glittered like themselves. To think that love must always go by blind instinct instead of merit—genuine, adoring passion!

This must be Phillipsburg coming into view! He couldn't mistake that high, round water tower!

Ah, the tragedy of seeing and knowing this and not being able to remedy it, of not being able to make oneself over into something like that! Somehow, Jessica had been betrayed by his bog-fire resemblance to the thing which she took him to be. He was a bog fire and nothing more, in so far as she was concerned, all she thought he was. Yet because he was so hungry, no doubt, for a woman of her type he had pretended that he was "the real thing," as she so liked to describe a gay character, a man of habits, bad or good, as you choose; one who liked to gamble, shoot, race, and do a lot of things which he really did not care for at all, but which the crowd or group with which he was always finding himself, or with whom he hoped to appear as somebody, was always doing and liking.

These poor countrymen, always loitering about their village stations!

And the women they ran with were just like them, like Jessica, like Idelle—smart, showy and liked that sort of man —and so—

Well, he had pretended to be all that and more, when she (Jessica) had appeared out of that gay group, petite, blonde (Idelle was darker), vivacious, drawn to him by his seeming reality as a man of the world and a gay cavalier. She had actually fallen in love with him at sight, as it were, or seemed to be at the time—she!—and then, see what had

happened! Those awful months in G—— after she had
returned with him! The agonies of mind and body!

*If only that stout traveling man in that gray suit would
cease staring at him! It must be the horn-rimmed glasses
he had on which interested him so! These mid-Western
people!*

Instantly almost, only a few weeks after they were
married, she seemed to realize that she had made a mistake. It seemed not to make the slightest difference to her,
after the first week or so, that they were married or that
he was infatuated with her or that he was who he was or
that her every move and thought were beautiful to him. On
the contrary, it seemed only to irritate her all the more.
She seemed to sense then—not before—that he was really
the one man not suited to her by temperament or taste or
ideas, not the kind she imagined she was getting, and from
then on there were the most terrible days, terrible—

That pretty girl turning in at that village gate!

Trying, depressing, degrading really. What dark frowns
used to flash across her face like clouds at that time—she
was nineteen to his twenty-four, and so pretty!—the realization, perhaps, that she had made a mistake. What she
really wanted was the gay, anachronistic, unthinking,
energetic person he had seemed to be under the stress of
the life at Ledgebrook's, not the quiet, reasoning, dreamy
person he really was. It was terrible!

Tall trees made such shadowy aisles at evening!

Finally she had run away, disappeared completely one
morning after telling him she was going shopping, and
then never seeing him any more—ever—not even once!
A telegram from Harrisburg had told him that she was going

to her mother's and for him not to follow her, please; and then before he could make up his mind really what to do had come that old wolf Caldwell, the famous divorce lawyer of G——, representing her mother, no doubt, and in smooth, ingratiating, persuasive tones had talked about the immense folly of attempting to adjust natural human antipathies, the sadness of all human inharmonies, the value of quiet in all attempts at separation, the need he had to look after his own social prestige in G——, and the like, until finally Caldwell had persuaded him to accept a decree of desertion in some Western state in silence and let her go out of his life forever! Think of that!

The first call for dinner! Perhaps he had better go at once and have it over with! He wanted to retire early to-night!

But Jessica—how she had haunted him for years after that! The whole city seemed to suggest her at times, even after he heard that she was married again and the mother of two children, so strong was the feeling for anything one lost. Even to this day certain corners in G——, the Brandingham, where they had lived temporarily at first; Mme. Gateley's dressmaking establishment, where she had had her gowns made, and the Tussockville entrance to the park —always touched and hurt him like some old, dear, poignant melody.

How this train lurched as one walked! The crashing couplings between these cars!

And then, after all these busy, sobering years, in which he had found out that there were some things he was not and could not be—a gay, animal man of the town, for instance, a "blood," a waster; and some things that he was— a fairly capable financial and commercial man, a lover of literature of sorts, and of horses, a genial and acceptable person in many walks of society—had come Idelle.

Think of the dining-car being crowded thus early! And such people!

He was just settling down to a semi-resigned acceptance of himself as an affectional, emotional failure in so far as women were concerned, when she had come—Idelle—this latest storm which had troubled him so much. Idelle had brains, beauty, force, insight—more than Jessica ever had had, or was he just older?—and that was what made her so attractive to men, so indifferent to women, so ready to leave him to do all the worshiping. She could understand him, apparently, at his time of life, with his sober and in some ways sad experiences, and sympathize with him most tenderly when she chose, and yet, strangely enough, she could ignore him also and be hard, cruel, indifferent. The way she could neglect him at times—go her own way! God!

Not a bad seat, only now it was too dark to see anything outside! These heavy forks!

But to return to that dreadful pagan youth of hers, almost half-savage: take that boy who shot himself at the age of sixteen for love of her, and all because she would not run away with him, not caring for him at all, as she said, or she would have gone! What a sad case that was, as she had told it, at least. The boy's father had come and denounced her to her parents in her own home, according to her, and still she denied that it had been her fault. And those other two youths, one of whom had embezzled $10,000 and spent it on her and several other boys and girls! And that other one who had stolen five hundred in small sums from his father's till and safe and then wasted it on her and her companions at country inns until he was caught! Those country clubs! Those little rivers she described, with their canoes—the automobiles of these youths—the dancing, eating, drinking life under the moon in the warmth of spring and summer under the trees! And he had never had anything like that, never! When one of the boys, being caught, complained of her to his parents as the cause of his evil ways she had denied it, or so she said, and did still to this day, saying she really did not know he was stealing the money and calling him coward or cry-baby. Idelle told him of this several years ago as though it had some humorous aspects, as possibly it had, to her—who knows? but with some remorse, too, for she was not wholly indifferent to the plight of these youths, although she contended that what she had given them of her time and youth and beauty was ample compensation. Yes, she was a bad woman, really, or had been—a bad girl, say what one would, a child of original evil impulse. One could not deny that really. But what fascination also, even yet, and then no doubt—terrible! He could understand the actions of those youths, their recklessness. There was something about sheer beauty, evil though it might be, which overcame moral prejudices or scruples. It had done so in his case, or why was he living with her? And so why not in theirs?

How annoying to have a train stop in a station while you were eating!

Beauty, beauty, beauty! How could one gainsay the charm or avoid the lure of it? Not he, for one. Trig, beautiful women, who carried themselves with an air and swing and suggested by their every movement passion, alertness, gayety of mind! The church bells might ring and millions of religionists preach of a life hereafter with a fixed table of rewards and punishments, but what did any one know of the future, anyhow? Nothing! Exactly nothing, in spite of all the churches. Life appeared and disappeared again; a green door opened and out you went, via a train wreck, for instance, on a night like this. All these farmers here tilling their fields and making their little homes and towns—where would they be in forty or fifty years, with all their moralities? No, here and now was life, here and now beauty—here and now Idelle, or creatures like her and Jessica.

He would pay his bill and go into the smoker for a change. It would be pleasant to sit there until his berth was made up.

Then, take that affair of the banker's son, young Gratiot it was, whom he knew well even now here in G——, only Gratiot did not know that he knew—or did he? Perhaps he was still friendly with Idelle, although she denied it. You could never really believe her. He it was, according to her, who had captured her fancy with his fine airs and money and car when she was only seventeen, and then robbed her (or could you call it robbery in Idelle's case, seeking, restless creature that she was?) of her indifferent innocence. No robbery there, surely, whatever she might say.

Those fascinating coke ovens blazing in the dark beside the track, mile after mile!

Somehow her telling him these things at first, or rather shortly after they were married and when she was going to make a clean breast of everything and lead a better life, had thrown a wonderful glamour over her past.

"Gay Stories"! What a name for a magazine! And that stout old traveling man reading it!

What a strange thing it was to be a girl like that—with passions and illusions like that! Perhaps, after all, life only came to those who sought it with great strength and natural gifts. But how hard it was on those who hadn't anything of that kind! Nevertheless, people should get

over the follies of their youth—Idelle should, anyhow. She
had had enough, goodness knows. She had been one of the
worst—hectic, vastly excited about life, irresponsible—and
she should have sobered by now. Why not? Look at all
he had to offer her! Was that not enough to effect a
change? While it made her interesting at times, this left-
over enthusiasm, still it was so ridiculous, and made her
non-desirable, too, either as wife or mother. Yet no doubt
that was what had made her so fascinating to him, too, at
this late day and to all those other men in B—— and elsewhere—that blazing youthfulness. Strange as it might
seem, he could condone Idelle's dreadful deeds even now,
just as her mother could, if she would only behave herself,
if she would only love him and him alone—but would she?
She seemed so determined to bend everything to her service,
regardless,—to yield nothing to him.

*No use! He couldn't stand these traveling men in this
smoking room! He must have the porter make up his
berth!*

And then had come Coulstone, the one who was still
hanging about her now, the one with whom she had had
that dreadful affair in Pittsburgh, the affair that always
depressed him to think about even now. Of course, there
was one thing to be said in extenuation of that, if you could
say anything at all—which you couldn't really—and that
was that Idelle was no longer a good girl then, but experienced and with all her blazing disposition aroused. She had
captured the reins of her life then and was doing as she
pleased—only why couldn't he have met her then instead of
Coulstone? He was alive then. And his own life had always been so empty. When she had confessed so much of
all this to him afterward—not this Coulstone affair exactly,
but the other things—why hadn't he left her then? He
might have and saved himself all this agony—or could he
have then? He was twice her age when he married her

and knew better, only he thought he could reform her—or did he? Was that the true reason? Could he admit the true reason to himself?

"Yes, make it up right away, if you will!" Now he *would have to wait about and be bored!*

But to come back to the story of Coulstone and all that hectic life in Pittsburgh. Coulstone, it seems, had been one of four or five very wealthy young managing vice-presidents of the Iverson-Centelever Frog and Switch Company, of Pittsburgh. And Idelle, because her father had suddenly died after her affair with young Gratiot, never knowing a thing about it, and her mother, not knowing quite what to do with her, had (because Idelle seemed to wish it) sent her to stay with an aunt in Pittsburgh. But the aunt having to leave for a time shortly after Idelle reached there, a girl friend had, at Idelle's instigation, apparently, suggested that she stay with her until the aunt's return, and Idelle had then persuaded her mother to agree to that.

That tall, lanky girl having to sleep in that upper berth opposite! European sleeping cars were so much better!

Her girl friend was evidently something like Idelle, or even worse. At any rate, Idelle appeared to have been able to wind her around her finger. For through her she had found some method of being introduced to (or letting them introduce themselves) a few of these smart new-rich men of the town, among them two of these same vice-presidents, one of whom was Coulstone. According to Idelle, he was a lavish and even reckless spender, wanting it to appear generally that he could do anything and have anything that money could buy, and liking to be seen in as many as a dozen public places in one afternoon or evening, especially at week-ends, only there weren't so many in Pittsburgh at the time.

This must be Centerfield, the state capital of E——, they were now passing without a pause! These expresses cut through so many large cities!

From the first, so Idelle said, he had made violent love to her, though he was already married (unhappily, of course), and she, caring nothing for the conventions and not being of the kind that obeys any laws (wilful, passionate, reckless), had received him probably in exactly the spirit in which he approached her, if not more so. That was the worst of her, her constant, wilful, pagan pursuit of pleasure, regardless of anybody or anything, and it still held her in spite of him. There was something revolting about the sheer animality of it, that rushing together of two people, regardless. Still, if it had been himself and Idelle now—

How fortunate that he had been able to obtain a section! At least he would have air!

There had been a wild season, according to her own admissions or boastings—he could never quite tell which—extending over six or seven months, during which time Idelle had pretended to her mother, so she said, to prefer to live with her girl friend rather than return home. She had had, according to her, her machine, her servants, clothes without end, and what-not—a dream-world of luxury and freedom which he had provided and from which she never expected to wake, and her mother totally ignorant of it all the while! There had been everything she wished at her finger tips—hectic afternoons, evenings and midnights; affairs at country clubs or hotel grills, where the young bloods of the city and their girls congregated; wild rides in automobiles; visits to the nearest smartest watering-places, and the like. Or was she lying? He could scarcely think so, judging by her career with him and others since.

Ah, what a comfort to fix oneself this way and rest, looking at the shadowy moonlit landscape passing by!

Idelle had often admitted or boasted that she had been wildly happy—that was the worst of it—that she had not quite realized what she was doing, but that she had no remorse either, even now—that she had lived! (And why should she have, perhaps? Weren't all people really selfish at bottom—or were they?) Only, owing to her almost insatiable pagan nature, there were other complications right then and there—think of that!—an older rival millionaire, if you please, richer by far than Coulstone, and more influential locally . . . and younger ones, too, who sought her but really did not win her, she having no time or plan for them. As it happened, the older one, having been worsted in the contest but being partially tolerated by her, had become frantically jealous and envious, although "he had no right," as she said, and had finally set about making trouble for the real possessor, and succeeded to the extent of exposing him and eventually driving him out of the great concern with which he was connected and out of Pittsburgh, too, if you please, on moral grounds (?), although he himself was trying to follow in Coulstone's footsteps! And all for the love or possession of a nineteen-year-old girl, a petticoat, a female ne'er-do-well! How little the world in general knew of such things—and it was a blessed thing, too, by George! Where would things be if everybody went on like that?

The rhythmic clack of these wheels and trucks over these sleeper joints—a poetic beat, of sorts!

But Idelle was so naïve about all this now, or pretended to be, so careless of what he or any one else might think in case they ever found out. She did not seem to guess how much he might suffer by her telling him all this, or how much pain thinking about it afterward might cause him.

She was too selfish intellectually. She didn't even guess, apparently, what his mood might be toward all this, loving her as he did. No—she really didn't care for him, or any one else—couldn't, or she couldn't have done anything like that. She would have lied to him rather. She had been, and was—although now semi-reformed—a heartless, careless wastrel, thinking of no one but herself. She had not cared about the wives of either of those two men who were pursuing her in B——, or what became of them, or what became of any of the others who had pursued her since. All she wanted was to be danced attendance on, to be happy, free, never bored. The other fellow never counted with Idelle much. In this case the wife of the younger lover, Coulstone, had been informed, the conservatives of the city appealed to, as it were. Coulstone, seeing the storm and being infatuated with his conquest, suggested Paris or a few years on the Riviera, but, strangely enough, Idelle would have none of it, or him, then. She wouldn't agree to be tied down for so long! She had suffered a reversal of conscience or mood—even—or so she said,—went to a priest, went into retirement here in G——, having fled her various evil pursuers.

How impressive the outlying slopes of these mountains they were just entering!

And yet he could understand that, too, in some people, anyhow,—the one decent thing in her life maybe, a timely revolt against a too great and unbroken excess. But, alas, it had been complicated with the fact that she wasn't ready to leave her mother or to do anything but stay in America. Besides things were becoming rather complicated. The war on J—— C—— threatened to expose her. Worse yet,—and so like her, life had won her back. Her beauty, her disposition, youth and age pursuing her—one slight concession to indulgence or pleasure after another and the new mood

or bent toward religiosity was entirely done away with.
Her sensual sex nature had conquered, of course.

*That little cabin on that slope, showing a lone lamp in
the dark!*

And then—then—

*Morning, by George! Ten o'clock! He had been asleep
all this time! He would have to hurry and dress now!*

But where was he in regard to Idelle? **Oh yes!** . . .
How she haunted him all the time these days! Coulstone,
angered at her refusal to come with him again (she could
not bring herself to do that, for all her religiosity, she said,
not caring for him so much any more), but frightened by
the presence of others, had eventually transferred all his
interests from Pittsburgh to G——, and at this very time,
on the ground of some form of virtue or duty—God only
knows what!—five years later, indeed—was here in G——
with his wife and attempting to persuade her that she ought
to give him a divorce in order to permit him to marry
Idelle and so legitimize her child! And he, Garrison,
already married to her! The insanity of mankind!

*He must be hurrying through his breakfast; they would
soon be nearing G—— now . . . and he must not forget
to stop in at Kiralfy's when he reached G—— and buy some
flowers for her!*

But Idelle was not to be taken that way. She did not
care for J—— C—— any more, or so she said. Besides
nothing would cure her varietism then or now but age,
apparently. And who was going to wait for age to overtake
her? Not he, anyhow. Why, the very event that threw
her into his arms—couldn't he have judged by that if he
had had any sense? Wasn't that just such another affair
as that of Coulstone and old Candia, only in this case it

concerned much younger men—wasters in their way, too—
one of whom, at least, was plainly madly in love with her,
while the other was just intensely interested. Why was it
that Idelle's affairs always had to be a complex of two or
more contending parties?

The condition of these washrooms in the morning!

According to her own story, she had first fallen in love,
or thought she had, with the younger of the two, Gaither
Browne, of the Harwood Brownes here in G—— and then
while he was still dancing attendance on her (and all the
while Coulstone was in the background, not entirely pushed
out of her life) young Gatchard Keene had come along
with his motor cars, his yacht, his stable of horses, and she
had begun to flirt with him also. Only, by then—and she
didn't care particularly for him, either—

*What a crowded breakfast car—all the people of last
night, and more from other cars attached since, probably!*

—she had half promised young Browne that she would
marry him, or let him think she might; had even confessed
a part of her past to him (or so she said) and he had forgiven her, or said it didn't matter. But when Keene came
along and she began to be interested in him Browne did not
like this new interest in the least, became furiously jealous
indeed. So great was his passion for her that he had threatened to kill her and himself if she did not give up Keene,
which, according to her, made her care all the more for
Keene. When Browne could stand it no longer and was
fearful lest Keene was to capture the prize—which he was
not, of course, Idelle being a mere trifler at all stages—he
had invited her out on that disastrous automobile ride—

*A mere form, eating, this morning! No appetite—due
to his troubled thoughts, of course, these days!*

—which had ended in her being carried into his presence at the Insull General. Browne must have been vividly in love with her to prefer to kill himself and her in that fashion rather than lose her, for, according to her, he had swung the car squarely into the rocks at Saltair Brook, only it never came out in the papers, and neither Idelle nor Browne would tell.

All railway cars seemed so soiled toward the end of a ride like this!

She professed afterwards to be sorry for Browne and inquired after him every day, although, of course, she had no sympathy for him or Keene, either,—for no man whom she could engage in any such contest. She was too wholly interested in following her own selfish bent. Afterward, when Keene was calling daily and trying to find out how it really did happen, and Coulstone was still in evidence and worrying over her condition (and old Candia also, he presumed—how could he tell whom all she had in tow at that time?), she refused to tell them, or any of a half dozen others who came to inquire. Yet right on top of all that she had encouraged him, Garrison, to fall in love with her, and had even imagined herself, or so she sneeringly charged, whenever they quarreled, in love with him, ready to reform and lead a better life, and had finally allowed him to carry her off and marry her in the face of them all! What were you to make of a creature like that? Insanity, on his or her part? Or both? Both, of course.

Kenelm! They were certainly speeding on! Those four wooden cows in that field, advertising a brand of butter!

But she could be so agreeable when she chose to be, and was so fascinatingly, if irritatingly, beautiful all the time! There was no doubt, though, that things were now reaching such a state that there would have to be a change. He couldn't stand this any longer. Women like Idelle were menaces, really, and shouldn't be tolerated. Most men wouldn't stand for her, although he had. But why? Why? Well, because he loved her, that was why, and you couldn't explain love. And the other reason—the worst of all—was the dread he had been suffering of late years of being left alone again if she left him. Alone! It was a terrible feeling, this fear of being left alone in the future, and especially when you were so drawn to some one who, whatever her faults, could make you idyllically happy if she only would. Lord, how peculiar these love passions of people were, anyhow! How they swayed one! Tortured one! Here he was haunted all the time now by the knowledge that he would be miserable if she left him, and that he needed some one like her to make him happy, a cheerful and agreeable beauty when she chose to be, fascinating even when she was not, and yet knowing that he would have to learn to endure to be alone if ever he was to get the strength to force her to better ways. Why couldn't he? Or why couldn't she settle down and be decent once? Well, he would have to face this out with her, once and for all now. He wasn't going to stand for her carrying on in this fashion. She must sober down. She had had her way long enough now, by God! He just wasn't going to pose as her husband and be a shield for her any longer! No sir, by George.

Only thirty-eight miles more! If she were not there now, as she promised!

Beginning to-day she would have to give him a decent deal or he would leave her. He wouldn't—he couldn't—stand for it any longer. Think of that last time he had come on from K——, just as he was coming to-day, and she had agreed to be at home—because he had made her promise before going that she would—and then, by George, when he got off the train and walked into the Brandingham with Arbuthnot to telephone, having just told Arbuthnot that he expected to find her out at the house, wasn't she there with young Keene and four or five others, drinking and dancing?

"Why, there's your wife now, Garrison," Arbuthnot had laughingly jested, and he had had to turn it all off with that "Oh, yes, that's right! I forgot! She was to meet me here. How stupid of me!"

Why hadn't he made a scene then? Why hadn't he broken things up then? Because he was a blank-blanked fool, that's why, allowing her to pull him around by the nose and do as she pleased! Love, that's why! He was a damned fool for loving her as much as he did, and in the face of all he knew!

Nearing Shively! Colonel Brandt's stock-farm! Home soon now! That little town in the distance, no connection with the railroad at all!

On that particular occasion, when at last they were in a taxi, she had begun one of her usual lies about having come downtown for something—a romper for Tatty—only when he ventured to show her what she was doing to herself and him socially, that he was being made a fool of, and that he really couldn't stand it, hadn't she flown into the usual rage and exclaimed: "Oh, all right! Why don't you leave me then? I don't care! I don't care! I'm bored! I can't help it! I can't always sit out in Sicard Avenue waiting for you!"

In Sicard Avenue. And that on top of always refusing to stay out there or to travel with him anywhere or to meet him and go places! Think of that for a happy married life, will you? Love! Love! Yes, love! Hell!

Well, here was Lawndale now, only eighteen miles—that meant about eighteen minutes from here, the way they were running now—and he would soon see her now if she was at home. If she only were, just this one time, to kiss him and laugh and ask about the trip and how he had made out, and let him propose some quiet dinner somewhere for just the two of them, a quiet dinner all to themselves, and then home again! How delightful that would be! Only— No doubt Charles would be at the station with the jitney, as he always called the yellow racer. He would have to summon all his ease to make his inquiry, for one had to keep one's face before the servants, you know—but then it was entirely possible that Charles wouldn't know whether she was home or not. She didn't always tell the servants. If she wasn't there, though—and after that letter and tele- gram— Well—now—this time!—by God!—

Wheelwright! They were running a little later, perhaps, but they would enter the station nearly on time!

But take, again, that last affair, that awful scene in the Shackamaxon at C——, when without his knowing it she had gone down there with Bodine and Arbuthnot and that wretched Aikenhead. Think of being seen in a public place like the Shackamaxon with Aikenhead and two such other wasters (even if Mrs. Bodine were along—she was no better than the others!), when she was already married and under so much suspicion as it was. If it weren't for him she would have been driven out of society long ago! Of course she would have! Hadn't General and Mrs. de Pasy cut her dead on that occasion?—only when they saw that he had joined her they altered their expressions and were polite enough, showing what they would do if they had to deal with her alone.

That brown automobile racing this train! How foolish some automobilists were!

Well, that time, coming home and finding her away, he had run down to C—— on the chance of finding her there— and sure enough there she was dancing with Aikenhead and Bodine by turns, and Mrs. Bodine and that free Mrs. Gildas and Belle Geary joining them later. And when he had sought her out to let her know he was back quite safe and anxious to see her, hadn't she turned on him with all the fury of a wildcat—"Always following me up and snooping around after me to catch me in something!" and that almost loud enough for all the others to hear! It was terrible! How could anybody stand for such a thing! He couldn't, and retain his self-respect. And yet he had—yes, he had, more shame to him! But if it hadn't been that he had been so lonely just beforehand and so eager to see her, and hadn't had those earrings for her in his pocket—thinking they would please her—perhaps he wouldn't have done as he did, backed down so. As it was—well, all he could think of at the moment was to apologize—to his own wife!—and plead that he hadn't meant to seem to follow her up and "snoop around." Think of that! Hang it all, why hadn't he left her then and there? Supposing she didn't come back? Supposing she didn't? What of it? What of it? Only—

"This way out, please."

Well, here was G—— at last, and there was Charles, well enough, waiting as usual. Would she be home now? Would she? Perhaps, after all, he had better not say anything yet, just go around to Kiralfy's and get the flowers. But to what end, really, if she weren't there again? What would he do this time? Surely this must be the end if she weren't there, if he had any strength at all. He wouldn't be put upon in this way again, would he?—after all he had told himself he would do the last time if ever it happened again! His own reputation was at stake now, really. It depended on what he did now. What must the servants think—his always following her up and she never being there or troubling about him in the least?

"Ah, Charles, there you are! To Kiralfy's first, then home!"

She was making him a laughing-stock, or would if he didn't take things in hand pretty soon to-day, really—a man who hung onto a woman because she was young and pretty, who tolerated a wife who did not care for him and who ran with other men—a sickening, heartless social pack—in his absence. She was pulling him down to her level, that's what she was doing, a level he had never deemed possible in the old days. It was almost unbelievable—and yet— But he would go in and get the flowers, anyway!

"Back in a minute, Charles!"

And now here was Sicard Avenue, again, dear old Sicaᵣᵤ, with its fine line of trees on either side of its b·oad roadway, and their own big house set among elms and with that French garden in front—so quiet and aristocratic! Why couldn't she be content with a place like this, with her present place in society? Why not? Why not be happy in it? She could be such an interesting social figure if she chose, if she would only try. But no, no—she wouldn't. It would always be the same until—until—

The gardener had trimmed the grass again, and nicely!

"No, suh, Mr. Garrison," George was already saying in that sing-song darky way of his as he walked up the steps ahead of him, and just as he expected or feared he would. It was always the way, and always would be until he had courage enough to leave once and for all—as he would to-day, by George! He wouldn't stand for this one moment longer—not one. "Mrs. Garrison she say she done gone to Mrs. Gildas'" (it might just as well have been the Bodines, the Del Guardias or the Cranes—they were all alike), "an' dat yo' was to call her up dere when yo' come in or come out. She say to say she lef' a note fo' yo' on yo' dresser."

Curse her! Curse her! Curse her! To be treated like

this all the time! He would fix her now, though, this time! Yes, he would. This time he wouldn't change his mind.

And the brass on the front door not properly cleaned, either!

"George," this to his servant as the latter preceded him into his room—their room—where he always so loved to be when things were well between them, "never mind the bags now. I'll call you later when I want you," and then, as the door closed, almost glaring at everything about him. There in the mirror, just above his military brushes, was stuck a note—the usual wheedling, chaffering rot she was inclined to write him when she wanted to be very nice on such occasions as this. Now he would see what new lying, fooling communication she had left for him, where he would be asked to come now, what do, instead of her being here to receive him as she had promised, as was her duty really, as any decent married woman would—as any decent married man would expect her to be. Oh, the devil!

That fly buzzing in the window there, trying to get out!

What was the use of being alive, anyway? What the good of anything—money or anything else? He wouldn't stand for this any longer, he couldn't—no, he couldn't, that was all there was to it! She could go to the devil now; he wouldn't follow her any more—never, never, never!—the blank-blank-blank-blank——! This was the end! This was the way she was always doing! But never again now, not once more! He'd get a divorce now! Now, by George, for once he would stand his ground and be a man, not a social door-mat, a humble beggar of love, hanging around hat in hand waiting for her favors! Never again, by God! Never!! Never!!! Only—

That letter of hers on the dresser there waiting for him, as usual!

"Dearest Old Judge: This isn't the real one. This is just a hundred-kiss one, this. The real one is pinned to your pillow over there—our pillow—where it ought to be, don't you think? I don't want you to be unhappy at not finding me home, Judgie, see? And I don't want you to get mad and quarrel. And I do want you to be sure to find the other letter. So don't be angry, see? But call me up at the Gildas'. I'm dying to see you, dearie, really and truly I am! I've been so lonesome without you! (Yes!) You're sure to find me out there. And you're not to be angry—not one little frown, do you hear? I just couldn't help it, dearest! So read the other letter now!

"IDELLE."

If only his hands wouldn't tremble so! Damn her! Damn her! Damn her! To think she would always treat him like this! To think he was never to have one decent hour of her time to himself, not one! Always this running here, there and everywhere away from him, as it were!

He crumpled up the note and threw it on the floor, then went to the window and looked out. There over the way at her own spacious door was young Mrs. Justus just entering her car—a simple, home-loving little woman, who would never dream of the treacheries and eccentricities of Idelle; who, if she even guessed what manner of woman she was, would never have anything more to do with her. Why couldn't he have loved a girl like her—why not? And just beyond, the large quiet house of the Walterses, those profoundly sober people of the very best ways and means, always so kind and helpful, anxious to be sociable, of whom Idelle could think of nothing better to say than "stuffy." Anything kind and gentle and orderly was just stuffy to her, or dull. That was what she considered him, no doubt. That's because she was what she was, curses on her! She couldn't stand, or even understand, profoundly worthy people like the Justuses or the Walterses. (There was May Walters now at her dining-room window.) And then there were the Hartleys. . . . But that other note of hers—what did it say? He ought to read that now, whether he left or no; but he would leave this time, well enough!

He turned to the twin bed and from the fretted counterpane unpinned the second lavender-colored and scented note—the kind Idelle was always scribbling when she was doing things she shouldn't. It didn't make one hanged bit of difference now what she wrote, of course—only— He wouldn't follow her this time; no, he wouldn't! He wouldn't have anything more to do with her ever! He would quit now, lock the doors in a few minutes, discharge the servants, cut off her allowance, tell her to go to blazes. He would go and live at a club, as he had so often threatened before to himself—or get out of G——, as he had also threatened. He couldn't stand the comment that would follow, anyhow. He had had enough of it. He hated the damned city! He had never had any luck in it. Never had he been happy here, in spite of the fact that he had been born and brought up here, and twice married here— never! Twice now he had been treated like this by women right here in this city, his home town, where everybody knew! Twice he had been made a fool of, but this time—

The letter, though!

"Dearest and best of hubbies, I know you're going to be disappointed at not finding me here, and in spite of anything I can say, probably terribly angry, too. (I wish you wouldn't be, darling!) But, sweetheart, if you'll only believe me this time (I've said that before when you wouldn't, I know, and it wasn't my fault, either), it wasn't premeditated, really, it wasn't! Honest, cross my heart, dear, twenty ways, and hope to die!"

(What did she really care for his disappointment or what he suffered, curse her!)

"Only yesterday at four Betty called up and insisted that I should come. There's a big house party on, and you're invited, of course, when you get back. Her cousin Frank is coming and some friends of his,"

(*Yes, he knew what friends!*)

"and four of my old girl chums, so I just couldn't get out of it, nor would I, particularly since she wanted me to help her, and I've asked her so many times to help us—now, could I?"

Idelle's way in letters, as in person, was always bantering. To the grave with Betty Gildas and all her house parties, in so far as he was concerned, the fast, restless, heartless thing! Why couldn't she have been here just this once, when he wanted her so much and had wired and written in plenty of time for her to be!

But no, she didn't care for him. She never had. She merely wanted to fool him along like this, to keep his name, his position, the social atmosphere he could give her. This whole thing was a joke to her—this house, his friends, himself, all—just nothing! Her idea was to fool him along in this way while she continued to run with these other shabby, swift, restless, insatiable creatures like herself, who liked cabarets, thés dansants, automobile runs to this, that and the other wretched place, country house parties, country clubs, country this, country that, or New York and all its shallow and heartless mockery of simplicity and peace. Well, he was through. She was always weary of him, never anxious to be with him for one moment even, but never weary of any of them, you bet—of seeking the wildest forms of pleasure! Well, this was the end now. He had had enough. She could go her own way from now on. Let the beastly flowers lie there—what did he care? He wouldn't carry them to her. He was through now. He was going to do what he said—leave. Only—

He began putting some things in another bag, in addition to the ones he had—his silk shirts, extra underwear, all his collars. Once and for all now he wouldn't stand this—never! Never!

Only—

As he fumed and glared, his eye fell on his favorite photo of Idelle—young, rounded, sensuous, only twenty-four to his forty-eight, an air and a manner flattering to any man's sense of vanity and possession—and then, as a contrast, he thought of the hard, smiling, self-efficiency of so many of her friends—J—— C——, for one, still dogging her heels in spite of him, and Keene, young and wealthy, and Arbuthnot—and who not else?—any one and all of whom would be glad to take her if he left her. And she knew this. It was a part of her strength, even her charm—curse her! Curse her! Curse her!

But more than that, youth, youth, the eternal lure of beauty and vitality, her smiling softness at times, her geniality, her tolerance, their long talks and pleasant evenings and afternoons. And all of these calling, calling now. And yet they were all at the vanishing point, perhaps never to come again, if he left her! She had warned him of that. "If I go," she had once said—more than once, indeed—"it's for good. Don't think I'll ever come back, for I won't." And he understood well enough that she would not. She didn't care for him enough to come back. She never would, if she really went.

He paused, meditating, biting his lips as usual, flushing, frowning, darkening—a changeable sky his face—and then—

"George," he said after the servant had appeared in answer to his ring, "tell Charles to bring the jitney around again, and you pack me the little brown kit bag out of these others. I'm going away for a day or two, anyhow."

"Yes, suh!"

Then down the stairs, saying that Idelle was a liar, a wastrel, a heartless butterfly, worthy to be left as he proposed to leave her now. Only, once outside in his car with Charles at the wheel, and ready to take him wherever he said, he paused again, and then—sadly— "To the Gildases, and better go by the Skillytown road. It's the shortest!"

Then he fell to thinking again.

IV

ST. COLUMBA AND THE RIVER

THE first morning that McGlathery saw the great river stretching westward from the point where the initial shaft had been sunk he was not impressed by it— or, rather, he was, but not favorably. It looked too gray and sullen, seeing that he was viewing it through a driving, sleety rain. There were many ferry boats and craft of all kinds, large and small, steaming across its choppy bosom, giant steamers, and long projecting piers, great and mysterious, and clouds of gulls, and the shriek of whistles, and the clang of fog-bells, . . . but he did not like water. It took him back to eleven wretched seasick days in which he had crossed on the steamer from Ireland. But then, glory be, once freed from the mysteries of Ellis Island, he had marched out on dry land at the Battery, cloth bags in hand, and exclaimed, "Thanks be, I'm shut av it!"

And he thought he was, for he was mortally afraid of water. But fate, alas! had not decreed it as a permanent thing. As a matter of fact, water in one form or another had persistently seemed to pursue him since. In Ireland, County Clare, from whence he hailed, he had been a ditcher—something remotely connected with water. Here in America, and once safely settled in Brooklyn, he had no sooner sought work than the best he could seemingly get was a job in connection with a marsh which was being drained, a very boggy and pool-y one—water again, you see. Then there was a conduit being dug, a great open sewer which once when he and other members of the construction gang were working on it, was flooded by a cloudburst, a tremendous afternoon rain-storm which drove them from it with a volume of water which threatened to drown them all. Still later, he and thirty others were engaged in cleaning out a two-compartment reservoir, old and stone-rotten, when, one-half being empty and the other full, the old dividing wall broke, and once more he barely escaped with his life by scrambling up a steep bank. It was then that the thought first took root in his mind that water—any kind of water, sea or fresh—was not favorable to him. Yet here he was, facing this great river on a gray rainy November morning, and with the avowed object of going to work in the tunnel which was about to be dug under it.

Think of it! In spite of his prejudices and fears, here he was, and all due to one Thomas Cavanaugh, a fellow churchman and his foreman these last three years, who had happened to take a fancy to him and had told him that if he came to work in the tunnel and prosecuted his new work thoroughly, and showed himself sufficiently industrious and courageous, it might lead to higher things—viz., bricklaying, or plastering, in the guise of cement moulding, down in this very tunnel, or timbering, or better yet, the steel-plate-joining trade, which was a branch of the ironworkers' guild and was rewarded by no less a compensation than twelve dollars a day. Think of it—twelve dollars a day! Men of this class and skill were scarce in tunnel work and in great demand in America. This same Cavanaugh was to be one of the foremen in this tunnel, his foreman, and would look after him. Of course it required time and patience. One had to begin at the bottom—the same being seventy-five feet under the Hudson River, where some very careful preliminary digging had to be done. McGlathery had surveyed his superior and benefactor at the time with uncertain and yet ambitious eyes.

"Is it as ye tell me now?" he commented at one place.

"Yis. Av course. What d'ye think I'm taalkin' to ye about?"

"Ye say, do ye?"

"Certainly."

"Well! Well! Belike it's a fine job. I dunno. Five dollars a day, ye say, to begin with?"

"Yis, five a day."

"Well, a man in my line could git no more than that, eh? It wouldn't hurt me fer once, fer a little while anyway, hey?"

"It would be the makin' av ye."

"Well, I'll be with ye. Yis, I'll be with ye. It's not five I can git everywhere. When is it ye'll be wantin' me?"

The foreman, a Gargantuan figure in yellow jeans and high rubber boots smeared to the buttocks with mud, eyed him genially and amiably, the while McGlathery surveyed his superior with a kind of reverence and awe, a reverence which he scarcely felt for any other man, unless perchance it might be his parish priest, for he was a good Catholic, or the political backer of his district, through whom he had secured his job. What great men they all were, to be sure, leading figures in his life.

So here he was on this particular morning shortly after the work had been begun, and here was the river, and down below in this new shaft, somewhere, was Thomas Cavanaugh, to whom he had to report before he could go to work.

"Sure, it's no colleen's job," he observed to a fellow worker who had arrived at the mouth of the shaft about the same time as himself, and was beginning to let himself down the ladder which sank darkly to an intermediate platform, below which again was another ladder and platform, and below that a yellow light. "Ye say Mr. Cavanaugh is below there?"

"He is," replied the stranger without looking up. "Ye'll find him inside the second lock. Arr ye workin' here?"

"Yis."

"Come along, then."

With a bundle which consisted of his rubber boots, a worn suit of overalls, and with his pick and shovel over his shoulder, he followed. He reached the bottom of the pit, boarded as to the sides with huge oak planks sustained by cross beams, and there, with several others who were waiting until the air pressure should be adjusted, entered the lock. The comparatively small and yet massive chamber, with its heavy iron door at either end, responding so slowly to pressure, impressed him. There was only a flickering light made by a gasoline torch here. There was a whistling sound from somewhere.

"Ever work under air pressure before, Paddy?" inquired a great hulking ironworker, surveying him with a genial leer.

"Air what?" asked McGlathery without the slightest comprehension of what was meant, but not to be outdone by mere words. "No, I never did."

"Well, ye're under it now, two thousand pounds to the square inch. Don't ye feel it?"

Dennis, who had been feeling an odd sensation about his ear-drums and throat, but had no knowledge that it was related to this, acknowledged that he did. "'Tis air, is it?" he inquired. "'Tis a quare feeling I have." The hissing ceased.

"Yuh want to look out fer that, new man," volunteered another, a skimpy, slithery, genial American. "Don't let 'em rush that stuff on yuh too fast. Yuh may git the 'bends.'"

Dennis, ignorant as to the meaning of "bends," made no reply.

"D'yuh know what the 'bends' is, new man?" persisted the other provocatively.

"Naw," replied Dennis awkwardly after a time, feeling himself the centre of a fire of curious observations and solicitation.

"Well, yuh will if yuh ever git 'em—haw! haw!" this from a waggish lout, a bricklayer who had previously not spoken. The group in the lock was large. "It comes from them lettin' the pressure be put on or took off too fast. It twists yer muscles all up, an' does sumpin' to yer nerves. Yuh'll know it if yuh ever git it."

"Member Eddie Slawder?" called another gaily. "He died of it over here in Bellevue, after they started the Fourteenth Street end. Gee, yuh oughta heerd him holler! I went over to see him."

Good news, indeed! So this was his introduction to the tunnel, and here was a danger not commented on by Cavanaugh. In his dull way McGlathery was moved by it. Well, he was here now, and they were forcing open the door at the opposite side of the lock, and the air pressure had not hurt him, and he was not killed yet; and then, after traversing a rather neatly walled section of tunnel, albeit badly littered with beams and plates and bags of cement and piles of brick, and entering another lock like the first and coming out on the other side—there, amid an intricate network of beams and braces and a flare of a half dozen great gasoline lamps which whistled noisily, and an overhanging mass of blackness which was nothing less than earth under the great river above, was Cavanaugh, clad in a short red sweater and great rubber boots, an old yellowish-brown felt hat pulled jauntily over one ear. He was conversing with two other foremen and an individual in good clothes, one of those mighties—an engineer, no doubt.

Ah, how remote to McGlathery were the gentlemen in smooth fitting suits! He viewed them as you might creatures from another realm.

Beyond this lock also was a group of night workers left over from the night before and under a strange foreman (ditchers, joiners, earth carriers, and steel-plate riveters), all engaged in the rough and yet delicate risk of forcing and safeguarding a passage under the river, and only now leaving. The place was full. It was stuffy from the heat of the lamps, and dirty from the smear of the black muck which was over everything. Cavanaugh spied Dennis as he made his way forward over the widely separated beams.

"So here ye arr! These men are just after comin' out,"

and he waved a hand toward the forward end of the tunnel. "Git in there, Dennis, and dig out that corner beyond the post there. Jerry here'll help ye. Git the mud up on this platform so we can git these j'ists in here."

McGlathery obeyed. Under the earthy roof whose surface he could see but dimly at the extreme forward end of the tunnel beyond that wooden framework, he took his position. With a sturdy arm and a sturdy back and a sturdy foot and leg, he pushed his spade into the thick mud, or loosened it with his pick when necessary, and threw it up on the crude platform, where other men shoveled it into a small car which was then trundled back over the rough boards to the lock, and so on out. It was slow, dirty, but not difficult work, so long as one did not think of the heavy river overhead with its ships and its choppy waves in the rain, and the gulls and the bells. Somehow, Dennis was fearfully disturbed as to the weight of this heavy volume of earth and water overhead. It really terrified him. Perhaps he had been overpersuaded by the lure of gold? Suppose it should break through, suppose the earth over his head should suddenly drop and bury him—that dim black earth overhead, as heavy and thick as this he was cutting with his shovel now.

"Come, Dennis, don't be standin' there lookin' at the roof. The roof's not goin' to hurt ye. Ye're not down here to be lookin' after the roof. I'll be doin' that. Just ye 'tend to yer shovelin'."

It was the voice of Cavanaugh near at hand. Unconsciously McGlathery had stopped and was staring upward. A small piece of earth had fallen and struck him on the back. Suppose! Suppose!

Know, O reader, that the business of tunneling is one of the most hazardous and dramatic, albeit interesting, of all known fields of labor. It consists, in these latter days at least, in so far as under-water tunneling is concerned, of sinking huge shafts at either end or side of a river, lake or channel (one hundred feet, perhaps, within the shore line) to a depth of, say, thirty feet below the water level, and from these two points tunneling outward under the bottom of the river until the two ends meet somewhere near the middle. The exact contact and precise joining of these outer ends is considered one of the true tests of skilful engineering. McGlathery personally understood all this but dimly. And even so it could not cheer him any.

And it should be said here that the safety of the men who did the work, and the possibility of it, depended first on the introduction at either end, just at the base of the shafts and then at about every hundred or so feet, as the tunnel progressed outward, of huge cylindrical chambers, or locks, of heavy iron—air locks, no less—fifteen feet in diameter, and closed at each end by massive doors swinging inward toward the shore line, so that the amazing and powerful pressure of air constantly forced outward from the shore by huge engines could not force them open. It was only by the same delicate system which causes water locks to open and close that they could be opened at all. That is, workingmen coming down into the shaft and desiring to pass into the head of the tunnel beyond the lock, would have to first enter one of these locks, which would then gradually be filled with air compressed up to the same pressure as that maintained in the main portion of the tunnel farther in. When this pressure had been reached they could easily open the inward swinging door and pass into the tunnel proper. Here, provided that so much had been completed, they might walk, say, so much as a hundred or more feet, when they would encounter another lock. The pressure in the lock, according to who had last used it, would be either that of the section of the tunnel toward the shore, or of the section beyond, toward the centre of the river. At first, bell cords, later telephones, and then electric signals controlled this—that is, the lowering or raising of the pressure of air in the locks so that one door or the other might be opened. If the pressure in the lock was different from that in your section, and you could not

open the door (which you could not), you pulled the cord
or pushed the button so many times, according to your position, and the air in the lock was adjusted to the section of
the tunnel in which you stood. Then you could open the
door. Once in, as in a water lock, the air was raised or
lowered, according to your signal, and you could enter the
next section outward or inward. All these things had been
adjusted to a nicety even in those days, which was years
ago.

*　　*　　*　　*　　*　　*　　*

The digging of this particular tunnel seemed safe enough
—for McGlathery at least, once he began working here. It
moved at the rate of two and even three feet a day, when
things were going well, only there were days and days when,
owing to the need of shoring and timbering and plate setting,
to say nothing of the accidental encountering of rock in front
which had to be drilled away, the men with picks and shovels
had to be given a rest, or better yet, set to helping the joiners
in erecting those cross beams and supports which made the
walls safe. It was so that Dennis learned much about joining and even drilling.

Nevertheless, in spite of the increased pay, this matter
of working under the river was a constant source of fear to
him. The earth in which he worked was so uncertain. One
day it would be hard black mud, another soft, another silt,
another sand, according as the tunnel sloped further and
further under the bed. In addition, at times great masses of
it fell, not enough to make a hole in the roof above, but
enough, had it chanced to fall on one of the workers, to
break his back or half bury him in mud. Usually it was
broken by the beams overhead. Only one day, some seven
months after he had begun and when he was becoming
fairly accustomed to the idea of working here, and when
his skill had increased to such an extent that he was considered one of the most competent workers in his limited
field, the unexpected happened.

He had come down one morning at eight with the rest of his gang and was working about the base of two new supports which had just been put in place, when he noticed, or thought he did, that the earth seemed wetter than usual, sticky, watery, and hard to manage. It could not have been much worse had a subterranean spring been encountered. Besides, one of the gasoline lamps having been brought forward and hung close by, he noticed by its light that the ceiling seemed to look silvery gray and beady. He spoke of it to Cavanagh, who stood by.

"Yis," said his foreman dubiously, staring upward, " 'tis wet. Maybe the air pumps is not workin' right. I'll just make sure," and he sent word to the engineer.

The shaft superintendent himself appeared.

"Everything's all right up above," he said. "Two thousand pounds to the square inch. I'll just put on a little more, if you say so."

"Ye'd better," replied Cavanaugh. "The roof's not actin' right. And if ye see Mr. Henderson, send him down. I'd like to talk to him."

"All right," and off he went.

McGlathery and the others, at first nervous, but now slightly reassured, worked on. But the ground under their feet became sloppy, and some of the silvery frosting on the roof began to drop and even trickle as water. Then a mass of sloppy mud fell.

"Back, men!"

It was the voice of Cavanaugh, but not quicker than the scampering of the men who, always keenly alive to the danger of a situation, had taken note of the dripping water and the first flop of earth. At the same time, an ominous creak from one of the beams overhead gave warning of the imminence of a catastrophe. A pell-mell rush for the lock some sixty feet away ensued. Tools were dropped, precedence disregarded. They fell and stumbled over the beams and between, pushing each other out of the way into the water and mud as they ran, McGlathery a fair second to none.

"Open the door! Open the door!" was the cry as they reached the lock, for some one had just entered from the other side—the engineer. "For Christ's sake, open the door!" But that could not be done so quicky. A few moments at least had to elapse.

"It's breakin' in!" cried some one in a panicky voice, an ironworker.

"Great God, it's comin down!" this from one of the masons, as three lamps in the distance were put out by the mud.

McGlathery was almost dying of fear. He was sweating a cold sweat. Five dollars a day indeed! He should stay away from water, once and for all. Didn't he know that? It was always bad luck to him.

"What's the trouble? What's the trouble?" called the amazed engineer as, unconscious of what was happening outside, he pushed open the door.

"Git out of the way!"

"Fer God's sake, let us in!"

"Shut the door!" this from a half dozen who had already reached safety assuming that the door could be instantly closed.

"Wait! Cavanaugh's outside!" This from some one— not McGlathery, you may be sure, who was cowering in a corner. He was so fearful that he was entirely unconscious of his superior's fate.

"To hell with Cavanaugh! Shut the door!" screamed another, a great ironworker, savage with fear.

"Let Cavanaugh in, I say!" this from the engineer.

At this point McGlathery, for the first time on this or any other job, awoke to a sense of duty, but not much at that. He was too fearful. This was what he got for coming down here at all. He knew Cavanaugh—Cavanaugh was his friend, indeed. Had he not secured him this and other jobs? Surely. But then Cavanaugh had persuaded him to come down here, which was wrong. He ought not to have done it. Still, even in his fear he had manhood enough to feel that it was not quite right to shut Cavanaugh out. Still, what could he do—he was but one. But even as he thought, and others were springing forward to shut Cavanaugh out, so eager were they to save themselves, they faced a gleaming revolver in the steady hand of the big foreman.

"I'll shoot down the first damned man that tries to shut the door before me and Kelly are in," the big foreman was calling, the while he was pulling this same Kelly from the mud and slime outside. Then fairly throwing him into the lock, and leaping after him, he turned and quietly helped closed the door.

McGlathery was amazed at this show of courage. To stop and help another man like that in the face of so much danger! Cavanaugh was even a better and kinder man than he had thought—really a great man—no coward like himself. But why had Cavanaugh persuaded him to come down here when he knew that he was afraid of water! And now this had happened. Inside as they cowered—all but Cavanaugh—they could hear the sound of crushing timber and grinding brick outside, which made it quite plain that where a few moments before had been beams and steel and a prospective passageway for men, was now darkness and water and the might of the river, as it had been since the beginning.

McGlathery, seeing this, awoke to the conviction that in the first place he was a great coward, and in the second that the tunnel digging was no job for him. He was by no means fitted for it, he told himself. " 'Tis the last," he commented, as he climbed safely out with the others after a distressing wait of ten minutes at the inward lock. "Begob, I thought we was all lost. 'Twas a close shave. But I'll go no more below. I've had enough." He was thinking of a small bank account—six hundred dollars in all—which he had saved, and of a girl in Brooklyn who was about to marry him. "No more!"

*   *   *   *   *   *   *

But, at that, as it stood, there was no immediate danger of work being offered. The cave-in had cost the contractors thousands and in addition had taught them that mere air pressure and bracing as heretofore followed were not sufficient for successful tunneling. Some new system would have to be devised. Work on both halves of the tunnel was suspended for over a year and a half, during which time McGlathery married, a baby was born to him, and his six hundred had long since diminished to nothing. The difference between two and five dollars a day is considerable. Incidentally, he had not gone near his old foreman in all this time, being somehow ashamed of himself, and in consequence he had not fared so well. Previously Cavanaugh had kept him almost constantly employed, finding him faithful and hard-working, but now owing to stranger associates there were weeks when he had no work at all and others when he had to work for as little as one-fifty a day. It was not so pleasant. Besides, he had a sneaking feeling that if he had behaved a little more courageously at that time, gone and talked to his old foreman afterward or at the time, he might now be working for good pay. Alas, he had not done so, and if he went now Cavanaugh would be sure to want to know why he had disappeared so utterly. Then, in spite of his marital happiness, poverty began to press him so. A second and a third child were born—only they were twins.

In the meantime, Henderson, the engineer whom Cavanaugh had wanted to consult with at the time, had devised a new system of tunneling, namely, what subsequently came to be known as the pilot tunnel. This was an iron tube ten feet in length and fifteen feet in diameter—the width of the tunnel, which was carried forward on a line with the axis of the tunnel into the ground ahead. When it was driven in far enough to be completely concealed by the earth about, then the earth within was removed. The space so cleared was then used exactly as a hub is used on a wagon wheel. Beams like spokes were radiated from its sides to its centre, and the surrounding earth sustained by heavy iron plates. On this plan the old company had decided to undertake the work again.

One evening, sitting in his doorway thumbing his way through an evening paper which he could barely read, McGlathery had made all this out. Mr. Henderson was to be in charge as before. Incidentally it was stated that Thomas Cavanaugh was going to return as one of the two chief foremen. Work was to be started at once. In spite of himself, McGlathery was impressed. If Cavanaugh would only take him back! To be sure, he had come very near losing his life, as he thought, but then he had not. No one had, not a soul. Why should *he* be so fearful if Cavanaugh could take such chances as he had? Where else could he make five dollars a day? Still, there was this haunting sensation that the sea and all of its arms and branches, wherever situated, were inimical to him and that one day one of them would surely do him a great injury—kill him, perhaps. He had a recurring sensation of being drawn up into water or down, he could not tell which, and of being submerged in ooze and choking slowly. It was horrible.

But five dollars a day as against one-fifty or two or none at all (seven, once he became very proficient) and an assured future as a tunnel worker, a "sand-hog," as he had now learned such men as himself were called, was a luring as well as a disturbing thought. After all, he had no trade other than this he had begun to learn under Cavanaugh. Worse he was not a union man, and the money he had once saved was gone, and he had a wife and three children. With the former he had various and sundry talks. To be sure, tunneling was dangerous, but still! She agreed with him that he had better not, but—after all, the difference that five, maybe seven, instead of two a day would make in their liv-

ing expenses was in both their minds. McGlathery saw it.
He decided after a long period of hesitation that perhaps he
had best return. After all, nothing had happened to him
that other time, and might it ever again, really? He meditated.

As has been indicated, a prominent element in Mc-
Glathery's nature was superstition. While he believed in the
inimical nature of water to him, he also believed in the
power of various saints, male and female, to help or hinder.
In the Catholic Church of St. Columba of South Brooklyn,
at which McGlathery and his young wife were faithful at-
tendants, there was a plaster statue of a saint of this same
name, a co-worker with St. Patrick in Ireland, it appears,
who in McGlathery's native town of Kilrush, County of
Clare, on the water's edge of Shannon, had been worshipped
for centuries past, or at least highly esteemed, as having
some merit in protecting people at sea, or in adventures
connected with water. This was due, perhaps, to the fact
that Kilrush was directly on the water and had to have a
saint of that kind. At any rate, among other things, he
had occasionally been implored for protection in that realm
when McGlathery was a boy. On his setting out for
America, for instance, some few years before at the suggestion of his mother, he had made a novena before this
very saint, craving of him a safe conduct in crossing the
sea, as well as prosperity once he had arrived in America.
Well, he had crossed in safety, and prospered well enough,
he thought. At least he had not been killed in any tunnel.
In consequence, on bended knees, two blessed candles burning before him in the rack, a half dollar deposited in the
box labeled "St. Columba's Orphans," he finally asked of
this saint whether, in case he returned to this underground
tunnel work, seeing that necessity was driving him, would
he be so kind as to protect him? He felt sure that Cavanaugh, once he applied to him, and seeing that he had
been a favorite worker, would not begrudge him a place

if he had one. In fact he knew that Cavanaugh had always favored him as a good useful helper.

After seven "Our Fathers" and seven "Hail Marys," said on his knees, and a litany of the Blessed Virgin for good measure, he crossed himself and arose greatly refreshed. There was a pleasant conviction in his mind now, newly come there before this image, that he would never come to real harm by any power of water. It was a revelation—a direct communication, perhaps. At any rate, something told him to go and see Cavanaugh at once, before the work was well under way, and not be afraid, as no harm would come to him, and besides, he might not get anything even though he desired it so much if he delayed. He bustled out of the church and over to the waterfront where the deserted shaft was still standing, and sure enough, there was Cavanaugh, conversing with Mr. Henderson.

"Yis—an' what arr ye here fer?" he now demanded to know of McGlathery rather amusedly, for he had sensed the cause of his desertion.

"I was readin' that ye was about to start work on the tunnel again."

"An' so we arr. What av it?"

"I was thinkin' maybe ye'd have a place fer me. I'm married now an' have three children."

"An' ye're thinkin' that's a reason fer givin' ye something, is it?" demanded the big foreman rather cynically, with a trace of amusement. "I thought ye said ye was shut av the sea—that ye was through now, once an' fer all?"

"So I did, but I've changed me mind. It's needin' the work I am."

"Very well, then," said Cavanaugh. "We're beginnin' in the mornin'. See that ye're here at seven sharp. An' mind ye, no worryin' or lookin' around. We've a safe way now. It's different. There's no danger."

McGlathery gratefully eyed his old superior, then departed, only to return the next morning a little dubious but willing. St. Columba had certainly indicated that all would be well with him—but still— A man is entitled to a few doubts even when under the protection of the best of saints. He went down with the rest of the men and began cleaning out that nearest section of the tunnel where first water and then earth had finally oozed and caked. That done he helped install the new pilot tunnel which was obviously a great improvement over the old system. It seemed decidedly safe. McGlathery attempted to explain its merits to his wife, who was greatly concerned for him, and incidentally each morning and evening on his way to and from his task he dropped in at St. Columba's to offer up a short silent prayer. In spite of his novena and understanding with the saint he was still suspicious of this dread river above him, and of what might happen to him in spite of St. Columba. The good saint, due to some error on the part of McGlathery, might change his mind.

Nothing happened, of course, for days and weeks and months. Under Cavanaugh's direction the work progressed swiftly, and McGlathery and he, in due time, became once more good friends, and the former an expert bracer or timberer, one of the best, and worth seven a day really, which he did not get. Incidentally, they were all shifted from day to night work, which somehow was considered more important. There were long conversations now and again between Cavanaugh and Henderson, and Cavanaugh and other officials of the company who came down to see, which enlightened McGlathery considerably as to the nature and danger of the work. Just the same, overhead was still the heavy river—he could feel it pushing at him at times, pushing at the thick layer of mud and silt above him and below which with the aid of this new pilot shield they were burrowing.

Yet nothing happened for months and months. They cleared a thousand feet without a hitch. McGlathery began to feel rather comfortable about it all. It certainly seemed reasonably safe under the new system. Every night he went down and every morning came up, as hale and healthy as ever, and every second week, on a Tuesday, a pay envelope containing the handsome sum of seventy-two dollars was handed him. Think of it! Seventy-two dollars! Naturally, as a token of gratitude to St. Columba, he contributed liberally to his Orphans' Home, a dollar a month, say, lit a fresh candle before his shrine every Sunday morning after high mass, and bought two lots out on the Goose Creek waterfront—on time—on which some day, God willing, he proposed to build a model summer and winter cottage. And then—! Well, perhaps, as he thought afterward, it might have been due to the fact that his prosperity had made him a little more lax than he should have been, or proud, or not quite as thoughtful of the saint as was his due. At any rate, one night, in spite of St. Columba—or could it have been with his aid and consent in order to show McGlathery his power?—the wretched sneaky river did him another bad turn, a terrible turn, really.

It was this way. While they were working at midnight under the new form of bracing, based on the pilot tunnel, and with an air pressure of two thousand pounds to the square inch which had so far sufficed to support the iron roof plates which were being put in place behind the pilot tunnel day after day, as fast as space permitted, and with the concrete men following to put in a form of arch which no river weight could break, the very worst happened. For it was just at this point where the iron roof and the mud of the river bottom came in contact behind the pilot tunnel that there was a danger spot ever since the new work began. Cavanaugh had always been hovering about that, watching it, urging others to be careful—"taking no chances with it," as he said.

"Don't be long, men!" was his constant urge. "Up with it now! Up with it! In with the bolts! Quick, now, with yer riveter—quick! quick!"

And the men! How they worked there under the river

whenever there was sufficient space to allow a new steel band to be segmentally set! For at that point it was, of course, that the river might break through. How they tugged, sweated, grunted, cursed, in this dark muddy hole, lit by a few glittering electric arcs—the latest thing in tunnel work! Stripped to the waist, in mud-soaked trousers and boots, their arms and backs and breasts mud-smeared and wet, their hair tousled, their eyes bleary—an artist's dream of bedlam, a heavenly inferno of toil—so they labored. And overhead was the great river, Atlantic liners resting upon it, thirty or fifteen or ten feet of soil only, sometimes, between them and this thin strip of mud sustained, supposedly, by two thousand pounds of air pressure to the square inch—all they had to keep the river from bleeding water down on them and drowning them like rats!

"Up with it! Up with it! Up with it! Now the bolts! Now the riveter! That's it! In with it, Johnny! Once more now!"

Cavanaugh's voice urging them so was like music to them, their gift of energy, their labor song, their power to do, their Ei Uchnam.

But there were times also, hours really, when the slow forward movement of the pilot tunnel, encountering difficult earth before it, left this small danger section unduly exposed to the rotary action of the water overhead which was constantly operating in the bed of the river. Leaks had been discovered from time to time, small tricklings and droppings of earth, which brought Cavanaugh and Henderson to the spot and caused the greatest tension until they had been done away with. The air had a tendency to bore holes upward through the mud. But these were invariably stanched with clay, or, if growing serious, bags of shavings or waste, the air pressure blowing outward from below being sufficient to hold these in place, provided the breach was not too wide. Even when "all hands" were working directly under a segment wide enough for a ring of plates, one man was told off to "kape an eye on it."

On the evening in question, however, after twenty-eight men, including Cavanaugh and McGlathery, had entered at six and worked until midnight, pushing the work as vigorously as usual, seven of the men (they were told off in lots of seven to do this) were allowed to go up to the mouth of the tunnel to a nearby all-night saloon for a drink and a bite of food. A half hour to each lot was allowed, when another group would depart. There was always a disturbing transition period every half hour between twelve and two, during which one group was going and another coming, which resulted at times in a dangerous indifference which Cavanaugh had come to expect at just about this time and in consequence he was usually watching for it.

On the other hand, John Dowd, ditcher, told off to keep an eye on the breach at this time, was replaced on this particular night by Patrick Murtha, fresh from the corner saloon, a glass of beer and the free lunch counter still in his mind. He was supposed to watch closely, but having had four glasses in rapid succession and meditating on their excellence as well as that of the hot frankfurters, the while he was jesting with the men who were making ready to leave, he forgot about it. What now—was a man always to keep his eye on the blanked thing! What was going to happen anyway? What could happen? Nothing, of course. What had ever happened in the last eight months?

"Sssst!"

What was that? A sound like the blowing off of steam. All at once Cavanaugh, who was just outside the pilot tunnel indicating to McGlathery and another just where certain braces were to be put, in order that the pilot tunnel might be pushed forward a few inches for the purpose of inserting a new ring of plates, heard it. At a bound he was back through the pilot hub, his face aflame with fear and rage. Who had neglected the narrow breach?

"Come now! What the hell is this?" he was about to exclaim, but seeing a wide breach suddenly open and water pour down in a swift volume, his spirit sank and fear over-came him.

"Back, men! Stop the leak!"

It was the cry of a frightened and yet courageous man at bay. There was not only fear, but disappointment, in it. He had certainly hoped to obviate anything like this this time. But where a moment before had been a hole that might have been stopped with a bag of sawdust (and Patrick Murtha was there attempting to do it) was now a rapidly widening gap through which was pouring a small niagara of foul river water, ooze and slime. As Cavanaugh reached it and seized a bag to stay it, another mass of muddy earth fell, striking both him and Murtha, and half blinding them both. Murtha scrambled away for his life. Mc-Glathery, who had been out in the front of the fatal tunnel with others, now came staggering back horribly frightened, scarcely knowing what to do.

"Quick, Dennis! Into the lock!" Cavanaugh called to him, while he himself held his ground. "Hurry!" and realizing the hopelessness of it and his own danger, Dennis thought to run past, but was stopped by the downpour of water and mud.

"Quick! Quick! Into the lock! For Christ's sake, can't ye see what's happenin'? Through with ye!"

McGlathery, hesitating by his chief's side, fearful to move lest he be killed, uncertain this time whether to leave his chief or not, was seized by Cavanaugh and literally thrown through, as were others after him, the blinding ooze and water choking them, but placing them within range of safety. When the last man was through Cavanaugh him-self plunged after, wading knee-deep in mud and water.

"Quick! Quick! Into the lock!" he called, and then see-ing McGlathery, who was now near it but waiting for him, added, "In, in!" There was a mad scramble about the door, floating timbers and bags interfering with many, and then, just as it seemed as if all would reach safety, an iron roof plate overhead, loosened by the breaking of plates beyond, gave way, felling one man in the half-open doorway of the lock and blocking and pinning it in such a way that it could be neither opened nor closed. Cavanaugh and others who came up after were shut out. McGlathery, who had just entered and saw it, could do nothing. But in this emergency, and unlike his previous attitude, he and several others on the inside seized upon the dead man and tried to draw him in, at the same time calling to Cavanaugh to know what to do. The latter, dumbfounded, was helpless. He saw very clearly and sadly that very little if anything could be done. The plate across the dead man was too heavy, and besides, the ooze was already pouring over him into the lock. At the same time the men in the lock, conscious that although they were partially on the road to safety they were still in danger of losing their lives, were frantic with fear.

Actually there were animal roars of terror. At the same time McGlathery, once more realizing that his Nemesis, water, had overtaken him and was likely to slay him at last, was completely paralyzed with fear. St. Columba had promised him, to be sure, but was not this that same vision that he had had in his dreams, that awful sense of encroaching ooze and mud? Was he not now to die this way, after all? Was not his patron saint truly deserting him? It certainly appeared so.

"Holy Mary! Holy St. Columba!" he began to pray, "what shall I do now? Mother of God! Our Father, who art in Heaven! Bejasus, it's a tight place I'm in now! I'll never get out of this! Tower of Ivory! House of Gold! Can't we git him in, boys? Ark of the Covenant! Gate of Heaven!"

As he gibbered and chattered, the others screaming about him, some pulling at the dead man, others pulling at the other door, the still eye of Cavanaugh outside the lock waist-deep in mud and water was surveying it all.

"Listen to me, men!" came his voice in rich, heavy, guttural tones. "You, McGlathery! Dennis!! Arr ye all crazy! Take aaf yer clothes and stop up the doorway! It's yer only chance! Aaf with yer clothes, quick! And those planks there—stand them up! Never mind us. Save yerselves first. Maybe ye can do something for us afterwards."

As he argued, if only the gap in the door could be closed and the compressed air pushing from the tunnel outward toward the river allowed to fill the chamber, it would be possible to open the other door which gave into the next section shoreward, and so they could all run to safety.

His voice, commanding, never quavering, even in the face of death, subsided. About and behind him were a dozen men huddled like sheep, waist-deep in mud and water, praying and crying. They had got as close to him as might be, still trying to draw upon the sustaining force of his courage, but moaning and praying just the same and looking at the lock.

"Yis! Yis!" exclaimed McGlathery of a sudden, awakening at last to a sense of duty and that something better in conduct and thought which he had repeatedly promised himself and his saint that he would achieve. He had been forgetting. But now it seemed to him once more that he had been guilty of that same great wrong to his foreman which had marked his attitude on the previous occasion—that is, he had not helped him or any one but himself. He was a horrible coward. But what could he do? he asked himself. What could he do? Tearing off his coat and vest and shirt as commanded, he began pushing them into the opening, calling to the others to do the same. In a twinkling, bundles were made of all as well as of the sticks and beams afloat in the lock, and with these the gap in the door was stuffed, sufficiently to prevent the air from escaping, but shutting out the foreman and his men completely.

"It's awful. I don't like to do it," McGlathery kept crying to his foreman but the latter was not so easily shaken.

"It's all right, boys," he kept saying. "Have ye no courage at aal?" And then to the others outside with him, "Can't ye stand still and wait? They may be comin' back in time. Kape still. Say yer prayers if ye know any, and don't be afraid."

But, although the air pressing outward toward Cavanaugh held the bundles in place, still this was not sufficient to keep all the air in or all the water out. It poured about the dead man and between the chinks, rising inside to their waists also. Once more it threatened their lives and now their one hope was to pull open the shoreward door and so release themselves into the chamber beyond, but this was not to be done unless the escaping air was completely blocked or some other method devised.

Cavanaugh, on the outside, his whole mind still riveted on the men whom he was thus aiding to escape, was the only one who realized what was to be done. In the panel of the door which confronted him, and the other, which they were trying to break open, were thick glass plates, or what were known as bull's eyes, through which one could see, and it was through the one at his end that Cavanaugh was peering. When it became apparent to him that the men were not going to be able to open the farthest door, a new thought occurred to him. Then it was that his voice was heard above the tumult, shouting:

"Break open the outside bull's eye! Listen to me, Dennis! Listen to me! Break open the outside bull's eye!"

Why did he call to Dennis, the latter often asked himself afterwards. And why did Dennis hear him so clearly? Through a bedlam of cries within, he heard, but also realized that if he or they knocked out the bull's eye in the other door, and the air escaped through it inward, the chances of their opening it would be improved, but the life of Cavanaugh and his helpless companions would certainly be destroyed. The water would rush inward from the river, filling up this chamber and the space in which stood Cavanaugh. Should he? So he hesitated.

"Knock it out!" came the muffled voice of his foreman from within where he was eyeing him calmly. "Knock it out, Dennis! It's yer only chance! Knock it out!" And then, for the first time in all the years he had been working for him, McGlathery heard the voice of his superior waver slightly: "If ye're saved," it said, "try and do what ye can fer the rest av us."

In that moment McGlathery was reborn spiritually. Although he could have wept, something broke in him—fear. He was not afraid now for himself. He ceased to tremble, almost to hurry and awoke to a new idea, one of undying, unfaltering courage. What! There was Cavanaugh outside there, unafraid, and here was he, Dennis McGlathery, scrambling about like a hare for his life! He wanted to go back, to do something, but what could he? It was useless. Instead, he assumed partial command in here. The spirit of Cavanaugh seemed to come over to him and possess him. He looked about, saw a great stave, and seized it.

"Here, men!" he called with an air of command. "Help knock it out!" and with a will born of terror and death a dozen brawny hands were laid on it. With a mighty burst of energy they assaulted the thick plate and burst it through. Air rushed in, and at the same time the door gave way before them, causing them to be swept outward by the accumulated water like straws. Then, scrambling to their feet, they tumbled into the next lock, closing the door behind them. Once in, they heaved a tremendous sigh of relief, for here they were safe enough—for the time being anyhow. McGlathery, the new spirit of Cavanaugh in him, even turned and looked back through the bull's eye into the chamber they had just left. Even as they waited for the pressure here to lower sufficiently to permit them to open the inner door he saw this last chamber they had left his foreman and a dozen fellow workers buried beyond. But what could he do? Only God, only St. Columba, could tell him, perhaps, and St. Columba had saved him—or had

he?—him and fifteen other men, the while he had chosen
to allow Cavanaugh and twelve men to perish! Had St.
Columba done that—or God—or who?

" 'Tis the will av God," he murmured humbly—but why
had God done that?

*   *   *   *   *   *   *

But somehow, the river was not done with him yet, and
that, seemingly, in spite of himself. Although he prayed
constantly for the repose of the soul of Thomas Cavanaugh
and his men, and avoided the water, until five years later,
still there was a sequel. By now McGlathery was the
father of eight children and as poor as any average laborer.
With the death of Cavanaugh and this accident, as has been
said, he had forsworn the sea—or water—and all its works.
Ordinary house shoring and timbering were good enough for
him, only—only—it was so hard to get enough of this at
good pay. He was never faring as well as he should. And
then one day when he was about as hard up as ever and as
earnest, from somewhere was wafted a new scheme in connection with this same old tunnel.

A celebrated engineer of another country—England, no
less—had appeared on the scene with a new device, according to the papers. Greathead was his name ,and he had invented what was known as "The Greathead Shield," which
finally, with a few changes and adaptations, was to rid tunnel work of all its dangers. McGlathery, sitting outside the
door of his cottage overlooking Bergen Bay, read it all in the
Evening *Clarion,* and wondered whether it could be true.
He did not understand very much about this new shield idea
even now, but even so, and in spite of himself, some of the
old zest for tunneling came back to him. What times he
had had, to be sure! What a life it had been, if a dog's one—
and Cavanaugh—what a foreman! And his body was still
down there entombed—erect, no doubt, as he was left. He
wondered. It would be only fair to dig him out and honor
his memory with a decent grave if it could be done. His

wife and children were still living in Flatbush. It stirred up all the memories, old fears, old enthusiasms, but no particular desire to return. Still, here he was now, a man with a wife and eight children, earning three a day, or less—mostly less—whereas tunneling paid seven and eight to such as himself, and he kept thinking that if this should start up again and men were advertised for, why shouldn't he go? His life had been almost miraculously saved these two times—but would it be again?—that was the great question. Almost unceasingly he referred the matter to his saint on Sundays in his church, but receiving no definite advice as yet and there being no work doing on the tunnel, he did nothing.

But then one day the following spring the papers were full of the fact that work would soon actually be resumed, and shortly thereafter, to his utter amazement, McGlathery received a note from that same Mr. Henderson under whom Cavanaugh had worked, asking him to call and see him. Feeling sure that it was the river that was calling him, he went over to St. Columba's and prayed before his saint, putting a dollar in his Orphans' box and a candle on his shrine, and then arising greatly refreshed and reassured, and after consulting with his wife, journeyed over to the river, where he found the old supervisor as before in a shed outside, considering one important matter and another.

What he wanted to know was this—did McGlathery want to take an assistant-foremanship under a new foreman who was going to be in charge of the day work here, one Michael Laverty by name, an excellent man, at seven dollars a day, seeing that he had worked here before and understood the difficulties, etc.? McGlathery stared in amazement. He an assistant-foreman in charge of timbering! And at seven dollars a day! He!

Mr. Henderson neglected to say that because there had been so much trouble with the tunnel and the difficulties so widely advertised, it was rather difficult to get just the right sort of men at first, although McGlathery was good enough any time. But the new shield made everything safe, he said. There could be no calamity this time. The work would be pushed right through. Mr. Henderson even went so far as to explain the new shield to him, its excellent points.

But McGlathery, listening, was dubious, and yet he was not thinking of the shield exactly now, nor of the extra pay he would receive, although that played a big enough part in his calculations, but of one Thomas Cavanaugh, mason foreman, and his twelve men, buried down below there in the ooze, and how he had left him, and how it would only be fair to take his bones out, his and the others', if they could be found, and give them a decent Christian burial. For by now he was a better Catholic than ever, and he owed that much to Cavanaugh, for certainly Cavanaugh had been very good to him—and anyhow, had not St. Columba protected him so far? And might he not in the future, seeing the position he was in? Wasn't this a call, really? He felt that it was.

Just the same, he was nervous and troubled, and went home and consulted with his wife again, and thought of the river and went over and prayed in front of the shrine of St. Columba. Then, once more spiritualized and strengthened, he returned and told Mr. Henderson that he would come back. Yes, he would come.

He felt actually free of fear, as though he had a mission, and the next day began by assisting Michael Laverty to get out the solid mass of earth which filled the tunnel from the second lock outward. It was slow work, well into the middle of the summer before the old or completed portion was cleared and the bones of Cavanaugh and his men reached. That was a great if solemn occasion—the finding of Cavanaugh and his men. They could recognize him by his big boots, his revolver, his watch, and a bunch of keys, all in position near his bones. These same bones and boots were then reverently lifted and transferred to a cemetery in Brooklyn, McGlathery and a dozen workers accompanying them, after which everything went smoothly. The new shield worked like a charm. It made eight feet a day in soft mud, and although McGlathery, despite his revived courage, was intensely suspicious of the river, he was really no longer afraid of it in the old way. Something kept telling him that from now on he would be all right—not to fear. The river could never hurt him any more, really.

But just the same, a few months later—eight, to be exact—the river did take one last slap at him, but not so fatally as might have appeared on the surface, although in a very peculiar way, and whether with or without St. Columba's aid or consent, he never could make out. The circumstances were so very odd. This new cutting shield, as it turned out, was a cylinder thirteen feet long, twenty feet in diameter, and with a hardened steel cutting edge out on front, an apron, fifteen inches in length and three inches thick at the cutting edge. Behind this came what was known as an "outside diaphragm," which had several openings to let in the mud displaced by the shield's advance.

Back of these openings were chambers four feet in length, one chamber for each opening, through which the mud was passed. These chambers in turn had hinged doors, which regulated the quantity of mud admitted, and were water tight and easily closed. It was all very shipshape.

Behind these little chambers, again, were many steel jacks, fifteen to thirty, according to the size of the shield, driven by an air pressure of five thousand pounds to the square inch, which were used to push the shield forward. Back of them came what was known as the tail end of the shield, which reached back into the completed tunnel and was designed to protect the men who were at work putting in the new plates (at that danger point which had killed Cavanaugh) whenever the shield had been driven sufficiently forward to permit of a new ring of them.

The only danger involved in this part of the work lay in the fact that between this lining and the tail end of the shield was always a space of an inch to an inch and a half which was left unprotected. This small opening would, under ordinary circumstances, be insignificant, but in some instances where the mud covering at the top was very soft and not very thick, there was danger of the compressed air from within, pushing at the rate of several thousand pounds to the square inch, blowing it away and leaving the aperture open to the direct action of the water above. This was not anticipated, of course, not even thought of. The shield was going rapidly forward and it was predicted by Henderson and Laverty at intervals that the tunnel would surely go through within the year.

Some time the following winter, however, when the shield was doing such excellent work, it encountered a rock which turned its cutting edge and, in addition, necessitated the drilling out of the rock in front. A bulkhead had to be built, once sufficient stone had been cut away, to permit the repairing of the edge. This took exactly fifteen days. In the meantime, at the back of the shield, at the little crevice described, compressed air, two thousand pounds to the square inch, was pushing away at the mud outside, gradually hollowing out a cup-like depression eighty-five feet long (Mr. Henderson had soundings taken afterwards), which extended backward along the top of the completed tunnel toward the shore. There was then nothing but water overhead.

It was at this time that the engineers, listening to the river, which, raked by the outpouring of air from below, was rolling gravel and stones above the tunnel top and pounding on it like a drum, learned that such was the case. It was easy enough to fix it temporarily by stuffing the crevice with bags, but one of these days when the shield was repaired it would have to be moved forward to permit the insertion of a new ring of plates, and then, what?

At once McGlathery scented trouble. It was the wretched river again (water), up to its old tricks with him. He was seriously disturbed, and went to pray before St.

Columba, but incidentally, when he was on duty, he hovered about this particular opening like a wasp. He wanted to know what was doing there every three minutes in the day, and he talked to the night foreman about it, as well as Laverty and Mr. Henderson. Mr. Henderson, at Laverty's and McGlathery's request, came down and surveyed it and meditated upon it.

"When the time comes to move the shield," he said, "you'll just have to keep plenty of bags stuffed around that opening, everywhere, except where the men are putting in the plates. We'll have extra air pressure that day, all we can stand, and I think that'll fix everything all right. Have plenty of men here to keep those bags in position, but don't let 'em know there's anything wrong, and we'll be all right. Let me know when you're ready to start, and I'll come down."

When the shield was eventually repaired and the order given to drive it just twenty-five inches ahead in order to permit the insertion of a new ring of plates, Mr. Henderson was there, as well as Laverty and McGlathery. Indeed, McGlathery was in charge of the men who were to stuff the bags and keep out the water. If you have ever seen a medium-sized red-headed Irishman when he is excited and determined, you have a good picture of McGlathery. He was seemingly in fifteen places at once, commanding, exhorting, persuading, rarely ever soothing—and worried. Yes, he was worried, in spite of St. Columba.

The shield started. The extra air pressure was put on, the water began to pour through the crevice, and then the bags were put in place and stopped most of it, only where the ironworkers were riveting on the plates it poured, poured so heavily at times that the workers became frightened.

"Come now! What's the matter wid ye! What arr ye standin' there fer? What arr ye afraid av? Give me that bag! Up with it! That's the idea! Do ye think ye're goin' to be runnin' away now?"

It was McGlathery's voice, if you please, commanding!—

McGlathery, after his two previous experiences! Yet in his vitals he was really afraid of the river at this very moment.

What was it that happened? For weeks after, he himself, writhing with "bends" in a hospital, was unable to get it straight. For four of the bags of sawdust burst and blew through, he remembered that—it was a mistake to have sawdust bags at all. And then (he remembered that well enough), in stuffing others in, they found that they were a bag short, and until something was secured to put in its place, for the water was streaming in like a waterfall and causing a flood about their ankles, he, McGlathery, defiant to the core, not to be outdone by the river this time, commanded the great thing to be done.

"Here!" he shouted, "the three av ye," to three gaping men near at hand, "up with me! Put me there! I'm as good as a bag of sawdust any day. Up with me!"

Astonished, admiring, heartened, the three of them jumped forward and lifted him. Against the small breach, through which the water was pouring, they held him, while others ran off for more bags. Henderson and Laverty and the ironworkers, amazed and amused and made braver themselves because of this very thing—filled with admiration, indeed, by the sheer resourcefulness of it, stood by to help. But then, if you will believe it, while they were holding him there, and because now there was nothing but water above it, one end of the shield itself—yes, that great iron invention—was lifted by the tremendous air pressure below— eleven or thirteen or fourteen inches, whatever space you can imagine a medium sized man being forced through— and out he went, McGlathery, and all the bags, up into the river above, the while the water poured down, and the men fled for their lives.

A terrific moment, as you can well imagine, not long in duration, but just long enough to swallow up McGlathery, and then the shield, having responded at first to too much air pressure, now responding to too little (the air pressure having been lessened by the escape), shut down like a safety valve, shutting off most of the water and leaving the tunnel as it was before.

But McGlathery!

Yes, what of him?

Reader—a miracle!

A passing tug captain, steaming down the Hudson at three one bright December afternoon was suddenly astonished to see a small geyser of water lift its head some thirty feet from his boat, and at the top of it, as it were lying on it, a black object which at first he took to be a bag or a log. Later he made it out well enough, for it plunged and bellowed.

"Fer the love av God! Will no one take me out av this? Git me out av this! Oh! Oh! Oh!"

It was McGlathery right enough, alive and howling lustily and no worse for his blow-out save that he was suffering from a fair case of the "bends'" and suffering mightily. He was able to scream, though, and was trying to swim. That old haunting sensation!—he had had it this time, sure enough. For some thirty or forty seconds or more he had been eddied swiftly along the top of the tunnel at the bottom of the river, and then coming to where the air richocheted upward had been hustled upward like a cork and literally blown through the air at the top of the great volume of water, out into space. The sudden shift from two thousand pounds of air pressure to none at all, or nearly none, had brought him down again, and in addition induced the severe case of "bends" from which he was now suffering. But St. Columba had not forgotten him entirely. Although he was suffering horribly, and was convinced that he was a dead man, still the good saint must have placed the tug conveniently near, and into this he was now speedily lifted.

"Well, of all things!" exclaimed Captain Hiram Knox, seeing him thoroughly alive, if not well, and eyeing him in astonishment. "Where do you come from?"

"Oh! Oh! Oh!" bawled McGlathery. "Me arms! Me ribs! Oh! Oh! Oh! The tunnel! The tunnel below, av course! Quick! Quick! It's dyin' av the bends I am! Git me to a hospital, quick!"

The captain, truly moved and frightened by his groans, did as requested. He made for the nearest dock. It took him but a few moments to call an ambulance, and but a few more before McGlathery was carried into the nearest hospital.

The house physician, having seen a case of this same disease two years before, and having meditated on it, had decided that the hair of the dog must be good for the bite. In consequence of this McGlathery was once more speedily carted off to one of the locks of this very tunnel, to the amazement of all who had known of him (his disappearance having aroused general excitement), and he was stared at as one who had risen from the grave. But, what was better yet, under the pressure of two thousand pounds now applied he recovered himself sufficiently to be host here and tell his story—another trick of his guardian saint, no doubt —and one rather flattering to his vanity, for he was now in no least danger of dying.

The whole city, if not the whole country, indeed, was astounded by the accident, and he was a true nine days' wonder, for the papers were full of the strange adventure. And with large pictures of McGlathery ascending heavenward, at the top of a geyser of water. And long and intelligent explanations as to the way and the why of it all.

But, better yet, four of the happiest weeks of his life were subsequently spent in that same hospital to which he had first been taken relating to all and sundry his amazing adventure, he being interviewed by no less than five representatives of Sunday editors and eleven reporters for city dailies, all anxious to discover just how it was that he had been blown through water and air up through so great a thing as a river, and how he felt while en route. A triumph.

Rivers may be smart, but saints are smarter, thanks be.

And, to top it all, seeing that his right hand and arm

might possibly be crippled for life, or at least an indefinite period (the doctors did not know), and in grateful appreciation of the fact that he had refused to deal with various wolfish lawyers who had now descended on him and urged him to sue for a large sum, he was offered a substantial pension by the company, or its equivalent, work with the company, no less, at good pay for the rest of his life, and a cash bonus into the bargain, a thing which seemed to solve his very uncertain future for him and put him at his ease. Once more the hand of the saint, you will certainly admit.

But, lastly, there was the peculiar spiritual consolation that comes with the feeling that you have done your duty and that a great saint is on your side. For if all these things did not prove that the good St. Columba had kept faith with him, what could? To be sure the river had attempted to do its worst, and had caused him considerable fear and pain, and perhaps St. Columba did not have as much control over the river as he should or as he might like to have, or —and this was far more likely—it was entirely possible that he (McGlathery) had not at all times deserved the good saint's support. But none the less, in the final extremity, had he not acted? And if not, how would you explain the fact that the tug *Mary Baker* was just at hand as he arose out of the water two thousand feet from shore? And why was it, if the saint had not been trying to help him, that the hospital doctor had seen to it that he was hustled off to a lock just in time—had seen, indeed, just such a case as this before, and known how to handle it? Incontrovertible facts all, aren't they?—or if not, why not?

At any rate McGlathery thought so, and on Sundays and holidays, whether there was or was not anything of importance being celebrated in his church, he might have been seen there kneeling before his favorite saint and occasionally eyeing him with both reverence and admiration. For, "Glory be," as he frequently exclaimed in narrating the wonderful event afterward, "I wasn't stuck between the shield and the tunnel, as I might 'a' been, and killed entirely, and sure, I've aaften thought 'tis a miracle that not enough water come in, just then, to drown 'em aal. It lifted up just enough to let me go out like a cork, and up I went, and then, God be praised, it shut down again. But, glory be, here I am, and I'm no worse fer it, though it do be that me hand wrenches me now and then."

And as for the good St. Columba—

Well, what about the good St. Columba?

V

CONVENTION

I

THIS story was told to me once by a very able newspaper cartoonist, and since it makes rather clear the powerfully repressive and often transforming force of convention, I set it down as something in the nature of an American social document. As he told it, it went something like this:

At one time I was a staff artist on the principal paper of one of the mid-Western cities, a city on a river. It was, and remains to this hour, a typical American city. No change. It had a population then of between four and five hundred thousand. It had its clubs and churches and its conventional goings-on. It was an excellent and prosperous manufacturing city; nothing more.

On the staff with me at this time was a reporter whom I had known a little, but never intimately. I don't know whether I ought to bother to describe him or not—physically, I mean. His physique is unimportant to this story. But I think it would be interesting and even important to take him apart mentally and look at him, if one could—sort out the various components of his intellectual machinery, and so find out exactly how his intellectual processes proceeded. However, I can't do that; I have not the skill. Barring certain very superficial characteristics which I will mention, he was then and remains now a psychological mystery to me. He was what I would describe as superficially clever, a good writer of a good, practical, matter-of-fact story. He appeared to be well liked by those who were above him officially, and he could write Sunday feature stories of a sort, no one of which, as I saw it, ever contained a moving touch of color or a breath of real poetry. Some humor he had. He was efficient. He had a nose for news. He dressed quite well and he was not ill-looking—tall, thin, wiry, almost leathery. He had a quick, facile smile, a genial word-flow for all who knew him. He was the kind of man who was on practical and friendly terms with many men connected with the commercial organizations and clubs about town, and from whom he extracted news bits from time to time. By the directing chiefs of the paper he was considered useful.

Well, this man and I were occasionally sent out on the same assignment, he to write the story, I to make sketches—usually some Sunday feature story. Occasionally we would talk about whatever was before us—newspaper work, politics, the particular story in hand—but never enthusiastically or warmly about anything. He lacked what I thought was the artistic and poetic point of view. And yet, as I say, we were friendly enough. I took him about as any newspaperman takes another newspaperman of the same staff who is in good standing.

Along in the spring or summer of the second year that I was on the paper the Sunday editor, to whom I was beholden in part for my salary, called me into his room and said that he had decided that Wallace Steele and myself were to do a feature story about the "love-boats" which plied Saturday and Sunday afternoons and every evening up and down the river for a distance of thirty-five miles or more. This distance, weather permitting, gave an opportunity to six or seven hundred couples on hot nights to escape the dry, sweltering heat of the city—and it was hot there in the summer—and to enjoy the breezes and dance, sometimes by the light of Chinese lanterns, sometimes by the light of the full moon. It was delightful. Many, many thousands took advantage of the opportunity in season.

It was delicious to me, then in the prime of youth and ambition, to sit on the hurricane or "spoon" deck, as our Sunday editor called it, and study not only the hundreds of boys and girls, but also the older men and women, who came principally to make love, though secondarily to enjoy the river and the air, to brood over the picturesque groupings of the trees, bushes, distant cabins and bluffs which rose steeply from the river, to watch the great cloud of smoke that trailed back over us, to see the two halves of the immense steel walking beam chuff-chuffing up and down, and to listen to the drive of the water-wheel behind. This was in the days before the automobile, and any such pleasant means of getting away from the city was valued much more than it is now.

But to return to this Sunday editor and his orders. I was to make sketches of spooning couples, or at least of two or three small distinctive groups with a touch of romance in them. Steele was to tell how the love-making went on. This, being an innocent method of amusement, relief from the humdrum of such a world as this was looked upon with suspicion if not actual disfavor by the wiseacres of the paper, as well as by the conservatives of the city. True conservatives would not so indulge themselves. The real object of the Sunday editor was to get something into his paper that would have a little kick to it. We were, without exaggerating the matter in any way, to shock the conservatives by a little picture of life and love, which, however innocent, was none the less taboo in that city. The story was to suggest, as I understand it, loose living, low ideals and the like. These outings did not have the lockstep of business or religion in them.

II

Well, to proceed. No sooner had the order been given than Steele came to me to talk it over. He liked the idea very much. It was a good Sunday subject. Besides, the opportunity for an outing appealed to him. We were to go on the boat that left the wharf at the foot of Beach street at eight o'clock that evening. He had been told to write anything from fifteen hundred to two thousand words. If I made three good sketches, that would make almost a three-fourths page special. He would make his story as lively and colorful as he could. He was not a little flattered, I am sure, by having been called to interpret such a gay, risqué scene.

It was about one-thirty when we had been called in. About four o'clock he came to me again. We had, as I had assumed, tentatively agreed to meet at the wharf entrance and do the thing together. By now, however, he had another plan. Perhaps I should say here that up to that moment I only vaguely knew that he had a wife and child and that he lived with them somewhere in the southwestern section of the city, whether in his own home or a rooming-house, I did not know. Come to think of it, just before this I believe I had heard him remark to others that his wife was out of the city. At any rate, he now said that since his wife was out of the city and as the woman of whom they rented their rooms was a lonely and a poor person who seldom got out anywhere, he had decided to bring her along for the outing. I needn't wait for him. He would see me on the boat, or we could discuss the story later.

I agreed to this and was prepared to think nothing of it except for one thing. His manner of telling me had something about it, or there was some mood or thought in connection with it in his own mind, which reached me telepathetically, and caused me to think that he was taking advantage of his wife's absence to go out somewhere with some one else. And yet, at that, I could not see why I thought about it. The thing had no real interest for me. And I had not the least proof and wanted none. As I say, I was not actually interested. I did not know his wife at all. I did not care for him or her. I did not care whether he flirted with some one else or not. Still, this silly, critical thought passed through my mind, put into it by him, I am sure, because he was thinking—at least, might have been thinking—that I might regard it as strange that he should appear anywhere with another woman than his wife. Apart from this, and before this, seeing him buzzing about here and there, and once talking to a girl on a street corner near the *Mail* office, I had only the vague notion that, married or not, he was a young man who was not averse to slipping away for an hour or two with some girl whom he knew or casually met, provided no one else knew anything about it, especially his wife. But that was neither here nor there. I never gave the man much thought at any time.

At any rate, seven o'clock coming, I had my dinner at a little restaurant near the office and went to the boat. It was a hot night, but clear and certain to bring a lovely full moon, and I was glad to be going. At the same time, I was not a little lonely and out of sorts with myself because I had no girl and was wishing that I had—wishing that some lovely girl was hanging on my arm and that now we two could go down to the boat together and sit on the spoon deck and look at the moon, or that we could dance on the cabin deck below, where were all the lights and musicians. My hope, if not my convinced expectation, was that somewhere on this boat I, too, should find some one who would be interested in me—I, too, should be able to sit about with the others and laugh and make love. But I didn't. The thought was futile. I was not a ladies' man, and few if any girls ever looked at me. Besides, women and girls usually came accompanied on a trip like this. I went alone, and I returned alone. So much for me.

Brooding in this fashion, I went aboard along with the earliest of the arrivals, and, going to the cabin deck, sat down and watched the others approach. It was one of my opportunities to single out interesting groups for my pen. And there were many. They came, so blithe, so very merry, all of them, in pairs or groups of four or six or eight or ten, boys and girls of the tenements and the slums—a few older couples among them,—but all smiling and chatting, the last ones hurrying excitedly to make the boat, and each boy with his girl, as I was keen to note, and each girl with her beau. I singled out this group and that, this type and that, making a few idle notes on my pad, just suggestions of faces, hats, gestures, swings or rolls of the body and the like. There was a strong light over the gangway, and I could sketch there. It was interesting and colorful, but, being very much alone, I was not very happy about it.

In the midst of these, along with the latter half of the crowd, came Steele and his lonely landlady, to whom, as he said, this proffer on his part was a kindness. Because of what he had said I was expecting a woman who would be somewhat of a frump—at least thirty-five or forty years old and not very attractive. But to my surprise, as they came up the long gangplank which led from the levee and was lighted by flaring gasoline torches, I saw a young woman who could not have been more than twenty-seven or -eight at most—and pretty, very. She had on a wide, floppy, lacy hat of black or dark blue, but for contrast a pale, cream-colored, flouncy dress. And she was graceful and plump and agreeable in every way. Some landlady, indeed, I thought, looking enviously down and wishing that it was myself and not he to whose arm she was clinging!

The bounder! I thought. To think that he should be able to interest so charming a girl, and in the absence of his wife! And I could get none! He had gone home and changed to a better suit, straw hat, cane and all, whereas I—I—dub!—had come as I was. No wonder no really interesting girl would look at me. Fool! But I remained in position studying the entering throng until the last couple was on and I listened to the cries of "Heave off, there!" "Loosen those stay lines, will you?" "Careful, there!" "Hurry with that gangplank!" Soon we were in midstream. The jouncy, tinny music had begun long before, and the couples, scores and scores of them, were already dancing on the cabin deck, while I was left to hang about the bar or saunter through the crowd, looking for types when I didn't want to be anywhere but close beside some girl on the spoon deck, who would hang on my arm, laugh into my eyes, and jest and dance with me.

III

Because of what he had said, I did not expect Steele to come near me, and he didn't. In sauntering about the two decks looking for arresting scenes I did not see him. Because I wanted at least one or two spoon deck scenes, I finally fixed on a couple that was half-hidden in the shadow back of the pilot-house. They had crumpled themselves up forward of an air-vent and not far from the two smoke-stacks and under the walking-beam, which rose and fell above them. The full moon was just above the eastern horizon, offering a circular background for them, and I thought they made a romantic picture outlined against it. I could not see their faces—just their outlines. Her head was upon his shoulder. His face was turned, and so concealed, and inclined toward hers. Her hat had been taken off and was held over her knee by one hand. I stepped back a little toward a companion-way, where was a light, in order to outline my impression. When I returned, they were sitting up. It was Steele and his rooming-house proprietress! It struck me as odd that of all the couple and group scenes that I had noted, the most romantic should have been that provided by Steele and this woman. His wife would be interested in his solicitude for her loneliness and her lack of opportunities to get out into the open air, I was sure. Yet, I was not envious then—just curious and a little amused.

Well, that was the end of that. The sketches were made, and the story published. Because he and this girl had provided my best scene I disguised it a little, making it not seem exactly back of the pilot-house, since otherwise he might recognize it. He was, for once, fascinated by the color and romance of the occasion, and did a better story than I thought he could. It dwelt on the beauty of the river, the freedom from heat, the loveliness of the moon, the dancing. I thought it was very good, quite exceptional for him, and I thought I knew the reason why.

And then one day, about a month or six weeks later, being in the city room, I encountered the wife of Steele and their little son, a child of about five years. She had stopped in about three or four in the afternoon, being downtown shopping, I presume. After seeing him with the young woman on the steamer, I was, I confess, not a little shocked. This woman was so pinched, so homely, so faded—veritably a rail of a woman, everything and anything that a woman, whether wife, daughter, mother or sweetheart, as I saw it then, should not be. As a matter of fact, I was too wrought up about love and youth and marriage and happiness at that time to rightly judge of the married. At any rate, after having seen that other woman on that deck with Steele, I was offended by this one.

She seemed to me, after the other, too narrow, too method-ical, too commonplace, too humdrum. She was a woman whose pulchritudinous favors, whatever they may have been, must have been lost at the altar. In heaven's name, I thought to myself, how could a man like this come to marry such a woman? He isn't so very good-looking himself, per-haps, but still . . . No wonder he wanted to take his rooming-house landlady for an outing! I would, too. I could understand it now. In fact, as little as I cared for Steele, I felt sorry that a man of his years and of his still restless proclivities should be burdened with such a wife. And not only that, but there was their child, looking not unlike him but more like her, one of those hostages to fortune by reason of which it is never easy to free oneself from the error of a mistaken marriage. His plight, as I saw it, was indeed unfortunate. And it was still summer and there was this other woman!

Well, I was introduced by him as the man who worked on some of his stories with him. I noticed that the woman had a thin, almost a falsetto voice. She eyed me, as I thought, unintelligently, yet genially enough. I was invited to come out to their place some Sunday and take dinner. Because of his rooming-house story I was beginning to wonder whether he had been lying to me, when she went on to explain that they had been boarding up to a few weeks ago, but had now taken a cottage for themselves and could have their friends. I promised. Yes, yes. But I never went— not to dinner, anyhow.

IV

Then two more months passed. By now it was late fall, with winter near. The current news, as I saw it, was decidedly humdrum. There was no local news to speak of. I scarcely glanced at the papers from day to day, no more than to see whether some particular illustration I had done was in and satisfactory or not. But then, of a sudden, came something which was genuine news. Steele's wife was laid low by a box of poisoned candy sent her through the mails, some of which she had eaten!

Just how the news of this first reached the papers I have almost forgotten now, but my recollection is that there was another newspaperman and his wife—a small editor or reporter on another paper—who lived in the same vicinity, and that it was to this newspaperman's wife that Mrs. Steele, after having called her in, confided that she believed she had been poisoned, and by a woman whose name she now gave as Mrs. Marie Davis, and with whom, as she then announced, her husband had long been intimate—the lady of the Steamer *Ira Ramsdell*. She had recognized the handwriting on the package from some letters written to her husband, but only after she had eaten of the candy and felt the pains—not before. Her condition was serious. She was, it appeared, about to die. In this predicament she had added, so it was said, that she had long been neglected by her husband for this other woman, but that she had suffered in silence rather than bring disgrace upon him, herself and their child. Now this cruel blow!

Forthwith a thrill of horror and sympathy passed over the city. It seemed too sad. At the same time a cry went up to find the other woman—arrest her, of course—see if she had really done it. There followed the official detention, if not legal arrest, of Mrs. Davis on suspicion of being the poisoner. Although the charge was not yet proved, she was at once thrown into jail, and there held to await the death or recovery of Mrs. Steele, and the proof or disproof of the charge that the candy had been sent by her. And cameras in hand, reporters and artists were packed off to the county jail to hear the accused's side of the story.

As I at once suspected on hearing the news, she proved to be none other than the lady of the *Ira Ramsdell,* and as charming as I had at first assumed her to be. I, being one of those sent to sketch her, was among the first to hear her story. She denied, and very vehemently, that she had sent any poisoned candy to any one. She had never dreamed of any such thing. But she did not deny, which at the time appeared to me to be incriminating, that she had been and was then in love with Steele. In fact, and this point interested me as much then as afterwards, she declared that this was an exceptional passion—her love for him, his love for her—and no mere passing and vulgar intimacy. A high and beautiful thing—a sacred love, the one really true and beautiful thing that had ever come to her—or him—in all their lives. And he would say so, too. For before meeting her, Wallace Steele had been very unhappy—oh, very. And her own marriage had been a failure.

Wallace, as she now familiarly called him, had confessed to her that this new, if secret, love meant everything to him. His wife did not interest him. He had married her at a time when he did not know what he was doing, and before he had come to be what he was. But this new love had resolved all their woes into loveliness—complete happiness. They had resolved to cling only to each other for life.

There was no sin in what they had done because they loved. Of course, Wallace had sought to induce Mrs. Steele to divorce him, but she would not; otherwise they would have been married before this. But as Mrs. Steele would not give him up, both had been compelled to make the best of it. But to poison her—that was wild! A love so beautiful and true as theirs did not need a marriage ceremony to sanctify it. So she raved. My own impression at the time was that she was a romantic and sentimental woman who was really very greatly in love.

Now as to Steele. Having listened to this blazoning of her passion by herself, the interviewers naturally hurried to Steele to see what he would have to say. In contrast to her and her grand declaration, they found a man, as every one agreed, who was shaken to the very marrow of his bones by these untoward events. He was, it appeared, a fit inhabitant of the environment that nourished him. He was in love, perhaps, with this woman, but still, as any one could see, he was not so much in love that, if this present matter were going to cost him his place in this commonplace, conventional world, he would not be able to surrender to it. He was horrified by the revelation of his own treachery. Up to this hour, no doubt, he had been slipping about, hoping not to be caught, and most certainly not wishing to be cast out for sin. Regardless of the woman, he did not wish to be cast out now. On the contrary, as it soon appeared, he had been doing his best in the past to pacify his wife and hold her to silence while he slaked his thirst for romance in this other way. He did not want his wife, but he did not want trouble, either. And now that his sin was out he shivered.

In short, as he confided to one of the men who went to interview him, and who agreed to respect his confidence to that extent, he was not nearly so much in love with Mrs. Davis as she thought he was—poor thing! True he had been infatuated for a while, but only a little while. She was pretty, of course, and naturally she thought she loved him—but he never expected anything like this to happen.

Great cripes! They had met at a river bathing-beach the year before. He had been smitten—well, you know. He had never got along well with his wife, but there was the little boy to consider. He had not intended any harm to any one; far from it. And he certainly couldn't turn on his wife now. The public wouldn't stand for it. It would make trouble for him. But he could scarcely be expected to turn on Mrs. Davis, either, could he, now that she was in jail, and suspected of sending poisoned candy to his wife? The public wouldn't stand for that, either.

It was terrible! Pathetic! He certainly would not have thought that Marie would go to the length of sending his wife poison, and he didn't really believe that she had. Still —and there may have been some actual doubt of her in that "still," or so the reporting newspapermen thought. At any rate, as he saw it now, he would have to stick to his wife until she was out of danger. Public opinion compelled it. The general impression of the newspapermen was that he was a coward. As one of them said of his courage, "Gee, it's oozing out of his hair!"

Nevertheless, he did go to see Mrs. Davis several times. But apart from a reported sobbing demonstration of affection on her part, I never learned what passed between them. He would not talk and she had been cautioned not to. Also, there were various interviews with his wife, who had not died, and now that the storm was on, admitted that she had intercepted letters between her husband and Mrs. Davis from time to time. The handwriting on the candy wrapper the day she received it so resembled the handwriting of Mrs. Davis that after she had eaten of it and the symptoms of poisoning had set in—not before—she had begun to suspect that the candy must have emanated from Mrs. Davis.

V

In the meantime Mrs. Davis, despite the wife's sad story, was the major attraction in the newspapers. She was young, she was beautiful, she had made, or at least attempted to make, a blood sacrifice on the altar of love. What more could a daily newspaper want? She was a heroine, even in this very moral, conservative, conventional and religious city. The rank and file were agog—even sympathetic. (How would the moralists explain that, would you say?) In consequence of their interest, she was descended upon by a corps of those women newspaper writers who, even in that day, were known as sob-sisters, and whose business it was—and this in advance of any proof of crime or indictment even—to psychologize and psychiatrize the suspect—to dig out if they could not only every vestige of her drama, but all her hidden and secret motives.

As I read the newspapers at the time, they revealed that she was and she was not a neurotic, a psychotic, who showed traces of being a shrewd, evasive and designing woman, and who did not. Also she was a soft, unsophisticated, passionate and deeply illusioned girl, and she was not. She was guilty, of course—maybe not—but very likely she was, and she must tell how, why, in what mood, etc. Also, it appeared that she had sent the poison deliberately, coldly, murderously. Her eyes and hands, also the shape of her nose and ears, showed it. Again, these very things proved she could not have done it. Had she been driven to it by stress of passionate emotion and yearning which had been too much for her to bear? Was she responsible for that—a great, destroying love? Of course she was! Who is not responsible for his deeds? A great, overwhelming, destroying love passion, indeed! Rot! She could help it. She could not help it. Could she help it? So it went.

Parallel with all this, of course, we were treated to various examinations of the Steele family. What sort of people were they, anyhow? It was said of Steele now that he was an average, fairly capable newspaperman of no very startling ability, but of no particular vices—one who had for some years been a serious and faithful employé of this paper. Mrs. Steele, on the other hand, was a good woman, but by no means prepossessing. She was without romance, imagination, charm. One could see by looking at her and then looking at so winsome and enticing a woman as Mrs. Davis why Steele had strayed. It was the old eternal triangle—the woman who was not interesting, the woman who was interesting, and the man interested by the more interesting woman. There was no solving it, but it was all very sad. One could not help sympathizing with Mrs. Steele, the wronged woman; and again one could not help sympathizing with Mrs. Davis, the beautiful, passionate, desirous, helpless beauty—helpless because she was desirious.

In the meantime, the District Attorney's office having taken the case in hand, there were various developments in that quarter. It was necessary to find out, of course, where the candy had been purchased, how it had been drugged, with what it had been drugged, where the drug had been purchased. Chemists, detectives and handwriting experts were all set to work. It was no trouble to determine that the drug was arsenic, yet where this arsenic was purchased was not so easy to discover. It was some time before it was found where it had been procured. Dissimilarly, it was comparatively easy to prove where the candy had come from. It had been sent in the original box of a well-known candy firm. Yet just who had purchased it was not quite so easy to establish. The candy company could not remember, and Mrs. Davis, although admitting that the handwriting did resemble hers, denied ever having addressed the box or purchased any candy from the firm in question. She was quite willing to go there and be identified, but no clerk in the candy-store was able to identify her as one woman who had purchased candy. There were one or two clerks who felt sure that there had been a woman there at some time or other who had looked like her, but they were not positive. However, there was one girl who had worked in the store during the week in which the candy had been purchased, and who was not there any longer. This was a new girl who had been tried out for that week only and had since disappeared. Her name was known, of course, and the newspapers as well as the District Attorney's office at once began looking for her.

There were some whispers to the effect that not only Mrs. Davis but Steele himself might have been concerned in the plot, or Steele alone, since apparently he had been anxious to get rid of his wife. Why not? He might have imitated the handwriting of Mrs. Davis or created an accidental like-ness to it. Also, there were dissenting souls, even in the office of the paper on which I worked, who thought that maybe Mrs. Steele had sent the candy to herself in order to injure the other woman. Why not? It was possible. Women were like that. There had been similar cases, had there not? Argument! Contention! "She might have wanted to die and be revenged on the other woman at the same time, might she not?" observed the railroad editor. "Oh, hell! What bunk!" called another. "No woman would kill herself to make a place for a rival. That's crazy." "Well," said a third, "she might have miscalculated the power of her own dope. Who knows? She may not have intended to take as much as she did." "Oh, Christ," called a fourth from somewhere, "just listen to the Sherlock Holmes Association in session over there! Lay off, will you?"

A week or more went by, and then the missing girl who had worked in the candy-store was found. She had left the city the following week and gone to Denver. Being shown the pictures of Mrs. Davis, Mrs. Steele and some others and asked whether on any given day she had sold any of them a two-pound box of candy, she seemed to recall no one of them save possibly Mrs. Steele. But she could not be sure from the photograph. She would have to see the woman. In consequence, and without any word to the newspapers who had been leading the case up to then, this girl was returned to the city. Here, in the District Attor-ney's office, she was confronted by a number of women gath-ered for the occasion, among whom was placed Mrs. Davis. But on looking them all over she failed to identify any one of them. Then Mrs. Steele, who was by then up and around, was sent for. She came, along with a representative of the office. On sight, as she entered the door, and although there were other women in the room at the time, this girl exclaimed: "There she is! That's the woman! Yes, that's the very woman!" She was positive.

VI

As is customary in such cases, and despite the sympathy that had been extended to her, Mrs. Steele was turned over to criminologists, who soon extracted the truth from her. She broke down and wept hysterically.

It was she who had purchased the candy and poisoned it. Her life was going to pieces. She had wanted to die, so she said now. She had addressed the wrapper about the candy, as some of the wiseacres of our paper had contended, only she had first made a tracing on the paper from Mrs. Davis' handwriting, on an envelope addressed to her husband, and had then copied that. She had put not arsenic, but rat poison, bought some time before, into the candy, and in order to indict Mrs. Davis, she had put a little in each piece, about as much as would kill a rat, so that it would seem as though the entire box had been poisoned by her. She had got the idea from a case she had read about years before in a newspaper. She hated Mrs. Davis for stealing her husband. She had followed them.

When she had eaten one of the pieces of candy she had thought, as she now insisted, that she was taking enough to make an end of it all. But before taking it she had made sure that Mrs. Dalrymple, the wife of the newspaperman whom she first called to her aid, was at home in order that she might call or send her little boy. Her purpose in doing this was to instil in the mind of Mrs. Dalrymple the belief that it was Mrs. Davis who had sent the poison. When she was gone, Mrs. Davis would be punished, her husband would not be able to have her, and she herself would be out of her misery.

Result: the prompt discharge of Mrs. Davis, but no charge against Mrs. Steele. According to the District Attorney and the newspapers who most truly reflected local sentiment, she had suffered enough. And, as the state of public feeling then was, the District Attorney would not have dared to punish her. Her broken confession so reacted on the public mind that now, and for all time, it was for Mrs. Steele, just as a little while before it was rather for Mrs. Davis. For, you see, it was now proved that it was Mrs. Steele and not Mrs. Davis who had been wrought up to that point emotionally where she had been ready and willing —had actually tried—to make a blood sacrifice of herself and another woman on the altar of love. In either case it was the blood sacrifice—the bare possibility of it, if you choose— that lay at the bottom of the public's mood, and caused it to turn sympathetically to that one who had been most willing to murder in the cause of love.

But don't think this story is quite ended. Far from it. There is something else here, and a very interesting something to which I wish to call your attention. I have said that the newspapers turned favorably to Mrs. Steele. They did. So did the sob-sisters, those true barometers of public moods. Eulogies were now heaped upon Mrs. Steele, her devotion, her voiceless, unbearable woe, the tragedy of her mood, her intended sacrifice of herself. She was now the darling of these journalistic pseudo-analysts.

As for Mrs. Davis—not a word of sympathy, let alone praise or understanding for her thereafter. Almost unmentioned, if you will believe it, she was, and at once allowed to slip back into the limbo of the unheralded, the subsequently-to-be-unknown. From then on it was almost as though she had never been. For a few weeks, I believe, she retired to the home in which she had lived; then she disappeared entirely.

But now as to Steele. Here was the third peculiar phase of the case. Subsequent to the exculpation of Mrs. Davis and her noiseless retirement from the scene, what would you say his attitude would have been, or should have been? Where would he go? What do? What attitude would he assume? One of renewed devotion to his wife? One of renewed devotion to Mrs. Davis? One of disillusion or indifference in regard to all things? It puzzled me, and I was a rank outsider with no least concern, except of course our general concern in all such things, so vital to all of us in our sex and social lives. But not only was it a puzzle to me; it was also a puzzle to others, especially those who were identified with the newspaper business in the city, the editors and the city editors and managing editors who had been following the wavering course of things with uncertain thoughts and I may say uncertain policy. They had been, as you may guess, as prepared to hang Steele as not, assuming that he had been identified with Mrs. Davis in a plot to do away with his wife. On the other hand, now that that shadow was removed and it was seen to be a more or less simple case of varietism on his part, resulting in marital unhappiness for his wife and a desire on her part to die, they were prepared to look upon him and this result with a more kindly eye. After all, she was not dead. Mrs. Davis had been punished. And say what you will, looking at Mrs. Steele as she was, and at Mrs. Davis as she was—well— with a certain amount of material if not spiritual provocation—what would you?

Indeed, the gabble about the newspaper offices was all to the above effect. What, if anything, finally asked some of the city editors and managing editors, was to be done about Steele? Now that everything had blown over, what of him? Go on hounding him forever? Nonsense! It was scarcely fair, and, anyhow, no longer profitable or worth while. Now that the storm was passing, might not something be done for him? After all, he had been a fairly respectable newspaper-

man and in good standing. Why not take him back? And
if not that, how was he to be viewed in future by his friends?
Was he to be let alone, dropped, forgotten, or what? Was
he going to stay here in G——, and fight it out, or leave?
And if he was going to leave or stay, with whom was he
going to leave or stay? Semikindly, semiselfish curiosity,
as you see.

VII

The thing to do, it was finally decided among several of
those on our paper and several on other papers who had
known him more or less intimately, was to go to Steele himself, and ask him, not for publicity but just between ourselves,
what was to be done, what he proposed to do, whether there
was anything now that the local newspapers could say or do
which would help him in any way? Did he want to be
restored to a staff position? Was he going to stick to his
wife? What, if anything, and with no malicious intent,
should they say about Mrs. Davis? In a more or less secret
and brotherly or professional spirit they were going to put
it up to him and then leave it there, doing whatever they
could in accordance with what he might wish.

Accordingly, two of the local newsmen whom he quite
honestly respected visited him and placed the above several
propositions before him. They found him, as I was told
afterwards, seated upon the front porch of the very small
and commonplace house in which after the dismissal of the
charge against Mrs. Davis, he and his wife had been dwell-
ing, reading a paper. Seated with him was Mrs. Steele,
thinner and more querulous and anemic and unattractive than
before. And upon the lot outside was their little son. Upon
their arrival, they hailed Steele for a private word, and Mrs.
Steele arose and went into the house. She looked, said one
of these men, as though she expected more trouble. Steele,
on his part, was all smiles and genial tenderings of hospi-
tality. He was hoping for the best, of course, and he was

anxious to do away with any new source of trouble. He even rubbed his hands, and licked his lips. "Come right in, boys. Come on up on the porch. Wait a minute and I'll bring out a couple of chairs." He hastened away but quickly returned, determined, as they thought, to make as good an impression as possible.

After he had heard what they had come for—most tactfully and artfully put, of course—he was all smiles, eager, apparently, to be well thought of once more. To their inquiry as to whether he proposed to remain or not, he replied: "Yes, for the present." He had not much choice. He had not saved enough money in recent days to permit him to do much of anything else, and his wife's illness and other things had used up about all he had. "And now, just between ourselves, Steele," asked one of the two men who knew him better than the other, "what about Mrs. Davis and your wife? Just where do you stand in regard to them? Are you going to stick to your wife or are you going with the other woman eventually? No trouble for you, you understand—no more publicity. But the fellows on the papers are in a little bit of a quandary in regard to this. They don't intend to publish anything more—nothing disparaging. They only want to get your slant on the thing so that if anything more does come up in connection with this they can fix it so that it won't be offensive to you, you see."

"Yes, I see," replied Steele cheerfully and without much reflection. "But so far as that Davis woman is concerned, though, you can forget her. I'm through with her. She was never much to me, anyhow, just a common——." Here he used the good old English word for prostitute. As for his wife, he was going to stick by her, of course. She was a good woman. She loved him. There was his little boy. He was through with all that varietistic stuff. There was nothing to it. A man couldn't get away with it—and so on.

The two men, according to their account of it afterward, winced not a little, for, as they said, they had thought from

too much; that damned memory of mine, illegitimate as it may seem to be, was too much. I could not help thinking of the *Ira Ramsdell* and of how much I had envied him the dances, the love, the music, the moonlight.

"By God!" I exclaimed as I walked away. "By God!"

And that is exactly how I feel now about all such miscarriages of love and delight—cold and sad.

VI

KHAT

"O, thou blessed that contains no demon, but a fairy! When I follow thee thou takest me into regions overlooking Paradise. My sorrows are as nothing. My rags are become as robes of silk. My feet are shod, not worn and bleeding. I lift up my head——O Flower of Paradise! O Flower of Paradise!"

Old Arabian Song.

"When the European is weary he calls for alcohol to revive him; when he is joyful he thinks of wine that he may have more joy. In like manner the Chinese wooes his 'white lady,' the poppy flower. The Indian chews bhang, and the West African seeks surcease in kola. To the Yemen Arab, khat, the poor man's happiness, his 'flower of paradise,' is more than any of these to its devotees. It is no narcotic compelling sleep, but a stimulant like alcohol, a green shrub that grows upon the hills in moist places. On the roads leading to the few cities of Arabia, and in the cities themselves, it may be seen being borne on the backs of camels to the market-place or the wedding feast—the wet and dripping leaves of the shrub. The poor and the well-to-do at once crave and adore it. They speak of it as 'the strength of the weak,' 'the inspiration of the depressed,' 'the dispeller of sorrow and too deep care.' All who may, buy and chew it, the poor by the anna's worth, the rich by the rupee. The beggar when he can beg or steal it—even he is happy too."

American Consular Report.

THE dawn had long since broken over the heat-weary cup and slopes of the Mugga Valley, in which lies Hodeidah. In the centre of the city, like a mass of upturned yellow cups and boxes surrounded by a ring of green and faced by the sea, were the houses, with their streets and among and in them the shopkeepers of streets or ways busy about the labors of the day. Al Hajjaj, the cook, whose place was near the mosque in the centre of the public square, had already set his pots and pans over the fire and washed his saucers and wiped his scales and swept his shop and sprinkled it. And indeed his fats and oils were clear and his spices fragrant, and he himself was standing behind his cooking pots ready to serve customers. Likewise those who dealt in bread, ornaments, dress goods, had put forth such wares as they had to offer. In the mosque a few of the faithful had entered to pray. Over the dust of the ill-swept street, not yet cleared of the rubbish of the day before, the tikka gharries of the better-to-do dragged their way along the road about various errands. The same was speckled with natives in bright or dull attire, some alive with the interest of business, others dull because of a life that offered little.

In his own miserable wattle-covered shed or hut, no more than an abandoned donkey's stall at the edge of the city, behold Ibn Abdullah. Beggar, ne'er-do-well, implorer of charity before the mosque, ex-water-carrier and tobacco seller in Mecca and Medina, from whence he had been driven years before by his extortions and adulterations, he now turned wearily, by no means anxious to rise although it was late. For why rise when you are old and weary and ragged, and life offers at best only a little food and sleep— or not so much food as (best and most loved of all earthly blessings) khat, the poor man's friend? For that, more than food or drink, he craved. Yet how to come by it was a mystery. There was about him not a single anna wherewith to sate his needs—not so much as a pice!

Indeed, as Ibn Abdullah now viewed his state, he had about reached the end of his earthly tether. His career was and had been a failure. Born in the mountain district back of Hodeidah, in the little village of Sabar, source of the finest khat, where formerly his father had been a khat farmer, his mother a farmer's helper, he had wandered far, here and there over Arabia and elsewhere, making a living as best he might: usually by trickery. Once for a little while he had been a herdsman with a Bedouin band, and had married a daughter of the tribe, but, restlessness and a lust of novelty overcoming him, he had, in time, deserted his wife and wandered hence. Thence to Jiddah, the port of debarkation for pilgrims from Egypt and Central Africa approaching Mecca and Medina, the birthplace and the burialplace of the Prophet. Selling trinkets and sacred relics, water and tobacco and fruit and food, and betimes indulging in trickery and robbery, he had finally been taken in the toils of the Cadis of both Mecca and Medina, by whose henchmen he had been sadly drubbed on his back and feet and ordered away, never to return. Venturing once more into the barren desert, a trailer of caravans, he had visited Taif, Taraba and Makhwa, but finding life tedious in these smaller places he had finally drifted southward along the coast of the Red Sea to the good city of Hodeidah, where, during as many as a dozen years now, he had been eking out a wretched existence, story-telling, selling tobacco (when he could get it) or occasionally false relics to the faithful. Having grown old in this labor, his tales commonplace, his dishonesty and lack of worth and truth well known, he was now weary and helpless, truly one near an unhonored end.

Time was, in his better days and greater strength, as he now bethought him on this particular morning, when he had had his full share of khat, and food too. Ay-ee! There had been some excellent days in the past, to be sure! Not even old Raschid, the khat drunkard, or Al Hajjaj, the cook, who might be seen of a late afternoon before his shop, his pillow and carpets and water chatties about him, his narghili lit, a bunch of khat by his side, his wife and daughter at the window above listening to him and his friends as they smoked or chewed and discoursed, had more of khat and food than had he. By Allah, things were different then! He had had his girls, too, his familiar places in the best of the mabrazes, where were lights and delightful strains of song, and dancing betimes. He had sung and applauded and recounted magnificent adventures with the best of them. Ay-ee!

But of late he had not done well—not nearly as well as in times past. He was very, very old now, that was the reason; his bones ached and even creaked. An undue reputation for evil things done in the past—Inshallah! no worse than those of a million others—pursued him wherever he went. It was remembered of him, unfortunately, here in Hodeidah, as in Mecca and Medina (due no doubt to the lying, blasting tongue—may it wither in his mouth!—of Tahrbulu, the carrier, whom he had known in Mecca) —that he had been bastinadoed there for adulterating the tobacco he sold—a little dried goats' and camels' dung, wind-blown and clean; and as for Taif, to which place he had gone after Mecca, Firaz, the ex-caravan guard who had known him in that place—the dog!—might his bones wither in the sun!—had recalled to various and sundry that at Mecca he had been imprisoned for selling water from a rain-pit as that of the sacred well of Jezer! Be it so; he was hard pressed at the time; there was no place to turn; business was poor—and great had been his yearning for khat.

But since then he had aged and wearied and all his efforts at an honest livelihood had served him ill. Betimes his craving for khat had grown, the while his ability to earn it—aye, even to beg it with any success!—had decreased. Here in Hodeidah he was too well known (alas, much too well known!), and yet where else was he to go? By sea it was all of three hundred miles to Aden, a great and generous place, so it was said, but how was he to get there at his time of life? No captain would carry him. He would be tossed into the sea like a rat. Had he not begged and been roundly cursed? And to Jiddah, whereby thousands came to Mecca, a full five hundred miles north, he dare not return. Were he there, no doubt he would do better: the faithful were generous. . . . But were he caught in the realm of the Grand Sherif— No; Hodeidah had its advantages.

He arose after a time, and, without ablutions, prostrating himself weakly in the direction of Mecca, adjusted his ragged loin- and shoulder-cloths and prepared to emerge for the day. Although hungry and weak, it was not food but khat that he desired, a few leaves of the green, succulent, life-giving plant that so restored his mood and strength and faculties generally. By Allah, if he had but a little, a handful, his thoughts concerning life would be so much more endurable. He might even, though cracked and wretched was his voice, tell a tale or two to idlers and so earn an honest anna. Or he would have more courage to beg, to lie, to mourn before the faithful. Yea, had he not done so often? With it he was as good as any man, as young, as hopeful; without it—well, he was as he was: feeble and worn.

As he went forth finally along the hot, dusty road which led into the city and the public market and mosque, lined on either side by low one-story mud houses of the poor, windowless, and with the roadway in front as yet unswept, his thoughts turned in eager seeking to the khat market, hard by the public square and beyond the mosque, whose pineapple-shaped dome he could even now see rising in the distance over the low roofs before him. Here it was that at about eleven o'clock in the morning the khat camels bearing their succulent loads would come winding along the isthmus road from the interior. He could see them now, hear their bells, the long striding camels, their shouting drivers, the green herb, wet and sweet, piled in refreshing masses upon their backs! How well he knew the process of its arrival—the great rock beyond the Jiddah gate casting a grateful shade, the two little black policemen ready to take custom toll of each load and give a receipt, the huge brutes halting before the door of the low kutcha-thatched inn, there to pick at some wisps of grass while their masters went inside to have a restful pull at a hubbuk (water-pipe) and a drink of kishr, or maybe a bowl of curds. Meanwhile, a flock of shrewd youngsters, bribelings of the merchants of the bazaars within the city, would flit about the loaded animals, seeking to steal a leaf or to thrust an appraising glance into the closely wrapped bundles, in order that they might report as to the sweetness and freshness of their respective loads.

"What, O *kowasji,* is the quality of your khat to-day? Which beast carries the best, and has thy driver stinted no water on the journey to keep it fresh?"

To find true answers to these questions had these urchins taken their bribe-money in the bazaars. But the barefoot policeman would chase them away, the refreshed drivers would come out again, fiercely breathing calumnies against the grandmothers of such brats, and the little caravan would pick its way upward and downward again into the market.

But to-day, too weary to travel so far, even though by sighs and groans and many prayers for their well-being he might obtain so little as a leaf or two from the comfortable drivers, he betook himself slowly toward the market itself. En route, and especially as he neared a better portion of the city, where tikka gharries might be seen, he was not spareful of "Alms, in the name of Allah! Allah! Alms!" or "May thy hours in paradise be endless!" But none threw him so much as a pice. Instead, those who recognized his familiar figure, the sad antithesis of all industry and well-being, turned away or called: "Out of the way, thou laggard! To one side, dog!"

When he reached the market, however, not without hav-ing cast a wishful eye at the shining pots and saucers of Al Hajjaj en route, the adjoining bazaar had heard of the coming of the green-laden caravan, and from the dark shops, so silent until now, cheerful cries were beginning to break forth. Indeed the streets were filled with singing and a stream of lean figures all headed one way. Like himself they were going to the khat market, only so much better equipped for the occasion—rupees and anna in plenty for so necessary and delectable an herb. Tikka gharries rattled madly past him, whips were waved and turbans pushed awry; there were flashes of color from rich men's gowns, as they hurried to select the choicest morsels, the clack of oryx-hide sandals, and the blunt beating of tom-toms. As the camels arrived in the near distance, the market was filled with a restless, yelling mob. Bedlam had broken loose, but a merry, good-natured bedlam at that. For khat, once obtained, would ease whatever ill feeling or morning unrest or weariness one might feel.

Although without a pice wherewith to purchase so much as a stalk, still Ibn could not resist the temptation of entering here. What, were none of the faithful merciful? By Allah, impossible! Perchance—who knows?—there might be a stranger, a foreigner, who in answer to his appealing glance, his outstretched hands, an expression of abject despair which long since he had mastered, would cast him an anna, or even a rupee (it had happened!), or some one, seeing him going away empty-handed or standing at the gate outside, forlorn and cast down, and asking always alms, alms, would cast him a delicious leaf or spray of the surpassing delight.

But no; this day, as on the day previous, and the one before that, he had absolutely no success. What was it— the hand of fate itself? Had Allah truly forsaken him at last? In a happy babel, and before his very eyes, the delicious paradisiacal stimulant was weighed on government scales and taxed again—the Emir must live! And then, divided into delicious bundles the thickness of a man's forearm, it was offered for sale. Ah, the beauty of those bundles—the delight therein contained—the surcease even now! The proud sellers, in turban and shirt, were mounting the small tables or stands about the place and beginning to auction it off, each bundle bringing its own price. "Min kam! Min kam!" Hadji, the son of Dodow, was now crying—Hadji, whom Ibn had observed this many a day as a seller here. He was waving a bunch above the outstretched hands of the crowd. "How much? How much will you give for this flower of paradise, this bringer of happiness, this dispeller of all weakness? 'Tis as a maiden's eyes. 'Tis like bees' breath for fragrance. 'Tis—"

"That I might buy!" sighed Ibn heavily. "That I might buy! Who will give me so much as a spray?"

"One anna" (two cents), yelled a mirthful and contemptuous voice, knowing full well the sacrilege of the offer.

"Thou scum! O thou miserable little tick on the back of a sick camel!" replied the seller irritably. "May my nose grow a beard if it is not worth two rupees at the very least!"

"Bismillah! There is not two rupees' worth in all thy filthy godown, *budmash!*"

"Thou dog! Thou detractor! But why should one pay attention to one who has not so much as an anna wherewith to ease himself? To those who have worth and many rupees—look, behold, how green, how fresh!"

And Al Hajjaj, the cook, and Ahmed, the carpet-weaver, stepped forward and took each a bunch for a rupee, the while Ibn Abdullah, hanging upon the skirt of the throng and pushed contemptuously here and there, eyed it all sadly. Other bundles in the hands of other sellers were held up and quickly disposed of—to Chudi, the baker, Azad Bakht, the barber, Izz-al-Din, the seller of piece goods, and so on, until within the hour all was exhausted and the place deserted. On the floor was now left only the litter and débris of stems and deadened leaves, to be haggled over by the hadjis (vendors of firewood), the sweepers, scavengers and beggars generally, of whom he was one; only for the want of a few pice, an anna at the most, he would not even now be allowed to carry away so much as a stem of this, so ill had been his fortunes these many, many days. In this pell-mell scene, where so many knew him and realized the craving wherewith he was beset, not one paused to offer him a sprig. He was as wretched as before, only hungrier and thirstier.

And then, once the place was finally deserted, not a leaf or a stem upon the ground, he betook himself slowly and wearily to his accustomed place in the shadow of one of the six columns which graced the entryway of the mosque (the place of beggars), there to lie and beseech of all who entered or left that they should not forget the adjuration of the Prophet "and give thy kinsman his due and the poor and the son of the road." At noon he entered with others and prayed, for there at least he was welcome, but alas, his thoughts were little on the five prescribed daily prayers and the morning and evening ablutions—no, not even upon food, but rather upon khat. How to obtain it—a leaf—a stem!

Almost perforce his thoughts now turned to the days of his youth, when as a boy living on the steep terraced slope of the mountains between Taiz and Yerim, he was wont literally to dwell among the small and prosperous plantations of the khat farmers who flourished there in great numbers. Indeed, before his time, his father had been one such, and Sabar and Hirwa, two little villages in the Taiz district, separated only by a small hill, and in the former of which he was born, were famous all over Arabia for the khat that was raised there. Next to that which came from Bokhari, the khat of Sabar, his home town, was and remained the finest in all Yemen. Beside it even that of Hirwa was coarse, thin and astringent, and more than once he had heard his mother, who was a khat-picker, say that one might set out Sabari plants in Hirwa and that they quickly became coarse, but remove Hirwa plants to Sabar, and they grew sweet and delicate.

And there as a child he—who could not now obtain even so much as a leaf of life-giving khat!—had aided his mother in picking or cutting the leaves and twigs of khat that constituted the crops of this region—great camel-loads of it! In memory now he could see the tasks of the cooler months, where, when new fields were being planted, they were started from cuttings buried in shallow holes four to six inches apart with space enough between the rows for pickers to pass; how the Yemen cow and the sad-eyed camel, whose maw was never full, had to be guarded against, since they had a nice taste in cuttings, and thorn twigs and spiny cactus leaves had to be laid over the young shoots to discourage the marauders.

At the end of a year the young shrubs, now two feet high, had a spread of thick green foliage eighteen inches in diameter. Behold now the farmer going out into the dawn of each morning to gaze at his field and the sky, in the hope of seeing the portents of harvest time. On a given morning the air would be thick with bulbuls, sparrows, weaver birds, shrilly clamoring; they would rise and fall above the plants, picking at the tenderest leaves. "Allah be praised!" would cry the farmer in delight. "The leaves are sweet and ripe for the market!" And now he would call his women and the wives of his neighbors to the crop-picking. Under a bower of jasmine vines, with plumes of the sweet smelling *rehan,* the farmer and his cronies would gather to drink from tiny cups and smoke the hubbuk, while the womenfolk brought them armfuls of the freshly cut khat leaves. What a joyous time it was for all the village, for always the farmer distributed the whole of his first crop among his neighbors, in the name of Allah, that Allah's blessings might thus be secured on all the succeeding ones. Would that he were in Sabar or Hirwa once more!

But all this availed him nothing. He was sick and weary, with little strength and no money wherewith to return; besides, if he did, the fame of his evil deeds would have preceded him perhaps. Again, here in Hodeidah, as elsewhere in Arabia, the cities and villages especially, khat-chewing was not only an appetite but a habit, and even a social custom or function, with the many, and re-quired many rupees the year to satisfy. Indeed one of the painful things in connection with all this was that, not unlike eating in other countries, or tea at least, it had come to involve a paraphernalia and a ritual all its own, one might say. At this very noon hour here in Hodeidah, when, because of his luck, he was here before the temple begging instead of having a comfortable home of his own, hundreds—aye, thousands—who an hour earlier might have been seen wending their way happily homeward from the market, their eyes full of a delicious content, their jaws working, a bundle of the precious leaves under their arms, might now be found in their private or public mabraz making themselves comfortable, chewing and digesting this same, and not until the second hour of the afternoon would they again be seen. They all had this, their delight, to attend to!

Aye, go to the house of any successful merchant, (only the accursed Jews and the outlanders did not use khat) between these hours and say that you had urgent news for him or that you had come to buy a lakh of rupees' worth of skins. . . . His servant would meet you on the verandah (accursed dogs! How well he knew them and their airs!) and offer the profoundest apologies . . . the master would be unutterably sick (here he would begin to weep), or his sister's husband's aunt's mother had died this very morning and full of unutterable woe as he was he would be doing no business; or certainly he had gone to Tawahi but assuredly would return by three. Would the caller wait? And at that very moment the rich dog would be in his mabraz at the top of his house smoking his hubbuk and chewing his leaves—he who only this morning had refused Ibn so much as a leaf! Bismillah! Let him rot like a dead jackal!

Or was it one who was less rich? Behold the public mabraz, such as he—Ibn—dared not even look into save as a wandering teller of tales, or could only behold from afar. For here these prosperous swine could take their ease in the heat of the day, cool behind trellised windows of these same, or at night could dream where were soft lights and faint strains of song, where sombre shadow-steeped figures swayed as though dizzy with the sound of their own voices, chanting benedictions out of the Koran or the Prophets. Had he not told tales for them in his time, the uncharitable dogs? Even now, at this noon hour, one might see them, the habitués of these same well-ventilated and well-furnished public rooms, making off in state for their favorite diversion, their khat tied up in a bright shawl and conspicuously displayed—for whom except himself, so poor or so low that he could not afford a little?—and all most anxious that all the world should know that they went thus to enjoy themselves. In the mabraz, each one his rug and pillow arranged for him, he would recline, occupying the space assigned him and no more. By his side would be the tall narghili or hubbuk, the two water-pots or chatties on copper stands, and a bowl of sweets. Bismillah, he was no beggar! When the mabraz was comfortably filled with customers a servant would come and light the pipes, some one would produce a Koran or commence a story—not he any more, for they would not have him, such was his state—and the afternoon's pleasure would begin. Occasionally the taraba (a kind of three-stringed viol) would be played, or, as it might happen, a favorite singer be present. Then the happy cries of *"Tai-eeb!"* or *"Marhabba! Marhabba!"* (Good!), or the more approbative "O friend, excellent indeed!" would be heard. How well he remembered his own share in all this in former years, and how little the knowledge of it all profited him now—how little! Ah, what a sadness to be old and a beggar in the face of so much joy!

But as he mused in the shade, uttering an occasional "Alms, alms, in the name of Allah!" as one or another of the faithful entered or left the mosque, there came from the direction of the Jiddah gate, the regular khat-bearing camel route, shrill cries and yells. Looking up now, he saw a crowd of boys racing toward the town, shouting as they ran: "Al khat aja!" (the khat has come), a thing which of itself boded something unusual—a marriage or special feast of some kind, for at this late hour for what other reason would khat be brought? The market was closed; the chewers of khat already in their mabrazes. From somewhere also, possibly in the house of a bridegroom, came the faint tunk-a-lunk of a tom-tom, which now seemed to take up the glad tidings and beat out its summons to the wedding guests.

"Bismillah! What means this?" commented the old beggar to himself, his eyes straining in the direction of the crowd; then folding his rags about him he proceeded to limp in the direction of the noise. At the turn of a narrow street leading into the square his eye was gladdened truly enough by the sight of a khat-bearing camel, encompassed by what in all likelihood, and as he well knew was the custom on such occasions, a cloud of "witnesses" (seekers of entertainment or food at any feast) to the probable approaching marriage. Swathed round the belly of the camel as it came and over its load of dripping green herbs, was laid a glorious silken cloth, blazing with gold and hung with jasmine sprays; and though tom-toms thumped and fifes squealed a furious music all about him, the solemn beast bore his burden as if it were some majesty of state.

"By Allah," observed the old beggar wearily yet eyeing the fresh green khat with zest, "that so much joy should be and I have not a pice, let alone an anna! Would that I might take a spray—that one might fall!"

"Friend," he ventured after a moment, turning to a water-carrier who was standing by, one almost as poor as himself if more industrious, "what means this? Has not Ramazan passed and is not Mohorrum yet to come?"

"Dost thou address me, thou bag of bones?" returned the carrier, irritated by this familiarity on the part of one less than himself.

"Sahib," returned the beggar respectfully, using a term which he knew would flatter the carrier, no more entitled to a "Sir" than himself, "use me not ill. I am in sore straits and weak. Is it for a marriage or a dance, perhaps?"

"Thou hast said," replied the carrier irritably, "—of

Zeila, daughter of old Bhori, the tin-seller in the bazaar, to Abdul, whose father is jemidar of chaprassies at the burra bungalow."

At the mere mention of marriage there came into the mind of Ibn the full formula for any such in Hodeidah—for had he not attended them in his time, not so magnificent as this perhaps but marriages of sorts? From noon on all the relatives and friends invited would begin to appear in twos and threes in the makhdara, where all preparations for the entertainment of the guests had no doubt been made. Here for them to sit on in so rich a case as this (or so he had heard in the rumored affairs of the rich), would be long benches of stone or teak, and upon them beautiful carpets and pillows. (In all the marriages he had been permitted to attend these were borrowed for the occasion from relatives or friends.) Madayeh, or water-bubbles, would be ready, although those well enough placed in the affairs of this world would prefer to bring their own, carried by a servant. A lot of little chatties for the pipes would be on hand, as well as a number of fire-pots, these latter outside the makhdara with a dozen boys, fan in hand, ready to refill for each guest his pipe with tobacco and fire on the first call of *"Ya yi-yall!"* How well he remembered his services as a pipe-filler on occasions of this kind in his youth, how well his pleasure as guest or friend, relative even on one occasion, in his earlier and more prosperous years and before he had become an outcast, when his own pipe had been filled. Oh, the music! the bowls of sweets! the hot kishr, the armful of delicious khat, and before and after those little cakes of wheat with butter and curds! When the makhdara was full and all the guests had been solemnly greeted by the father of the bride, as well as by the prospective husband, khat would be distributed, and the pleasure of chewing it begin. Ah! Yes, weddings were wonderful and very well in their way indeed, provided one came by anything through them.

Alas, here, as in the case of the market sales, his opportunities for attending the same with any profit to himself, the privilege of sharing in the delights and comforts of the same, were over. He had no money, no repute, not even respect. Indeed the presence of a beggar such as he on an occasion of this kind, and especially here in Hodeidah where were many rich, would be resented, taken almost as an evil omen. Not only the guests within but those poorer admirers without, such as these who but now followed the camel, would look upon his even so much as distant approach as a vile intrusion, lawless, worthless dog that he was, come to peek and pry and cast a shadow upon what would otherwise be a happy occasion.

Yet he could not resist the desire to follow a portion of the way, anyhow. The escorted khat looked too enticing. Bismillah! There must be some one who would throw him a leaf on so festal an occasion, surely! By a slow and halting process therefore he came finally before the gate of the residence, into which already the camel had disappeared. Before it was the usual throng of those not so vastly better than himself who had come to rejoice for a purpose, and within, the sound of the tom-tom and voices singing. Over the gate and out of the windows were hung silken carpets and jasmine sprays, for old Bhori was by no means poor in this world's goods.

While recognizing a number who might have been tolerant of him, Ibn Abdullah also realized rather painfully that of the number of these who were most friendly, having known him too long as a public beggar, there were few.

"What! Ne'er-do-well!" cried one who recognized him as having been publicly bastinadoed on one occasion here years before, when he had been younger and healthy enough to be a vendor of tobacco, for adulterating his tobacco. "Do you come here, too?" Then turning to another he called: "Look who comes here—Ibn, the rich man! A friend of the good Bhori, no doubt, mayhap a relative, or at least one of his invited guests!"

"Ay-ee, a friend of the groom at least!" cried another.

"Or a brother or cousin of the bride!" chaffed still a third.

"A rich and disappointed seeker after her hand!" declared a fourth titteringly.

"He brings rich presents, as one can see!" proclaimed a fifth. "But look now at his hands!" A chortle followed, joined in by many.

"And would he be content with so little as a spray of khat in return?" queried a sixth.

"By Allah, an honest tobacco-merchant! Bismillah! One whom the Cadi loves!" cried a seventh.

For answer Ibn turned a solemn and craving eye upon them, thinking only of khat. "Inshallah! Peace be with thee, good citizens!" he returned. "Abuse not one who is very low in his state. Alms! Alms! A little khat, of all that will soon generously be bestowed upon thee! Alms!"

"Away, old robber!" cried one of them. "If you had ever been honest you would not now be poor."

"What, old jackal, dost thou come here to beg? What brings thee from the steps of the mosque? Are the praying faithful so ungenerous? By Allah! Likely they know thee—not?"

"Peace! Peace! And mayst thou never know want and distress such as mine! Food I have not had for three days. My bones yearn for so much as a leaf of khat. Be thou generous and of all that is within, when a portion is given thee give me but a leaf!"

"The Cadi take thee!"

"Dog!"

"Beggar!"

"Come not too near, thou bag of decay!"

So they threatened him and he came no closer, removing rather to a safe distance and eyeing as might a lorn jackal a feast partaken of by lions.

Yet having disposed of this objectionable intruder in this fashion, no khat was as yet forthcoming, the reason being that it was not yet time. Inside, the wedding ceremony and feast, a matter of slow and ordered procedure, was going forward with great care. Kishr was no doubt now being drunk, and there were many felicitations to be extended and received. But, once it was all over and the throng without invited to partake of what was left, Ibn was not one of those included. Rather, he was driven off with curses by a servant, and being thus entirely shut out could only wait patiently in the distance until those who had entered should be satisfied and eventually come forth wiping their lips and chewing khat—in better humor, perchance— or go his way. Then, if he chose to stay, and they were kind—

But, having eaten and drunk, they were in no better mood in regard to him. As they came forth, singly or in pairs, an hour or more later, they saw in him only a pest, one who would take from them a little of that which they themselves had earned with difficulty. Therefore they passed him by unheeding or with jests.

And by now it was that time in the afternoon when the effect on the happy possessor of khat throughout all Arabia was only too plainly to be seen. The Arab servant who in the morning had been surly and taciturn under the blazing sun was now, with a wad of the vivifying leaves in his cheek, doing his various errands and duties with a smile and a light foot. The bale which the ordinary coolie of the waterfront could not lift in the morning was now but a featherweight on his back. The coffee merchant who in the morning was acrid in manner and sharp at a bargain, now received your orders gratefully and with a pleasantry, and even a bid for conversation in his eye. Abdullah, the silk merchant, dealing with his customers in sight of the mosque, bestowed compliments and presents. By Allah, he would buy your horse for the price of an elephant and find no favor too great to do for you. Yussuf, the sambuk-carrier, a three-hundred-weight goatskin on his back, and passing Ibn near the mosque once more, assured Ali, his familiar of the same world and of equal load, as they trudged along together, "Cut off my strong hand, and I will become Hadji, the sweeper" (a despised caste), "but take away my khat, and let me die!" Everywhere the evasive, apathetic atmosphere of the morning had given way to the valor of sentient life. Chewing the life-giving weed, all were sure that they could perform prodigies of energy and strength, that life was a delicious thing, the days and years of their troubles as nothing.

But viewing this and having none, and trudging moodily along toward his waiting-place in front of the mosque, Ibn was truly depressed and out of sorts. The world was not right. Age and poverty should command more respect. To be sure, in his youth perhaps he had not been all that he might have been, but still, for that matter, had many others so been? Were not all men weak, after their kind, or greedy or uncharitable? By Allah, they were, and as he had reason to know! Waidi, the water-seller? A thief really, no whit better than himself, if the world but knew. Hussein, the peddler of firewood; Haifa, the tobacco tramp —a wretched and swindling pack, all, not a decent loin- or shoulder-cloth among them, possessed of no better places of abode than his own really, yet all, even as the richest of men, had their khat, could go to their coffee places this night and enjoy it for a few anna. Even they! And he!

In Hodeidah there was still another class, the strictly business or merchant class, who, unlike men of wealth or the keepers of the very small shops, wound up their affairs at four in the afternoon and returning to their homes made a kind of public show of their ease and pleasure in khat from then on until the evening prayers. Charpoys, water-pipes and sweetmeats were brought forth into the shade before the street door. The men of the household and their male friends sprawled sociably on the charpoys, the ingredients for the promotion of goodly fellowship ready to their hands. A graybeard or two might sit among them expounding from the sacred book, or conversation lively in character but sub-dued in tone entertained the company. Then the aged, the palsied, even the dying of the family, their nearest of kin, were brought down on their beds from the top of the house to partake of this feast of reason and flow of wit. Inside the latticed windows the women sat, munching the second-best leaves and listening to the scraps of wisdom that floated up to them from the company below.

It was from this hour on that Ibn found it most difficult to endure life. To see the world thus gay while he was hungry was all but too much. After noting some of this he wandered wearily down the winding market street which led from the mosque to the waterfront, and where in view of the sea were a few of the lowest coffee-houses, frequented by coolies, bhisties and hadjis. Here in some one of them, though without a single pice in his hand, he proposed to make a final effort before night should fall, so that thereafter in some one of them, the very lowest of course, he himself might sit over the little khat he would (if fortunate) be permitted to purchase, and a little kishr. Perhaps in one of these he would receive largess from one of these lowest of mabraz masters or his patrons, or be permitted to tell an old and hoarse and quavering tale. His voice was indeed wretched.

On his way thence, however, via the Street of the Seven Blessings, he came once more before the door of Al Hajjaj, the cook, busy among his pots and pans, and paused rather disconsolately in the sight of the latter, who recognized him but made no sign.

"Alms, O Hajjaj, in the name of the Prophet, and mayst thou never look about thy shop but that it shall be full of customers and thy profit large!" he voiced humbly.

"Be off! Hast thou no other door than mine before which to pause and moan?"

"Ever generous Hajjaj," he continued, "'tis true thou hast been kind often, and I deserve nothing more of thee. Yet wilt thou believe me that for days I have had neither food nor drink—nor a leaf of khat—nay, not so much as an wheaten cake, a bowl of curds or even a small cup of kishr. My state is low. That I shall not endure another day I know."

"And well enough, dog, since thou hast not made more of thy life than thou hast. Other men have affairs and children, but thou nothing. What of all thy years? Hast thou aught to show? Thou knowest by what steps thou hast come so. There are those as poor as thyself who can sing in a coffee-house or tell a tale. But thou— Come, canst thou think of nothing better than begging? Does not Hussein, the beggar, sing? And Ay-eeb tell tales? Come!"

"Do thou but look upon me! Have I the strength? Or a voice? Or a heart for singing? It is true; I have sung in my time, but now my tales are known, and I have not the strength to gather new ones. Yet who would listen?"

The restaurant-keeper eyed him askance. "Must I therefore provide for thee daily? By Allah, I will not! Here is a pice for thee. Be off, and come not soon again! I do not want thee before my door. My customers will not come here if thou dost!"

With slow and halting steps Ibn now took himself off, but little the better for the small gift made him. There was scarcely any place where for a pice, the smallest of coins, he could obtain anything. What, after all, was to be had for it—a cup of kishr? No. A small bowl of curds? No. A sprig of khat? No. And so great was his need, his distress of mind and body, that little less than a good armful of khat, or at least a dozen or more green succulent sprays, to be slowly munched and the juice allowed to sharpen his brain and nerves, would have served to strengthen and rest him. But how to come by so much now? How?

The character of the places frequented by the coolies, bhisties (water-carriers), hadjis and even beggars like Ibn, while without any of the so-called luxuries of these others, and to the frequenters of which the frequenters of these were less than the dust under their feet, were still, to these latter, excellent enough. Yea, despised as they were, they contained charpoys on which each could sit with his little water-chatty beside him, and in the centre of the circle one such as even the lowly Ibn, a beggar, singing his loudest or reciting some tale—for such as they. It was in such places as these, before his voice had wholly deserted him, that Ibn had told his tales. Here, then, for the price of a few anna, they could munch the leavings of the khat market, drink kishr and discuss the state of the world and their respective fortunes. Compared to Ibn in his present state, they were indeed as lords, even princes.

But, by Allah, although having been a carrier and a vendor himself in his day, and although born above them, yet having now no voice nor any tales worth the telling, he was not even now looked upon as one who could stand up and tell of the wonders of the Jinn and demons and the great kings and queens who had reigned of old. Indeed, so low had he fallen that he could not even interest this despised caste. His only gift now was listening, or to make a pathetic picture, or recite the ills that were his.

Nevertheless necessity, a stern master, compelled him to think better of his quondam tale-telling art. Only, being, as he knew, wholly unsuited to recite any tale now, he also knew that the best he could do would be to make the effort, a pretense, in the hope that those present, realizing his age and unfitness, would spare him the spectacle he would make of himself and give him a few anna wherewith to ease himself then and there. Accordingly, the hour having come when the proffered services of a singer or story-teller would be welcomed in any mabraz, he made his way to this region of many of them and where beggars were so common. Only, glancing through the door of the first one, he discovered that there were far too few patrons for his mood. They would be in nowise gay, hence neither kind nor generous as yet, and the keeper would be cold. In a second, a little farther on, a tom-tom was beginning, but the guests were only seven in number and but newly settled in their pleasure. In a third, when the diaphanous sky without was beginning to pale to a deep steel and the evening star was hanging like a solitaire from the pure breast of the western firmament, he pushed aside the veiling cords of beads of one and entered, for here was a large company resting upon their pillows and charpoys, their chatties and hubbuks beside them, but no singer or beater of a tom-tom or teller of tales as yet before them.

"O friends," he began with some diffidence and imaginings, for well he knew how harsh were the moods and cynical the judgments of some of these lowest of life's offerings, "be generous and hearken to the tale of one whose life has been long and full of many unfortunate adventures, one who although he is known to you—"

"What!" called Hussein, the peddler of firewood, reclining at his ease in his corner, a spray of all but wilted khat in his hand. "Is it not even Ibn Abdullah? And has he turned tale-teller once more? By Allah, a great teller of tales—one of rare voice! The camels and jackals will be singing in Hodeidah next!"

"An my eyes deceive me not," cried Waidi, the water-carrier, at his ease also, a cup of kishr in his hands, "this is not Ibn Abdullah, but Sindbad, fresh from a voyage!"

"Or Ali Baba himself," cried Yussuf, the carrier, hoarsely. "Thou hast a bag of jewels somewhere about thee? Now indeed we shall hear things!"

"And in what a voice!" added Haifa the tobacco-tramp, noting the husky, wheezy tones with which Ibn opened his plea. "This is to be a treat, truly. And now we may rest and have wonders upon wonders. Ibn of Mecca and Jiddah, and even of marvelous Hodeidah itself, will now tell us much. A cup of kishr, ho! This must be listened to!"

But now Bab-al Oman, the keeper, a stout and cumbrous soul, coming forth from his storeroom, gazed upon Ibn with mingled astonishment and no little disfavor, for it was not customary to permit any of his customers of the past to beg in here, and as for a singer or story-teller he had never thought of Ibn in that light these many years. He was too old, without the slightest power to do aught but begin in a wheezy voice.

"Hearken," he called, coming over and laying a hand on him, the while the audience gazed and grinned, "hast thou either anna or rupee wherewith to fulfill thy account in case thou hast either khat or kishr?" The rags and the mummy-like pallor of the old man offended him.

"Do but let him speak," insisted Hussein the peddler gaily, "or sing," for he was already feeling the effects of his ease and the restorative power of the plant. "This will be wonderful. By the voices of eleven hundred elephants!"

"Yea, a story," called Waidi, "or perhaps that of the good Cadi of Taiz and the sacred waters of Jezer!"

"Or of the Cadi of Mecca and the tobacco that was too pure!"

Ibn heard full well and knew the spectacle he was making of himself. The references were all too plain. Only age and want and a depressing feebleness, which had been growing for days, caused him to forget, or prevented, rather, his generating a natural rage and replying in kind. These wretched enemies of his, dogs lower than himself, had never forgiven him that he had been born out of their caste, or, having been so, that he had permitted himself to sink to labor and beg with them. But now his age and weakness were too great. He was too weary to contend.

"O most generous Oman, best of keepers of a mabraz— and thou, O comfortable and honorable guests," he insisted wheezily, "I have here but one pice, the reward of all my seekings this day. It is true that I am a beggar and that my coverings are rags, yet do but consider that I am old and feeble. This day and the day before and the day before that—"

"Come, come!" said Oman restlessly and feeling that

the custom and trade of his mabraz were being injured,
"out! Thou canst not sing and thou canst not tell a tale,
as thou well knowest. Why come here when thou hast but
a single pice wherewith to pay thy way? Beg more, but
not here! Bring but so much as half a rupee, and thou
shalt have service in plenty!"

"But the pice I have here—may not I—O good sons of
the Prophet, a spray of khat, a cup of kishr—suffer me not
thus be cast forth! '—and the poor and the son of the
road!' Alms—alms—in the name of Allah!"

"Out, out!" insisted Oman gently but firmly. "So much
as ten anna, and thou mayst rest here; not otherwise."

He turned him forth into the night.

And now, weak and fumbling, Ibn stood there for a time,
wondering where else to turn. He was so weak that at last
even the zest for search or to satisfy himself was departing.
For a moment, a part of his old rage and courage returning, he threw away the pice that had been given him, then
turned back, but not along the street of the bazaars. He
was too distrait and disconsolate. Rather, by a path which
he well knew, he circled now to the south of the town,
passing via the Bet-el-Fakin gate to the desert beyond the
walls, where, ever since his days as a pack servant with the
Bedouins, he had thought to come in such an hour. Overhead were the stars in that glorious æther, lit with a light
which never shines on other soils or seas. The evening
star had disappeared, but the moon was now in the west,
a thin feather, yet transfiguring and transforming as by
magic the homely and bare features of the sands. Out here
was something of that beauty which as a herdsman among
the Bedouins he had known, the scent of camels and of
goats' milk, the memory of low black woolen tents, dot-
ting the lion-tawny sands and gazelle-brown gravels with
a warm and human note, and the camp-fire that, like a
glowworm, had denoted the village centre. Now, as in a
dream, the wild weird songs of the boys and girls of the
desert came back, the bleating of their sheep and goats in

the gloaming. And the measured chant of the spearsmen, gravely stalking behind their charges, the camels, their song mingling with the bellowing of their humpy herds.

"It is finished," he said, once he was free of the city and far into the desert itself. "I have no more either the skill nor the strength wherewith to endure or make my way. And without khat one cannot endure. What will be will be, and I am too old. Let them find me so. I shall not move. It is better than the other."

Then upon the dry, warm sands he laid himself, his head toward Mecca, while overhead the reremouse circled and cried, its tiny shriek acknowledging its zest for life; and the rave of a jackal, resounding through the illuminated shade beyond, bespoke its desire to live also. Most musical of all music, the palm trees now answered the whispers of the night breeze with the softest tones of falling water.

"It is done," sighed Ibn Abdullah, as he lay and wearily rested. "Worthless I came, O Allah, and worthless I return. It is well."

VII

TYPHOON

INTO a singularly restricted and indifferent environment Ida Zobel was born. Her mother, a severe, prim German woman, died when she was only three, leaving her to the care of her father and his sister, both extremely reserved and orderly persons. Later, after Ida had reached the age of ten, William Zobel took unto himself a second wife, who resembled Zobel and his first wife in their respect for labor and order.

Both were at odds with the brash gayety and looseness of the American world in which they found themselves. Being narrow, sober, workaday Germans, they were annoyed by the groups of restless, seeking, eager, and as Zobel saw it, rather scandalous young men and women who paraded the neighborhood streets of an evening without a single thought apparently other than pleasure. And these young scamps and their girl friends who sped about in automobiles. The loose, indifferent parents. The loose, free ways of all these children. What was to become of such a nation? Were not the daily newspapers, which he would scarcely tolerate in his home longer, full of these wretched doings? The pictures of almost naked women that filled them all! Jazz! Petting parties! High school boys with flasks on their hips! Girls with skirts to their knees, rolled-down stockings, rolled-down neck-bands, bare arms, bobbed hair, no decent concealing underwear!

"What—a daughter of his grow up like that! Be permitted to join in this prancing route to perdition! Never!" And in consequence, the strictest of rules with regard to

Ida's upbringing. Her hair was to grow its natural length, of course. Her lips and cheeks were never to know the blush of false, suggestive paint. Plain dresses. Plain underwear and stockings and shoes and hats. No crazy, idiotic finery, but substantial, respectable clothing. Work at home and, when not otherwise employed with her studies at school, in the small paint and color store which her father owned in the immediate vicinity of their home. And last, but not least, a schooling of such proper and definite character as would serve to keep her mind from the innumerable current follies which were apparently pulling at the foundations of decent society.

For this purpose Zobel chose a private and somewhat religious school conducted by an aged German spinster of the name of Elizabeth Hohstauffer, who had succeeded after years and years of teaching in impressing her merits as a mentor on perhaps as many as a hundred German families of the area. No contact with the careless and shameless public school here. And once the child had been inducted into that, there followed a series of daily inquiries and directions intended to guide her in the path she was to follow.

"Hurry! You have only ten minutes now in which to get to school. There is no time to lose!" . . . "How comes it that you are five minutes late to-night? What were you doing?" . . . "Your teacher made you stay? You had to stop and look for a blank book?" . . . "Why didn't you come home first and let me look for it with you afterwards?" (It was her stepmother talking.) "You know your father doesn't want you to stay after school." . . . "And just what were you doing on Warren Avenue between twelve and one to-day? Your father said you were with some girl." . . . "Vilma Balet? And who is Vilma Balet? Where does she live? And how long has it been that you have been going with her? Why is it that you have not mentioned her before? You know what your father's rule is. And now I shall have to tell him. He will be angry.

You must obey his rules. You are by no means old enough to decide for yourself. You have heard him say that."

Notwithstanding all this, Ida, though none too daring or aggressive mentally, was being imaginatively drawn to the very gayeties and pleasures that require courage and daring. She lived in a mental world made up of the bright lights of Warren Avenue, of which she caught an occasional glimpse. The numerous cars speeding by! The movies and her favorite photographs of actors and actresses, some of the mannerisms of whom the girls imitated at school. The voices, the laughter of the boys and girls as they walked to and fro along the commonplace thoroughfare with its street-cars and endless stores side by side! And what triumphs or prospective joys they planned and palavered over as they strolled along in their easy manner—arms linked and bodies swaying—up the street and around the corner and back into the main street again, gazing at their graceful ankles and bodies in the mirrors and windows as they passed, or casting shy glances at the boys.

But as for Ida—despite her budding sensitivity—at ten, eleven, twelve, thirteen, fourteen—there was no escape from the severe regimen she was compelled to follow. Breakfast at seven-thirty sharp because the store had to be opened by her father at eight; luncheon at twelve-thirty, on the dot to satisfy her father; dinner invariably at six-thirty, because there were many things commercial and social which fell upon the shoulders of William Zobel at night. And between whiles, from four to six on weekdays and later from seven to ten at night, as well as all day Saturdays, store duty in her father's store. No parties, no welcome home atmosphere for the friends of her choice. Those she really liked were always picked to pieces by her stepmother, and of course this somewhat influenced the opinion of her father. It was common gossip of the neighborhood that her parents were very strict and that they permitted her scarcely any liberties. A trip to a movie, the choice of which was properly supervised by her parents; an occasional ride in an automobile with her parents, since by the time she had attained her fifteenth year he had purchased one of the cheaper cars.

But all the time the rout of youthful life before her eyes. And in so far as her home life and the emotional significance of her parents were concerned, a sort of depressing grayness. For William Zobel, with his gray-blue eyes gleaming behind gilt-rimmed glasses, was scarcely the person to whom a girl of Ida's temperament would be drawn. Nor was her stepmother, with her long, narrow face, brown eyes and black hair. Indeed, Zobel was a father who by the very solemnity of his demeanor, as well as the soberness and practicability of his thoughts and rules, was constantly evoking a sense of dictatorship which was by no means conducive to sympathetic approach. To be sure, there were greetings, acknowledgments, respectful and careful explanations as to this, that and the other. Occasionally they would go to a friend's house or a public restaurant, but there existed no understanding on the part of either Zobel or his wife—he never having wanted a daughter of his own and she not being particularly drawn to the child of another—of the growing problems of adolescence that might be confronting her, and hence none of that possible harmony and enlightenment which might have endeared each to the other.

Instead, repression, and even fear at times, which in the course of years took on an aspect of careful courtesy supplemented by accurate obedience. But within herself a growing sense of her own increasing charm, which, in her father's eyes, if not in her stepmother's, seemed to be identified always with danger—either present or prospective. Her very light and silky hair—light, grayish-blue eyes—a rounded and intriguing figure which even the other girls at Miss Hohstauffer's school noticed and commented on. And in addition a small straight nose and a full and yet small and almost pouting mouth and rounded chin. Had she not a mirror and were there not boys from her seventh year on who looked at her and sought to attract her attention? Her father could see this as well as his second wife. But she dared not loiter here and there as others did, for those vigorous, bantering, seeking, intriguing contacts. She must hurry home—to store or house duty or more study in such fields as Zobel and his wife thought best for her. If it was to run errands she was always timed to the minute.

And yet, in spite of all these precautions, the swift telegraphy of eyes and blood. The haunting, seeking moods of youth, which speaks a language of its own. In the drugstore at the corner of Warren and Tracy, but a half-block from her home, there was at one time in her twelfth year Lawrence Sullivan, a soda clerk. He seemed to her the most beautiful thing she had ever seen. The dark, smooth hair lying glossed and parted above a perfect white forehead; slim, graceful hands—or so she thought—a care and smartness in the matter of dress which even the clothing of the scores of public school boys passing this way seemed scarcely to match. And such a way where girls were concerned—so smiling and at his ease. And always a word for them as they stopped in on their way home from school.

"Why, hello, Della! How's Miss McGinnis to-day? I bet I know what you're going to have. I think pretty blonde girls must like chocolate sundaes—they contrast with their complexions." And then smiling serenely while Miss McGinnis panted and smiled: "A lot you know about what blonde girls like."

And Ida Zobel, present on occasion by permission for a soda or a sundae, looking on and listening most eagerly. Such a handsome youth. All of sixteen. He would as yet pay no attention to so young a girl as she, of course, but when she was older! Would she be as pretty as this Miss McGinnis? Could she be as assured? How wonderful to be attractive to such a youth! And what would he say to her, if he said anything at all? And what would she say in return? Many times she imitated these girls mentally and held imaginary conversations with herself. Yes, despite this passive admiration, Mr. Sullivan went the way of all soda-clerks, changing eventually to another job in another neighborhood.

But in the course of time there were others who took her eye and for a time held her mind—around whose differing charms she erected fancies which had nothing to do with reality. One of these was Merton Webster, the brisk, showy, vain and none too ambitious son of a local state senator, who lived in the same block she did and attended Watkins High School, which she was not permitted to attend. So handsome was he—so debonair. "Hello, kid! Gee, you look cute, all right. One of these days I'll take you to a dance if you want to go." Yet, because of her years and the strict family espionage, blushes, her head down, but a smile none the less.

And she was troubled by thoughts of him until Walter Stour, whose father conducted a realty and insurance business only a little way west of her father's store, took her attention—a year later. Walter was a tall, fair complexioned youth, with gay eyes and a big, laughing mouth, who, occasionally with Merton Webster, Lawrence Cross, a grocer's son, Sven Volberg, the dry-cleaner's son, and some others, hung about the favorite moving-picture theatre or the drugstore on the main corner and flirted with the girls as they passed by. As restricted as she was still, because of her trips to and fro between home and school and her service as a clerk in her father's store, she was not unfamiliar with these several figures or their names. They came into the store occasionally and even commented on her looks: "Oh, getting to be a pretty girl, isn't she?" Whereupon she would flush with excitement and nervously busy herself about filling a customer's order.

It was through Etelka Shomel, the daughter of a German neighbor who was also a friend of William Zobel, that she learned much of these boys and girls. Her father thought Etelka a safe character for Ida to chum with, chiefly on account of her unattractiveness. But through her, as well as their joint pilgrimages here and there, she came to hear much gossip about the doings of these same. Walter Stour, whom she now greatly admired, was going with a girl by the name of Edna Strong, who was the daughter of a milk-dealer. Stour's father was not as stingy as some fathers. He had a good car and occasionally let his son use it. Stour often took Edna and some of her friends to boathouse resorts on the Little Shark River. A girl friend of Etelka's told her what a wonderful mimic and dancer he was. She had been on a party with him. And, of course, Ida lent a willing and eager ear to all this. Oh, the gayety of such a life! Its wonders! Beauties!

And then one night, as Ida was coming around the corner to go to her father's store at about seven-thirty and Stour was on his favorite corner with several other boys, he called: "I know who's a sweet kid, but her daddy won't let her look at a guy. Will he?" This last aimed directly at her as she passed, while she, knowing full well who was meant and how true it was, hurried on all the faster. If her father had heard that! Oh, my! But it thrilled her as she walked. "Sweet kid." "Sweet kid"— kept ringing in her ears.

And then at last, in her sixteenth year, Edward Hauptwanger moved into a large house in Grey Street. His father, Jacob Hauptwanger, was a well-to-do coal-dealer who had recently purchased a yard on the Absecon. It was about this time that Ida became keenly aware that her normal girlhood, with its so necessary social contacts, was being set at naught and that she was being completely frustrated by the stern and repressive attitude of her father and stepmother. The wonder and pain, for instance, of spring and summer evenings just then, when she would stand gazing at the moon above her own commonplace home—shining down into the narrow, commonplace garden at the back, where still were tulips, hyacinths, honeysuckle and roses. And the stars shining above Warren Avenue, where were the cars, the crowds, the moving-picture theatres and restaurants which held such charm for her. There was a kind of madness, an ache, in it all. Oh, for pleasure—pleasure! To go, run, dance, play, kiss with some one—almost any one, really, if he were only young and handsome. Was she going to know no one—no one? And, worse, the young men of the neighborhood calling to her as she passed: "Oh, look who's here! Shame her daddy won't let her out." "Why don't you bob your hair, Ida? You'd be cute." Even though she was out of school now, she was clerking as before and dressing as before. No short skirts, bobbed hair, rolled-down stockings, rouge.

But with the arrival of this Edward Hauptwanger, there came a change. For here was a youth of definite and drastic impulses—a beau, a fighter, a fellow of infinite guile where girls of all sorts were concerned—and, too, a youth of taste in the matter of dress and manner—one who stood out as a kind of hero to the type of youthful male companions with whom he chose to associate. Did he not live in a really large, separate house on Grey Street? And were not his father's coal-pockets and trucks conspicuously labelled outstanding features of the district? And, in addition, Hauptwanger, owing to the foolish and doting favor of his mother (by no means shared by his father), always supplied with pocket money sufficient to meet all required expenditures of such a world as this. The shows to which he could take his "flames"; the restaurants, downtown as well as here. And the boat club on the Little Shark which at once became a rendezvous of his. He had a canoe of his own, so it was said. He was an expert swimmer and diver. He was allowed the use of his father's car and would often gather up his friends on a Saturday or Sunday and go to the boat club.

More interesting still, after nearly a year's residence here, in which he had had time to establish himself socially after this fashion, he had his first sight of Ida Zobel passing one evening from her home to the store. Her youthful if repressed beauty was at its zenith. And some remarks concerning her and her restricted life by youths who had neither the skill nor the daring to invade it at once set him thinking. She was beautiful, you bet! Hauptwanger, because of a certain adventurous fighting strain in his blood, was at once intrigued by the difficulties which thus so definitely set this girl apart. "These old-fashioned, dictatorial Germans! And not a fellow in the neighborhood to step up and do anything about it! Well, whaddya know?"

And forthwith an intensive study of the situation as well as of the sensitive, alluring Ida Zobel. And with the result that he was soon finding himself irresistibly attracted to her. That pretty face! That graceful, rounded figure! Those large, blue-gray, shy and evasive eyes! Yet with yearning in them, too.

And in consequence various brazen parades past the very paint store of Zobel, with the fair Ida within. And this despite the fact that Zobel himself was there—morning, noon and night—bent over his cash register or his books or doing up something for a customer. And Ida, by reason of her repressed desires and sudden strong consciousness of his interest in her as thus expressed, more and more attracted to him. And he, because of this or his own interest, coming to note the hours when she was most likely to be alone. These were, as a rule, Wednesdays and Fridays, when because of a singing society as well as a German social and commercial club her father was absent from eight-thirty on. And although occasionally assisted by her stepmother she was there alone on these nights.

And so a campaign which was to break the spell which held the sleeping beauty. At first, however, only a smile in the direction of Ida whenever he passed or she passed him, together with boasts to his friends to the effect that he would "win that kid yet, wait and see." And then, one evening, in the absence of Zobel, a visit to the store. She was behind the counter and between the business of waiting on customers was dreaming as usual of the life outside. For during the past few weeks she had become most sharply conscious of the smiling interest of Hauptwanger. His

straight, lithe body—his quick, aggressive manner—his as-
sertive, seeking eyes! Oh, my! Like the others who had
gone before him and who had attracted her emotional interest, he was exactly of that fastidious, self-assured and
self-admiring type toward which one so shy as herself
would yearn. No hesitancy on his part. Even for this
occasion he had scarcely troubled to think of a story. What
difference? Any old story would do. He wanted to see
some paints. They might be going to repaint the house
soon—and in the meantime he could engage her in conversation, and if the "old man" came back, well, he would talk
paints to him.

And so, on this particularly warm and enticing night
in May, he walked briskly in, a new gray suit, light tan
fedora hat and tan shoes and tie completing an ensemble
which won the admiration of the neighborhood. "Oh,
hello. Pretty tough to have to work inside on a night like
this, ain't it?" (A most irresistible smile going with this.)
"I want to see some paints—the colors of 'em, I mean.
The old man is thinking of repainting the house."

And at once Ida, excited and flushing to the roots of her
hair, turning to look for a color card—as much to conceal
her flushing face as anything else. And yet intrigued as
much as she was affrighted. The daring of him! Suppose
her father should return—or her stepmother enter? Still,
wasn't he as much of a customer as any one else—although
she well knew by his manner that it was not paint that had
brought him. For over the way, as she herself could and
did see, were three of his admiring companions ranged in
a row to watch him, the while he leaned genially and
familiarly against the counter and continued: "Gee, I've
seen you often enough, going back and forth between your
school and this store and your home. I've been around
here nearly a year now, but I've never seen you around
much with the rest of the girls. Too bad! Otherwise
we mighta met. I've met all the rest of 'em so far," and
at the same time by troubling to touch his tie he managed

to bring into action one hand on which was an opal ring, his wrist smartly framed in a striped pink cuff. "I heard your father wouldn't even let you go to Warren High. Pretty strict, eh?" And he beamed into the blue-gray eyes of the budding girl before him, noted the rounded pink cheeks, the full mouth, the silky hair, the while she trembled and thrilled.

"Yes, he is pretty strict."

"Still, you can't just go nowhere all the time, can you?" And by now the color card, taken into his own hand, was lying flat on the counter. "You gotta have a little fun once in a while, eh? If I'da thought you'da stood for it, I'da introduced myself before this. My father has the big coal-dock down here on the river. He knows your father, I'm sure. I gotta car, or at least my dad has, and that's as good as mine. Do you think your father'd letcha take a run out in the country some Saturday or Sunday—down to Little Shark River, say, or Peck's Beach? Lots of the fellows and girls from around here go down there."

By now it was obvious that Hauptwanger was achieving a conquest of sorts and his companions over the way were abandoning their advantageous position, no longer hopefully interested by the possibility of defeat. But the nervous Ida, intrigued though terrified, was thinking how wonderful it was to at last interest so handsome a youth as this. Even though her father might not approve, still might not all that be overcome by such a gallant as this? But her hair was not bobbed, her skirts not short, her lips not rouged. Could it really be that he was attracted by her physical charms? His dark brown and yet hard and eager eyes— his handsome hands. The smart way in which he dressed. She was becoming conscious of her severely plain blue dress with white trimmings, her unmodish slippers and stockings. At the same time she found herself most definitely reply-ing: "Oh, now, I couldn't ever do anything like that, you know. You see, my father doesn't know you. He wouldn't let me go with any one he doesn't know or to whom I haven't been properly introduced. You know how it is."

"Well, couldn't I introduce myself then? My father knows your father, I'm sure. I could just tell him that I want to call on you, couldn't I? I'm not afraid of him, and there's sure no harm in that, is there?"

"Well, that might be all right, only he's very strict— and he might not want me to go, anyhow."

"Oh, pshaw! But you would like to go, wouldn't you? Or to a picture show? He couldn't kick against that, could he?"

He looked her in the eye, smiling, and in doing so drew the lids of his own eyes together in a sensuous, intriguing way which he had found effective with others. And in the budding Ida were born impulses of which she had no consciousness and over which she had no control. She merely looked at him weakly. The wonder of him! The beauty of love! Her desire toward him! And so finding heart to say: "No, maybe not. I don't know. You see I've never had a beau yet."

She looked at him in such a way as to convince him of his conquest. "Easy! A cinch!" was his thought. "Nothing to it at all." He would see Zobel and get his permission or meet her clandestinely. Gee, a father like that had no right to keep his daughter from having any fun at all. These narrow, hard-boiled German parents—they ought to be shown—awakened—made to come to life.

And so, within two days brazenly presenting himself to Zobel in his store in order to test whether he could not induce him to accept him as presumably at least a candidate for his daughter's favor. Supposing the affair did not prove as appealing as he thought, he could drop the contact, couldn't he? Hadn't he dropped others? Zobel knew of his father, of course. And while listening to Hauptwanger's brisk and confident explanation he was quite consciously evaluating the smart suit, new tan shoes and gathering, all in all, a favorable impression.

"You say you spoke to her already?"

"I asked her if I might call on her, yes, sir."

"Uh-uh! When was this?"

"Just two days ago. In the evening here."

"Uh-uh!"

At the same time a certain nervous, critical attitude toward everything, which had produced many fine lines about the eyes and above the nose of Mr. Zobel, again taking hold of him: "Well, well—this is something I will have to talk over with my daughter. I must see about this. I am very careful of my daughter and who she goes with, you know." Nevertheless, he was thinking of the many coal trucks delivering coal in the neighborhood, the German name of this youth and his probable German and hence conservative upbringing. "I will let you know about it later. You come in some other time."

And so later a conference with his daughter, resulting finally in the conclusion that it might be advisable for her to have at least one male contact. For she was sixteen years old and up to the present time he had been pretty strict with her. Perhaps she was over the worst period. At any rate, most other girls of her age were permitted to go out some. At least one beau of the right kind might be essential, and somehow he liked this youth who had approached him in this frank, fearless manner.

And so, for the time being, a call permitted once or twice a week, with Hauptwanger from the first dreaming most daring and aggressive dreams. And after a time, having conducted himself most circumspectly, it followed that an evening at one of the neighborhood picture houses was suggested and achieved. And once this was accomplished it became a regularity for him to spend either Wednesday or Friday evening with Ida, it depending on her work in the store. Later, his courage and skill never deserting him, a suggestion to Mr. Zobel that he permit Ida to go out with him on a Saturday afternoon to visit Peck's Beach nine miles below the city, on the Little Shark. It was very nice there, and a popular Saturday and Sunday resort for most of the residents of this area. After a time, having by degrees gained the complete confidence of Zobel, he was granted permission to take Ida to one or another of the theatres downtown, or to a restaurant, or to the house of a boy friend who had a sister and who lived in the next block.

Despite his stern, infiltrating supervision, Zobel could not prevent the progressive familiarities based on youth, desire, romance. For with Edward Hauptwanger, to contact was to intrigue and eventually demand and compel. And so by degrees hand pressures, stolen or enforced kisses. Yet, none the less, Ida, still fully dominated by the mood and conviction of her father, persisting in a nervous evasiveness which was all too trying to her lover.

"Ah, you don't know my father. No, I couldn't do that. No, I can't stay out so late. Oh, no—I wouldn't dare go there—I wouldn't dare to. I don't know what he would do to me."

This, or such as this, to all of his overtures which hinted at later hours, a trip to that mysterious and fascinating boat club on the Little Shark twenty-five miles out, where, as he so glibly explained, were to be enjoyed dancing, swimming, boating, music, feasting. But as Ida who had never done any of these things soon discovered for herself, this would require an unheard-of period of time—from noon until midnight—or later Saturday, whereas her father had fixed the hour of eleven-thirty for her return to the parental roof.

"Ah, don't you want to have any fun at all? Gee! He don't want you to do a thing and you let him get away with it. Look at all the other girls and fellows around here. There's not one that's as scary as you are. Besides, what harm is there? Supposing we don't get back on time? Couldn't we say the car broke down? He couldn't say anything to that. Besides, no one punches a time clock any more." But Ida nervous and still resisting, and Hauptwanger, because of this very resistance, determined to win her to his mood and to outwit her father at the same time.

And then the lure of summer nights—Corybantic—dithyrambic—with kisses, kisses, kisses—under the shadow of the trees in King Lake Park, or in one of the little boats of its lake which nosed the roots of those same trees on the shore. And with the sensitive and sensual, and yet restricted and inexperienced Ida, growing more and more lost in the spell which youth, summer, love, had generated. The beauty of the face of this, her grand cavalier! His clothes, his brisk, athletic energy and daring! And with him perpetually twittering of this and that, here and there, that if she only truly loved him and had the nerve, what wouldn't they do? All the pleasures of the world before them, really. And then at last, on this same lake—with her lying in his arms—himself attempting familiarities which scarcely seemed possible in her dreams before this, and which caused her to jump up and demand to be put ashore, the while he merely laughed.

"Oh, what had he done that was so terrible? Say, did she really care for him? Didn't she? Then, why so uppish? Why cry? Oh, gee, this was a scream, this was. Oh, all right, if that was the way she was going to feel about it." And once ashore, walking briskly off in the gayest and most self-sufficient manner while she, alone and tortured by her sudden ejection from paradise, slipped home and into her room, there to bury her face in her pillow and to whisper to it and herself of the danger—almost the horror—that had befallen her. Yet in her eyes and mind the while the perfect Hauptwanger. And in her heart his face, hands, hair. His daring. His kisses. And so brooding even here and now as to the wisdom of her course— her anger—and in a dreary and hopeless mood even, dragging herself to her father's store the next day, merely to wait and dream that he was not as evil as he had seemed— that he could not have seriously contemplated the familiarities that he had attempted; that he had been merely obsessed, bewitched, as she herself had been.

Oh, love, love! Edward! Edward! Edward! Oh, he would not, could not remain away. She must see him—give him a chance to explain. She must make him understand that it was not want of love but fear of life—her father, everything, everybody—that kept her so sensitive, aloof, remote.

And Hauptwanger himself, for all of his bravado and craft, now nervous lest he had been too hasty. For, after all, what a beauty! The lure! He couldn't let her go this way. It was a little too delicious and wonderful to have her so infatuated—and with a little more attention, who knew? And so conspicuously placing himself where she must pass on her way home in the evening, at the corner of Warren and High—yet with no sign on his part of seeing her. And Ida, with yearning and white-faced misery, seeing him as she passed. Monday night! Tuesday night! And worse, to see him pass the store early Wednesday evening without so much as turning his head. And then the next day a note handed the negro errand boy of her father's store to be given to him later, about seven, at the corner where he would most surely be.

And then later, with the same Edward taking it most casually and grandly and reading it. So she had been compelled to write him, had she? Oh, these dames! Yet with a definite thrill from the contents for all of that, for it read: "Oh, Edward, darling, you can't be so cruel to me. How can you? I love you so. You didn't mean what you said. Tell me you didn't. I didn't. Oh, please come to the house at eight. I want to see you."

And Edward Hauptwanger, quite triumphant now, saying to the messenger before four cronies who knew of his present pursuit of Ida: "Oh, that's all right. Just tell her I'll be over after a while." And then as eight o'clock neared, ambling off in the direction of the Zobel home. And as he left one of his companions remarking: "Say, whaddya know? He's got that Zobel girl on the run now. She's writing him notes now. Didn't ya see the coon bring it up? Don't it beat hell?" And the others as enviously, amazedly and contemptuously inquiring: "Whaddya know?"

And so, under June trees in King Lake Park, once more another conference. "Oh, darling, how could you treat me so, how could you? Oh, my dear, dear darling." And he replying— "Oh, sure, sure, it was all right, only what do you think I'm made of? Say, have a heart, I'm human, ain't I? I've got some feelings same as anybody else. Ain't I crazy about you and ain't you crazy about me? Well, then— besides—well, say . . ." A long pharisaical and deluding argument as one might guess, with all the miseries and difficulties of restrained and evaded desire most artfully suggested—yet with no harm meant, of course. Oh, no.

But again, on her part, the old foolish, terrorized love plea. And the firm assurance on his part that if anything went wrong —why, of course. But why worry about that now? Gee, she was the only girl he knew who worried about anything like that. And finally a rendezvous at Little Shark River, with his father's car as the conveyance. And later others and others. And she—because of her weak, fearsome yielding in the first instance—and then her terrorized contemplation of possible consequences in the second—clinging to him in all too eager and hence cloying fashion. She was his now—all his. Oh, he would never, never desert her, now, would he?

But he, once satisfied—his restless and overweening ego comforted by another victory—turning with a hectic and chronic, and for him uncontrollable sense of satiety, as well as fear of complications and burden—to other phases of beauty—other fields and relationships where there was no such danger. For after all—one more girl. One more experience. And not so greatly different from others that had gone before it. And this in the face of the magic of her meaning before capitulation. He did not understand it. He could not. He did not even trouble to think about it much. But so it was. And with no present consciousness or fear of being involved in any early and unsatisfactory complications which might require marriage—on the contrary a distinct and definite opposition to any such complication at any time, anywhere.

Yet, at last, after many, many perfect hours throughout July and August, the fatal complaint. There was something wrong, she feared. She had such strange moods—such strange spells, pains, fears—recently. Could there be? Did he think there could be any danger? She had done what he said. Oh, if there was! What was she to do then? Would he marry her? He must, really, then. There was no other way. Her father—his fierce anger. Her own terrors. She could not live at home any more. Could they not—would they not—be married now if anything were wrong? He had said he would if anything like this ever happened, had he not?

And Hauptwanger, in the face of this, suffering a nervous and cold reaction. Marriage! The mere thought of such a thing! Impossible! His father! His hitherto free roving life! His future! Besides, how did she know? How could she be sure? And supposing she was! Other girls got out of such things without much trouble. Why not she? And had he not taken all the usual customary and necessary precautions that he knew! She was too easily frightened—too uninformed—not daring enough. He knew of lots of cases where girls got through situations of this kind with ease. He would see about something first.

But conjoined with this, as she herself could see and feel, a sudden definite coolness never before sensed or witnessed by her, which was based on his firm determination not to pursue this threatening relationship any longer, seeing that to do so meant only to emphasize responsibility. And in addition, a keen desire to stay away. Were there not other girls? A whole world full. And only recently had he not been intrigued by one who was more aware of the free, smart ways of pleasure and not so likely ever to prove a burden?

But on the other hand, in the face of a father as strict as Zobel himself and a mother who believed in his goodness, his course was not absolutely clear either. And so from this hour on an attempt to extricate himself as speedily and as gracefully as possible from this threatening position. But before this a serious, if irritated, effort on his part to find a remedy among his friends of the boating club and street corners. But with the result merely of a vivid advertisement of the fact that this gay and successful adventure of his had now resulted most unsuccessfully for Ida. And thereafter hints and nods and nudges among themselves whenever she chanced to pass. And Ida, because of fear of scandal, staying in as much as she could these days, or when she did appear trying to avoid Warren Avenue at High as much as possible. For by now she was truly terrified, seized indeed with the most weakening emotions based on the stern and unrelenting countenance of her father which loomed so threateningly beyond the immediate future. "If me no ifs," and "but me no buts." Oh, how to do? For throughout the trial of this useless remedy, there had been nothing to do but wait. And the waiting ended in nothing—only greater horrors. And between all this, and enforced work at the store and enforced duties at home, efforts to see her beloved—who, because of new and more urgent duties, was finding it harder and harder to meet her anywhere or at any time.

"But you must see how it is with me, don't you, dear? I can't go on like this, can't you see that? You said you'd marry me, didn't you? And look at all the time that's gone already. Oh, I'm almost mad. You must do something. You must! You must! If father should find out, what in the world would I do? What would he do to me, and to you, too? Can't you see how bad it is?"

Yet in the face of this tortured plea on the part of this frantic and still love-sick girl, a calm on the part of Hauptwanger that expressed not indifference but cruelty. She be damned! He would not. He could not. He must save himself now at whatever cost. And so a determined attempt not to see her any more at all—never to speak to her openly anywhere—or to admit any responsibility as to all this. Yet, because of her inexperience, youth and faith thus far, no willingness on her part to believe this. It could not be. She had not even so much as sensed it before. Yet his continuing indifference which could only be interpreted one way. The absences—the excuses! And then one day, when pains and terror seized on her and thereby drove her to him, he looking her calmly and brazenly in the eye and announcing: "But I didn't really promise to marry you, and you know I didn't. Besides, I'm not to blame any more than you are. You don't suppose that just because you don't know how to take care of yourself I've got to marry you now, do you?"

His eyes now for the first time were truly hard. His intention to end this by one fell blow was very definite. And the blow was sufficient at the moment to half unseat the romantic and all but febrile reason of this girl, who up to this hour had believed so foolishly in love. Why, how could this be? The horror of it! The implied disaster. And then half in understanding, half in befuddled unreason, exclaiming: "But, Ed! Ed! You can't mean that. Why, it isn't true! You know it isn't! You promised. You swore. You know I never wanted to—until you made me. Why . . . oh, what'll I do now? My father! I don't know what he'll do to me or to you either. Oh, dear! Oh, dear!" And frantically, and without sufficient balance to warrant the name of reason, beginning to wring her hands and twist and sway in a kind of physical as well as mental agony.

At this Hauptwanger, more determined than ever to frighten her away from him once and for all, if possible, exclaiming: "Oh, cut that stuff! I never said I'd marry you, and you know it!" and turning on his heel and leaving her to rejoin the chattering group of youths on the corner, with whom, before her arrival, he had been talking. And as much to sustain himself in this fatal decision as well as to carry it off before them all, adding: "Gee, these skirts! It does beat hell, don't it?"

Yet now a little fearsome, if vain and contemptuous, for the situation was beginning to take on a gloomy look. But just the same when Johnny Martin, one of his companions and another aspirant for street corner and Lothario honors, remarked: "I saw her here last night lookin' for you, Ed. Better look out. One of these skirts is likely to do somepin to you one of these days"—he calmly extracted a cigarette from a silver cigarette case and without a look in the direction of the half-swooning Ida, said: "Is that so? Well, maybe. We'll see first." And then with a nonchalant nod in the direction of Ida, who, too tortured to even retreat, was standing quite still, exclaimed: "Gee, these Germans! She's got an old man that wouldn't ever let her find out anything and now because she thinks there's something wrong with her she blames me." And just then, another intimate approaching, and with news of two girls who were to meet them somewhere later, exclaiming: "Hello, Skate! Everything set? All right, then. We might as well go along. S'long, fellas." And stepping briskly and vigorously away.

But the stricken and shaken Ida still loitered under the already partially denuded September trees. And with the speeding street and auto cars with their horns and bells and the chattering voices and shuffling feet of pedestrians and the blazing evening lights making a kind of fanfare of color and sound. Was it cold? Or was it only herself who was numb and cold? He would not marry her! He had never said he would! How could he say that now? And her father to deal with—and her physical condition to be considered!

As she stood there without moving, there flashed before her a complete panorama of all the paths and benches of

King Lake Park—the little boats that slipped here and there under the trees at night in the summertime—a boy and a girl—a boy and a girl—a boy and a girl—to each boat. And the oars dragging most inconsequentially—and infatuated heads together—infatuated hearts beating ecstatically—suffocatingly strong. Yet now—after so many kisses and promises, the lie given to her dreams, her words—his words on which her words had been based—the lie given to kisses —hours, days, weeks, months of unspeakable bliss—the lie given to her own security and hopes, forever. Oh, it would be best to die—it would—it would.

And then a slow and dragging return to her room, where because of the absence of her father and stepmother she managed to slip into her bed and lie there, thinking. But with a kind of fever, alternating with chills—and both shot through with most menacing pains due to this most astounding revelation. And with a sudden and keener volume of resentment than she had ever known gathering in her brain. The cruelty! The cruelty! And the falsehood! He had not only lied but insulted her as well. He who only five months before had sought her so eagerly with his eyes and intriguing smile. The liar! The brute! The monster! Yet linked and interwoven with such thoughts as these, a lacerating desire not to believe them—to turn back a month —two—three—to find in his eyes somewhere a trace of something that would gainsay it all. Oh, Ed! Ed!

And so the night going—and the dawn coming. A horrible lacerating day. And after that other days. And with no one to talk to—no one. If only she could tell her stepmother all. And so other days and nights—all alone. And with blazing, searing, whirling, disordered thoughts in unbroken procession stalking her like demons. The outside world in case she were to be thrust into it! Her own unfamiliarity and hence fear of it! Those chattering, gaping youths on the corners—the girls she knew—their thoughts, since they must all soon know. Her loneliness without love. These and a hundred related thoughts dancing a fantastic, macabre mental dance before her.

But even so, within her own brain the persistent and growing illusion that all she had heard from him was not true—a chimera—and so for the time being at least continued faith in the value of pleading. Her wonderful lover. It must be that still some understanding could be reached. Yet with growing evidence that by no plea or plaint was he to be restored to his former attitude. For, in answer to notes, waiting at the corners, at the end of the street which led down to his father's coal-dock, in the vicinity of his home—silence, evasions, or direct insults, and sneers, even.

"What's the big idea, following me around, anyhow? You think I haven't anything else to do but listen to you? Say, I told you in the first place I couldn't marry, didn't I? And now because you think there's something wrong with you, you want to make me responsible. Well, I'm not the only fellow in this neighborhood. And everybody knows that."

He paused there, because as he saw this last declaration had awakened in her a latent strength and determination never previously shown in any way. The horror of that to her, as he could see. The whiteness of her face afterwards and on the instant. The blazing electric points within the pupils of her eyes. "That's a lie, and you know it! It's not true! Oh, how terrible! And for you to say that to me! I see it all now. You're just a sneak and a coward. You were just fooling with me all the time, then! You never intended to marry me, and now because you're afraid you think you can get out of it that way— by trying to blame it on some one else. You coward! Oh, aren't you the small one, though! And after all the things you said to me—the promises! As though I even thought of any one else in my life! You dare to say that to me, when you know so well!"

Her face was still lily white. And her hands. Her eyes

flashed with transcendent and yet helpless and defeated
misery. And yet, despite her rage—in the center of this
very misery—love itself—strong, vital, burning love—
the very core of it. But so tortured that already it
was beginning to drive the tears to her eyes.

And he knowing so thoroughly that this love was still
there, now instantly seizing on these latest truthful words
of hers as an insult—something on which to base an assumed grievance.

"Is that so? A coward, eh? Well, let's see what you
draw down for that, you little dumb-bell." And so turning on his heel—the strongest instinct in him—his own
social salvation in this immediate petty neighborhood at the
present time uppermost in his mind. And without a look
behind.

But Ida, her fear and terror at its height, calling: "Ed!
Ed! You come back here! Don't you dare to leave me
like this! I won't stand for it. I tell you, I won't! You
come back here now! Do you hear me?" And seeing that
he continued on briskly and indifferently, running after
him, unbelievably tense and a little beside herself—almost
mentally unaccountable for the moment. And he, seeing
her thus and amazed and troubled by this new turn his
problem had taken, turning abruptly with: "Say! You cut
out o' this now before I do something to you, do you hear?
I'm not the one to let you pull this stuff on me. You got
yourself into this and now you can get yourself out of it.
Beat it before I do something to you, do you hear?" And
now he drew nearer—and with such a threatening and
savage look in his eyes that for the first time in all her contact with him Ida grew fearful of him. That angry, sullen
face. Those fierce, cruel, savage eyes. Was it really true
that in addition to all the rest he would really do her physical harm? Then she had not understood him at all, ever.
And so pausing and standing quite still, that same fear of
physical force that had kept her in subjection to her father
overawing her here. At the same time, Hauptwanger,

noting the effect of his glowering rage, now added: "Don't come near me any more, do you hear? If you do, you're goin' to get something you're not going to like. I'm through, and I'm through for good, see."

Once more he turned and strode away, this time toward the central business district of the High and Warren Avenue region—the while Ida, too shaken by this newest development to quite grasp the full measure of her own necessity or courage, stood there. The horror of it! The disgrace! The shame! For now, surely, tragedy was upon her!

For the time being, in order to save herself from too much publicity, she began to move on—walk—only slowly and with whirling, staggering thoughts that caused her to all but lurch. And so, shaking and pale, she made her way once more to her home, where she stole into her room unnoticed. Yet, now, too tortured to cry but thinking grimly—fiercely at moments—at other times most weakly and feebly even—on all that had so recently occurred.

Her father! Her stepmother! If he—she—they should come to know! But no—something else must happen before ever that should be allowed to happen. She must leave—or—or, better yet—maybe drown herself— make way with herself in some way—or—

In the garret of this home, to which as a child on certain days she had frequently resorted to play, was an old wire clothes-line on which was hung an occasional wash. And now—might not that—in the face of absolute fiasco here—might not that—she had read of ending one's life in that manner. And it was so unlikely that any one would trouble to look there—until—until—well—

But would she? Could she? This strange budding of life that she sensed—feared. Was it fair to it? Herself? To life that had given it to her? And when she desired so to live? And when he owed her something—at least help to her and her—her—her— No, she could not—would not think of that yet, especially when to die this way would be but to clear the way to easier and happier conquests for him. Never! Never! She would kill him first—and then herself. Or expose him and so herself—and then—and then—

But again her father! Her stepmother! The disgrace! And so—

In her father's desk at the store was a revolver—a large, firm, squarish mechanism which, as she had heard him say, fired eight shots. It was so heavy, so blue, so cold. She had seen it, touched it, lifted it once—but with a kind of terror, really. It was always so identified with death—anger—not life— But now—supposing—supposing, if she desired to punish Edward and herself—or just herself alone. But no, that was not the way. What was the way, anyhow? What was the way?

And so now brooding in a tortured and half-demented way until her father, noting her mental state, inquired solemnly as to what had come over her of late. Had she had a quarrel with Hauptwanger? He had not seen him about recently. Was she ill in any way? Her appetite had certainly fallen off. She ate scarcely anything. But receiving a prompt "No" to both inquiries he remained curious but inclined to suspend further inquiry for the time being. There was something, of course, but no doubt it would soon come out.

But now—in the face of this—of course there must be action—decision. And so, in view of the thoughts as to self-destruction and the revolver, a decision to try the effect of a physical threat upon Hauptwanger. She would just frighten him. She might even point the gun at him—and see what he would do then. Of course, she could not kill him—she knew that. But supposing—supposing—one aimed—but not at him, really—and—and—(but, oh no!) a spit of fire, a puff of smoke, a deadly bullet—into his heart—into hers afterward, of course. No, no! For then what? Where?

A dozen, a score, of times in less than two days she

approached the drawer that held the revolver and looked at it—finally lifting it up but with no thought of doing more than just that at the moment. It was so heavy, so cold, so blue. The very weight and meaning of it terrorized her, although at last—after the twentieth attempt—she was able to fit it into her bosom in such a way that it lay quite firm and still. The horror of it—cold against her breast, where so often during the summer his head had lain.

And then one afternoon, when she could scarcely endure the strain longer—her father demanding: "What is the matter with you, anyhow? Do you know what you're doing half the time? Is there anything wrong between you and that beau of yours? I see he doesn't come around any more. It is time that you either married or had nothing more to do with him, anyway. I don't want any silly nonsense between you and him, you know." And this effected the very decision which she had most dreaded. Now . . . now . . . she must act. This evening—at least she must see him again and tell him that she was going to see his father and reveal all—furthermore, that if he did not marry her she would kill him and herself. Show him the gun, maybe, and frighten him with it—if she could— but at any rate make a last plea as well as a threat. If only—if only he would listen this time—not turn on her— become frightened, maybe, and help her,—not curse—or drive her away.

There was the coal-yard of his father that was at the end of an inlet giving into the river. Or his own home. She might go first to the coal office. He would be sure to be leaving there at half past five, or at six he would be nearing his home. At seven or half past departing from that again very likely to see—to see—whom? But best—best to go to the coal office first. He would be coming from there alone. It would be the quickest.

And Hauptwanger coming out of the coal office on this particular evening in the mood and with the air of one with whom all was well. But in the windy dusk of this November evening, arc lights blazing in the distance, the sound of distant cars, distant life, the wind whipping crisp leaves along the ground—the figure of a girl—a familiar cape about her shoulders, suddenly emerging from behind a pile of brick he was accustomed to pass.

"Ed! I want to talk to you a minute."

"You again! What the hell did I tell you? I ain't got no time to talk to you, and I won't! What did I . . ."

"Now listen, Ed, stop that, now! I'm desperate. *I'm desperate,* Ed, do you hear? Can't you see?" Her voice was staccato—almost shrill and yet mournful, too. "I've come to tell you that you've got to marry me now. *You've got* to—do you hear?" She was fumbling at her breast where lay that heavy blue thing—no longer so cold as when she had placed it there. The handle was upward. She must draw it now—show it—or hold it under her cloak ready so that at the right moment she could show it—and make him understand that unless he did something. . . . But her hand shaking so that she could scarcely hold it. It was so heavy—so terrible. She could scarcely hear herself adding: "Otherwise, I'm going to your father and mine, now. My father may do something terrible to me but he'll do more to you. And so will your father when he knows. . . . But, anyway . . ." She was about to add: "You've got to marry me, and right away too, or, or, I'm going to kill you and myself, that's all—" and then to produce the revolver, and wave it before him in a threatening dramatic manner.

But before that the uncalculated and non-understanding fury of Hauptwanger. "Well, of all the nerve! Say, cut this out, will ya? Who do you think you are? What did I tell you? Go to my father, if you want to. Go to yours! Who's afraid? Do you think they're going to believe a —— like you? I never had anything to do with you, and that's that!" And then in his anger giving her a push—as much to overawe her as anything.

But then, in spite of her desire not to give way, fury, blindness, pain,—whirling, fiery sparks, such as never in all her life before had she seen—and executing strange, rhythmic, convoluting orbits in her brain—swift, eccentric, red and yet beautiful orbits. And in the center of them the face of Hauptwanger—her beloved—but not as it was now—oh, no—but rather haloed by a strange white light— as it was under the trees in the spring. And herself turning, and in spite of the push, jumping before him.

"You will marry me, Ed, you will! You will! You see this? You will marry me!"

And then, as much to her astonishment as to his—yet with no particular terror to either of them—the thing spitting flame—making a loud noise—jumping almost out of her hand—so much so that before she could turn it away again there was another report—another flash of red in the dusk. And then Hauptwanger, too astonished quite for words at the moment, exclaiming: "Jesus! What are you . . ." And then, because of a sharp pain in his chest, putting his hand there and adding: "Oh, Christ! I'm shot!" and falling forward to one side of her. . . .

And then herself—those same whirling red sparks in her brain, saying: "Now, now—I must kill myself, too. I must. I must. I must run somewhere and turn this on myself," only quite unable to lift it at the moment—and because of some one—a man—approaching—a voice—footsteps, running—herself beginning to run—for some tree— some wall—some gate or doorway where she might stop and fire on herself. But a voice: "Hey! Stop that girl!" "Murder!" And another voice from somewhere else: "Hey! Murder! Stop that girl!" And footsteps, hard, quick ones, immediately behind her. And a hand grabbing hers in which was still the pistol, wildly and yet unwittingly held. And as the other hand wrenched at her hand— "Gimme that gun!" And then a strong youth whom she had never seen before—and yet not unlike Eddie either— turning her about—restraining her— "Say, you! What the devil is this, anyhow? Come back here. You can't get away with this."

And yet at the same time not unfriendly eyes looking into hers, strong hands holding her, but not too roughly, and herself exclaiming: "Oh, let me go! Let me go! I want to die, too, I tell you! Let me go!" And sobbing great, dry, shaking sobs.

But after that—and all so quickly—crowds—crowds— men and women, boys and girls, and finally policemen gathering about her, each with the rules of his training firmly in mind to get as much general information as possible; to see that the wounded man was hurried to a hospital, the girl to a precinct police station; the names and addresses of various witnesses secured. But with the lorn Ida in a state of collapse—seated upon a doorstep in a yard surrounded by a pushing crowd, while voices rang in her ears: "Where? What? How?" "Sure, sure! Just now, right back there. Sure, they're calling the ambulance." "He's done for, I guess. Twice in the breast. He can't live." "Gee! He's all covered with blood." "Sure, she did. With a revolver—a great big one. The cop's got it. She was tryin' to get away. Sure, Jimmie Allen caught her. He was just comin' home." "Yeah. She's the daughter of old Zobel who keeps the paint store up here in Warren Avenue. I know her. An' he's the son of this Hauptwanger here who owns the coal-yard. I used to work for 'em. He lives up in Grey Street."

But in the meantime young Hauptwanger unconscious and being transferred to an operating table at Mercy Hospital— his case pronounced hopeless—twenty-four hours of life at the very most. And his father and mother hearing the news and running there. And in the same period the tortured Ida transferred to Henderson Avenue Police Station, where in a rear inquisitorial chamber, entirely surrounded by policemen and detectives, she was questioned and requestioned. "Yah say yah seen this fella for the first time over a year ago? Is that right? He just moved into the

neighborhood a little while before? Ain't that so?" And
the disconsolate, half-conscious Ida nodding her head. And
outside a large, morbid, curious crowd. A beautiful girl!
A young man dying! Some sex mystery here.

And in the interim Zobel himself and his wife, duly informed by a burly policeman, hurrying white-faced and
strained to the station. My God! My God! And both
rushing in breathless. And beads of perspiration on Zobel's
forehead and hands—and misery, misery eating at his vitals.
What! His Ida had shot some one! Young Hauptwanger!
And in the street, near his office! Murder! Great God!
Then there was something between them. There was.
There was. But might he not have known? Her white face.
Her dreary, forsaken manner these later days. She had
been betrayed. That was it. Devils! Devils! That was
it! Eighty thousand hells! And after all he had said to
her! And all his and his wife's care of her! And now
the neighbors! His business! The police! A public trial!
Possibly a sentence—a death sentence! God in heaven!
His own daughter, too! And that young scoundrel with
his fine airs and fine clothes! Why—why was it that he
had let her go with him in the first place? When he might
have known—his daughter so inexperienced. "Where is
she? My God! My God! This is terrible!"

But seeing her sitting there, white, doleful-looking, and
looking up at him when spoken to with an almost meaningless look—a bloodless, smileless face—and saying: "Yes, I
shot him. Yes. Yes. He wouldn't marry me. He should
have but he wouldn't—and so—" And then at once crushing her hands in a sad, tortured way and crying: "Oh, Ed!
Ed!" And Zobel exclaiming: "Ach, God! Ida! Ida! In
God's name, it can't be so. Why didn't you tell me? Why
didn't you come to me? Am I not your father! I would
have understood. Of course! Of course! I would have
gone to his father—to him. But now—this—and now—"
and he began to wring his own hands.

Yet the principal thought in his mind that now the world would know all— And after all his efforts. And beginning volubly to explain to the desk lieutenant and the detectives and policemen all that he knew. But the only thought afloat in the unhappy Ida's brain, once she awakened again, was: Was this really her father? And was he talking so—of help? That she might have come to him— for what—when she had thought—that—that he would not be like that to her. But . . . after a time again . . . there was Ed to be thought of. That terrible scene. That terrible accident. She had not intended to do that—really. She had not. She had not. No! But was he really dead? Had she really killed him? That push—almost a blow it was—those words. But still— Oh, dear! Oh, dear! And then beginning to cry to herself, silently and deeply, while Zobel and his wife bent over her for the first time in true sympathy. The complications of life! The terrors! There was no peace for any one on this earth—no peace— no peace. All was madness, really, and sorrow. But they would stand by her now—yes, yes.

But then the reporters. A public furore fanned by the newspapers, with their men and women writers, pen and ink artists, photographers. Their editorials: "Beautiful girl of seventeen shoots lover, twenty-one. Fires two bullets into body of man she charges with refusing to keep faith. About to become a mother. Youth likely to die. Girl admits crime. Pleads to be left alone in misery. Parents of both in despair." And then columns and columns, day after day—since on the following afternoon at three Hauptwanger did die—admitting that he had wronged her. And a coroner's jury, called immediately afterwards, holding the girl for subsequent action by the Grand Jury, and without bail. Yet, because of her beauty and the "pathos" of the case—letters to the newspapers, from ministers, society men and women, politicians and the general public, demanding that this wronged girl about to become a mother, and who had committed no wrong other than that of loving too well—if not wisely—be not severely dealt with—be forgiven—be admitted to bail. No jury anywhere would convict her. Not in America. Indeed, it would "go hard" with any jury that would attempt to "further punish" a girl who had already suffered so much. Plainly it was the duty of the judge in this case to admit this poor wronged soul to bail and the peace and quiet of some home or institution where her child might be born, especially since already a woman of extreme wealth and social position, deeply stirred by the pathos of this drama, had not only come forward to sympathize with this innocent victim of love and order and duty, but had offered any amount of bail that she might be released to the peace and quiet of her own home—there to await the outcome of her physical condition as well as the unavoidable prosecution which must fix her future.

And so, to her wonder and confusion, Ida finally released in the custody of this outwardly sober and yet inwardly emotional woman, who ever since the first day of her imprisonment in the central county jail had sought to ingratiate herself into her good graces and emotions—a woman middle-aged and plain but soft-voiced and kindly-mannered, who over and over repeated that she understood, that she also had suffered—that her heart had been torn, too—and that she, Ida, need never worry. And so Ida finally transferred (a bailed prisoner subject to return upon demand) to the wide acres and impressive chambers of a once country but now city residence, an integral part of the best residence area of the city. And there, to her astonishment and wonder—and this in spite of her despair—all needful equipment and service provided—a maid and servants, her food served to her in her room when she wished—silence or entertainment as she chose. And with her own parents allowed to visit her whenever she chose. Yet she was so uncomfortable in their presence always now. True, they were kind—gentle, whenever they came. They spoke of the different life that was to be after this great crisis was truly past—the birth of the child, which was never other than indirectly referred to, or the trial, which was to follow later. There was to be a new store in a new neighborhood. The old one had already been offered for sale. And after that . . . well, peace perhaps, or a better life. But even in her father's eyes as he spoke could she not see the weight of care which he now shouldered? She had sinned! She had killed a man! And wrecked another family—the hearts of two other parents as well as her father's own peace of mind and commercial and social well-being. And in all his charity, was there room for that? In the solemnity of his manner, as well as that of her stepmother, could she feel that there was?

Yet in the main, and because her mood and health seemed to require it, she was now left to contemplate the inexplicable chain of events which her primary desire for love had brought about. The almost amazing difference in the mental attitude of her parents toward her now and before this dreadful and unfortunate event in her life! So considerate and sympathetic now as to result in an offer of a happier home for her and her child in the future, whereas before all was—or as she sensed it—so threatening and desperate. The strange and to her inexplicable attitude of this woman even—so kind and generous—and this in the face of her sin and shame.

And yet, what peace or quiet could there be for her here or anywhere now? The terrible torture that had preceded that terrible accident! Her Edward's cry! His death! And when she loved him so! Had! Did now! And yet by his dread perverseness, cruelty, brutality, he had taken himself from her. But still, still—now that he was gone—now that in dying, as she heard he had said, he had been "stuck on her" at first, that she had "set him crazy," but that afterwards, because of his parents, as well as hers, he had decided that he would not marry her—she could not help but feel more kindly to him. He had been cruel. But had he not died? And at her hands. She had killed him— murdered him. Oh, yes, she had. Oh! Oh! Oh! For in connection with the actual scene did she not recall some one crying that his shirt front had been all bloody. Oh! Oh! Oh! And in her heart, no doubt, when she had jumped in front of him there in the dusk had been rage—rage and hate even, too, for the moment. Oh, yes. But he had cried: "Oh, Christ! I'm shot!" (Her Edward's cry.)

And so, even in the silence of these richly furnished rooms, with a servant coming to her call, hot, silent tears and deep, racking sobs—when no one was supposed to see or hear— and thoughts, thoughts, thoughts—sombre, bleak—as to her lack of sense, her lack of courage or will to end it all for herself on that dreadful evening when she so easily might have. And now here she had plighted her word that she would do nothing rash—would not attempt to take her life. But the future! The future! And what had she not seen since that dreadful night! Edward's father and mother at the inquest! And how they had looked at her! Haupt- wanger, senior—his strong, broad German face marked with a great anguish. And Mrs. Hauptwanger—small and all in black, and with great hollow rings under her eyes. And crying silently nearly all the time. And both had sworn that they knew nothing of Edward's conduct, or of his definite interest in her. He was a headstrong, virile, rest- less boy. They had a hard time controlling him. And yet he had not been a bad boy, either—headstrong but willing to work—and gay—their only son.

At one point in these extensive grounds—entirely sur- rounded by Lombardy poplars now leafless—there stood a fountain drained of its water for the winter. But upon the pedestal, upon a bronze rock, at the foot of which washed bronze waves of the Rhine, a Rhine maiden of the blonde German Lorelei type, standing erect and a-dream, in youth, in love. And at her feet, on his knees, a German lover of the Ritter type—vigorous, uniformed, his fair blond head and face turned upward to the beauty about whose hips his arms were clasped—his look seeking, urgent. And upon his fair bronze hair, her right hand, the while she bent on

him a yearning, yielding glance. Oh, Edward! Oh, love!
Spring! She must not come out here any more. And yet
evening after evening in early December, once the first
great gust of this terrific storm had subsided and she was
seeing things in a less drastic light, she was accustomed to
return to look at it. And sometimes, even in January, a
new moon overhead would suggest King Lake Park! The
little boats gliding here and there! She and Edward in
one. Herself leaning back and dreaming as now—now—
this figure of the girl on the rock was doing. And he—
he—at her knees. To be sure, he had cursed her. He
had said the indifferent, cruel words that had at last driven
her to madness. But once he had loved her just this way.
It was there, and only there, that she found spiritual comfort in her sorrow—

But then, in due course, the child—with all these
thoughts, moods enveloping it. And after that the trial,
with her prompt acquittal. A foreseen conclusion. And
with loud public acclaim for that verdict also, since it was
all for romance and drastic drama. And then the final
leaving of these great rooms and this personal intimate
affection that had been showered upon her. For after all
the legal, if not the emotional problem, had now been
solved. And since her father was not one who was poor
or welcomed charity—a contemplated and finally accomplished return to a new world—the new home and store
which had been established in a very different and remote
part of the city. The child a boy. That was good, for
eventually he could care for himself. He would not need
her. The new paint shop was near another cross business
street, near another moving-picture theatre. And boys and
girls here as elsewhere—on the corners—going arm in
arm—and herself again at home cooking, sewing, cleaning
as before. And with Mrs. Zobel as reserved and dubious
as before. For after all, had she not made a mess of her
life, and for what? What now? Here forever as a fixture?
And even though Zobel, in spite of his grimness, was be-

coming fond of the child. How wretched, how feeble life really was!

But far away King Lake Park and the old neighborhood. And thoughts that went back to it constantly. She had been so happy the summer before. And now this summer! And other summers to come—even though perhaps some time—once little Eric was grown—there might be some other lover—who would not mind— But, no—no, not that. Never! She did not want that. Could not—would not endure it.

And so at last of a Saturday afternoon, when she had the excuse of certain things needed for Eric, a trip to presumably the central business heart—whereas, in reality, it was to King Lake Park she was going. And once there— the little boats, the familiar paths—a certain nook under the overarching bushes and trees. She knew it so well. It was here that she had demanded to be let out in order that she might go home by herself—so shocked, so ashamed. Yet now seeking it.

The world does not understand such things. It is so busy with so many, many things.

And then dusk—though she should have been returning. Her boy! He would miss her! And then a little wind with a last faint russet glow in the west. And then stars! Quite all the world had gone to its dinner now. The park was all but empty. The water here was so still—so agate. (The world—the world—it will never understand, will it?) Where would Edward be? Would he be meeting her somewhere? Greeting her? Would he forgive,— when she told him all—could she find him, perchance? (The world—the busy, strident, indifferent, matter-of-fact world—how little it knows.)

And then a girl in the silence, in the shadow, making her way down to the very spot that the nose of their boat had nuzzled but one short summer before. And calmly stepping into the water and wading out to her knees—to her waist— her breasts—in the mild, caressing water—and then to her lips and over them—and finally, deliberately—conclusively —sinking beneath its surface and without a cry or sigh.

The world does not understand such things. The tide of life runs too fast. So much that is beautiful—terrible— sweeps by—by—by—without thought—without notice in the great volume.

And yet her body was found—her story retold in great, flaring headlines. (Ida Zobel—Girl Slayer of Hauptwanger a Suicide.) And then . . . and then . . . forgotten.

VIII

THE OLD NEIGHBORHOOD

HE came to it across the new bridge, from the south where the greater city lay—the older portion—and where he had left his car, and paused at the nearer bridge-head to look at it—the eddying water of the river below, the new docks and piers built on either side since he had left, twenty years before; the once grassy slopes on the farther shore, now almost completely covered with factories, although he could see too, among them, even now, traces of the old, out-of-the-way suburb which he and Marie had known. Chadds Bridge, now an integral part of the greater city, connected by car lines and through streets, was then such a simple, unpretentious affair, a little suburban village just on the edge of this stream and beyond the last straggling northward streets of the great city below, where the car lines stopped and from which one had to walk on foot across this bridge in order to take advantage of the rural quiet and the cheaper—much cheaper—rents, so all-important to him then.

Then he was so poor—he and Marie—a mere stripling of a mechanic and inventor, a student of aeronautics, electricity, engineering, and what not, but newly married and without a dollar, and no clear conception of how his future was to eventuate, whereas now—but somehow he did not want to think of now. Now he was so very rich, comparatively speaking, older, wiser, such a forceful person commercially and in every other way, whereas then he was so lean and pathetic and worried and wistful—a mere uncertain stripling, as he saw himself now, with ideas and ambitions and dreams which were quite out of accord with his immediate prospects or opportunities. It was all right to say, as some one had—Emerson, he believed—"hitch your wagon to a star." But some people hitched, or tried to, before they were ready. They neglected some of the slower moving vehicles about them, and so did not get on at all—or did not seem to, for the time being.

And that had been his error. He was growing at the time, of course, but he was so restless, so dissatisfied with himself, so unhappy. All the world was apparently tinkling and laughing by, eating, drinking, dancing, growing richer, happier, every minute; whereas he—he and Marie, and the two babies which came a little later—seemed to make no progress at all. None. They were out of it, alone, hidden away in this little semi-rural realm, and it was all so disturbing when elsewhere was so much—to him, at least, if not to her—of all that was worth while—wealth, power, gayety, repute. How intensely, savagely almost, he had craved all of those things in those days, and how far off they still were at that time!

Marie was not like him, soft, clinging little thing that she was, inefficient in most big ways, and yet dear and helpful enough in all little ones—oh, so very much so.

When first he met her in Philadelphia, and later when he brought her over to New York, it seemed as though he could not possibly have made a better engagement for himself. Marie was so sweet, so gentle, with her waxy white pallor, delicately tinted cheeks, soft blackish brown eyes that sought his so gently always, as if seeming to ask, "And what can I do for my dearie now? What can he teach me to do for him?" She was never his equal, mentally or spiritually—that was the dreadful discovery he had made a few months after the first infatuation had worn off, after the ivory of her forehead, the lambent sweetness of her eyes, her tresses, and her delicately rounded figure, had ceased to befuddle his more poetical brain. But how delightful she seemed then in her shabby little clothes and her shabbier little home—all the more so because her delicate white blossom of a face was such a contrast to the drear surroundings in which it shone. Her father was no more than a mechanic, she a little store clerk in the great Rand department store in Philadelphia when he met her, he nothing more than an experimental assistant with the Culver Electric Company, with no technical training of any kind, and only dreams of a technical course at some time or other. The beginnings of his career were so very vague.

His parents were poor too, and he had had to begin to earn his own living, or share, at fourteen. And at twenty-four he had contracted this foolish marriage when he was just beginning to dream of bigger things, to see how they were done, what steps were necessary, what studies, what cogitations and hard, grinding sacrifices even, before one finally achieved anything, especially in the electrical world. The facts which had begun to rise and take color and classify themselves in his mind had all then to develop under the most advantageous conditions thereafter. His salary did not rise at once by any means, just because he was beginning to think of bigger things. He was a no better practical assistant in a laboratory or the equipment department of the several concerns for which he worked, because in his brain were already seething dim outlines of possible improvements in connection with arms, the turbine gun, electro-magnetic distance control, and the rotary excavator. He had ideas, but also as he realized at the time he would have to study privately and long in order to make them real; and his studies at night and Sundays and holidays in the libraries and everywhere else, made him no more helpful, if as much so, in his practical, everyday corporation labors. In fact, for a long time when their finances were at the lowest ebb and the two children had appeared, and they all needed clothes and diversion, and his salary had not been raised, it seemed as though he were actually less valuable to everybody.

But in the meantime Marie had worked for and with him, dear little thing, and although she had seemed so wonderful at first, patient, enduring, thoughtful, later because of their poverty and so many other things which hampered and seemed to interfere with his work, he had wearied of her a little. Over in Philadelphia, where he had accompanied her home of an evening and had watched her help her mother, saw her set the table, wash the dishes, straighten up the house after dinner, and then if it were pleasant go for a walk with him, she seemed ideal, just the wife for him, indeed. Later as he sensed the world, its hardness, its innate selfishness, the necessity for push, courage, unwillingness to be a slave and a drudge, these earlier qualities and charms were the very things that militated against her in his mind. Poor little Marie!

But in other ways his mind was not always on his work, either. Sometimes it was on his dreams of bigger things. Sometimes it was on his silly blindness in wanting to get married so soon, in being betrayed by the sweet innocence and beauty of Marie into saddling himself with this burden when he was scarcely prepared, as he saw after he was married, to work out his own life on a sensible, economic basis. A thought which he had encountered somewhere in some book of philosophy or other (he was always reading in those days) had haunted him—"He that hath wife and children hath given hostages to fortune"—and that painful thought seemed to grow with each succeeding day. Why had he been so foolish, why so very foolish, as to get married when he was so unsuitably young! That was a thing the folly of which irritated him all the time.

Not that Marie was not all she should be—far from it!—nor the two little boys (both boys, think of that!), intensely precious to him at first. No, that was not it, but this, that whatever the values and the charms of these (and they were wonderful at first), he personally was not prepared to bear or enjoy them as yet. He was too young, too restless, too nebulous, too inventively dreamful. He did not, as he had so often thought since, know what he wanted—only, when they began to have such a very hard time, he knew he did not want that. Why, after the first year of their marriage, when Peter was born, and because of better trade conditions in the electrical world, they had moved over here (he was making only twenty-two dollars a week at the time), everything had seemed to go wrong. Indeed, nothing ever seemed to go right any more after that, not one thing.

First it was Marie's illness after Peter's birth, which kept him on tenterhooks and took all he could rake and scrape and save to pay the doctor's bill, and stole half her beauty, if not more. She always looked a little pinched and weak after that. (And he had charged that up to her, too!) Then it was some ailment which affected Peter for months and which proved to be undernourishment, due to a defect in Marie's condition even after she had seemingly recovered. Then, two years later, it was the birth of Frank, due to another error, of course, he being not intended in Marie's frail state; and then his own difficulties with the manager of the insulating department of the International Electric, due to his own nervous state, his worries, his consciousness of error in the manipulation of his own career—and Marie's. Life was slipping away, as he saw it then and he kept thinking he was growing older, was not getting on as he had thought he should, was not achieving his technical education; he was saddled with a family which would prevent him from ever getting on. Here, in this neighborhood, all this had occurred—this quiet, run-down realm, so greatly changed since he had seen it last. Yes, it had all happened here.

But how peaceful it was to-day, although changed. How the water ran under this bridge now, as then, eddying out to sea. And how this late October afternoon reminded him of that other October afternoon when they had first walked up here—warm, pleasant, colorful. Would he ever forget that afternoon? He had thought he was going to do so much better—was praying that he would, and they had done so much worse. He, personally, had grown so restless and dissatisfied with himself and her and life. And things seemed to be almost as bad as they could be, drifting in-

definitely on to nothing. Indeed, life seemed to gather
as a storm and break. He was discharged from the International Electric, due supposedly to his taking home for
a night a battery for an experiment he was making but
in reality because of the opposition of his superior, based on
the latter's contempt for his constantly (possibly) depressed
and dissatisfied air, his brooding mien, and some minor in-
attentions due to the state of his mind at the time.

Then, quite as swiftly (out of black plotting or evil
thoughts of his own, perhaps), Peter had died of pneumonia.
And three days later Frank. There were two funerals, two
dreary, one-carriage affairs—he remembered that so well!—
for they had no money; and his pawned watch, five dollars
from Marie's mother, and seven chemical and electrical
works sold to an old book man had provided the cash advance required by the undertaker! Then, spiritually, something seemed to break within him. He could not see this
world, this immediate life in which he was involved, as having any significance in it for himself or any one after that.
He could not stand it any more, the weariness, the boredom,
the dissatisfaction with himself, the failure of himself, the
sickening chain of disasters which had befallen this earlier
adventure. And so—

But that was why he was here to-day, after all these
years—twenty-four, to be exact—with his interest in this old
region so keen, if so sad. Why, there—there!—was a flock
of pigeons, just like those of old Abijah Hargot's, flying
around the sky now, as then. And a curl of smoke creeping
up from Tanzer's blacksmith shop, or the one that had succeeded it, just one block from this bridge. How well he
remembered old Tanzer and his forge, his swelling muscles
and sooty face! He had always nodded in such a friendly
way as he passed and talked of the pest of flies and heat in
summer. That was why he was pausing on this bridge
to-day, just to see once more, to feel, standing in the pleasant afternoon sun of this October day and gazing across the
swirling waters below at the new coal-pockets, the enlarged

lamp works of the George C. Woodruff Company, once a mere shed hidden away at a corner of this nearest street and rented out here no doubt because it was cheap and Woodruff was just beginning—just as he did twenty-four years before. Time had sped by so swiftly. One's ideals and ideas changed so. Twenty years ago he would have given so much to be what he was now—rich and fairly powerful—and now—now— The beauty of this old neighborhood, to-day, even.

The buff school which crowned the rise beyond, and the broad asphalt of Edgewood Avenue leading up to the old five-story flat building—the only one out here, and a failure financially—in which he and Marie had had their miserable little apartment—here it was, still to be seen. Yes, it and so many other things were all here; that group of great oaks before old Hargot's door; the little red—if now rusted—weather-vane over his carriage house; the tall romantic tower of St. George's Episcopal Church—so far to the west over the river, and the spars and masts of vessels that still docked here for a while. But dark memories they generated, too, along with a certain idyllic sweetness, which had seemed to envelop the whole at first. For though it had had sweetness and peace at first, how much that had been bitter and spiritually destroying had occurred here, too.

How well he recalled, for instance, the day he and Marie had wandered up here, almost hand in hand, across this very bridge and up Edgewood Avenue, nearly twenty-four years before! They had been so happy at first, dreaming their little dream of a wonderful future for them—and now—well, his secret agency had brought him all there was to know of her and her mother and her little world after he had left. They had suffered so much, apparently, and all on account of him. But somehow he did not want to think of that now. It was not for that he had come to-day, but to see, to dream over the older, the better, the first days.

He crossed over, following the old road which had then been a cobble wagon trail, and turned into Edgewood Avenue which led up past the line of semi-country homes which he used to dread so much, homes which because of their superior prosperity, wide lawns, flowers and walks, made the life which he and Marie were compelled to lead here seem so lean and meagre by contrast. Why, yes, here was the very residence of Gatewood, the dentist, so prosperous then and with an office downtown; and that of Dr. Newton, whom he had called in when Peter and Frank were taken ill that last time; and Temple, the druggist, and Stoutmeyer, the grocer—both of whom he had left owing money; and Dr. Newton, too, for that matter—although all had subsequently been paid. Not a sign of the names of either Gatewood or Newton on their windows or gates now; not a trace of Temple's drug store. But here was Stoutmeyer's grocery just the same. And Buchspiel, the butcher. (Could he still be alive, by any chance—was that his stout, aged figure within?) And Ortman, the baker—not a sign of change there. And over the way the then village school, now Public School No. 261, as he could see. And across from it, beyond, the slim little, almost accidental (for this region) five-story apartment house—built because of an error in judgment, of course, when they thought the city was going to grow out this way—a thing of grayish-white brick. On the fifth floor of this, in the rear, he and Marie had at last found a tiny apartment of three rooms and bath, cheap enough for them to occupy in the growing city and still pay their way. What memories the mere sight of the building evoked! Where were all the people now who used to bustle about here of a summer evening when he and Marie were here, boys and girls, grown men and women of the neighborhood? It had all been so pleasant at first, Marie up there preparing dinner and he coming home promptly at seven and sometimes whistling as he came! He was not always unhappy, even here.

Yes, all was exactly as it had been in the old days in regard to this building and this school, even—as he lived!—a "For Rent" sign in that very same apartment, four flights up, as it had been that warm October day when they had first come up here seeking.

But what a change in himself—stouter, so much older, gray now. And Marie—dying a few years after in this very region without his ever seeing her again or she him—and she had written him such pathetic letters. She had been broken, no doubt, spiritually and in every other way when he left her,—no pointless vanity in that, alas—it was too sad to involve vanity. Yes, he had done that. Would it ever be forgiven him? Would his error of ambition and self-dissatisfaction be seen anywhere in any kindly light—on earth or in heaven? He had suffered so from remorse in regard to it of late. Indeed, now that he was rich and so successful the thought of it had begun to torture him. Some time since—five years ago—he had thought to make amends, but then—well, then he had found that she wasn't any more. Poor little Marie!

But these walls, so strong and enduring (stone had this advantage over human flesh!), were quite as he had left them, quite as they were the day he and Marie had first come here—hopeful, cheerful, although later so depressed, the two of them. (And he had charged her spiritually with it all, or nearly so—its fatalities and gloom, as though she could have avoided them!)

The ruthlessness of it!

The sheer brutality!

The ignorance

If she could but see him now, his great shops and factories, his hundreds of employés, his present wife and children, his great new home—and still know how he felt about her! If he could only call her back and tell her, apologize, explain, make some amends! But no; life did not work that way. Doors opened and doors closed. It had no consideration for eleventh-hour repentances. As though they mattered to life, or anything else! He could tell her something now, of course, explain the psychology, let her know how pathetically depressed and weary he had felt then. But

would she understand, care, forgive? She had been so
fond of him, done so much for him in her small, sweet way.
And yet, if she only knew, he could scarcely have helped
doing as he did then, so harried and depressed and eager for
advancement had he been, self-convinced of his own error
and failure before ever his life had a good start. If she could
only see how little all his later triumphs mattered now, how
much he would be glad to do for her now! if only—only—
he could. Well, he must quit these thoughts. They did not
help at all, nor his coming out here and feeling this way!

But life was so automatic and unconsciously cruel at
times. One's disposition drove one so, shutting and bolting
doors behind one, driving one on and on like a harried steer
up a narrow runway to one's fate. He could have been
happy right here with Marie and the children—as much so
as he had ever been since. Or, if he had only taken Marie
along, once the little ones were gone—they might have been
happy enough together. They might have been! But no,
no; something in him at that time would not let him.
Really, he was a victim of his own grim impulses, dreams,
passions, mad and illogical as that might seem. He was
crazy for success, wild with a desire for a superior, contemptuous position in the world. People were so, at times.
He had been. He had had to do as he did, so horribly
would he have suffered mentally if he had not, all the theo-
ries of the moralists to the contrary notwithstanding. The
notions of one's youth were not necessarily those of age, and
that was why he was here to-day in this very gloomy and
contrite mood.

He went around the corner now to the side entrance of
the old apartment house, and paused. For there, down the
street, almost—not quite—as he had left it, was the residence
of the quondam old Abijah Hargot, he of the pigeons,—iron
manufacturer and Presbyterian, who even in his day was
living there in spite of the fact that the truly princely residence suburbs had long since moved much farther out and
he was being entirely surrounded by an element of cheaper

life which could not have been exactly pleasant to him. In those days he and Marie had heard of the hardwood floors, the great chandeliers, the rugs and pictures of the house that had once faced a wide sward leading down to the river's edge itself. But look at it now! A lumber-yard between it and the river! And some sort of a small shop or factory on this end of the lawn! And in his day, Abijah had kept a pet Jersey cow nibbling the grass under the trees and fantailed pigeons on the slate roof of his barn, at the corner where now was this small factory, and at the back of his house an immense patch of golden glow just outside the conservatory facing the east, and also two pagodas down near the river. But all gone! all gone, or nearly so. Just the house and a part of the lawn. And occupied now by whom? In the old days he had never dared dream, or scarcely so, that some day, years later—when he would be much older and sadder, really, and haunted by the ghosts of these very things—he would be able to return here and know that he had far more imposing toys than old Hargot had ever dreamed of, as rich as he was.

Toys!

Toys!

Yes, they were toys, for one played with them a little while, as with so many things, and then laid them aside forever.

Toys!

Toys!

But then, as he had since come to know, old Hargot had not been without his troubles, in spite of all his money. For, as rumor had it then, his oldest son, Lucien, his pride, in those days, a slim, artistic type of boy, had turned out a drunkard, gambler, night-life lover; had run with women, become afflicted with all sorts of ills, and after his father had cut him off and driven him out (refusing to permit him even to visit the home), had hung about here, so the neighbors had said, and stolen in to see his mother, especially on dark or rainy nights, in order to get aid from her. And, like all mothers, she had aided him secretly, or so they said, in spite of her fear of her husband. Mothers were like that —his mother, too. Neighbors testified that they had seen her whispering to him in the shade of the trees of the lawn or around the corner in the next street—a sad, brooding, care-worn woman, always in black or dark blue. Yes, life held its disappointments for every one, of course, even old Abijah and himself.

He went on to the door and paused, wondering whether to go up or not, for the atmosphere of this building and this neighborhood was very, very sad now, very redolent of old, sweet, dead and half-forgotten things. The river there, running so freshly at the foot of the street; the school where the children used to play and shout, while he worked on certain idle days when there was no work at the factory; the little church up the street to which so many common- place adherents used to make their way on Sunday; the shabby cabin of the plumber farther up this same street, who used to go tearing off every Saturday and Sunday in a rattle-trap car which he had bought second-hand and which squeaked and groaned, for all the expert repairing he had been able to do upon it.

The color, the humor, the sunshine of those old first days, in spite of their poverty!

He hesitated as to whether to ring the bell or no—just as he and Marie had, twenty-odd years before. She was so gay then, so hopeful, so all-unconscious of the rough fate that was in store for her here. . . . How would it be in- side? Would Marie's little gas stove still be near the win- dow in the combined kitchen, dining-room and laundry— almost general living-room—which that one room was? Would the thin single gas jet still be hanging from the ceil- ing over their small dining-room table (or the ghost of it) where so often after their meals, to save heat in the other room—because there was no heat in the alleged radiator, and their oil stove cost money—he had sat and read or worked on plans of some of the things he hoped to perfect—and had since, years since, but long after he had left her and this place? How sad! He had never had one touch of luck or opportunity with her here,—not one. Yet, if only she could, and without pain because of it, know how brilliantly he had finished some of them, how profitably they had resulted for him if not her.

But he scarcely looked like one who would be wanting to see so small an apartment, he now felt, tall and robust and prosperous as he was. Still might he not be thinking of buying this place? Or renting quarters for a servant or a relative? Who should know? What difference did it make? Why should he care?

He rang the bell, thinking of the small, stupid, unfriendly and self-defensive woman who, twenty or more years before, had come up from the basement below, wiping her hands on a gingham apron and staring at them querulously. How well he remembered her—and how unfriendly she had always remained in spite of their efforts to be friendly, because they had no tips to give her. She could not be here any longer, of course; no, this one coming was unlike her in everything except stupidity and grossness. But they were alike in that, well enough. This one was heavy, beefy. She would make almost two of the other one.

"The rooms," he had almost said "apartment," "on the top floor—may I see them?"

"Dey are only t'ree an' bat'—fourteen by der mont'."

"Yes, I know," he now added almost sadly. So they had not raised the rent in all this time, although the city had grown so. Evidently this region had become worse, not better. "I'll look at them, if you please, just the same," he went on, feeling that the dull face before him was wondering why he should be looking at them at all.

"Vait; I getcha der key. You can go up py yerself."

He might have known that she would never climb any four flights save under compulsion.

She returned presently, and he made his way upward, remembering how the fat husband of the former janitress had climbed up promptly every night at ten, if you please, putting out the wee lights of gas on the return trip (all but a thin flame on the second floor: orders from the landlord, of course), and exclaiming as he did so, at each landing, "Ach Gott, I go me up py der secon' floor ant make me der lights out. Ach Gott, I go me py der t'ird floor ant make me der lights out. Ach Gott, I go me py der fourt' floor ant make me der lights out," and so on until he reached the fifth, where they lived. How often he had listened to him, puffing and moaning as he came!

Yes, the yellowish-brown paper that they had abhorred then, or one nearly as bad, covered all these hall walls to-day. The stairs squeaked, just as they had then. The hall gas jets were just as small and surmounted by shabby little pink imitation glass candles—to give the place an air, no doubt! He and Marie would never have taken this place at all if it had depended on the hall, or if the views from its little windows had not been so fine. In the old days he had trudged up these steps many a night, winter and summer, listening, as he came, for sounds of Marie in the kitchen, for the prattle of the two children after they were with them, for the glow of a friendly light (always shining at six in winter) under the door and through the keyhole. His light! His door! In those early dark winter days, when he was working so far downtown and coming home this way regularly, Marie, at the sound of his key in the lock, would always come running, her heavy black hair done in a neat braid about her brow, her trim little figure buttoned gracefully into a house-dress of her own making. And she always had a smile and a "Hello, dearie; back again?" no matter how bad things were with them, how lean the little larder or the family purse. Poor little Marie!

It all came back to him now as he trudged up the stairs and neared the door. God!

And here was the very door, unchanged—yellow, painted to imitate the natural grain of oak, but the job having turned out a dismal failure as he had noted years before.

And the very lock the same! Could he believe? Scarcely any doubt of it. For here was that other old hole, stuffed with putty and painted over, which he and Marie had noted as being the scar of some other kind of a lock or knob that had preceded this one. And still stuffed with paper! Marie had thought burglars (!) might make their way in via that, and he had laughed to think what they would steal if they should. Poor little Marie!

But now, now—well, here he was all alone, twenty-four years later, Marie and Peter and Frank gone this long time, and he the master of so many men and so much power and so much important property. What was life, anyhow? What was it?

Ghosts! Ghosts!

Were there ghosts?

Did spirits sometimes return and live and dream over old, sad scenes such as this? Could Marie? Would she? Did she?

Oh, Marie! . . . Marie! Poor little weak, storm-beaten, life-beaten soul. And he the storm, really.

Well, here was the inside now, and things were not a bit different from what they had been in his and her day, when they had both been so poor. No, just the same. The floor a little more nail-marked, perhaps, especially in the kitchen here, where no doubt family after family had tacked down oil-cloth in place of other pieces taken up—theirs, for instance. And here in the parlor—save the mark!—the paper as violent at it had ever been! Such paper—red, with great bowls of pinkish flowers arranged in orderly rows! But then they were paying so little rent that it was ridiculous for them to suggest that they wanted anything changed. The landlord would not have changed it anyhow.

And here on the west wall, between the two windows, overlooking Abijah Hargot's home and the river and the creeping city beyond, was where he had hung a wretched little picture, a print of an etching of a waterscape which he had admired so much in those days and had bought somewhere second-hand for a dollar—a house on an inlet near the sea, such a house as he would have liked to have occupied, or thought he would—then. Ah, these windows! The northernmost one had always been preferred by him and her because of the sweep of view west and north. And how often he had stood looking at a soft, or bleak, or reddening, sunset over the river; or, of an early night in winter, at the lights on the water below. And the outpost apartments and homes of the great city beyond. Life had looked very dark then, indeed. At times, looking, he had been very sad. He was like some brooding Hamlet of an inventor as he stood there then gazing at the sweet little river, the twinkling stars in a steely black sky overhead; or, in the fall when it was still light, some cold red island of a cloud in the sky over the river and the city, and wondering what was to become of him—what was in store for him! The fallacy of such memories as these! Their futility!

But things had dragged and dragged—here! In spite of the fact that his mind was full of inventions, inventions, inventions, and methods of applying them in some general way which would earn him money, place, fame—as they subsequently did—the strange mysteries of ionic or electronic action, for instance, of motion, of attraction and polarity, of wave lengths and tensile strengths and adhesions in metals, woods and materials of all kinds—his apparent error in putting himself in a position where failure might come to him had so preyed on his mind here, that he could do nothing. He could only dream, and do common, ordinary day labor—skeleton wiring and insulating, for instance, electrical mapping, and the like. Again, later, but while still here, since he had been reading, reading, reading after marriage, and working and thinking, life had gone off into a kind of welter of conflicting and yet organized and plainly directed powers which was confusing to him, which was not to be explained by anything man could think of and which no inventor had as yet fully used, however great he was—

Edison, Kelvin, or Bell. Everything as he knew then and hoped to make use of in some way was alive, everything full of force, even so-called dead or decaying things. Life was force, that strange, seemingly (at times) intelligent thing, and there was apparently nothing but force—everywhere—amazing, perfect, indestructible. (He had thought of all that here in this little room and on the roof overhead where he made some of his experiments, watching old Hargot's pigeons flying about the sky, the sound of their wings coming so close at times that they were like a whisper of the waves of the sea, dreams in themselves.)

But the little boundaries of so-called health and decay, strength and weakness, as well as all alleged *fixity* or changelessness of things,—how he had brooded on all that, at that time. And how all thought of fixity in anything had disappeared as a ridiculous illusion intended, maybe, by something to fool man into the belief that his world here, his physical and mental state, was real and enduring, a greater thing than anything else in the universe, when so plainly it was not. But not himself. A mere shadow—an illusion—nothing. On this little roof, here, sitting alone at night or by day in pleasant weather or gray, Saturdays and Sundays when it was warm and because they had no money and no particular place to go, and looking at the stars or the lights of the city or the sun shining on the waters of the little river below,—he had thought of all this. It had all come to him, the evanescence of everything, its slippery, protean changefulness. Everything was alive, and everything was nothing, in so far as its seeming reality was concerned. And yet everything was everything but still capable of being undermined, changed, improved, or come at in some hitherto undreamed-of way—even by so humble a creature as himself, an inventor—and used as chained force, if only one knew how. And that was why he had become a great inventor since—because he had thought so—had chained force and used it—even he. He had become conscious of anterior as well as ulterior forces and immensities and fathomless wells of wisdom and energy, and had enslaved a minute portion of them, that was all. But not here! Oh, no. Later!

The sad part of it, as he thought of it now, was that poor little Marie could not have understood a thing of all he was thinking, even if he had explained and explained, as he never attempted to do. Life was all a mystery to Marie—deep, dark, strange—as it was to him, only he was seeking and she was not. Sufficient to her to be near him, loving him in her simple, dumb way, not seeking to understand. Even then he had realized that and begun to condemn her for it in his mind, to feel that she was no real aid and could never be—just a mother-girl, a housewife, a social fixture, a cook, destined to be shoved back if ever he were really successful; and that was sad even then, however obviously true.

But to her, apparently, he was so much more than just a mere man—a god, really, a dream, a beau, a most wonderful person, dreaming strange dreams and thinking strange thoughts which would lead him heaven knows where; how high or how strange, though, she could never guess, nor even he then. And for that very reason—her blind, non-understanding adoration—she had bored him then, horribly at times. All that he could think of then, as he looked at her at times—after the first year or two or three, when the novelty of her physical beauty and charm had worn off and the children had come, and cares and worries due to his non-success were upon them—was that she was an honest, faithful, patient, adoring little drudge, but no more, and that was all she would ever be. Think of that! That was the way life was—the way it rewarded love! He had not begun to dislike her—no, that was not it—but it was because, as the philosopher had said, that in and through her and the babies he had given hostages to fortune, and that she was not exactly the type of woman who could further him as fast as he wished—that he had begun to weary of her. And that was practically the whole base of his objection to her,—not anything she did.

Yes, yes—it was that, *that,* that had begun to plague him as though he had consciously fastened a ball and chain on one foot and now never any more could walk quickly or well or be really free. Instead of being able to think on his inventions he was constantly being compelled to think on how he would make a living for her and them, or find ten more dollars, or get a new dress for Marie and shoes for the children! Or how increase his salary. That was the great and enduring problem all the time, and over and over here. Although healthy, vigorous and savagely ambitious, at that time, it was precisely because he was those things that he had rebelled so and had desired to be free. He was too strong and fretful as he could see now to endure so mean a life. It was that that had made him savage, curt, remote, indifferent so much of the time in these later days—here— And to her. And when she could not help it at all—poor little thing—did not know how to help it and had never asked him to marry her! Life had tinkled so in his ears then. It had called and called. And essentially, in his own eyes then, he was as much of a failure as a husband as he was at his work, and that was killing him. His mind had been too steadily depressed by his mistake in getting married, in having children so soon, as well as by his growing knowledge of what he might be fitted to do if only he had a chance to go off to a big technical school somewhere and work his way through alone and so get a new and better position somewhere else—to have a change of scene. For once, as he knew then, and with all his ideas, he was technically fitted for his work, with new light and experience in his mind, what wonders might he not accomplish! Sitting in this little room, or working or dreaming upstairs in the air, how often he had thought of all that!

But no; nothing happened for ever so long here. Days and weeks and months, and even years went by without perceptible change. Nature seemed to take a vicious delight in torturing him, then, in so far as his dreams were concerned, his hopes. Hard times came to America, blasting ones—a year and a half of panic really—in which every one hung on to his pathetic little place, and even he was afraid to relinquish the meagre one he had, let alone ask for more pay. At the same time his dreams, the passing of his youth, this unconscionable burden of a family, tortured him more and more. Marie did not seem to mind anything much, so long as she was with him. She suffered, of course, but more for him than for herself, for his unrest, and his dissatisfaction, which she feared. Would he ever leave her? Was he becoming unhappy with her? Her eyes so often asked what her lips feared to frame.

Once they had seventy dollars saved toward some inventive work of his. But then little Peter fell from the top of the washtub, where he had climbed for some reason, and broke his arm. Before it was healed and all the bills paid, the seventy was gone. Another time Marie's mother was dying, or so she thought, and she had to go back home and help her father and brother in their loneliness. Again, it was brother George who, broke, arrived from Philadelphia and lived with them a while because he had no place else to go. Also once he thought to better himself by leaving the International Electric, and joining the Winston Castro Generator Company. But when he had left the first, the manager of the second, to whom he had applied and by whom he had been engaged, was discharged ("let out," as he phrased it), and the succeeding man did not want him. So for three long months he had been without anything, and, like Job, finally, he had been ready to curse God and die.

And then—right here in these rooms it was—he had rebelled, spiritually, as he now recalled, and had said to himself that he could not stand this any longer, that he was ruining his life, and that however much it might torture Marie—ruin her even—he must leave and do something to better his state. Yes quite definitely, once and for all, then, he had wished that he had not married Marie, that they had never been so foolish as to have children, that Marie was not dependent on him any more, that he was free to go, be, do, all the things he felt that he could go do, be—no matter where, so long as he went and was free. Yes, he had wished that in a violent, rebellious, prayerful way, and then—

Of all the winters of his life, the one that followed that was the blackest and bleakest, that last one with Marie. It seemed to bring absolutely nothing to either him or her or the children save disaster. Twenty-five dollars was all he had ever been able to make, apparently, while he was with her. The children were growing and constantly requiring more; Marie needed many things, and was skimping along on God knows what. Once she had made herself some corset slips and other things out of his cast-off underwear—bad as that was! And then once, when he was crossing Chadds Bridge, just below here, and had paused to meditate and dream, a new hat—his very best, needless to say, for he had worn his old one until it was quite gone—had blown off into the water, a swift wind and some bundles he was compelled to carry home aiding, and had been swiftly carried out by the tide. So much had he been harried in those days by one thing and another that at first he had not even raged, although he was accustomed so to do. Instead then he had just shut his teeth and trudged on in the biting wind, in danger of taking cold and dying of something or other—as he had thought at the time—only then he had said to himself that he did not really mind now. What difference did it make to himself or anybody whether he died or not? Did anybody care really, God or anybody else, what became of him? Supposing he did it? What of it? Could it be any worse than this? To hell with life itself, and its Maker,—this brutal buffeting of winds and cold and harrying hungers and jealousies and fears and brutalities, arranged to drive and make miserable these crawling, beggarly creatures—men! Why, what had he ever had of God or any creative force so far? What had God ever done for him or his life, or his wife and children?

So he had defiantly raged.

And then life—or God, or what you will—had seemed to strike at last. It was as if some Jinnee of humane or inhuman power had said, "Very well, then, since you are so dissatisfied and unhappy, so unworthy of all this (perhaps) that I have given you, you shall have your will, your dreams. You have prayed to be free. Even so—this thing that you see here now shall pass away. You have sinned against love and faith in your thoughts. You shall be free! Look! Behold! You shall be! Your dreams shall come true!"

And then, at once, as if in answer to this command of the Jinnee, as though, for instance, it had waved its hand, the final storm began which blew everything quite away. Fate struck. It was as if black angels had entered and stationed themselves at his doors and windows, armed with the swords of destruction, of death. Harpies and furies beset his path and perched on his roof. One night—it was a month before Peter and Frank died, only three days before they contracted their final illness—he was crossing this same bridge below here and was speculating, as usual, as to his life and his future, when suddenly, in spite of the wind and cold and some dust flying from a coal barge below, his eye was attracted by two lights which seemed to come dancing down the hill from the direction of his apartment and passed out over the river. They rose to cross over the bridge in front of him and disappeared on the other side. They came so close they seemed almost to brush his face, and yet he could not quite accept them as real. There was something too eerie about them. From the moment he first laid eyes on them in the distance they seemed strange. They came so easily, gracefully, and went so. From the first moment he saw them there below Tegetmiller's paint shop, he wondered about them. What were they? What could they mean? They were so bluish clear, like faint, grey stars, so pale and watery. Suddenly it was as if something whispered to him, "Behold! These are the souls of your children. They are going—never to return! See! Your prayers are being answered!"

And then it was that, struck with a kind of horror and numb despair, he had hurried home, quite prepared to ask Marie if the two boys were dead or if anything had happened to them. But, finding them up and playing as usual he had tried to put away all thought of this fact as a delusion, to say nothing. But the lights haunted him. They would not stay out of his mind. Would his boys really die? Yet the first and the second day went without change. But on the third both boys took sick, and he knew his dread was well founded.

For on the instant, Marie was thrown into a deep, almost inexplicable, depression, from which there was no arousing her, although she attempted to conceal it from him by waiting on and worrying over them. They had to put the children in the one little bedroom (theirs), while they used an extension cot in the "parlor," previously occupied by the children. Young Dr. Newton, the one physician of repute in the neighborhood, was called in, and old Mrs. Wertzel, the German woman in front, who, being old and lonely and very fond of Marie, had volunteered her services. And so they had weathered along, God only knows how. Marie prepared the meals—or nearly all of them—as best she could. He had gone to work each day, half in a dream, wondering what the end was to be.

And then one night, as he and Marie were lying on the cot pretending to sleep, he felt her crying. And taking her in his arms he had tried to unwish all the dark things he had wished, only apparently then it was too late. Something told him it was. It was as though in some dark mansion somewhere—some supernal court or hall of light or darkness—his prayer had been registered and answered, a decision made, and that that decision could not now be unmade. No. Into this shabby little room where they lay and where she was crying had come a final black emissary, scaled, knightly, with immense arms and wings and a glittering sword, all black, and would not leave until all this should go before him. Perhaps he had been a little deranged in his mind at the time, but so it had seemed.

And then, just a few weeks after he had seen the lights and a few days after Marie had cried so, Peter had died—poor weak little thing that he was—and, three days later, Frank. Those terrible hours! For by then he was feeling so strange and sad and mystical about it all that he could neither eat nor sleep nor weep nor work nor think. He had gone about, as indeed had Marie, in a kind of stupor of misery and despair. True, as he now told himself—and then too, really,—he had not loved the children with all the devotion he should have or he would never have had the thoughts he had had—or so he had reasoned afterward. Yet then as now he suffered because of the love he should have given them, *and had not*—and now could not any more, save in memory. He recalled how both boys looked in those last sad days, their pinched little faces and small weak hands! Marie was crushed, and yet dearer for the time being than ever before. But the two children, once gone, had seemed the victims of his own dark thoughts as though his own angry, resentful wishes had slain them. And so, for the time, his mood changed. He wished, if he could, that he might undo it all, go on as before with Marie, have other children to replace these lost ones in her affection —but no. It was apparently not to be, not ever any more.

For, once they were gone, the cords which had held him and Marie together were weaker, not stronger—almost broken, really. For the charm which Marie had originally had for him had mostly been merged in the vivacity and vitality and interest of these two prattling curly-headed boys. Despite the financial burden, the irritation and drain they had been at times, they had also proved a binding chain, a touch of sweetness in the relationship, a hope for the future, a balance which had kept even this uneven scale. With them present he had felt that however black the situation it must endure because of them, their growing interests; with them gone, it was rather plain that some modification of their old state was possible—just how, for the moment, he scarcely dared think or wish. It might be that he could go away and study for awhile now. There was no need of his staying here. The neighborhood was too redolent now of the miseries they had endured. Alone somewhere else, perhaps, he could collect his thoughts, think out a new program. If he went away he might eventually succeed in doing better by Marie. She could return to her parents in Philadelphia for a little while and wait for him, working there at something as she had before until he was ready to send for her. The heavy load of debts could wait until he was better able to pay them. In the meantime, also, he could work and whatever he made over and above his absolute necessities might go to her— or to clearing off these debts.

So he had reasoned.

But it had not worked out so of course. No. In the broken mood in which Marie then was it was not so easy. Plainly, since he had run across her that April day in Philadelphia when he was wiring for the great dry goods store, her whole life had become identified with his, although his had not become merged with hers. No. She was, and would be, as he could so plainly see, then, nothing without him, whereas he—he— Well, it had long since been plain that he would be better off without her—materially, anyhow. But what would she do if he stayed away a long time—or never came back? What become? Had he thought of that then? Yes, he had. He had even thought that once away he might not feel like renewing this situation which had proved so disastrous. And Marie had seemed to sense that, too. She was so sad. True he had not thought of all these things in any bold outright fashion then. Rather they were as sly, evasive shadows skulking in the remote recesses of his brain, things which scarcely dared show their faces to the light, although later, once safely away—they had come forth boldly enough. Only at that time, and later—even now, he could not help feeling that however much Marie might have lacked originally, or then, the fault for their might was his,—that if he himself had not been so dull in the first instance all these black things would not have happened to him or to her. But could she go on without him? Would she? he had asked himself then. And answered that it would be better for him to leave and build himself up in a different world, and then return and help her later. So he fretted and reasoned.

But time had solved all that, too. In spite of the fact that he could not help picturing her back there alone with her parents in Philadelphia, their poor little cottage in Leigh Street in which she and her parents had lived—not a cottage either, but a minute little brick pigeon-hole in one of those long lines of red, treeless, smoky barracks flanking the great mills of what was known as the Reffington District, where her father worked—he had gone. He had asked himself what would she be doing there? What thinking, all alone without him—the babies dead? But he had gone.

He recalled so well the day he left her—she to go to Philadelphia, he to Boston, presumably—the tears, the depression, the unbelievable sadness in her soul and his. Did she suspect? Did she foreknow? She was so gentle, even then, so trustful, so sad. "You will come back to me, dearie, won't you, soon?" she had said, and so sadly. "We will be happy yet, won't we?" she had asked between sobs. And he had promised. Oh yes; he had done much promising in his life, before and since. That was one of the darkest things in his nature, his power of promising.

But had he kept that?

However much in after months and years he told himself that he wanted to, that he must, that it was only fair, decent, right, still he had not gone back. No. Other things had come up with the passing of the days, weeks, months, years, other forces, other interests. Some plan, person, desire had always intervened, interfered, warned, counseled,

delayed. Were there such counselors? There had been
times during the first year when he had written her and sent
her a little money—money he had needed badly enough
himself. Later there was that long period in which he felt
that she must be getting along well enough, being with her
parents and at work, and he had not written. A second
woman had already appeared on the scene by then as a
friend. And then—

The months and years since then in which he had not
done so! After his college course—which he took up after
he left Marie, working his way—he had left Boston and
gone to K—— to begin a career as an assistant plant manager and a developer of ideas of his own, selling the rights
to such things as he invented to the great company with
which he was connected. And then it was that by degrees
the idea of a complete independence and a much greater life
had occurred to him. He found himself so strong, so interesting to others. Why not be free, once and for all? Why
not grow greater? Why not go forward and work out all
the things about which he had dreamed? The thing from
which he had extricated himself was too confining, too
narrow. It would not do to return. The old shell could
not now contain him. Despite her tenderness, Marie was
not significant enough. So— He had already seen so
much that he could do, be, new faces, a new world, women
of a higher social level.

But even so, the pathetic little letters which still followed
from time to time—not addressed to him in his new world
(she did not know where he was), but to him in the old
one—saying how dearly she loved him, how she still awaited
his return, that she knew he was having a hard time, that
she prayed always, and that all would come out right yet,
that they would be able to be together yet!—she was working, saving, praying for him! True, he had the excuse that
for the first four years he had not really made anything
much, but still he might have done something for her,—
might he not have?—gone back, persuaded her to let him go,

made her comfortable, brought her somewhat nearer him
even? Instead he had feared, feared, reasoned, argued.

Yes, the then devil of his nature, his ambition, had held
him completely. He was seeing too clearly the wonder of
what he might be, and soon, what he was already becoming.
Everything as he argued then and saw now would have
had to be pushed aside for Marie, whereas what he really
desired was that his great career, his greater days, his
fame, the thing he was sure to be now—should push everything aside. And so— Perhaps he had become sharper,
colder, harder, than he had ever been, quite ready to sacrifice everything and everybody, or nearly, until he should be
the great success he meant to be. But long before this he
might have done so much. And he had not—had not until
very recently decided to revisit this older, sweeter world.

But in the meantime, as he had long since learned, how
the tragedy of her life had been completed. All at once
in those earlier years all letters had ceased, and time slipping
by—ten years really—he had begun to grow curious. Writing back to a neighbor of hers in Philadelphia in a disguised
hand and on nameless paper, he had learned that nearly two
years before her father had died and that she and her mother
and brother had moved away, the writer could not say
where. Then, five years later, when he was becoming truly
prosperous, he had learned, through a detective agency, that
she and her mother and her ne'er-do-well brother had moved
back into this very neighborhood—this old neighborhood of
his and hers!—or, rather, a little farther out near the grave-
yard where their two boys were buried. The simplicity of
her! The untutored homing instinct!

But once here, according to what he had learned recently,
she and her mother had not prospered at all. They had
occupied the most minute of apartments farther out, and
had finally been compelled to work in a laundry in their
efforts to get along—and he was already so well-to-do,
wealthy, really! Indeed three years before his detectives
had arrived, her mother had died, and two years after that,

she herself, of pneumonia, as had their children. Was it a message from her that had made him worry at that time? Was that why, only six months since, although married and rich and with two daughters by this later marriage, he had not been able to rest until he had found this out, returned here now to see? Did ghosts still stalk the world?

Yes, to-day he had come back here, but only to realize once and for all now how futile this errand was, how cruel he had been, how dreary her latter days must have been in this poor, out-of-the-way corner where once, for a while at least, she had been happy—he and she.

"Been happy!"

"By God," he suddenly exclaimed, a passion of self-reproach and memory overcoming him, "I can't stand this! It was not right, not fair. I should not have waited so long. I should have acted long, long since. The cruelty—the evil! There is something cruel and evil in it all, in all wealth, all ambition, in love of fame—too cruel. I must get out! I must think no more—see no more."

And hurrying to the door and down the squeaking stairs, he walked swiftly back to the costly car that was waiting for him a few blocks below the bridge—that car which was so representative of the realm of so-called power and success of which he was now the master—that realm which, for so long, had taken its meaningless lustre from all that had here preceded it—the misery, the loneliness, the shadow, the despair. And in it he was whirled swiftly and gloomily away.

IX

PHANTOM GOLD

YOU would have to have seen it to have gathered a true impression—the stubby roughness of the country, the rocks, the poverty of the soil, the poorness of the houses, barns, agricultural implements, horses and cattle and even human beings, in consequence—especially human beings, for why should they, any more than any other product of the soil, flourish where all else was so poor?

It was old Judge Blow who first discovered that "Jack," or zinc, was the real riches of Taney, if it could be said to have had any before "Jack" was discovered. Months before the boom began he had stood beside a smelter in far-off K—— one late winter afternoon and examined with a great deal of care the ore which the men were smelting, marveling at its resemblance to certain rocks or boulders known as "slug lumps" in his home county.

"What is this stuff?" he asked of one of the bare-armed men who came out from the blazing furnace after a time to wipe his dripping face.

"Zinc," returned the other, as he passed his huge, soiled palm over his forehead.

"We have stuff down in our county that looks like that," said the judge as he turned the dull-looking lump over and considered for a while. "I'm sure of it—any amount." Then he became suddenly silent, for a thought struck him.

"Well, if it's really 'Jack,'" said the workman, using the trade or mining name for it, "there's money in it, all right. This here comes from St. Francis."

The old judge thought of this for a little while and quietly turned away. He knew where St. Francis was. If this was so valuable that they could ship it all the way from southeast B——, why not from Taney? Had he not many holdings in Taney?

The result was that before long a marked if secret change began to manifest itself in Taney and regions adjacent thereto. Following the private manipulations and goings to and fro of the judge one or two shrewd prospectors appeared, and then after a time the whole land was rife with them. But before that came to pass many a farmer who had remained in ignorance of the value of his holdings was rifled of them.

Old Bursay Queeder, farmer and local ne'er-do-well in the agricultural line, had lived on his particular estate or farm for forty years, and at the time that Judge Blow was thus mysteriously proceeding to and fro and here and there upon the earth, did not know that the rocks against which his pair of extra large feet were being regularly and bitterly stubbed contained the very wealth of which he had been idly and rather wistfully dreaming all his life. Indeed, the earth was a very mysterious thing to Bursay, containing, as it did, everything he really did not know. This collection of seventy acres, for instance—which individually and collectively had wrung more sweat from his brow and more curses from his lips than anything else ever had—contained, unknown to him, the possibility of the fulfilment of all his dreams. But he was old now and a little queer in the head at times, having notions in regard to the Bible, when the world would come to an end, and the like, although still able to contend with nature, if not with man. Each day in the spring and summer and even fall seasons he could be seen on some portion or other of his barren acres, his stubby beard and sparse hair standing out roughly, his fingers like a bird's claws clutching his plough handles, turning the thin and meagre furrows of his fields and rattling the stony soil, which had long ceased to yield him even a modicum of profit. It was a bare living now which he expected, and a bare living which he received. The house, or cabin, which he occupied with his wife and son and daughter, was dilapidated beyond the use or even need of care. The fences were all decayed save for those which had been built of these same impediments of the soil which he had always considered a queer kind of stone, useless to man or beast—a "hendrance," as he would have said. His barn was a mere accumulation of patchboards, shielding an old wagon and some few scraps of machinery. And the alleged corn crib was so aged and lopsided that it was ready to fall. Weeds and desolation, bony horses and as bony children, stony fields and thin trees, and withal solitude and occasional want—such was the world of his care and his ruling.

Mrs. Queeder was a fitting mate for the life to which he was doomed. It had come to that pass with her that the monotony of deprivation was accepted with indifference. The absence or remoteness of even a single modest school, meeting house or town hall, to say nothing of convenient neighbors, had left her and hers all but isolated. She was irascible, cantankerous, peculiar; her voice was shrill and her appearance desolate. Queeder, whom she understood or misunderstood thoroughly, was a source of comfort in one way—she could "nag at him," as he said, and if they quarreled frequently it was in a fitting and harmonious way. Amid such a rattletrap of fields and fences bickering was to be expected.

"Why don't yuh take them thar slug lumps an' make a fence over thar?" she asked of Queeder for something like the thousandth time in ten years, referring to as many as thirty-five piles of the best and almost pure zinc lying along the edges of the nearest field, and piled there by Bursay,—this time because two bony cows had invaded one of their corn patches. The "slug lumps" to which she referred could not have been worth less than $2,000.

For as many as the thousandth time he had replied:

"Well, fer the land sakes, hain't I never got nuthin' else tuh do? Yuh'd think them thar blame-ding rocks wuz wuth more nor anythin' else. I do well enough ez 'tis to git 'em outen the sile, I say, 'thout tryin' tuh make fences outen 'em."

"So yuh say—yuh lazy, good-fer-nuthin' ole tobacco-chewin' ——," here a long list of expletives which was usually succeeded by a stove lid or poker or a fair-sized stick of wood, propelled by one party or the other, and which was as deftly dodged. Love and family affection, you see, due to unbroken and unbreakable propinquity, as it were.

But to proceed: The hot and rainy seasons had come and gone in monotonous succession during a period of years, and the lumps still lay in the field. Dode, the eldest child and only son—a huge, hulking, rugged and yet bony igno-ramus, who had not inherited an especially delicate or agreeable disposition from his harried parents—might have removed them had he not been a "consarned lazy houn'," his father said, or like his father, as his mother said, and Jane, the daughter, might have helped, but these two par-took of the same depressed indifference which characterized the father. And why not, pray? They had worked long, had had little, seen less and hoped for no particular outlet for their lives in the future, having sense enough to know that if fate had been more kind there might have been. Useless contention with an unyielding soil had done its best at hardening their spirits.

"I don't see no use ploughin' the south patch," Dode had now remarked for the third time this spring. "The blamed thing don't grow nuthin'."

"Ef yuh only half 'tended it instid o' settin' out thar under them thar junipers pickin' yer teeth an' meditatin', mebbe 'twould," squeaked Mrs. Queeder, always petulant or angry or waspish—a nature soured by long and hopeless and useless contention.

"No use shakin' up a lot uv rocks, ez I see," returned

Dode, wearily and aimlessly slapping at a fly. "The hull place ain't wuth a hill o' beans," and from one point of view he was right.

"Why don't yuh git off'n hit then?" suggested Queeder in a tantalizing voice, with no particular desire to defend the farm, merely with an idle wish to vary the monotony. "Ef hit's good enough tuh s'port yuh, hit's good enough to work on, I say."

"S'port!" sniffed the undutiful Dode, wearily, and yet humorously and scornfully. "I ain't seed much s'port, ez I kin remember. Mebbe ye're thinkin' uv all the fine schoolin' I've had, er the places I've been." He slapped at another fly.

Old Queeder felt the sneer, but as he saw it it was scarcely his fault. He had worked. At the same time he felt the futility of quarreling with Dode, who was younger and stronger and no longer, owing to many family quarrels, bearing him any filial respect. As a matter of fact it was the other way about. From having endured many cuffs and blows in his youth Dode was now much the more powerful physically, and in any contest could easily outdo his father; and Queeder, from at first having ruled and seen his word law, was now compelled to take second, even third and fourth, place, and by contention and all but useless snarling gain the very little consideration that he received.

But in spite of all this they lived together indifferently. And day after day—once Judge Blow had returned to Taney —time was bringing nearer and nearer the tide of mining and the amazing boom that went with it. Indeed every day, like a gathering storm cloud, it might have been noted by the sensitive as approaching closer and closer, only these unwitting holders were not sensitive. They had not the slightest inkling as yet of all that was to be. Here in this roadless, townless region how was one to know. Prospectors passed to the north and the south of them; but as yet none had ever come directly to this wonderful patch upon which Queeder and his family rested. It was in too out-of-the-way a place—a briary, woodsy, rocky corner.

Then one sunny June morning—

"Hi, thar!" called Cal Arnold, their next neighbor, who lived some three miles further on, who now halted his rickety wagon and bony horses along the road opposite the field in which Queeder was working. "Hyur the news?" He spoke briskly, shifting his cud of tobacco and eyeing Queeder with the chirpiness of one who brings diverting information.

"No; what?" asked Queeder, ceasing his "cultivating" with a worn one-share plough and coming over and leaning on his zinc fence, rubbing a hand through his sparse hair the while.

"Ol' Dunk Porter down here to Newton's sold his farm," replied Cal, shrewdly and jubilantly, as though he were relating the tale of a great battle or the suspected approach of the end of the world. "An' he got three thousan' dollars fer it." He rolled the sum deliciously under his tongue.

"Yuh don't say!" said Queeder quietly but with profound and amazed astonishment. "Three thousan'?" He stirred as one who hears of the impossible being accomplished and knows it can't be true. "Whut fer?"

"They 'low now ez how thar's min'l onto it," went on the farmer wisely. "They 'low ez how now this hyur hull kentry round hyur is thick an' spilin' with it. Hit's uvrywhar. They tell me ez how these hyur slug lumps"—and he flicked at one of the large piles of hitherto worthless zinc against which Queeder was leaning—"is this hyur min'l—er 'Jack,' ez they call hit—an' that hit's wuth two cents a pound when it's swelted" ("smelted," he meant) "an' even more. I see yuh got quite a bit uv hit. So've I. Thar's a lot layin' down around my place. I allus 'lowed ez how 'twant wuth much o' anythin,' but they say 'tis. I hyur from some o' the boys 'at's been to K—— that when hit's fixed up, swelted and like o' that, that hit's good fer lots of things."

He did not know what exactly, so he did not stop to explain. Instead he cocked a dreamful eye, screwed up his mouth preparatory to expectorating and looked at Queeder. The latter, unable to adjust his thoughts to this new situation, picked up a piece of the hitherto despised "slug" and looked at it. To think that through all these years of toil and suffering he should have believed it worthless and now all of a sudden it was worth two cents a pound when "swelted" and that neighbors were beginning to sell their farms for princely sums!—and his farm was covered with this stuff, this gold almost! Why, there were whole hummocks of it raising slaty-gray backs to the hot sun further on, a low wall in one place where it rose sheer out of the ground on this "prupetty," as he always referred to it. Think of that! Think of that! But although he thought much he said nothing, for in his starved and hungry brain was beginning to sprout and flourish a great and wondrous idea. He was to have money, wealth—ease, no less! Think of it! Not to toil and sweat in the summer sun any more, to loaf and dream at his ease, chew all the tobacco he wished, live in town, visit far-off, mysterious K——, see all there was to see!

"Well, I guess I'll be drivin' on," commented Arnold after a time, noting Queeder's marked abstraction. "I cal'-late tuh git over tuh Bruder's an' back by sundown. He's got a little hay I traded him a pig fer hyur a while back," and he flicked his two bony horses and was off up the rubbly, dusty road.

For a time Queeder was scarcely satisfied to believe his senses. Was it really true? Had Porter really sold his place? For days thereafter, although he drove to Arno—sixteen miles away—to discover the real truth, he held his own counsel, nursing a wonderful fancy. This property was his, not his wife's, nor his two children's. Years before he had worked and paid for it, a few lone dollars at a time, or their equivalent in corn, pigs, wheat, before he had married. Now—now—soon one of those strange creatures—a "prowspector," Arnold had called him—who went about with money would come along and buy up his property. Wonderful! Wonderful! What would he get for it?—surely five thousand dollars, considering that Porter had received three for forty acres, whereas he had seventy. Four thousand, anyhow—a little more than Dunk. He could not figure it very well, but it would be more than Dunk's, whatever it was—probably five thousand!

The one flaw in all this though—and it was a great flaw—was the thought of his savage and unkindly family—the recalcitrant Dode, the angular Jane and his sour better half, Emma—who would now probably have to share in all this marvelous prosperity, might even take it away from him and push him into that background where he had been for so long. They were so much more dogmatic, forceful than he. He was getting old, feeble even, from long years of toil. His wife had done little this long time but sneer and jeer at him, as he now chose most emphatically to remember; his savage son the same. Jane, the indifferent, who looked on him as a failure and a ne'er-do-well, had done nothing but suggest that he work harder. Love, family tenderness, family unity—if these had ever existed they had long since withered in the thin, unnourishing air of this rough, poverty-stricken world. What did he owe any of them? Nothing. And now they would want to share in all this, of course. Having lived so long with them, and under such disagreeable conditions, he now wondered how they would dare suggest as much, and still he knew they would. Fight him, nag him, that's all they had ever done. But now that wealth was at his door they would be running after him, fawning upon him—demanding it of him, perhaps! What should he do? How arrange for all of this?—for wealth was surely close to his hands. It must be. Like a small, half-intelligent rat he peeked and perked. His demeanor changed to such an extent that even his family noticed it and began to wonder, although (knowing nothing of all that had transpired as yet) they laid it to the increasing queerness of age.

"Have yuh noticed how Pap acts these hyur days?" Dode inquired of Jane and his mother one noontime after old Queeder had eaten and returned to the fields. "He's all the time standin' out thar at the fence lookin' aroun' ez if he wuz a-waitin' fer somebody er thinkin' about somepin. Mebbe he's gittin' a little queer, huh? Y' think so?"

Dode was most interested in anything which concerned his father—or, rather, his physical or mental future—for once he died this place would have to be divided or he be called upon to run it, and in that case he would be a fitting catch for any neighborhood farming maiden, and as such able to broach and carry through the long-cherished dream of matrimony, now attenuated and made all but impossible by the grinding necessities he was compelled to endure.

"Yes, I've been noticin' somepin," returned Mrs. Queeder. "He hain't the same ez he wuz a little while back. Some new notion he's got into his mind, I reckon, somepin he wants tuh do an' kain't, er somepin new in 'ligion, mebbe. Yuh kain't ever tell whut's botherin' him."

Jane " 'lowed" as much and the conversation ended. But still Queeder brooded, trying to solve the knotty problem, which depended, of course, on the open or secret sale of the land—secret, if possible, he now finally decided, seeing that his family had always been so unkind to him. They deserved nothing better. It was his—why not?

In due time appeared a prospector, mounted on horseback and dressed for rough travel, who, looking over the fields of this area and noting the value of these particular acres, the surface outcropping of a thick vein, became intensely interested. Queeder was not to be seen at the time, having gone to some remote portion of the farm, but Mrs. Queeder, wholly ignorant of the value of the land and therefore of the half-suppressed light in the stranger's eye, greeted him pleasantly enough.

"Would you let me have a drink of water?" inquired the stranger when she appeared at the door.

"Sartinly," she replied with a tone of great respect. Even comparatively well-dressed strangers were so rare here.

Old Queeder in a distant field observing him at the well, now started for the house.

"What is that stuff you make your fences out of?" asked the stranger agreeably, wondering if they knew.

"Well, now, I dunno," said Mrs. Queeder. "It's some kind o' stone, I reckon—slug lumps, we uns always call hit aroun' hyur."

The newcomer suppressed a desire to smile and stooped to pick up a piece of the zinc with which the ground was scattered. It was the same as he had seen some miles back, only purer and present in much greater quantities. Never had he seen more and better zinc near the surface. It was lying everywhere exposed, cultivation, frosts and rains having denuded it, whereas in the next county other men were digging for it. The sight of these dilapidated holdings, the miserable clothing, old Queeder toiling out in the hot fields, and all this land valueless for agriculture because of its wondrous mineral wealth, was almost too much for him.

"Do you own all this land about here?" he inquired.

"'Bout seventy acres," returned Mrs. Queeder.

"Do you know what it sells at an acre?"

"No. It ain't wuth much, though, I reckon. I ain't heerd o' none bein' sold aroun' hyur fer some time now."

The prospector involuntarily twitched at the words "not wuth much." What would some of his friends and rivals say if they knew of this particular spot? What if some one should tell these people? If he could buy it now for a song, as he well might! Already other prospectors were in the neighborhood. Had he not eaten at the same table at Arno with three whom he suspected as such? He must get this, and get it now.

"I guess I'll stroll over and talk to your husband a moment," he remarked and ambled off, the while Mrs. Queeder and Jane, the twain in loose blue gingham bags of dresses much blown by the wind, stood in the tumbledown doorway and looked after him.

"Funny, ain't he?" said the daughter. "Wonder whut he wants o' Paw?"

Old Queeder looked up quizzically from his ploughing, to which he had returned, as he saw the stranger approaching, and now surveyed him doubtfully as he offered a cheery "Good morning."

"Do you happen to know if there is any really good farming land around here for sale?" inquired the prospector after a few delaying comments about the weather.

"Air yuh wantin' it fer farmin'?" replied Queeder cynically and casting a searching look upon the newcomer, who saw at once by Queeder's eye that he knew more than his wife. "They're buyin' hit now mostly fer the min'l ez is onto it, ez I hyur." At the same time he perked like a bird to see how this thrust had been received.

The prospector smiled archly if wisely. "I see," he said. "You think it's good for mining, do you? What would you hold your land at as mineral land then if you had a chance to sell it?"

Queeder thought for a while. Two wood doves cooed mournfully in the distance and a blackbird squeaked rustily before he answered.

"I dunno ez I keer tuh sell yit." He had been getting notions of late as to what might be done if he were to retain his land, bid it up against the desires of one and another, only also the thought of how his wife and children might soon learn and insist on dividing the profits with him if he did sell it was haunting him. Those dreams of getting out in the world and seeing something, of getting away from his family and being happy in some weird, free way, were actually torturing him.

"Who owns the land just below here, then?" asked the

stranger, realizing that his idea of buying for little or nothing might as well be abandoned. But at this Queeder winced. For after all, the land adjoining had considerable mineral on it also, as he well knew.

"Why, let me see," he replied waspishly, with mingled feelings of opposition and indifference. "Marradew," he finally added, grudgingly. It was no doubt true that this stranger or some other could buy of other farmers if he refused to sell. Still, land around here anywhere must be worth something, his as much as any other. If Dunk Porter had received $3,000—

"If you don't want to sell, I suppose he might," the prospector continued pleasantly. The idea was expressed softly, meditatively, indifferently almost.

There was a silence, in which Queeder calmly leaned on his plough handles thinking. The possibility of losing this long-awaited opportunity was dreadful. But he was not floored yet, for all his hunger and greed. Arnold had said that the metal alone, these rocks, was worth two cents a pound, and he could not get it out of his mind that somehow the land itself, the space of soil aside from the metal, must be worth something. How could it be otherwise? Small crops of sorts grew on it.

"I dunno," he replied defiantly, if internally weakly. "Yuh might ast. I ain't heerd o' his wantin' to sell." He was determined to risk this last if he had to run after the stranger afterward and beg him to compromise, although he hoped not to have to do that, either. There were other prospectors.

"I don't know yet whether I want this," continued the prospector heavily and with an air of profound indifference, "but I'd like to have an option on it, if you'd like to sell. What'll you take for an option at sixty days on the entire seventy acres?"

The worn farmer did not in the least understand what was meant by the word option, but he was determined not to admit it. "Whut'll yuh give?" he asked finally, in great doubt as to what to say.

"Well, how about $200 down and $5,000 more at the end of sixty days if we come to terms at the end of that time?" He was offering the very lowest figure that he imagined Queeder would take, if any, for he had heard of other sales in this vicinity this very day.

Queeder, not knowing what an option was, knew not what to say. Five thousand was what he had originally supposed he might be offered, but sixty days! What did he mean by that? Why not at once if he wanted the place—cash—as Dunk Porter, according to Arnold, had received? He eyed the stranger feverishly, fidgeted with his plough handles, and finally observed almost aimlessly: "I 'low ez I could git seven thousan' any day ef I wanted to wait. The feller hyur b'low me a ways got three thousan', an' he's got thirty acres less'n I got. Thar's been a feller aroun' hyur offerin' me six thousan'."

"Well, I might give you $6,000, providing I found the ground all right," he said.

"Cash down?" asked Queeder amazedly, kicking at a clod.

"Within sixty days," answered the prospector.

"Oh!" said Queeder, gloomily. "I thort yuh wanted tuh buy t'day."

"Oh, no," said the other. "I said an option. If we come to terms I'll be back here with the money within sixty days or before, and we'll close the thing up—six thousand in cash, minus the option money. Of course I don't bind myself absolutely to buy—just get the privilege of buying at any time within sixty days, and if I don't come back within that time the money I turn over to you to-day is yours, see, and you're free to sell the land to some one else."

"Huh!" grunted Queeder. He had dreamed of getting the money at once and making off all by himself, but here was this talk of sixty days, which might mean something or nothing.

"Well," said the prospector, noting Queeder's dissatisfaction and deciding that he must do something to make the deal seem more attractive, "suppose we say seven thousand, then, and I put down $500 cash into your hands now? How's that? Seven thousand in sixty days and five hundred in cash right now. What do you say?"

He reached in his pocket and extracted a wallet thick with bills, which excited Queeder greatly. Never had so much ready money, which he might quickly count as his if he chose, been so near him. After all, $500 in cash was an amazing amount in itself. With that alone what could he not do? And then the remainder of the seven thousand within sixty days! Only, there were his wife and two children to consider. If he was to carry out his dream of decamping there must be great secrecy. If they learned of this—his possession of even so much as five hundred in cash—what might not happen? Would not Dode or his wife or Jane, or all three, take it away from him—steal it while he was asleep? It might well be so. He was so silent and puzzled that the stranger felt that he was going to reject his offer.

"I'll tell you what I'll do," he said, as though he were making a grand concession. "I'll make it eight thousand and put up eight hundred. How's that? If we can't arrange it on that basis we'll have to drop the matter, for I can't offer to pay any more," and at that he returned the wallet to his pocket.

But Queeder still gazed, made all but dumb by his good fortune and the difficulties it presented. Eight thousand! Eight hundred in cash down! He could scarcely understand.

"T'day?" he asked.

"Yes, to-day—only you'll have to come with me to Arno. I want to look into your title. Maybe you have a deed, though—have you?"

Queeder nodded.

"Well, if it's all right I'll pay you the money at once. I have a form of agreement here and we can get some one to witness it, I suppose. Only we'll have to get your wife to sign, too."

Queeder's face fell. Here was the rub—his wife and two children! "She's gotta sign, hez she?" he inquired grimly, sadly even. He was beside himself with despair, disgust. To work and slave so all these years! Then, when a chance came, to have it all come to nothing, or nearly so!

"Yes," said the prospector, who saw by his manner and tone that his wife's knowledge of it was not desired. "We'll have to get her signature, too. I'm sorry if it annoys you, but the law compels it. Perhaps you could arrange all that between you in some way. Why not go over and talk to her about it?"

Queeder hesitated. How he hated it—this sharing with his wife and son! He didn't mind Jane so much. But now if they heard of it they would quarrel with him and want the larger share. He would have to fight—stand by his "rights." And once he had the money—if he ever got it— he would have to watch it, hide it, to keep it away from them.

"What's the matter?" asked the prospector, noting his perturbation. "Does she object to your selling?"

"'Tain't that. She'll sell, well enough, once she hyurs. I didn't 'low ez I'd let 'er know at fust. She'll be wantin' the most uv it—her an' Dode—an' hit ain't ther'n, hit's mine. I wuz on hyur fust. I owned this hyur place fust, 'fore ever I saw 'er. She don't do nuthin' but fuss an' fight, ez 'tis."

"Supposing we go over to the house and talk to her. She may not be unreasonable. She's only entitled to a third, you know, if you don't want to give her more than that. That's the law. That would leave you nearly five thousand. In fact, if you want it, I'll see that you get five thousand whatever she gets." He had somehow gathered the impression that five thousand, for himself, meant a great deal to Queeder.

And true enough, at that the old farmer brightened a

little. For five thousand? Was not that really more than he had expected to get for the place as a whole but an hour before! And supposing his wife did get three thousand? What of it? Was not his own dream coming true? He agreed at once and decided to accompany the prospector to the house. But on the way the farmer paused and gazed about him. He was as one who scarcely knew what he was doing. All this money—this new order of things—if it went through! He felt strange, different, confused. The mental ills of his many years plus this great fortune with its complications and possibilities were almost too much for him. The stranger noted a queer metallic and vacant light in the old farmer's eyes as he now turned slowly about from west to east, staring.

"What's the matter?" he asked, a suspicion of insanity coming to him.

The old man seemed suddenly to come to. " 'Tain't nuthin'," he said. "I wuz just thinkin'."

The prospector meditated on the validity of a contract made with a lunatic, but the land was too valuable to bother about trifles. Once a contract was made, even with a half-wit, the legal difficulties which could be made over any attempt to break the agreement would be very great.

In the old cabin Jane and her mother wondered at the meaning of the approaching couple, but old Queeder shooed off the former as he would have a chicken. Once inside the single room, which served as parlor, sitting-room, bedroom and all else convenient, Queeder nervously closed the door leading into the kitchen, where Jane had retired.

"Go on away, now," he mumbled, as he saw her there hanging about. "We want a word with yer Maw, I tell yuh."

Lank Jane retired, but later clapped a misshapen ear to the door until she was driven away by her suspicious father. Then the farmer began to explain to his wife what it was all about.

"This hyur stranger—I don't know your name yit—"

"Crawford! Crawford!" put in the prospector.

"Crawford—Mr. Crawford—is hyur tuh buy the place ef he kin. I thought, seein' ez how yuh've got a little int'est in it—third"—he was careful to add—"we'd better come an' talk tuh yuh."

"Int'est!" snapped Mrs. Queeder, sharply and suspiciously, no thought of the presence of the stranger troubling her in her expression of her opinion, "I should think I had —workin' an' slavin' on it fer twenty-four year! Well, whut wuz yuh thinkin' uv payin' fer the place?" she asked of the stranger sharply.

A nervous sign from Queeder, whose acquisitiveness was so intense that it was almost audible, indicated that he was not to say.

"Well, now what do you think it would be worth?"

"Dunno ez I kin say exackly," replied the wife slyly and greedily, imagining that Queeder, because of his age and various mental deficiencies was perhaps leaving these negotiations to her. "Thar's ben furms aroun' hyur ez big's this sold fer nigh onto two thousan' dollars." She was quoting the topmost figure of which she had ever heard.

"Well, that's pretty steep, isn't it?" asked Crawford solemnly but refusing to look at Queeder. "Ordinarily land around here is not worth much more than twenty dollars an acre and you have only seventy, as I understand."

"Yes, but this hyur land ain't so pore ez some, nuther," rejoined Mrs. Queeder, forgetting her original comment on it and making the best argument she could for it. "Thar's a spring on this hyur one, just b'low the house hyur."

"Yes," said Crawford, "I saw it as I came in. It has some value. So you think two thousand is what it's worth, do you?" He looked at Queeder wisely, as much as to say, "This is a good joke, Queeder."

Mrs. Queeder, fairly satisfied that hers was to be the dominant mind in this argument, now turned to her husband for counsel. "What do yuh think, Bursay?" she asked.

Queeder, shaken by his duplicity, his fear of discovery, his greed and troublesome dreams, gazed at her nervously. "I sartinly think hit's wuth that much anyhow."

Crawford now began to explain that he only wanted an option on it at present, an agreement to sell within a given time, and if this were given, a paper signed, he would pay a few dollars to bind the bargain—and at this he looked wisely at Queeder and half closed one eye, by which the latter understood that he was to receive the sum originally agreed upon.

"If you say so we'll close this right now," he said ingratiatingly, taking from his pockets a form of agreement and opening it. "I'll just fill this in and you two can sign it." He went to the worn poplar table and spread out his paper, the while Queeder and his wife eyed the proceeding with intense interest. Neither could read or write but the farmer, not knowing how he was to get his eight hundred, could only trust to the ingenuity of the prospector to solve the problem. Besides, both were hypnotized by the idea of selling this worthless old land so quickly and for so much, coming into possession of actual money, and moved and thought like people in a dream. Mrs. Queeder's eyelids had narrowed to thin, greedy lines.

"How much did yuh cal'late yuh'd give tuh bind this hyur?" she inquired tensely and with a feverish gleam in her eye.

"Oh," said the stranger, who was once more looking at Queeder with an explanatory light in his eye, "about a hundred dollars, I should say. Wouldn't that be enough?"

A hundred dollars! Even that sum in this lean world was a fortune. To Mrs. Queeder, who knew nothing of the value of the mineral on the farm, it was unbelievable, an unexplainable windfall, an augury of better things. And besides, the two thousand to come later! But now came the question of a witness and how the paper was to be signed. The prospector, having filled in (in pencil) a sample acknowledgment of the amount paid—$100—and then having said, "Now you sign here, Mr. Queeder," the latter replied, "But I kain't write an' nuther kin my wife."

"Thar wuzn't much chance fer schoolin' around' hyur when I wuz young," simpered his better half.

"Well then, we'll just have to let you make your marks, and get some one to witness them. Can your son or daughter write?"

Here was a new situation and one most unpleasant to both, for Dode, once called, would wish to rule, being so headstrong and contrary. He could write his name anyhow, read a little bit also—but did they want him to know yet? Husband and wife looked at each dubiously and with suspicion. What now? The difficulty was solved by the rumble of a wagon on the nearby road.

"Maybe that is some one who could witness for you?" suggested Crawford.

Queeder looked out. "Yes, I b'lieve he kin write," he commented. "Hi, thar, Lester!" he called. "Come in hyur a minute! We wantcha fer somepin.'"

The rumbling ceased and in due time one Lester Botts, a farmer, not so much better in appearance than Queeder, arrived at the door. The prospector explained what was wanted and the agreement was eventually completed, only Botts, not knowing of the mineral which Queeder's acres represented, was anxious to tell the prospector of better land than this, from an agricultural view, which could be had for less money, but he did not know how to go about it. Before she would sign, Mrs. Queeder made it perfectly clear where she stood in the matter.

"I git my sheer uv this hyur money now, don't I," she demanded, "paid tuh me right hyur?"

Crawford, uncertain as to Queeder's wishes in this, looked at him; and he, knowing his wife's temper and being moved by greed, exclaimed, "Yuh don't git nuthin' 'ceptin I die. Yuh ain't entitled tuh no sheer unless'n we're separatin', which we hain't."

"Then I don't sign nuthin'," said Mrs. Queeder truculently.

"Of course I don't want to interfere," commented the prospector, soothingly, "but I should think you'd rather give her her share of this—thirty-three dollars," he eyed Queeder persuasively—"and then possibly a third of the two thousand —that's only six hundred and sixty—rather than stop the sale now, wouldn't you? You'll have to agree to do something like that. It's a good bargain. There ought to be plenty for everybody."

The farmer hearkened to the subtlety of this. After all, six hundred and sixty out of eight thousand was not so much. Rather than risk delay and discovery he pretended to soften, and finally consented. The marks were made and their validity attested by Botts, the one hundred in cash being counted out in two piles, according to Mrs. Queeder's wish, and the agreement pocketed. Then the prospector accompanied by Mr. Botts, was off—only Queeder, following and delaying him, was finally handed over in secret the difference between the hundred and the sum originally agreed upon. When he saw all the money the old farmer's eyes wiggled as if magnetically operated. Trembling with the agony of greed he waited, and then his hard and knotted fingers closed upon the bills like the claws of a gripping hawk.

"Thank yuh," he said aloud. "Thank yuh," and he jerked doorward in distress. "See me alone fust when yuh come ag'in. We gotta be mighty keerful er she'll find out, an' ef she does she'll not sign nuthin', an' raise ol' Harry, too."

"Oh, that's all right," replied the prospector archly. He was thinking how easy it would be, in view of all the dishonesty and chicanery already practised, to insist that the two thousand written in in pencil was the actual sale price and efface old Queeder by threatening to expose his duplicity. However, there were sixty days yet in which to consider this. "In sixty days, maybe less, I'll show up." And he slipped gracefully away, leaving the old earth-scraper to brood alone.

But all was not ended with the payment of this sum, as any one might have foretold. For Dode and Jane, hearing after a little while from their mother of the profitable sale of the land, were intensely moved. Money—any money, however small in amount—conjured up visions of pleasure and ease, and who was to get it, after all the toil here on the part of all? Where was their share in all this? They had worked, too. They demanded it in repeated ways, but to no avail. Their mother and father were obdurate, insisting that they wait until the sale was completed before any further consideration was given the matter.

While they were thus arguing, however, quarreling over even so small a sum as $100, as they thought, a new complication was added by Dode learning, as he soon did, that this was all mineral land, that farms were being sold in Adair— the next township—and even here; that it was rumored that Queeder had already sold his land for $5,000, and that if he had he had been beaten, for the land was worth much more —$200 an acre even, or $14,000. At once he suspected his father and mother of some treachery in connection with the sale—that there had been no option given, but a genuine sale made, and that Queeder or his mother, or both, were concealing a vast sum from himself and Jane. An atmosphere of intense suspicion and evil will was at once introduced.

"They've sold the furm fer $5,000 'stid uv $2,000; that's whut they've gone an' done," insisted Dode one day to Jane in the presence of his father and mother. "Ev'rybody aroun' hyur knows now what this hyur land's wuth, an' that's whut they got, yuh kin bet."

"Yuh lie!" shrieked Queeder shrilly, who was at once struck by the fact that if what Dode said was true he had walked into a financial as well as a moral trap from which he could not well extricate himself. "I hain't sold nuthin'," he went on angrily. "Lester Botts wuz hyur an' seed whut we done. He signed onto it."

"Ef the land's wuth more'n $2,000, that feller 'twuz hyur

didn' agree tuh pay no more'n that fer it in hyur," put in Mrs. Queeder explantorily, although, so little did she trust her husband, she was now beginning to wonder if there might not have been some secret agreement between him and this stranger. "Ef he had any different talk with yer Paw," and here she eyed old Queeder suspiciously, beginning to recall the prospector's smooth airs and ways, "he didn' say nuthin' 'bout it tuh me. I do rec'leck yer Paw'n him talkin' over by the fence yander near an hour afore they come in hyur. I wondered then whut it wuz about." She was beginning to worry as to how she was to get more seeing that the price agreed upon was now, apparently, inconsequential.

And as for Dode, he now eyed his father cynically and sus-piciously. "I cal'late he got somepin more fer it than he's tellin' us about," he insisted. "They ain't sellin' land down to Arno right now fer no $200 an acre an' him not knowin' it—an' land not ez good ez this, nuther. Ye're hidin' the money whut yuh got fer it, that's whut!"

Mrs. Queeder, while greatly disturbed as to the possibility of duplicity on her husband's part in connection with all this, still considered it policy to call Heaven to witness that in her case at least no duplicity was involved. If more had been offered or paid she knew nothing of it. For his part Queeder boiled with fear, rage, general opposition to all of them and their share in this.

"Yuh consarned varmint!" he squealed, addressing Dode and leaping to his feet and running for a stick of stovewood, "I'll show yuh whuther we air er not! Yuh 'low I steal, do yuh?"

Dode intercepted him, however, and being the stronger, pushed him off. It was always so easy so to do—much to Queeder's rage. He despised his son for his triumphant strength alone, to say nothing of his dour cynicism in regard to himself. The argument was ended by the father being put out of the house and the mother pleading volubly that in so far as she knew it was all as she said, that in signing the secret agreement with her husband she had meant no harm to her children, but only to protect them and herself.

But now, brooding over the possibility of Queeder's deception, she began to lay plans for his discomfiture in any way that she might—she and Dode and Jane. Queeder himself raged secretly between fear and hatred of Dode and what might follow because of his present knowledge. How was he to prevent Dode from being present at the final transaction, and if so how would the secret difference be handed him? Besides, if he took the sum mentioned, how did he know that he was not now being overreached? Every day nearly brought new rumors of new sales at better prices than he had been able to fix. In addition, each day Mrs. Queeder cackled like an irritable hen over the possible duplicity of her husband, although that creature in his secretive greed and queerness was not to be encompassed. He fought shy of the house the greater part of each day, jerked like a rat at every sound or passing stranger and denied himself words to speak or explain, or passed the lie if they pressed him too warmly. The seven hundred extra he had received was wrapped in paper and hidden in a crevice back of a post in the barn, a tin can serving as an outer protection for his newly acquired wealth. More than once during the day he returned to that spot, listened and peeked before he ventured to see whether it was still safe.

Indeed, there was something deadly in the household order from now on, little short of madness in fact, for now mother and children schemed for his downfall while all night long old Queeder wakened, jerking in the blackness and listening for any sounds which might be about the barn. On more than one occasion he changed the hiding place, even going so far as to keep the money on his person for a time. Once he found an old rusty butcher knife and, putting that in his shirt bosom, he slept with it and dreamed of trouble.

Into the heart of this walked another prospector one morning rejoicing, like the first one, at his find. Like all good business men he was concerned to see the owner only and demanded that Queeder be called.

"Oh, Paw!" called Jane from the rickety doorway. "Thar's some one hyur wants tuh see yuh!"

Old Queeder looked warily up from his hot field, where he had been waiting these many days, and beheld the stranger. He dropped his weed fighting and came forward. Dode drifted in from somewhere.

"Pretty dry weather we're having, isn't it?" remarked the stranger pleasantly meeting him halfway in his approach.

"Yes," he replied vacantly, for he was very, very much worn these days, mentally and physically. "It's tol'able dry! Tol-able dry!" He wiped his leathery brow with his hand.

"You don't know of any one about here, do you, who has any land for sale?"

"Ye're another one uv them min'l prowspecters, I projeck, eh?" inquired Queeder, now quite openly. There was no need to attempt to conceal that fact any longer.

The newcomer was taken aback, for he had not expected so much awareness in this region so soon. "I am," he said frankly.

"I thought so," said Queeder.

"Have you ever thought of selling the land here?" he inquired.

"Well, I dunno," began the farmer shrewdly. "Thar've been fellers like yuh aroun' hyar afore now lookin' at the place. Whut do yuh cal-late it might be wuth tuh yuh?" He eyed him sharply the while they strolled still further away from the spot where Dode, Jane and the mother formed an audience in the doorway.

The prospector ambled about the place examining the surface lumps, so very plentiful everywhere.

"This looks like fairly good land to me," he said quietly after a time. "You haven't an idea how much you'd want an acre for it, have you?"

"Well, I hyur they're gettin' ez much ez three hundred down to Arno," replied Queeder, exaggerating fiercely. Now that a second purchaser had appeared he was eager to learn how much more, if any, than the original offer would be made.

"Yes—well, that's a little steep, don't you think, considering the distance the metal would have to be hauled to the railroad? It'll cost considerable to get it over there."

"Not enough, I 'low, tuh make it wuth much less'n three hundred, would it?" observed Queeder, sagely.

"Well, I don't know about that. Would you take two hundred an acre for as much as forty acres of it?"

Old Queeder pricked his ears at the sound of bargain. As near as he could figure, two hundred an acre for forty acres would bring him as much as he was now to get for the entire seventy, and he would still have thirty to dispose of. The definiteness of the proposition thrilled him, boded something large for his future—eight thousand for forty, and all he could wring from the first comer had been eight thousand for seventy!

"Huh!" he said, hanging on the argument with ease and leisure. "I got an offer uv a option on the hull uv it fer twelve thousan' now."

"What!" said the stranger, surveying him critically. "Have you signed any papers in the matter?"

Queeder looked at him for the moment as if he suspected treachery, and then seeing the gathered family surveying them from the distant doorway he made the newcomer a cabalistic sign.

"Come over hyur," he said, leading off to a distant fence. At the safe distance they halted. "I tell yuh just how 'tis," he observed very secretively. "Thar wuz a feller come along hyur three er four weeks ago an' at that time I didn't know ez how this hyur now wuz min'l, see? An' he ast me, 'thout sayin' nuthin' ez tuh whut he knowed, whut I'd take for it, acre fer acre. Well, thar wuz anuther feller, a neighbor o' mine, had been along hyur an' he wuz sayin' ez how a piece o' land just below, about forty acres, wuz sold fer five thousan' dollars. Seein' ez how my land wuz the same kind o' land, only better, I 'lowed ez how thar bein' seventy acres

hyur tuh his forty I oughta git nearly twicet ez much, an'
I said so. He didn't 'low ez I ought at fust, but later on he
kind o' come roun' an' we agreed ez how I bein' the one that
fust had the place—I wuz farmin' hyur 'fore ever I married
my wife—that ef any sale wuz made I orter git the biggest
sheer. So we kind o' fixed it up b'tween us, quiet-like an'
not lettin' anybody else know, that when it come tuh makin'
out the papers an' sich at the end uv the sixty days he was to
gimme a shade the best o' the money afore we signed any
papers. Course I wouldn't do nuthin' like that ef the place
hadn't b'longed tuh me in the fust place, an' ef me an' my
wife an' chil'n got along ez well's we did at fust, but she's
allers a-fightin' an' squallin'. Ef he come back hyur, ez he
'lowed he would, I wuz t' have eight thousan' fer myself,
an' me an' my wife wuzta divide the rest b'tween us ez best
we could, her to have her third, ez the law is."

The stranger listened with mingled astonishment, amusement and satisfaction at the thought that the contract, if
not exactly illegal, could at least to Queeder be made to appear so. For an appeal to the wife must break it, and besides
because of the old man's cupidity he might easily be made to
annul the original agreement. For plainly even now this
farmer did not know the full value of all that he had so
foolishly bartered away. About him were fields literally
solid with zinc under the surface. Commercially $60,000
would be a mere bagatelle to give for it, when the East was
considered. One million dollars would be a ridiculously low
capitalization for a mine based on this property. A hundred
thousand might well be his share for his part in the transaction. Good heavens, the other fellow had bought a fortune
for a song! It was only fair to try to get it away from him.

"I'll tell you how this is, Mr. Queeder," he said after a
time. "It looks to me as though this fellow, whoever he is,
has given you a little the worst end of this bargain. Your
land is worth much more than that, that's plain enough. But
you can get out of that easily enough on the ground that you
really didn't know what you were selling at the time you

made this bargain. That's the law, I believe. You don't have to stick by an agreement if it's made when you don't understand what you're doing. As a matter of fact, I think I could get you out of it if you wanted me to. All you would have to do would be to refuse to sign any other papers when the time comes and return the money that's been paid you. Then when the time came I would be glad to take over your whole farm at three hundred dollars an acre and pay cash down. That would make you a rich man. I'd give you three thousand cash in hand the day you signed an agreement to sell. The trouble is you were just taken in. You and your wife really didn't know what you were doing."

"That's right," squeaked Queeder, "we wuz. We didn't 'low ez they wuz any min'l on this when we signed that air contrack."

Three hundred dollars an acre, as he dumbly figured it out, meant $21,000—twenty-one instead of a wretched eight thousand! For the moment he stood there quite lost as to what to do, say, think, a wavering, element-worn figure. His bent and shriveled body, raked and gutted by misfortune, fairly quivered with the knowledge that riches were really his for the asking, yet also that now, owing to his early error and ignorance in regard to all this, he might not be able to arrange for their reception. His seared and tangled brain, half twisted by solitude, balanced unevenly with the weight of this marvelous possibility. It crossed the wires of his mind and made him see strabismically.

The prospector, uncertain as to what his silence indicated, added: "I might even do a little better than that, Mr. Queeder—say, twenty-five thousand. You could have a house in the city for that. Your wife could wear silk dresses; you yourself need never do another stroke of work; your son and daughter could go to college if they wanted to. All you have to do is to refuse to sign that deed when he comes back—hand him the money or get his address and let me send it to him."

"He swindled me, so he did!" Queeder almost shouted now, great beads of sweat standing out upon his brow. "He tried tuh rob me! He shan't have an acre, by God—not an acre!"

"That's right," said the newcomer, and before he left he again insinuated into the farmer's mind the tremendous and unfair disproportion between twelve (as he understood Queeder was receiving) and twenty-five thousand. He pictured the difference in terms of city or town opportunities, the ease of his future life.

Unfortunately, the farmer possessed no avenue by which to escape from his recent duplicity. Having deceived his wife and children over so comparatively small a sum as eight thousand, this immensely greater sum offered many more difficulties—bickering, quarreling, open fighting, perhaps, so fierce were Dode and his wife in their moods, before it could be attained. And was he equal to it? At the same time, although he had never had anything, he was now feeling as though he had lost a great deal, as if some one were endeavoring to take something immense away from him, something which he had always had!

During the days that followed he brooded over this, avoiding his family as much as possible, while they, wondering when the first prospector would return and what conversation or arrangement Queeder had had with the second, watched him closely. At last he was all but unbalanced mentally, and by degrees his mind came to possess but one idea, and that was that his wife, his children, the world, all were trying to rob him, and that his one escape lay in flight with his treasure if only he could once gain possession of it. But how? How? One thing was sure. They should not have it. He would fight first; he would die. And alone in his silent field, with ragged body and mind, he brooded over riches and felt as if he already had them to defend.

In the meanwhile the first prospector had been meditating as to the ease, under the circumstances, with which Queeder's land could be taken from him at the very nominal price of two thousand, considering the secrecy which, according to Queeder's own wish, must attach to the transfer of all moneys over that sum. Once the deed was signed—the same reading for two thousand—in the presence of the wife and a lawyer who should accompany him, how easy to walk off and pay no more, standing calmly on the letter of the contract!

It was nearing that last day now and the terrible suspense was telling. Queeder was in no mental state to endure anything. His hollow eyes showed the wondering out of which nothing had come. His nervous strolling here and there had lost all semblance of reason. Then on the last of the sixty allotted days there rode forward the now bane of his existence, the original prospector, accompanied by Attorney Giles, of Arno, a veritable scamp and rascal of a lawyer.

At first on seeing them Queeder felt a strong impulse to run away, but on second consideration he feared so to do. The land was his. If he did not stay Dode and Mrs. Queeder might enter on some arrangement without his consent—something which would leave him landless, moneyless—or they might find out something about the extra money he had taken and contracted for, the better price he was now privately to receive. It was essential that he stay, and yet he had no least idea as to how he would solve it all.

Jane, who was in the doorway as they entered the yard, was the one to welcome them, although Dode, watchful and working in a nearby patch, saluted them next. Then Mrs. Queeder examined them cynically and with much opposition. These, then, were the twain who were expecting to misuse her financially!

"Where's your father, Dode?" asked Attorney Giles familiarly, for he knew them well.

"Over thar in the second 'tater patch," answered Dode sourly. A moment later he added with rough calculation, "Ef ye're comin' about the land, though, I 'low ez 'twon't do yuh no good. Maw an' Paw have decided not tuh sell. The place is wuth a heap more'n whut you all're offerin'. They're sellin' land roun' Arno with not near ez much min'l onto hit ez this hez for three hundred now, an' yuh all only wanta give two thousan' fer the hull place, I hyur. Maw'n Paw'd be fools ef they'd agree tuh that."

"Oh, come now," exclaimed Giles placatively and yet irritably—a very wasp who was always attempting to smooth over the ruffled tempers of people on just such trying occasions as this. "Mr. Crawford here has an option on this property signed by your mother and father and witnessed by a Mr."—he considered the slip—"a Mr. Botts—oh, yes, Lester Botts. You cannot legally escape that. All Mr. Crawford has to do is to offer you the money—leave it here, in fact—and the property is his. That is the law. An option is an option, and this one has a witness. I don't see how you can hope to escape it, really."

"They wuzn't nuthin' said about no min'l when I signed that air," insisted Mrs. Queeder, "an' I don't 'low ez no paper whut I didn't know the meanin' uv is goin' tuh be good anywhar. Leastways, I won't put my name onto nuthin' else."

"Well, well!" said Mr. Giles fussily, "We'd better get Mr. Queeder in here and see what he says to this. I'm sure he'll not take any such unreasonable and illegal view."

In the meantime old Queeder, called for lustily by Jane, came edging around the house corner like some hunted animal—dark, fearful, suspicious—and at sight of him the prospector and lawyer, who had seated themselves, arose.

"Well, here we are, Mr. Queeder," said the prospector, but stopped, astonished at the weird manner in which Queeder passed an aimless hand over his brow and gazed almost dully before him. He had more the appearance of a hungry bird than a human being. He was yellow, emaciated, all but wild.

"Look at Paw!" whispered Jane to Dode, used as she was to all the old man's idiosyncrasies.

"Yes, Mr. Queeder," began the lawyer, undisturbed by the whisper of Jane and anxious to smooth over a very troublesome situation, "here we are. We have come to settle this sale with you according to the terms of the option. I suppose you're ready?"

"Whut?" asked old Queeder aimlessly, then, recovering himself slightly, began, "I hain't goin' tuh sign nuthin'! Nuthin' 'tall! That's whut I hain't! Nuthin'!" He opened and closed his fingers and twisted and craned his neck as thought physically there were something very much awry with him.

"What's that?" queried the lawyer incisively, attempting by his tone to overawe him or bring him to his senses, "not sign? What do you mean by saying you won't sign? You gave an option here for the sum of $100 cash in hand, signed by you and your wife and witnessed by Lester Botts, and now you say you won't sign! I don't want to be harsh, but there's a definite contract entered into here and money passed, and such things can't be handled in any such light way, Mr. Queeder. This is a contract, a very serious matter before the law, Mr. Queeder, a very serious matter. The law provides a very definite remedy in a case of this kind. Whether you want to sign or not, with this option we have here and what it calls for we can pay over the money before witnesses and enter suit for possession and win it."

"Not when a feller's never knowed whut he wuz doin' when he signed," insisted Dode, who by now, because of his self-interest and the appearance of his father having been misled, was coming round to a more sympathetic or at least friendly attitude.

"I'll not sign nuthin'," insisted Queeder grimly. "I hain't a-goin' tuh be swindled out o' my prupetty. I never knowed they wuz min'l onto hit, like they is—leastways not whut it wuz wuth—an' I won't sign, an' yuh ain't a-goin' tuh make me. Ye're a-tryin' tuh get it away from me fur nuthin', that's whut ye're a-tryin' tuh do. I won't sign nuthin'!"

"I had no idee they wuz min'l onto hit when I signed," whimpered Mrs. Queeder.

"Oh, come, come!" put in Crawford sternly, deciding to deal with this eccentric character and believing that he could overawe him by referring to the secret agreement between them, "don't forget, Mr. Queeder, that I had a special agreement with you concerning all this." He was not quite sure now as to what he would have to pay—the two or the eight. "Are you going to keep your bargain with me or not? You want to decide quick now. Which is it?"

"Git out!" shouted Queeder, becoming wildly excited and waving his hands and jumping backward. "Yuh swindled me, that's whutcha done! Yut thort yuh'd git this place fer nuthin'. Well, yuh won't—yuh kain't. I won't sign nuthin'. I won't sign nuthin'." His eyes were red and wild from too much brooding.

Now it was that Crawford, who had been hoping to get it all for two thousand, decided to stick to his private agreement to pay eight, only instead of waiting to adjust it with Queeder in private he decided now to use it openly in an attempt to suborn the family to his point of view by showing them how much he really was to have and how unjust Queeder had planned to be to himself and them. In all certainty the family understood it as only two. If he would now let them know how matters stood, perhaps that would make a difference in his favor.

"You call eight thousand for this place swindling, and after you've taken eight hundred dollars of my money and kept it for sixty days?"

"Whut's that?" asked Dode, edging nearer, then turning and glaring at his father and eyeing his mother amazedly. This surpassed in amount and importance anything he had imagined had been secured by them, and of course he assumed that both were lying. "Eight thousan'! I thort yuh said it wuz two!" He looked at his mother for confirmation.

The latter was a picture of genuine surprise. "That's the fust I hearn uv any eight thousan'," she replied dumbly, her own veracity in regard to the transaction being in question.

The picture that Queeder made under the circumstances was remarkable. Quite upset by this half-unexpected and yet feared revelation, he was now quite beside himself with rage, fear, the insolvability of the amazing tangle into which he had worked himself. The idea that after he had made an agreement with this man, which was really unfair to himself, he should turn on him in this way was all but mentally upsetting. Besides, the fact that his wife and son now knew how greedy and selfish he had been weakened him to the point of terror.

"Well, that's what I offered him, just the same," went on Crawford aggressively and noting the extreme effect, "and that's what he agreed to take, and that's what I'm here to pay. I paid him $800 in cash to bind the bargain, and he has the money now somewhere. His saying now that I tried to swindle him is too funny! He asked me not to say anything about it because the land was all his and he wanted to adjust things with you three in his own way."

"Git outen hyur!" shouted Queeder savagely, going all but mad, "before I kill yuh! I hain't signed nuthin'! We never said nuthin' about no $8,000. It wuz $2,000—that's what it wuz! Ye're trin' tuh swindle me, the hull varmint passel o' yuh! I won't sign nuthin'!" and he stooped and attempted to seize a stool that stood near the wall.

At this all retreated except Dode, who, having mastered his father in more than one preceding contest, now descended on him and with one push of his arm knocked him down, so weak was he, while the lawyer and prospector, seeing him prone, attempted to interfere in his behalf. What Dode was really thinking was that now was his chance. His father had lied to him. He was naturally afraid of him. Why not force him by sheer brute strength to accept this agreement and take the money? Once it was paid here before him, if he could make his father sign, he could take his share without let or hindrance. Of what dreams might not this be the fulfilment? "He agreed on't, an' now he's gotta do it," he thought; "that's all."

"No fighting, now," called Giles. "We don't want any fighting—just to settle this thing pleasantly, that's all."

After all, Queeder's second signature or *mark* would be required, peaceably if possible, and besides they wished no physical violence. They were men of business, not of war.

"Yuh say he agreed tuh take $8,000, did he?" queried Dode, the actuality of so huge a sum ready to be paid in cash seeming to him almost unbelievable.

"Yes, that's right," replied the prospector.

"Then, by heck, he's gotta make good on whut he said!" said Dode with a roll of his round head, his arms akimbo, heavily anxious to see the money paid over. "Here you," he now turned to his father and began—for his prostrate father, having fallen and injured his head, was still lying semi-propped on his elbows, surveying the group with almost non-comprehending eyes, too confused and lunatic to quite realize what was going on or to offer any real resistance. "Whut's a-gittin' into yuh, anyhow, Ol' Spindle Shanks? Git up hyur!" Dode went over and lifted his father to his feet and pushed him toward a chair at the table. "Yuh might ez well sign fer this, now 'at yuh've begun it. Whar's the paper?" he asked of the lawyer. "Yuh just show him whar he orter sign, an' I guess he'll do it. But let's see this hyur money that ye're a-goin' tuh pay over fust," he added, "afore he signs. I wanta see ef it's orl right."

The prospector extracted the actual cash from a wallet, having previously calculated that a check would never be accepted, and the lawyer presented the deed to be signed. At the same time Dode took the money and began to count it.

"All he has to do," observed Giles to the others as he did so, "is to sign this second paper, he and his wife. If you can read," he said to Dode when the latter had concluded, and seeing how satisfactorily things were going, "you can see for yourself what it is." Dode now turned and picked it up and looked at it as though it were as simple and clear as daylight. "As you can see," went on the lawyer, "we agreed to buy this land of him for eight thousand dollars. We have already paid him eight hundred. That leaves seven thousand two hundred still to pay, which you have there," and he touched the money in Dode's hands. The latter was so moved by the reality of the cash that he could scarcely speak for joy. Think of it—seven thousand two hundred dollars—and all for this wretched bony land!

"Well, did yuh ever!" exclaimed Mrs. Queeder and Jane in chorus. "Who'd 'a' thort! Eight thousan'!"

Old Queeder, still stunned and befogged mentally, was yet recovering himself sufficiently to rise from the chair and look strangely about, now that Dode was attempting to make him sign, but his loving son uncompromisingly pushed him back again.

"Never mind, Ol' Spindle Shanks," he repeated roughly. "Just yuh stay whar yuh air an' sign as he asts yuh tuh. Yuh agreed tuh this, an' yuh might ez well stick tuh it. Ye're gittin' so yuh don't know what yuh want no more," he jested, now that he realized that for some strange reason he had his father completely under his sway. The latter was quite helplessly dumb. "Yuh agreed tuh this, he says. Did ja? Air yuh clean gone?"

"Lawsy!" put in the excited Mrs. Queeder. "Eight thousan'! An' him a-walkin' roun' hyur all the time sayin' hit wuz only two an' never sayin' nuthin' else tuh nobody! Who'd 'a' thort hit! An' him a-goin' tuh git hit all ef he could an' say nuthin'!"

"Yes," added Jane, gazing at her father greedily and vindictively, "tryin' tuh git it all fer hisself! An' us a-workin' hyur year in an' year out on this hyur ol' place tuh keep him comfortable!" She was no less hard in her glances than her brother. Her father seemed little less than a thief, attempting to rob them of the hard-earned fruit of their toil.

As the lawyer took the paper from Dode and spread it upon the old board table and handed Queeder a pen the latter took it aimlessly, quite as a child might have, and made his mark where indicated, Mr. Giles observing very cautiously, "This is of your own free will and deed, is it, Mr. Queeder?" The old man made no reply. For the time being anyhow, possibly due to the blow on his head as he fell, he had lost the main current of his idea, which was not to sign. After signing he looked vaguely around, as though uncertain as to what else might be requested of him, while Mrs. Queeder made her mark, answering "yes" to the same shrewd question. Then Dode, as the senior intelligence of this institution and the one who by right of force now dominated, having witnessed the marks of his father and mother, as did Jane, two signatures being necessary, he took the money and before the straining eyes of his relatives proceeded to recount it. Meanwhile old Queeder, still asleep to the significance of the money, sat quite still, but clawed at it as though it were something which he ought to want, but was not quite sure of it.

"You find it all right, I suppose?" asked the lawyer, who was turning to go. Dode acknowledged that it was quite correct.

Then the two visitors, possessed of the desired deed, departed. The family, barring the father, who sat there still in a daze, began to discuss how the remarkable sum was to be divided.

"Now, I just wanta tell yuh one thing, Dode," urged the mother, all avarice and anxiety for herself, "a third o' that, whutever 'tis, b'longs tuh me, accordin' tuh law!"

"An' I sartinly oughta git a part o' that thar, workin' the way I have," insisted Jane, standing closely over Dode.

"Well, just keep yer hands off till I git through, cantcha?" asked Dode, beginning for the third time to count it. The mere feel of it was so entrancing! What doors would it not open? He could get married now, go to the city, do a hundred things he had always wanted to do. The fact that his father was entitled to anything or that, having lost his wits, he was now completely helpless, a pathetic figure and very likely from now on doomed to wander about alone or to do his will, moved him not in the least. By right of strength and malehood he was now practically master here, or so he felt himself to be. As he fingered the money he glowed and talked, thinking wondrous things, then suddenly remembering the concealed eight hundred, or his father's part of it, he added, "Yes, an' whar's that other eight hundred, I'd like tuh know? He's a-carryin' it aroun' with him er hidin' it hyurabout mebbe!" Then eyeing the crumpled victim suspiciously, he began to feel in the old man's clothes, but, not finding anything, desisted, saying they might get it later. The money in his hands was finally divided: a third to Mrs. Queeder, a fourth to Jane, the balance to himself as the faithful heir and helper of his father, the while he speculated as to the whereabouts of the remaining eight hundred.

Just then Queeder, who up to this time had been completely bereft of his senses, now recovered sufficiently to guess nearly all of what had so recently transpired. With a bound he was on his feet, and, looking wildly about him, exclaiming as he did so in a thin, reedy voice, "They've stole my prupetty! They've stole my prupetty! I've been robbed, I have! I've been robbed! Eh! Eh! Eh! This hyur land ain't wuth only eight thousan'—hit's wuth twenty-five thousan', an' that's whut I could 'a' had for it, an' they've gone an' made me sign it all away! Eh! Eh! Eh!" He jigged and moaned, dancing helplessly about until, seeing Dode with his share of the money still held safely in his hand, his maniacal chagrin took a new form, and, seizing it and running to the open door, he began to throw a portion of the precious bills to the winds, crying as he did so, "They've stole my prupetty! They've stole my prupetty! I don't want the consarned money—I don't want it! I want my prupetty! Eh! Eh! Eh!"

In this astonishing situation Dode saw but one factor— the money. Knowing nothing of the second prospector's offer, he could not realize what it was that so infuriated the old man and had finally completely upset his mind. As the latter jigged and screamed and threw the money about he fell upon him with the energy of a wildcat and, having toppled him over and wrested the remainder of the cash from him, he held him safely down, the while he called to his sister and mother, "Pick up the money, cantcha? Pick up the money an' git a rope, cantcha? Git a rope! Cantcha see he's done gone plum daffy? He's outen his head, I tell yuh. He's crazy, he is, shore! Git a rope!" and eyeing the money now being assembled by his helpful relatives, he pressed the struggling maniac's body to the floor. When the latter was safely tied and the money returned, the affectionate son arose and, having once more recounted his share in order to see that it was all there, he was content to look about him somewhat more kindly on an all too treacherous world. Then, seeing the old man where he was trussed like a fowl for market, he added, somewhat sympathetically, it may be:

"Well, who'd 'a' thort! Pore ol' Pap! I do b'lieve he's outen his mind for shore this time! He's clean gone—plum daffy."

"Yes, that's whut he is, I do b'lieve," added Mrs. Queeder with a modicum of wifely interest, yet more concerned at that with her part of the money than anything else.

Then Dode, his mother and sister began most unconcernedly to speculate as to what if anything was next to be done with the old farmer, the while the latter rolled a vacant eye over a scene he was no longer able to interpret.

X

MARRIAGE—FOR ONE

WHENEVER I think of love and marriage I think of Wray. That clerkly figure. That clerkly mind. He was among the first people I met when I came to New York and, like so many of the millions seeking to make their way, he was busy about his affairs. Fortunately, as I saw it, with the limitations of the average man he had the ambitions of the average man. At that time he was connected with one of those large commercial agencies which inquire into the standing of business men, small and large, and report their findings, for a price, to other business men. He was very much interested in his work and seemed satisfied that should he persist in it he was certain to achieve what was perhaps a fair enough ambition: a managership in some branch of this great concern, which same would pay him so much as five or six thousand a year. The thing about him that interested me, apart from a genial and pleasing disposition, was the fact that with all his wealth of opportunity before him for studying the human mind, its resources and resourcefulness, its inhibitions and liberations, its humor, tragedy, and general shiftiness and changefulness, still he was largely concerned with the bare facts of the differing enterprises whose character he was supposed to investigate. Were they solvent? Could and did they pay their bills? What was their capital stock? How much cash did they have on hand? . . . Such was the nature of the data he needed, and to this he largely confined himself.

Nevertheless, by turns he was amused or astonished or made angry or self-righteous by the tricks, the secretiveness, the errors and the downright meanness of spirit of so many he had to deal with. As for himself, he had the feeling that he was honest, straightforward, not as limited or worthless as some of these others, and it was on this score that he was convinced he would succeed, as he did eventually, within his limitations, of course. What interested me and now makes me look upon him always as an excellent illustration of the futility of the dream of exact or even suitable rewards was his clerkly and highly respectable faith in the same. If a man did as he should do, if he were industrious and honest and saving and courteous and a few more of those many things we all know we ought to be, then in that orderly nature of things which he assumed to hold one must get along better than some others. What—an honest, industrious, careful man not do better than one who was none of these things—a person who flagrantly disregarded them, say? What nonsense. It must be so. Of course there were accidents and sickness, and men stole from one another, as he saw illustrated in his daily round. And banks failed, and there were trusts and combinations being formed that did not seem to be entirely in tune with the interests of the average man. But even so, all things considered, the average man, if he did as above, was likely to fare much better than the one who did not. In short, there was such a thing as approximate justice. Good did prevail, in the main, and the wicked were punished, as they should be.

And in the matter of love and marriage he held definite views also. Not that he was unduly narrow or was inclined to censure those whose lives had not worked out as well as he hoped his own would, but he thought there was a fine line of tact somewhere in this matter of marriage which led to success there quite as the qualities outlined above led, or should lead, to success in matters more material or practical. One had to understand something about women. One had to be sure that when one went a-courting one selected a woman of sense as well as of charm, one who came of good stock and hence would be possessed of good taste and good principles. She need not be rich; she might even be poor. And one had to be reasonably sure that one loved her. So many that went a-courting imagined they loved and were loved when it was nothing more than a silly passing passion. Wray knew. And so many women were designing, or at least light and flighty; they could not help a serious man to succeed if they would. However, in many out-of-the-way corners of the world were the really sensible and worthy girls, whom it was an honor to marry, and it was one of these that he was going to choose. Yet even there it was necessary to exercise care: one might marry a girl who was too narrow and conventional, one who would not understand the world and hence be full of prejudices. He was for the intelligent and practical and liberal girl, if he could find her, one who was his mental equal.

It was when he had become secretary to a certain somebody that he encountered in his office a girl who seemed to him to embody nearly all of the virtues or qualities which he thought necessary. She was the daughter of very modestly circumstanced parents who dwelt in the nearby suburb of O——, and a very capable and faithful stenographer, of course. If you had seen the small and respectable suburb from which she emanated you would understand. She was really pretty and appeared to be practical and sensible in many ways, but still very much in leash to the instructions and orders and tenets of her home and her church and her family circle, three worlds as fixed and definite and worthy and respectable in her thought as even the most enthusiastic of those who seek to maintain the order and virtue of the world would have wished. According to him, as he soon informed me—since we exchanged nearly all our affairs whenever me met, she was opposed to the theatre, dancing, any form of night dining or visiting in the city on week-days, as well as anything that in her religious and home world might be construed as desecration of the Sabbath. I recall him describing her as narrow "as yet," but he hoped to make her more liberal in the course of time. He also told me with some amusement and the air of a man of the world that it was impossible for him to win her to so simple an outing as rowing on the Sabbath on the little river near her home because it was wrong; on the contrary, he had to go to church with her and her parents. Although he belonged to no church and was mildly interested in socialism, he kept these facts from her knowledge. The theatre could not even be mentioned as a form of amusement and she could not and would not dance; she looked upon his inclination for the same as not only worldly but loose and sinful. However, as he told me, he was very fond of her and was doing his best to influence and enlighten her. She was too fine and intelligent a girl to stick to such notions. She would come out of them.

By very slow degrees (he was about his business of courting her all of two or three years) he succeeded in bringing her to the place where she did not object to staying downtown to dinner with him on a weekday, even went with him to a sacred or musical concert of a Sunday night, but all unbeknown to her parents or neighbors, of course. But what he considered his greatest triumph was when he succeeded in interesting her in books, especially bits of history and philosophy that he thought very liberal and which no doubt generated some thin wisps of doubt in her own mind. Also, because he was intensely fond of the theatre and had always looked upon it as the chiefest of the sources of his harmless entertainment, he eventually induced her to attend one performance, and then another and another. In short, he emancipated her in so far as he could, and seemed to be delighted with the result.

With their marriage came a new form of life for both of them, but more especially for her. They took a small apartment in New York, a city upon which originally she had looked with no little suspicion, and they began to pick up various friends. It was not long before she had joined a literary club which was being formed in their vicinity, and here she met a certain type of restless, pushing, seeking woman for whom Wray did not care—a Mrs. Drake and a Mrs. Munshaw, among others, who, from the first, as he afterward told me, he knew could be of no possible value to any one. But Bessie liked them and was about with them here, there, and everywhere.

It was about this time that I had my first suspicion of anything untoward in their hitherto happy relations. I did not see him often now, but when I did visit them at their small apartment, could not help seeing that Mrs. Wray was proving almost too apt a pupil in the realm in which he had interested her. It was plain that she had been emancipated from quite all of her old notions as to the sinfulness of the stage, and in regard to reading and living in general. Plainly, Wray had proved the Prince Charming, who had entered the secret garden and waked the sleeping princess to a world of things she had never dreamed of. She had reached the place where she was criticizing certain popular authors, spoke of a curiously enlightened history of France she was reading, of certain bits of philosophy and poetry which her new club were discussing. From the nature of the conversation being carried on by the three of us I could see that Wray was beginning to feel that the unsophisticated young girl he had married a little while before might yet outstrip him in the very realm in which he had hoped to be her permanent guide. More than once, as I noticed, she chose to question or contradict him as to a matter of fact, and I think he was astonished if not irritated by the fact that she knew more than he about the import of a certain plot or the relativity of certain dates in history. And with the force and determination that had caused her to stand by her former convictions, she now aired and defended her new knowledge. Not that her manner was superior or irritating exactly; she had a friendly way of including and consulting him in regard to many things which indicated that as yet she had no thought of manifesting a superiority which she did not feel. "That's not right, dearest. His name is Bentley. He is the author of a play that was here last year

—*The Seven Rings of Manfred*—don't you remember?"
And Wray, much against his will, was compelled to confess
that she was right.

Whenever he met me alone after this, however, he would
confide the growing nature of his doubts and perplexities.
Bessie was no more the girl she had been when he first met
her than he was like the boy he had been at ten years of age.
A great, a very great change was coming over her. She was
becoming more aggressive and argumentative and self-cen-
tred all the time, more this, more that. She was reading a
great deal, much too much for the kind of life she was called
upon to lead. Of late they had been having long and unnecessary arguments that were of no consequence however
they were settled, and yet if they were not settled to suite
her she was angry or irritable. She was neglecting her home
and running about all the time with her new-found friends.
She did not like the same plays he did. He wanted a play
that was light and amusing, whereas she wanted one with
some serious moral or intellectual twist to it. She read only
serious books now and was attending a course of lectures,
whereas he, as he now confessed, was more or less bored by
serious books. What was the good of them? They only
stirred up thoughts and emotions which were better left un-
stirred. And she liked music, or was pretending she did,
grand opera, recitals and that sort of thing, whereas he was
not much interested in music. Grand opera bored him, and
he was free to admit it, but if he would not accompany her
she would go with one or both of those two wretched women
he was beginning to detest. Their husbands had a little
money and gave them a free rein in the matter of their social
and artistic aspirations. They had no household duties to
speak of and could come and go as they chose, and Wray now
insisted that it was they who were aiding and abetting Bessie
in these various interests and enthusiasms and stirring her
up to go and do and be. What was he to do? No good
could come if things went on as they were going. They
were having frequent quarrels, and more than once lately

she had threatened to leave him and do for herself here in New York, as he well knew she could. He was doing very well now and they could be happy together if only these others could be done away with.

It was only a month or two after this that Wray came to see me, in a very distrait state of mind. After attempting to discuss several other things quite casually he confessed that his young wife had left him. She had taken a room somewhere and had resumed work as a stenographer, and although he met her occasionally in the subway she would have nothing to do with him. She wanted to end it all. And would I believe it? She was accusing him of being narrow and ignorant and stubborn and a number of other things! Only think of it! And three or four years ago she had thought he was all wrong when he wanted to go rowing on Sunday or stay downtown to dinner of an evening. Could such things be possible? And yet he loved her, in spite of all the things that had come up between them. He couldn't help it. He couldn't help thinking how sweet and innocent and strange she was when he first met her, how she loved her parents and respected their wishes. And now see. "I wish to God," he suddenly exclaimed in the midst of the "oldtime" picture he was painting of her, "that I hadn't been so anxious to change her. She was all right as she was, if I had only known it. She didn't know anything about these new-fangled things then, and I wasn't satisfied till I got her interested in them. And now see. She leaves me and says I'm narrow and stubborn, that I'm trying to hold her back intellectually. And all because I don't want to do all the things she wants to do and am not interested in the things that interest her, now."

I shook my head. Of what value was advice in such a situation as this, especially from one who was satisfied that the mysteries of temperament of either were not to be unraveled or adjusted save by nature—the accidents of chance and affinity, or the deadly opposition which keep apart those unsuited to each other? Nevertheless, being appealed to for advice, I ventured a silly suggestion, borrowed from another. He had said that if he could but win her back he would be willing to modify the pointless opposition and contention that had driven her away. She might go her intellectual way as she chose if she would only come back. Seeing him so tractable and so very wishful, I now suggested a thing that had been done by another in a somewhat related situation. He was to win her back by offering her such terms as she would accept, and then, in order to bind her to him, he was to induce her to have a child. That would capture her sympathy, very likely, as well as insinuate an image of himself into her affectionate consideration. Those who had children rarely separated—or so I said.

The thought appealed to him intensely. It satisfied his practical and clerkly nature. He left me hopefully and I saw nothing of him for several months, at the end of which time he came to report that all was once more well with him. She had come back, and in order to seal the new pact he had taken a larger apartment in a more engaging part of the city. Bessie was going on with her club work, and he was not opposing her in anything. And then within the year came a child and there followed all those simple, homey, and seemingly binding and restraining things which go with the rearing and protection of a young life.

But even during that period, as I was now to learn, all was not as smooth as I had hoped. Talking to me in Wray's absence once Bessie remarked that, delightful as it was to have a child of her own, she could see herself as little other than a milch cow with an attendant calf, bound to its service until it should be able to look after itself. Another time she remarked that mothers were bond-servants, that even though she adored her little girl she could not help seeing what a chain and a weight a child was to one who had ambitions beyond those of motherhood. But Wray, clerkly soul that he was, was all but lost in rapture. There was a small park nearby, and here he could be found trundling his infant in a handsome baby-carriage whenever his duties would permit.

He would sit or walk where were others who had children of about the age of his own so that he might compare them. He liked to speculate on the charm and innocence of babyhood and was amused by a hundred things which he had never noticed in the children of others. Already he was beginning to formulate plans for little Janet's future. It was hard for children to be cooped up in an apartment house in the city. In a year or two, if he could win Bessie to the idea, they would move to some suburban town where Janet could have the country air.

They were prospering now and could engage a nursemaid, so Mrs. Wray resumed her intellectual pursuits and her freedom. Throughout it all one could see that, respect Wray as she might as a dutiful and affectionate and methodical man, she could not love or admire him, and that mainly because of the gap that lay between them intellectually. Dissemble as he might, there was always the hiatus that lies between those who think or dream a little and those who aspire and dream much. Superiority of intellect was not altogether the point; she was not so much superior as different, as I saw it. Rather, they were two differing rates of motion, flowing side by side for the time being only, his the slower, hers the quicker. And it mattered not that his conformed more to the conventional thought and emotions of the majority. Hers was the more satisfactory to herself and constituted an urge which he feared rather than despised; and his was more satisfactory to himself, compromise as he would. Observing them together one could see how proud he was of her and of his relationship to her, how he felt that he had captured a prize, regardless of the conditions by which it was retained; and on the other hand one could easily see how little she held him in her thought and mood. She was forever talking to others about those things which she knew did not interest him or to which he was opposed.

For surcease she plunged into those old activities that had so troubled him at first, and now he complained that little Janet was being neglected. She did not love her as she should or she could not do as she was doing. And what was more and worse, she had now taken to reading Freud and Kraft-Ebbing and allied thinkers and authorities, men and works that he considered dreadful and shameful, even though he scarcely grasped their true significance.

One day he came to me and said: "Do you know of a writer by the name of Pierre Loti?"

"Yes," I replied, "I know his works. What about him?"

"What do you think of him?"

"As a writer? Why, I respect him very much. Why?"

"Oh, I know, from an intellectual point of view, as a fine writer, maybe. But what do you think of his views of life—of his books as books to be read by the mother of a little girl?"

"Wray," I replied, "I can't enter upon a discussion of any man's works upon purely moral grounds. He might be good for some mothers and evil for others. Those who are to be injured by a picture of life must be injured, or kept from its contaminating influence, and those who are to be benefited will be benefited. I can't discuss either books or life in any other way. I see worthwhile books as truthful representations of life in some form, nothing more. And it would be unfair to any one who stood in intellectual need to be restrained from that which might prove of advantage to him. I speak only for myself, however."

It was not long after that I learned there had been a new quarrel and that Bessie had left him once more, this time, as it proved, for good. And with her, which was perhaps illegal or unfair, she had taken the child. I did not know what had brought about this latest rupture but assumed that it was due to steadily diverging views. They could not agree on that better understanding of life which at one time he was so anxious for her to have—his understanding. Now that she had gone beyond that, and her method of going was unsatisfactory to him, they could not agree, of course.

Not hearing from him for a time I called and found him living in the same large apartment they had taken. Its equipment was better suited to four than to one, yet after seven or eight months of absence on her part here he was, living alone, where every single thing must remind him of her and Janet. As for himself, apart from a solemnity and reserve which sprang from a wounded and disgruntled spirit, he pretended an indifference and a satisfaction with his present state which did not square with his past love for her. She had gone, yes; but she had made a mistake and would find it out. Life wasn't as she thought it was. She had gone with another man—he was sure of that, although he did not know who the man was. It was all due to one of those two women she had taken up with, that Mrs. Drake. They were always interested in things which did not and could not interest him. After a time he added that he had been to see her parents. I could not guess why, unless it was because he was lonely and still very much in love and thought they might help him to understand the very troublesome problem that was before him.

It was a year and a half before I saw him again, during which time, as I knew, he continued to live in the apartment they had occupied together. He had become manager of a department of the agency by this time and was going methodically to and fro between his home and office. After living alone and brooding for more than a year, he came to see me one rainy November night. He looked well enough materially, quite the careful person who takes care of his clothes, but thinner, more tense and restless. He seated himself before my fire and declared that he was doing very well and was thinking of taking a long vacation to visit some friends in the West. (He had once told me that he had heard that Bessie had gone to California.) Yes, he was still living in the old place. I might think it strange, but he had not thought it worth while to move. He would only have to find another place to live in; the furniture was hard to pack; he didn't like hotels.

Then of a sudden, noting that I studied him and wondered, he grew restless and finally stood up, then walked about looking at some paintings and examining a shelf of books. His manner was that of one who is perplexed and undetermined, of one who has stood out against a silence and loneliness of which he was intensely weary. Then of a sudden he wheeled and faced me: "I can't stand it. That's what's the matter. I just can't stand it any longer. I've tried and tried. I thought the child would make things work out all right, but she didn't. She didn't want a child and never forgave me for persuading her to have Janet. And then that literary craze—that was really my own fault, though. I was the one that encouraged her to read and go to theatres. I used to tell her she wasn't up-to-date, that she ought to wake up and find out what was going on in the world, that she ought to get in with intelligent people. But it wasn't that either. If she had been the right sort of woman she couldn't have done as she did." He paused and clenched his hands nervously and dramatically. It was as though he were denouncing her to her face instead of to me.

"Now, Wray," I interposed, "how useless to say that. Which of us is as he should be? Why will you talk so?"

"But let me tell you what she did," he went on fiercely. "You haven't an idea of what I've been through, not an idea. She tried to poison me once so as to get rid of me." And here followed a brief and sad recital of the twists and turns and desperation of one who was intensely desirous of being free of one who was as desirous of holding her. And then he added: "And she was in love with another man, only I could never find out who he was." And his voice fell to a low, soft level, as though he was even then trying to solve the mystery of who it was. "And I know she had an operation performed, though I could never prove it." And he gave me details of certain mysterious goings to and fro, of secret pursuits on his part, actions and evidences and moods and quarrels that pointed all too plainly to a breach that could never be healed. "And what's more," he exclaimed at last, "she tortured me. You'll never know. You couldn't. But I loved her. . . . And I love her now."

Once more the tensely gripped fingers, the white face, the flash of haunted eyes.

"One afternoon I stood outside of a window of an apartment house when I knew she was inside, and I knew the name of the man who was supposed to occupy it, only he had re-sublet it, as I found out afterwards. And she had Janet with her—think of that!—our own little girl! I saw her come to the window once to look out—I actually saw her in another man's rooms. I ran up and hammered at the door —I tried to break it open. I called to her to come out but she wouldn't, and I went to get a policeman to make him open the door. But when I got back a servant was coming up as though she had been out, and she unlocked the door and went in. It was all a ruse, and I know it. They weren't inside. She had slipped out with Janet. And she had told me they were going to Westchester for the day.

"And another time I followed her to a restaurant when she said she was going to visit a friend. I suspected there was a man—the man I thought she was going with, but it was some one I had never seen before. When they came out and were getting into a cab I came up and told them both what I thought of them. I threatened to kill them both. And she told him to go and then came home with me, but I couldn't do anything with her. She wouldn't talk to me. All she would say was that if I didn't like the way she was doing I could let her go. She wanted me to give her a divorce. And I couldn't let her go, even if I had wanted to. I loved her too much. And I love her too much now. I do. I can't help it." He paused. The pain and regret were moving.

"Another time," he went on, "I followed her to a hotel— yes, to a hotel. But when I got inside she was waiting for me; she had seen me. I even saw a man coming toward her—but not the one I believed was the one—only when he saw me he turned away and I couldn't be sure that he was there to meet her. And when I tried to talk to her about him she turned away from me and we went back home in silence. I couldn't do anything with her. She would sit and read and ignore me for days—days, I tell you—without ever a word."

"Yes," I said, "but the folly of all that. The uselessness, the hopelessness. How could you?"

"I know, I know," he exclaimed, "but I couldn't help it. I can't now. I love her. I can't help that, can I? I'm miserable without her. I see the folly of it all, but I'm crazy about her. The more she disliked me the more I loved her. And I love her now, this minute. I can't help it. There were days when she tortured me so that I vomited, from sheer nervousness. I was sick and run down. I have been cold with sweat in her presence and when she was away and I didn't know where she was. I have walked the streets for hours, for whole days at a time, because I couldn't eat or sleep and didn't know what to do. By God!" Once more the pause and a clenching of the hands. "And all I could do was think and think and think. And that is all I do now really—think and think and think. I've never been myself since she went away. I can't shake it off. I live up there, yes. But why? Because I think she might come back some day, and because we lived there together. I wait and wait. I know it's foolish, but still I wait. Why? God only knows. And yet I wait. Oh," he sighed, "and it's three years now. Three years!"

He paused and gazed at me and I at him, shaken by a fact that was without solution by any one. Here he was—the one who had understood so much about women. But where was she, the one he had sought to enlighten, to make more up-to-date and liberal? I wondered where she was, whether she ever thought of him even, whether she was happy in her new freedom. And then, without more ado, he slipped on his raincoat, took up his umbrella, and stalked out into the rain, to walk and think, I presume. And I, closing the door on him, studied the walls, wondering. The despair, the passion, the rage, the hopelessness, the love. "Truly," I thought, "this is love, for one at least. And this is marriage, for one at least. He is spiritually wedded to that woman, who despises him, and she may be spiritually wedded to another man who may despise her. But love and marriage, for one, at least, I have seen here in this room to-night, and with mine own eyes."

XI

FULFILMENT

HEARING the maid tap lightly on her door for the third or fourth time, Ulrica uttered a semiconscious "Come." It was her usual rising hour but to-day she was more depressed than usual, although the condition was common enough at all times. The heavy drag of a troubled mental state was upon her. Was it never to end? Was she never to be happy again? After several weeks of a decidedly acceptable loneliness, during which Harry had been in the west looking after his interminable interests, he was about to return. The weariness of that, to begin with! And while she could not say that she really hated or even disliked him deeply (he was too kind and considerate for that), still his existence, his able and different personality, constantly forced or persuaded upon her, had come to be a bore. The trouble was that she did not truly love him and never could. He might be, as he was, rich, resourceful and generous to a fault in her case, a man whom the world of commerce respected, but how did that avail her? He was not her kind of man. Vivian before him had proved that. And other men had been and would be as glad to do as much if not more.

Vivian had given all of himself in a different way. Only Harry's seeking, begging eyes pleading with her (after Vivian's death and when she was so depressed) had preyed upon and finally moved her to sympathy. Life had not mattered then, (only her mother and sister), and she had

become too weary to pursue any career, even for them. So
Harry with his wealth and anxiety to do for her—

> (The maid entered softly, drew back the curtains and
> raised the blinds, letting in a flood of sunshine, then
> proceeded to arrange the bath.)

It had been, of course, because of the magic of her
beauty—how well she knew the magic of that!—plus an
understanding and sympathy she had for the miseries Harry
had endured in his youth, that had caused him to pursue
her with all the pathetic vehemence of a man of fifty. He
was not at all like Vivian, who had been shy and retiring.
Life had seemed to frighten poor Vivian and drive him
in upon himself in an uncomplaining and dignified way.
In Harry's case it had acted contrariwise. Some men were
so, especially the old and rich, those from whom life was
slipping away and for whom youth, their lost youth, seemed
to remain a colored and enthralling spectacle however
wholly gone. The gifts he had lavished upon her, the cars,
the jewels, this apartment, stocks and bonds, even that house
in Seadale for her sister and mother! And all because of a
beauty that meant so little to her now that Vivian was gone,
and in the face of an indifference so marked that it might
well have wearied any man.

How could she go on? (She paused in her thoughts
to survey and follow her maid, who was calling for the
second time.) Though he hung upon her least word or
wish and was content to see her at her pleasure, to run her
errands and be ever deferential and worshipful, still she
could not like him, could barely tolerate him. Before her
always now was Vivian with his brooding eyes and elusive,
sensitive smile; Vivian, who had never a penny to bless
himself with. She could see him now striding to and fro in
his bare studio, a brush in one hand, or sitting in his crippled
chair meditating before a picture or talking to her of ways

and means which might be employed to better their state. The pathos!

"I cannot endure that perfume, Olga!"

In part she could understand her acceptance of Harry after Vivian (only it did not seem understandable always, even to her), for in her extreme youth her parents had been so very poor. Perhaps because of her longings and childish fears in those days she had been marked in some strange way that had eventually led her to the conviction that wealth was so essential. For her parents were certainly harassed from her sixth to her thirteenth years, when they recovered themselves in part. Some bank or concern had failed and they had been thrown on inadequate resources and made to shift along in strange ways. She could remember an old brick house with a funereal air and a weedy garden into which they had moved and where for a long time they were almost without food. Her mother had cried more than once as she sat by the open window looking desolately out, while Ulrica, not quite comprehending what it was all about, had stared at her from an adjacent corner.

"Will madame have the iris or the Japanese lilac in the water?"

She recalled going downtown once on an errand and slipping along shyly because her clothes were not good. And when she saw some schoolgirls approaching, hid behind a tree so they should not see her. Another time, passing the Pilkington at dinner-time, the windows being open and the diners visible, she had wondered what great persons they must be to be able to bask in so great a world. It was then perhaps that she had developed the obsession for wealth which had led to this. If only she could have seen herself as she now was she would not have longed so. (She paused, looking gloomily back into the past.) And then had come the recovery of her father in some way or other. He had managed to get an interest in a small stove factory and they were no longer so poor—but that was after her youth had been spoiled, her mind marked in this way.

And to crown it all, at seventeen had come Byram the inefficient. And because he was "cute" and had a suggestion of a lisp; was of good family and really insane over her, as nearly every youth was once she had turned fourteen, she had married him, against her parents' wishes, running away with him and lying about her age, as did he about his. And then had come trying times. Byram was no money-maker, as she might have known. He was inexperienced, and being in disfavor with his parents for ignoring them in his hasty choice of a wife, he was left to his own devices. For two whole years what had she not endured—petty wants which she had concealed from her mother, furniture bought on time and dunned for, collectors with whom she had to plead not to take the stove or the lamp or the parlor table, and grocery stores and laundries and meat-markets which had to be avoided because of unpaid bills. There had even been an ejectment for non-payment of rent, and job after job lost for one reason and another, until the whole experiment had been discolored and made impossible even after comfort had been restored.

"I cannot endure the cries of the children, Olga. You will have to close that window."

No; Byram was no money-maker, not even after his parents in far-distant St. Paul had begun to help him to do better. And anyhow by then, because she had had time to sense how weak he was, what a child, she was weary of him, although he was not entirely to blame. It was life. And besides, during all that time there had been the most urgent pursuit of her by other men, men of the world and of means, who had tried to influence her with the thought of how easily her life could be made more agreeable. Why remain faithful to so young and poor a man when so much could be done

for her. But she had refused. Despite Byram's lacks she
had small interest in them, although their money and skill
had succeeded in debasing Byram in her young and un-
trained imagination, making him seem even weaker and more
ridiculous than he was. But that was all so long ago now
and Vivian had proved so much more important in her life.
While even now she was sorry for Harry and for Byram she
could only think of Vivian, who was irretrievably gone.
Byram was successful now and out of her life, but maybe
if life had not been so unkind and they so foolish——

"You may have Henry serve breakfast and call the car!"

And then after Byram had come Newton, big, successful,
important, a quondam employer of Byram, who had met her
on the street one day when she was looking for work, just
when she had begun to sense how inefficient Byram really
was, and he had proved kind without becoming obnoxious
or demanding. While declaring, and actually proving,
that he wished nothing more of her than her good-will, he
had aided her with work, an opportunity to make her own
way. All men were not selfish. He had been the vice-
president of the Dickerson Company and had made a place
for her in his office, saying that what she did not know he
would teach her since he needed a little sunshine there.
And all the while her interest in Byram was waning, so
much so that she had persuaded him to seek work elsewhere
so that she might be rid of him, and then she had gone home
to live with her mother. And Newton would have married
her if she had cared, but so grieved was she by the outcome
of her first love and marriage that she would not.

"The sedan, yes. And I will take my furs."

And then, living with her mother and making her own
way, she had been sought by others. But there had been
taking root and growing in her an ideal which somehow in

the course of time had completely mastered her and would not even let her think of anything else, save in moments of loneliness and the natural human yearning for life. This somehow concerned some one man, not any one she knew, not any one she was sure she would ever meet, but one so wonderful and ideal that for her there could be no other like him. He was not to be as young or unsophisticated as Byram, nor as old and practical as Newton, though possibly as able (though somehow this did not matter), but wise and delicate, a spirit-mate, some such wondrous thing as a great musician or artist might be, yet to whom in spite of his greatness she was to be all in all. She could not have told herself then how she was to have appealed to him, unless somehow surely, because of her great desire for him, her beauty and his understanding of her need. He was to have a fineness of mind and body, a breadth, a grasp, a tenderness of soul such as she had not seen except in pictures and dreams. And such as would need her.

"To Thorne and Company's first, Fred."

Somewhere she had seen pictures of Lord Byron, of Shelley, Liszt and Keats, and her soul had yearned over each, the beauty of their faces, the record of their dreams and seekings, their something above the common seeking and clayiness (she understood that now). They were of a world so far above hers. But before Vivian appeared, how long a journey! Life had never been in any hurry for her. She had gone on working and seeking and dreaming, the while other men had come and gone. There had been, for instance, Joyce with whom, had she been able to tolerate him, she might have found a life of comfort in so far as material things went. He was, however, too thin or limited spiritually to interest a stirring mind such as hers, a material man, and yet he had along with his financial capacity more humanity than most, a kind of spiritual tenderness and generosity at times towards some temperaments. But no art, no true romance. He was a plunger in real estate, a developer of tracts. And he lacked that stability and worth of temperament which even then she was beginning to sense as needful to her, whether art was present or not. He was handsomer than Byram, a gallant of sorts, active and ebullient, and always he seemed to sense, as might a homing pigeon, the direction in which lay his own best financial opportunities and to be able to wing in that direction. But beyond that, what? He was not brilliant mentally, merely a clever "mixer" and maker of money, and she was a little weary of men who could think only in terms of money. How thin some clever men really were!

"I rather like that. I'll try it on."

And so it had been with him as it had been with Byram and Newton, although he sought her eagerly enough! and so it was afterward with Edward and Young. They were all worthy men in their way. No doubt some women would be or already had been drawn to them and now thought them wonderful. Even if she could have married any one of them it would only have been to have endured a variation of what she had endured with Byram; with them it would have been of the mind instead of the purse, which would have been worse. For poor Byram, inefficient and inexperienced as he was, had had some little imagination and longings above the commonplace. But these, as contrasted with her new ideal——

"Yes, the lines of this side are not bad."

Yes, in those days there had come to her this nameless unrest, this seeking for something better than anything she had yet known and which later, without rhyme or reason, had caused her to be so violently drawn to Vivian. Why had Vivian always grieved so over her earlier affairs? They were nothing, and she regretted them once she knew him.

"Yes, you may send me this one, and the little one with the jade pins."

And then after Young had come Karel, the son of rich parents and well-placed socially in Braleigh. He was young, well-informed, a snob of sorts, although a gentle one. The only world he knew was that in which his parents had been reared. Their ways had been and always would be his, conservatism run mad. At thirty the only place to go in summer was Macomber Beach, and in winter the only place to be was in Braleigh. There he could meet his equals twenty times a day. They went to the same homes, the same hotels, the same parties the year round. It was all the life he wanted, and it was all the life she would have been expected to want. But by then she was being hopelessly held by this greater vision and something within had said: "No, no, no!"

"You were making over my ermine cape. Is it finished?"

And Loring! He, for a change, was a physician there in Braleigh and lived with his sister in Lankester Way, near her home, only hers was in a cheaper street. He was young and good-looking but seemed to think only of his practice, how it was to make him and achieve her perhaps, although it had all seemed so commonplace and practical to her. He was so keen as to his standing with the best people, always so careful of his ways and appearance, as though his life depended upon it. He might have married more to his social and financial advantage but he had wanted her. And she had never been able to endure him —never seriously tolerate his pursuit.

"Yes, if you would alter these sleeves I might like it."

Whenever he saw her he would come hustling up. "My, but it's nice to see you again, Ulrica. You are always the same, always charming, always beautiful—now don't frown. Have you changed your mind yet, Ulrica? You don't want to forget that I'm going to be one of the successful men here some day. Please do smile a little for me. I'll be just as successful as Joyce or any of them."

"And is it just success you think I want?" she had asked.

"Oh, I know it isn't just that, but I've had a hard time and so have you. I know it wouldn't do any good to offer you only success, but what I mean is that it makes everything so much easier. With you I could do anything—" and so he would ramble on.

"To McCafferey's, the Post Street entrance."

But the shrewd hard eyes and dapper figure and unvaried attention to *his interests* had all bored and after a time alienated her, since her ideal seemed to dwarf and discolor every one and everything. Was there not something somewhere much bigger than all this, these various and unending men, she had asked herself, some man not necessarily so successful financially but different? She had felt that she would find him somewhere, must indeed if her life was to mean anything to her. Always her great asset, her beauty, had been looked upon as the one thing she must keep for this other. And so it had gone, man after man and flirtation after flirtation. It had seemed as though it would never end. Even after she had transferred her life to the great city, to work, to go upon the stage if need be, there were more of these endless approaches and recessions; but, like the others, they had come and gone, leaving only a faint impression. Not until that day at Althea's party in the rooming-house in which they both lived had she found the one who touched her.

And then—

"And now to the Willoughby."

It was late afternoon and just as she was returning from her task of seeking work in connection with the stage that they met. There he was in Althea's room, tall, spare, angular, slightly sallow and cloisterish, his heavy eyebrows low above his sunken eyes as though he sought to shut himself in to himself, and with those large dark eyes fixed ruminatively and yet somewhat uncertainly upon all, even her when she came. And from Althea she gathered that he was a painter of strange dark landscapes and decorations which many of those who knew seemed to think were wonderful but which as yet had achieved no recognition at all. Worse, he was from the Rockies, a sheep-rancher's son, but had not been able to endure ranching. His future was still very far before him, and, as one could sense, he was so innocent of any desire to be put forward; he seemed half the time to be a—dream. By some strange freak of luck he was still there when she entered, sitting in a corner not entirely at ease, because, as he told her later, he was strange to such affairs and did not know when to go.

The brightness of the buildings in the spring sun!

And she had looked at his hands, at his commonplace clothes, and then, a little troubled by his gaze, had withdrawn hers. Again and again her eyes sought his or his hers, as though they were furtively surveying each other; as though each was unable to keep his eyes off the other. And by degrees there was set up in her a tremendous something that was like music and fear combined, as though all at once she had awakened and comprehended. She was no longer the complete master of herself, as she had always imagined, but was now seized upon and possessed by this stranger! In brief, here he was, her dream, and now she could do nothing save gaze nervously and appealingly—for what? Those dark, sombre eyes, the coarse black hair and sallow skin! Yes, it was he indeed, her love, her star, the one by whose mystic light she had been steering her course these many years. She sensed it. Knew it. He was here before her now as though saying: "Come." And she could only smile foolishly without speaking. Her hands trembled and her throat tightened until she almost choked. "I never saw any one more beautiful than you," he had said afterwards when they talked, and she had thrilled so that it was an effort not to cry out. And then he had sighed like a child and said: "Talk to me, about anything—but don't go, will you?"

The air—the air—this day!

And so, realizing that he valued her for this one gift at least, her beauty, she had sought now to make him understand that she was his without, however, throwing herself beggingly before him. With her eyes, her smile, her every gesture, she had said: "I am yours! I am yours! Can't you see?" At last, in his shy way, he had seemed to comprehend, but even then, as he afterwards confessed, he could not believe that anything so wonderful could follow so speedily upon contact, that one could love, adore, at sight. She had asked where he lived and if she might come and see his work, and with repressed intensity he had said: "I wish you would! I wish you could come to-day!" It had made her sad and yet laugh, too, for joy.

That single tree blooming in this long, hard block!

There and then, with only the necessary little interludes which propriety seemed to demand, and with longing and seeking on the part of each, had begun that wondrous thing, their love. Only it seemed to have had no fixed beginning,— to have been always—just been. For the day she had called him up his voice had so thrilled her that she could scarcely speak. She had still felt she had known him for so long. How could that have been?

"I was afraid you might not call," he had said tremulously, and she had replied: "And I was wondering if you really wanted me to."

And when she sought him out in his studio she had found it to be such a poor mean room over a stable, in a mean street among a maze of mean streets, and yet had thought it heaven. It was so like him, so bare and yet wonderful—a lovely spiritual mood set over against tawdry materials and surroundings.

"Drive me through the East Side, Fred."

Better, she had found him painting or perhaps merely pretending to. He had on that old long gray linen duster which later became so familiar a thing to her. And to one side of him and his easel on a table were some of the colors of his palette, greens and purples and browns and blues. He had said so softly as he opened the door to her: "My painting is all bluffing to-day. I haven't been able to think of anything but you, how you might not come, how you would look—" And then, without further introduction or explanation, under the north light of his roof window filtering down dustily upon them, he had put his arms about her and she her lips to his, and they had clung together, thinking only of each other, their joy and their love. And he had sighed, a tired sigh, or one of great relief after a strain, such a strain as she herself had been under.

That one little cloud in the sky!

And then after a time, he had shown her the picture he was painting, a green lush sea-marsh with a ribbon of dark enamel-like water laving the mucky strand, and overhead heavy, sombre, smoky clouds, those of a sultry summer day over a marsh. And in the distance, along the horizon, a fringe of trees showing as a filigree. But what a mood! Now it hung in the Wakefield Gallery—and— (Harry had helped to place it there for her!) But then he had said, putting his brushes aside: "But what is the use of trying to paint now that you are here?" And she had sighed for joy, so wonderful was it all.

The crowds in these East Side streets!

Yet what had impressed her most was that he made no apology for the bareness and cheapness of his surroundings. Outside were swarming push carts and crowds, the babble of the great foreign section, but it was all as though he did not hear. Over a rack at the back of the large bare room he had hung a strip of faded burnt orange silk and another of clear light green, which vivified what otherwise would have been dusty and gray. Behind this, as she later discovered, were his culinary and sleeping worlds.

And then, of course, had come other days.

But how like that first day was this one, so fresh and bright!

There was no question here of what was right or wrong, conventional or otherwise. This was love, and this her beloved. Had she not sought him in the highways and the byways? At the close of one afternoon, as she was insisting that she must continue her search for work, now more than ever since neither he nor she had anything, he had said sadly: "Don't go. We need so little, Ulrica. Don't. I can't stand it now." And she had come back. "No," she had replied, "I won't—I can't—not any more, if you want me."

And she had stayed.

And that wondrous, beautiful love-life! The only love-life she had ever known.

But just the same she had seen that she must redouble her efforts to make her way, and had. Six hundred dollars she had brought to the city was nearly all gone, and as for Vivian, his allotment was what he could earn, a beggar's dole. During the days that followed, each bringing them closer, he had confessed more and more of the difficulties that confronted him, how hard it was to sell his wares. And she—it was needful for her to reopen the pages of her past. She had not been happy or prosperous, she told him; fortune might have been hers for the taking but she could not endure those who came with it. Now that she had the misery of her soul's ache removed she must find something to do. The stage was her great opportunity. And plainly his life was one which had always been and must be based on the grudged dole that life offers to those who love its beauty and lift their eyes. So few, as yet, knew of his work or had been arrested by it. Yet if he persisted, as she felt,—if that wondrous something in his work which had attracted the sensitive and selective did not fail—

The hot, bare redness of the walls of these streets, so flowerless, so bleak, and yet so alive and human!

But all too well she understood that his life, unless changed by her, would ever be the meagre thing it had been. Beauty was his, but no more,—a beauty of mind and of dreams and of the streets and the night and the sea and the movements of life itself, but of that which was material he had nothing. That was for those whom she had been unable to endure. Only by a deft synthesis of those wondrous faculties which concern beauty was he able to perceive, respond to, translate the things which he saw and felt, and these were not of matter. Rather, they were epitomes, his pictures, of lands and skies and seas and strange valleys of dreams, worlds in miniature. But what transmutations and transferences! She was never weary of the pictures he made. Nor was she ever weary of the picture he made before his easel, tenuous and pale and concerned, his graceful hands at work with the colors he synthetized. The patience, the stability, the indifference to all but that which was his to do!

"Into Bartow Street, Fred."

And in him, too, was no impatience with life for anything

it might have failed to provide. Instead, he seemed ever to be thinking of its beauties and harmonies, the wonder of its dawns and sunsets, the colors and harmonies of its streets, buildings, crowds, silences. Often of a morning when it was yet dark he would arise and open a door that gave out onto a balcony and from there gaze upon the sky and city. And at any time it was always an instinct with him to pause before anything that appealed to either of them as beautiful or interesting. And in his eye was never the estimating glint of one who seeks to capture for profit that which is elemental and hence evanescent, but only the gaze of the lover of beauty, the worshiper of that which is profitable to the soul only.

The very street! The very studio!

Although she was ignorant of the spirit or the technique of art she had been able to comprehend it and him, all that he represented as a portion of beauty itself, the vast and supernal beauty toward which the creative forces of life in their harsh and yet tender ways seem impelled at times.

Had she not understood very well that it was as beauty that she appealed to him, at first anyhow, an artistry of face and form plus a certain mood of appreciation or adoration or understanding which was of value to him? How often had he spoken of her lavender-lidded eyes, the whiteness and roundness of her arms, the dark gold of her hair, the sombre unrevealing blue of the iris of her eyes! Here strange it was that these seemed to enthrall and hold him at times, leaving him, if not weak, at least childlike in her hands. He had never seemed to weary of her and during all their days together she could feel his unreasoning joy in her.

His one-time yellow curtains exchanged for green ones!

That she had proved and remained irresistible to him was evidenced by his welcoming and gratified eyes, the manner in which he paused to survey her whenever she came near, seeming to re-estimate her every least attribute with loving interest. Indeed, he seemed to need her as much as she needed him, to yearn with an intense hunger over her as a thing of beauty,—he who to her was strength, beauty, ideals, power, all the substance of beauty and delight that she could crave.

Yes, here was where they had come to gaze at the towers of the bridge beyond.

And so for over a year it was that they clung together, seeking to make of their lives an ideal thing. Only it was after she came into his life that he had begun to worry— and because of what? It was no hardship for him to live upon what he could make, but now that she had come, with her beauty and her beauty's needs, it was no longer the same. As soon as she appeared he had seemed to sense his inefficiency as a creator of means. Bowdler, the wealthy dealer, had once told him that if he pleased him with something it might be worth five hundred dollars. Five hundred dollars! But when he took a painting to Bowdler he said he was overstocked, had too many of his things on hand— the very things that to-day—(now that Vivian was gone)— were selling for as much as ten and twelve thousand! And a single one of all those now being sold would have made them both happy for a whole year or more!

He had called this tree her parasol!

And she had been able to do so little for him! Realizing how little life had done for him she had decided then and there that all her efforts must be bent toward correcting this injustice. Life owed him more. And so it was that at last she had turned to the stage and sought earnestly, day after day and week after week, only to obtain very little of all she needed to make them happy, a small part in one of Wexford's many productions, he of the comedies and farces and beauty shows. Yet after some effort she had made him admit that she was distinctive and that he could use her. But then had come that long wait of nearly three months before the work began! And in the meantime what labor, the night and day work of rehearsals and appearances, the trying to get back to him each afternoon or night. And he had been so patient and hopeful and helpful, waiting for her after late hours of rehearsal to walk home with her and encouraging her in every way. And yet always there was a tang of something unreal about it all, hopes, as she so truly feared, that were never to be realized, dreams too good to come true. The hours had flown. The very pressure of his hand had suggested paradise, present and yet not to be.

She must be returning now. It was not wise for her to sit here alone.

And while those three months were dragging their slow days she had borrowed what money she could to keep them going. She had even borrowed from her mother! Yet they had been happy, wandering here and there, he always rejoicing in the success which her work promised to bring her. The studios facing the great park where she now lived at which they had looked, he seeming to think they were not for such as he. (The creatures who really dwelt there!)

Yes, she must be going. His train was due at four.

And then at last, her trial period was over, Wexford had complimented her and her salary had been increased. She had begun to buy things for Vivian and his studio, much as he protested. But best of all for her the hope of better days still to come, greater fame for herself and so better days for Vivian, a real future in which he was to share— money,—comfort for them both.

"To the apartment, Fred."

And then— In spite of all her wishes and fears, had come the necessity for her to go on the road with the show. And owing to their limited means he was compelled to remain behind. Worse, despite the fact that each knew that every thought was for the other, the thought of separation tortured them both. Wherever she was there was the thought of him, alone, at his easel and brooding. And herself alone. It had seemed at times as though she must die unless this separation could be ended.

If only Harry were not coming into her life again!

But it was not ended—for weeks. And then one day, after a brief silence had come the word that he had been ill. A wave of influenza was sweeping the city and had seized him. She was not to worry. But she did worry—and returned immediately, only to find him far along the path which he was never to retrace. He was so ill. And worse, a strange despondency based on the thought that he was never to get well, had seized him. He had felt when she left, or so he said, that something were sure to happen. They might not ever, really, be together again. It had been so hard for him to do without her.

He had added that he was sorry to be so poor a fighter, to bring her back from her work. Her work! And he ill!

The immense wall these hotels made along the park!

And then against the utmost protest of her soul had come the end, a conclusion so sudden and unexpected that it had driven despair like metal into her very soul. Hour after hour and under her very eyes, her protesting if not restraining hands and thoughts, he had grown weaker. Though he knew, he seemed to wish to deny it, until at last his big dear eyes fixed upon her, he had gone, looking as though he wished to say something.

This wretchedly wealthy West Side!

It was that look, the seeking in it, that wishing to remain with her that was written there, that had haunted her and did still. It was as though he had wished to say: "I do not want to go! I do not want to go!"

And then, half-dead, she had flung herself upon him. With her hands she had tried to draw him back, until she was led away. For days she was too ill to know, and only his grave—chosen by strangers!—had brought it all back. And then the long days! Never again would life be the same. For the first time in her life she had been happy. A bowl of joy had been placed in her eager fingers, only to be dashed from them. Yes, once more now she was alone and would remain so, thrust back upon herself. And worse, with the agonizing knowledge of what beauty might be. Life had lost its lustre. What matter if others told of her beauty, if one or many sought to make her life less bare?

This stodgy porter always at the door in his showy braid! Why might not such as he die instead?

But then her mother and sister, learning of her despair, had come to her. Only since there was nothing that any pleasure, or aspect of life could offer her, the days rolled drearily,—meaninglessly. And only because of what was still missing in her mother's life, material comfort, had she changed. It had been with the thought of helping her mother that after a year she had returned to the city and the stage, but exhausted, moping, a dreary wanderer amid old and broken dreams.

By degrees of course she had managed to pick up the

threads of her life again. Who did not? And now nature, cynical, contemptuous of the dreams and longings which possess men, now lavished upon her that which she and Vivian had longed for in vain. Fame? It was hers. Money? A Score of fortunes had sought her in vain. Friendship? She could scarcely drive it from the door. She was successful.

But what mattered it now? Was it not a part of the routine, shabby method of life to first disappoint one—sweat and agonize one—and then lavish luxury upon one,—afterwards?

"I want nothing. And if any one calls, I am not in."

And so it was that after a time Harry descending upon her with his millions, and seeking solace for himself through her sympathy, she had succumbed to that—or him—as a kindly thing to do. He too had confessed to a wretched dole of difficulties that had dogged his early years. He too had been disappointed in love, comfort—almost everything until too late. In his earliest years he had risen at four in a mill-town to milk cows and deliver milk, only later to betake himself, barefooted and in the snow, to a mill to work. Later still he had worked in a jewelry factory, until his lungs had failed. And had then taken to the open road as a peripatetic photographer of street children in order to re-cover his health. But because of this work—the chemistry, and physics of photography—he had interested himself in chem-istry and physics—later taking a "regular job," as he phrased it, in a photographic supply house and later still opening a store of his own. It was here that he had met Kesselbloom, who had solved the mystery of the revolving shutter and the selenium bath. Financing him and his patents, he had been able to rise still more, to fly really, as though others were standing still. The vast Dagmar Optical and Photo-graphic Company. It was now his, with all its patents. And the Baker-Wile Chemical Company. Yes, now he was a multimillionaire, and lonely—as lonely as she was. Strange that he and she should have met.

"No, I will not see any one."

So now, through her, he was seeking the youth which could be his no more. Because of some strange sense of comradeship in misery, perhaps, they had agreed to share each other's unhappiness!

"You say Mr. Harris telephoned from the station?"

Yes, as he had told her in his brooding hours, at fifty it had suddenly struck him that his plethora of wealth was pointless. As a boy he had not learned to play, and now it was too late. Already he was old and lonely. Where lay his youth or any happiness?

And so now—nearly icy-cold the two of them, and contemning life dreams—they were still facing life together. And here he was this day, at her door or soon would be, fresh from financial labors in one city and another. And returning to what? With a kind of slavish and yet royal persistence he still pursued her—to comfort—as well as to be comforted, and out of sheer weariness she endured him. Perhaps because he was willing to await her mood, to accept the least crumb of her favor as priceless. The only kinship that existed between them was this unhappy youth of his and her sympathy for it, and his seeming understanding of and sympathy for the ills that had beset her. Supposing (so his argument had run) that the burden of this proposed friendship with him were to be made very light, the lightest of all burdens, that upon closer contact he proved not so hopeless or dull as he appeared, could she not—would she not—endure him? (The amazing contrarieties and strangenesses of things!) And so friendship, and later marriage under these strange conditions. Yet she could not love him, never had and never would. However

it might have seemed at first—and she did sympathize with
and appreciate him—still only because of her mother and
sister and the fact that she herself needed some one to fall
back upon, a support in this dull round of living, had caused
her to go on as long as she had.

*How deserted that wading-pool looked at evening, with
all the children gone!*

And now at this very moment he was below stairs waiting
for her, waiting to learn whether she had smiled or her
mood had relaxed so that he might come up to plead afresh
for so little as she could give—her worthless disinterested
company somewhere!

Well, perhaps it was unfair to serve one so who wished
nothing more than to be kind and who had striven in every
way for several years now to make himself useful if not
agreeable to her, and yet— True, she had accepted of his
largess, not only for herself but for her mother; but had she
not had things of her own before that? And had she not
been content? Was it charity from her or from him?
And still—

Those darkening shadows in the sky in the east!

And yet it was always "Ulrica" here and "Ulrica" there.
Did she so much as refer to an old-time longing was it not
he who attempted to make amends in some way or to bring
about a belated fulfilment? Vivian's painting now in the
museum, the talk as to his worth, his monument but now
being erected—to whom, to whom were those things due—
this belated honoring of her darling—?

*"Oh, well, tell him to come up. And you may lay out my
green evening dress, Olga."*

XII

THE VICTOR

I

Some excerpts from an article on the late J. H. Osterman, by C. A. Gridley, Chief Engineer of the Osterman Development Company. This article appeared in the Engineering Record, for August last.

"MY admiration for the late J. H. Osterman was based on his force and courage and initiative, rather than upon his large fortune and the speed with which he had accumulated it after he had passed the age of forty. Mr. Osterman was not always a pleasant person to be near. Not that he was given to violent rages, but in the prosecution of his various enterprises he had the faculty of giving one the impression that but a fraction of his thoughts was being revealed and that he was sitting apart and in judgment upon one, as it were, even while he talked. He had the habit of extracting the most carefully thought-out opinions of all those about him, and when all had been said of shaking his head and dismissing the whole matter as negligible, only to make use of the advice in some form later. At such times he was apt to convince himself, and quite innocently, I am sure, that his final opinion was his own.

"In so far as I could judge from hearsay and active contact with him for a period of something like fourteen years, Mr. Osterman was one who required little if any rest and at all times much work to keep him content. His was an intense and always dominant personality. Even after he had passed the age of sixty-five, when most men of means are content to rest and let others assume the strenuous burdens of the world, he was always thinking of some new thing to do. It was only the week before he died, stricken while walking upon his verandah, that he was in my office with a plan to subsidize the reigning authorities of a certain minor Asiatic state, in order that certain oil and other properties there might be developed under peaceful conditions. A part of this plan contemplated a local army to be organized and equipped and maintained at his expense. Of a related nature was his plan for the double-screw platform descents and exits for the proposed New York-New Jersey traffic tunnel, which he appears to have worked out during the spring which preceded his sudden demise and plans for which he was most anxious to have this department prepare in order that they might be submitted to the respective states. It is hardly needful to state, since the fact is generally known, that those plans have been accepted. Of a related nature were those Argentine-Chilean Trans-Andean railway projects so much discussed in the technical engineering as well as the trade papers of a few years since, and which recently have been jointly financed by the two governments. Only the natural tact and diplomacy of a man like Mr. Osterman, combined with his absolute genius for detecting and organizing the natural though oftentimes difficult resources of a country, would have been capable of making anything out of that very knotty problem. It was too much identified with diplomacy and the respective ambitions and prejudices of the countries involved. Yet it was solved and he succeeded in winning for his South American organization the confidence and friendship of the two governments."

II

The facts concerning the founding and development of the fortune of the late J. H. Osterman, as developed by C. B. Cummings, quondam secretary to Mr. Osterman, special investigator for E. X. Bush, of counsel for the minority stockholders of the C. C. and Q. L., in their suit to compel the resale of the road to the original holders and the return of certain moneys alleged to have been illegally abstracted by J. H. Osterman and Frank O. Parm, of Parm-Baggott and Company, and by him set forth in his reminiscences of Mr. Bush and the Osterman-Parm-C. C. & Q. L. imbroglio.

1. The details of the Osterman-De Malquit matter were, as near as I have been able to gather, or recall, since I was Mr. Osterman's secretary until that time, as follows: De Malquit was one of the many curb brokers in New York dabbling in rubber and other things at the time Osterman returned from Honduras and executed his very dubious coup. The afternoon before De Malquit killed himself—and this fact was long held against Mr. Osterman in connection with his sudden rise—he had come to Osterman's office in Broad Street, and there, amid rosewood and mahogany and an unnecessary show of luxury which Osterman appeared to relish even at that time, had pleaded for time in which to meet a demand for one hundred thousand dollars due for ten thousand shares of Calamita Rubber, which Osterman then entirely controlled and for which he was demanding the par or face value. And this in spite of the fact that it had been selling on "curb" only the day before for seven and one-fourth and seven and three-fourths. De Malquit was one of those curb brokers whom Osterman, upon coming to New York and launching Calamita (which was built on nothing more solid than air), had deliberately plotted to trap in this way. Unwitting of Osterman's scheme, he had sold ten thousand shares of Calamita on margin at the above low price without troubling to have the same in his safe, as Osterman well knew. That was what Osterman had been counting on and it had pleased him to see De Malquit, along with many others just at that moment, in the very same difficult position. For up to that day Calamita, like many another of its kind, had been a wildcat

stock. Only "wash sales" were traded in by brokers in order to entrap the unwary from the outside. They traded in it without ever buying any of it. It had to fluctuate so that the outsider might be induced to buy, and that was why it was traded in. But when it did fluctuate and the lamb approached, he was sold any quantity he wished, the same being entered upon their books as having been sold or bought on his order. When a quotation sufficiently low to wipe out the margin exacted had been engineered among friends, the lamb was notified that he must either post more money to cover the decline or retire. In quite all cases the lamb retired, leaving the broker with a neat profit.

This was the very situation upon which Osterman had been counting to net him the fortune which it eventually did, and overnight at that. Unknown to the brokers, he had long employed agents whose business it was to permit themselves to be fleeced for small sums in order that these several brokers, growing more and more careless and finding this stock to be easy and a money-maker, should sell enough of it without actually having it in their safes to permit him to pounce upon them unexpectedly and make them pay up. And so they did. The promoters of the stock seeming indifferent or unable to manage their affairs, these fake sales became larger and larger, a thousand and finally a ten thousand share margin sale being not uncommon. When the stage was set the trap was sprung. Overnight, as it were, all those who at Osterman's order had bought the stock on margin (and by then some hundreds of thousands of dollars' worth had been disposed of) decided that they would not lose their margins but would follow up their cash with more and take the stock itself, holding it as an investment. It then became the duty of these brokers to deliver the stock within twenty-four hours or take the consequences—say, a petition in bankruptcy or a term in jail. Naturally there was a scrambling about to find any loose blocks of the stock. But these had been carefully garnered into the safe of Mr. Osterman, who was the sole owner of the stock, and they were compelled to hurry eventually to him. Here they were met by the genial eye of the cat that is expecting the mouse. They wanted Calamita, did they? Well, they could have it, all they wanted . . . at par or a little more. Did that seem harsh, seeing that it had been selling only the day before for seven and three-fourths or seven-eighths? Sorry. That was the best he could do. They could take it at that price or leave it.

Naturally there was a panic among those who were short. The trick was obvious, but so was the law. Those who could, pocketed their losses without undue complaint and departed; some who could not, and were financially unimportant, decamped, leaving Osterman's agents to collect as best they might. Only one, Mr. De Malquit, finding himself faced by complications which he could not meet, took his own life. He had unfortunately let himself in for much more money than had the others and at a time when he could least stand the strain.

The day De Malquit came to see Osterman, he was behind his desk expecting many, and because, as I afterwards learned from Mr. Osterman himself, Mr. De Malquit had been so wary, making agreements at first, which made it hard to trap him, Osterman saw him as one of those who had made it most difficult for him to win, and therefore deserving to be sheared the closest. "One hundred per share, take it or leave it," was his only comment in reply to Mr. De Malquit's statement that he found himself in a bit of a hole and would like to explain how a little time would see him through.

"But, Mr. Osterman," I recall De Malquit replying, "I haven't so much now, and I can't get it. These shares were being quoted at seven and three-fourths only yesterday. Can't you let me off easier than that, or give me a few months in which to pay? If I could have six months or a year—I have some other matters that are pressing me even more than this. They will have to come first, but I might pull through if I had a little time."

"One hundred, on the nail. That's the best I can do," Osterman replied, for I was in the room at the time. And then signaled me to open the door for him.

But at that Mr. De Malquit turned and bent on him a very troubled look, which, however, did not move Mr. Osterman any. "Mr. Osterman," he said, "I am not here to waste either your time or mine. I am in a corner, and I am desperate. Unless you can let me have some of this stock at a reasonable price I am done for. That will bring too much trouble to those who are near and dear to me for me to care to live any longer. I am too old to begin over again. Let me have some of it now. To-morrow will be too late. Perhaps it won't make any difference to you, but I won't be here to pay anybody. I have a wife who has been an invalid for two years. I have a young son and daughter in school. Unless I can go on——" He turned, paused, swallowed, and then moistened his lips.

But Mr. Osterman was not inclined to believe any broker or to be worked by sentiment. "Sorry. One hundred is the best I can do."

At that De Malquit struck his hands together, a resounding smack, and then went out, turning upon Osterman a last despairing glance. That same night De Malquit killed himself, a thing which Osterman had assumed he would not do—or so he said, and I resigned. The man had really been in earnest. And, to make matters worse, only three months later De Malquit's wife killed herself, taking poison in the small apartment to which she had been forced to remove once the breadwinner of the family was gone. According to the pictures and descriptions published in the newspapers at the time she was, as De Malquit had said, an invalid, practically bedridden. Also, according to the newspapers, De Malquit had in more successful days been charitably inclined, having contributed liberally to the support of an orphan asylum, the Gratiot Home for Orphans, the exterior appearance of which Osterman was familiar with. This fact was published in all of the papers and was said to have impressed Osterman, who was said always to have had a friendly leaning toward orphans. I have since heard that only his very sudden death three years ago prevented his signing a will which contained a proviso leaving the bulk of his great fortune to a holding company instructed to look after orphans. Whether this is truth or romance I do not know.

2. The case of Henry Greasadick, another of Mr. Osterman's competitors, was similar. Mr. Greasadick has been described to me as a very coarse and rough man, without any education of any kind, but one who understood oil prospecting and refining, and who was finally, though rather unfortunately for himself, the cause of the development by Osterman of the immensely valuable Arroya Verde field. It is not likely that Greasadick would ever have made the fortune from this field that Osterman and his confrères were destined to reap. However, it is equally true that he was most shabbily treated in the matter, far more so than was De Malquit in regard to his very questionable holdings and sales. The details of the Arroya Verde field and Greasadick are as follows: Greasadick has been described to me as a big, blustery, dusty soul, uncouth in manners and speech, but one who was a sound and able prospector. And Osterman, it appears, having laid the foundation of his fortune by treating De Malquit and others as he had, had come west, first to the lumber properties of Washington and Oregon, where he bought immense tracts; and later, to the oil lands of California and Mexico, in which state and country he acquired very important and eventually (under him) productive holdings. Now it chanced that in his wanderings through southern California and Arizona he came across Greasadick, who had recently chanced upon a virgin oil field which, although having very little capital himself, he was secretly attempting to develop. In fact, Greasadick had no money when he discovered this oil field and was borrowing from L. T.

Drewberry, of the K. B. & B., and one or two others on the strength of his prospects. It also appears that Drewberry it was who first called the attention of Osterman to Greasdick and his find and later plotted with him to oust Greasadick. Osterman was at that time one of three or four men who were interested in developing the K. B. & B. into a paying property by extending it into Arizona.

At any rate, Greasadick's holdings were one hundred miles from any main line road, and there was very little water, only a thin trickle that came down through a cut. True, the K. B. & B. was about to build a spur to Larston in order to aid him, but Larston, once the line was built to it, was fourteen miles away and left Greasadick with the problem of piping or hauling his oil to that point. Once he heard of it Osterman saw at a glance that by a little deft manœuvring it could be made very difficult for Greasadick to do anything with his property except sell, and this manœuvring he proceeded to do. By buying the land above Greasadick's, which was a mountain slope, and then because of a thin wall of clay and shale dividing the Arroya Verde, in which lay Greasadick's land, from the Arroya Blanco, which was unwatered and worthless, being able to knock the same through, he was able to divert the little water upon which Greasadick then depended to do his work. Only it was all disguised as a landslide—an act of God—and a very expensive one for Greasadick to remedy. As for the proposed spur to Larston—well, that was easy to delay indefinitely. There was Drewberry, principal stockholder of the K. B. & B., who joined with Osterman in this adroit scheme. Finally, there was the simple device of buying in the mortgage given by Greasadick to Drewberry and others and waiting until such time as he was hard-pressed to force him to sell out. This was done through Whitley, Osterman's efficient assistant, who in turn employed another to act for him. Throughout, Osterman saw to it that he personally did not appear.

Of course Greasadick, when he discovered what the plot

was, roared and charged like a bull. Indeed before he was eventually defeated he became very threatening and dangerous, attempting once even to kill Drewberry. Yet he was finally vanquished and his holdings swept away. With no money to make a new start and seeing others prosper where he had failed for want of a little capital, he fell into a heavy gloom and finally died there in Larston in the bar that had been erected after the K. B. & B. spur had been completed. Through all of this Mr. Osterman appears to have been utterly indifferent to the fate of the man he was undermining. He cared so little what became of him afterwards that he actually admitted, or remarked to Whitley, who remained one of his slaves to the end, that one could scarcely hope to build a large fortune without indulging in a few such tricks.

3. Lastly, there was the matter of the C. C. and Q. L. Railroad, the major portion of the stock of which he and Frank O. Parm, of the Parm-Baggott chain of stores, had managed to get hold of by the simple process of buying a few shares and then bringing stockholders' suits under one and another name in order to embarrass President Doremus and his directors, and frighten investors so they would let go of the stock. And this stock, of course, was picked up by Osterman and Parm, until at last these two became the real power behind the road and caused it to be thrown into the hands of a receiver and then sold to themselves. That was two years before ever Michael Doremus, the first president of the road, resigned. When he did he issued a statement saying that he was being hounded by malign financial influences and that the road was as sound as ever it had been, which was true. Only it could not fight all of these suits and the persistent rumors of mismanagement that were afoot. As a matter of fact, Mr. Doremus died only a year after resigning, declaring at that time that a just God ruled and that time would justify himself. But Mr. Osterman and Mr. Parm secured the road, and finally incorporated it with the P. B. & C. as is well known.

III

Some data taken from the biographic study of the late J. H. Osterman, multimillionaire and oil king, prepared for Lingley's Magazine and by it published in its issue for October, 1917.

In order to understand the late J. H. Osterman and his great success and his peculiar faults one would first have to have known and appreciated the hard and colorless life that had surrounded him as a boy. His father, in so far as I have been able to ascertain, was a crude, hard, narrow man who had been made harder and, if anything, cruder by the many things which he had been compelled to endure. He was not a kind or soft-spoken man to his children. He died when John Osterman, the central figure of this picture, was eleven. Osterman's mother, so it is said, was a thin and narrow and conventional woman, as much harried and put upon by her husband as ever he was by life. Also there was one sister, unattractive and rough-featured, an honest and narrow girl who, like her mother, worked hard up to nineteen, when her mother died. After that, both parents being dead, she and her brother attempted to manage the farm, and did so fairly successfully for two years when the sister decided to marry; and Osterman consenting, she took over the farm. This falling in with his mood and plans, he ceased farming for good and betook himself to the Texas oil fields, where he appears to have mastered some of the details of oil prospecting and refining.

But before that, what miseries had he not endured! He was wont to recount how, when grasshoppers and drought took all of their crops for two years after his father's death, he and his mother and sister were reduced to want and he had actually been sent to beg a little cornmeal and salt from the local store on the promise to pay, possibly a year later. Taxes mounted up. There was no money to buy seed or to plant or replace stock, which had had to be sold.

The family was without shoes or clothes. Osterman himself appeared to be of the fixed opinion that the citizens and dealers of Reamer, from near which point in Kansas he hailed, were a hard and grasping crew. He was fond of telling how swift they were to point out that there was no help for either himself or his mother or sister as farmers and to deny them aid and encouragement on that score. He once said that all he ever heard in the local branch of his mother's church, of which he was never a confessing communicant, was "an eye for an eye, a tooth for a tooth"; also "with whatsoever measure ye mete it shall be measured to you again." Obviously such maxims taken very much to heart by a boy of his acquisitive and determined nature might bring about some of the shrewd financial tricks later accredited to him. Yet he appears to have been a man of some consideration and sympathy where boys were concerned, for it was said that he made it a rule in all his adventures to select the poorest if most determined youths of his organization for promotion and to have developed all of his chief lieutenants from the ranks of farm or orphan boy beginners whom he encouraged to work for him. How true this is the writer is not able to state. However, of the forty or more eminent men who have been connected with him in his enterprises, all but four were farm or orphan boys who had entered his enterprises as clerks or menials at the very bottom, and some seven of the total were from his native State, Kansas.

IV

The private cogitations of the late John H. Osterman in his mansion at 1046 Fifth Avenue, New York, and elsewhere during the last five years of his life.

Oh, but those days when he had been working and scheming to get up in the world and was thinking that money was the great thing—the only thing! Those impossible wooden towns in the Northwest and elsewhere in which he had lived and worked, and those worse hotels and boarding-houses—always hunting, hunting for money or the key to it. The greasy, stinking craft in which he had made his way up weedy and muddy rivers in Honduras and elsewhere —looking for what? Snakes, mosquitoes, alligators, tarantulas, horned toads and lizards. In Honduras he had slept under chiqua trees on mats of chiqua leaves, with only a fire to keep away snakes and other things. And of a morning he had chased away noisy monkeys and parroquets from nearby branches with rotten fruit so as to sleep a little longer. Alone, he had tramped through fever swamps, pursued by Pequi Indians, who wanted only the contents of his wretched pack. And he had stared at huge coyal palms, a hundred feet high, with the great feathery leaves fifteen feet long and their golden flowers three feet high. Ah, well, that was over now. He had shot the quetzal with its yellow tail feathers three feet long and had traded them for food. Once he had all but died of fever in a half-breed's hut back of Cayo. And the halfbreed had then stolen his gun and razor and other goods and left him to make his way onward as best he might. That was life for you, just like that. People were like that.

And it was during that time that he had come to realize that by no honest way at his age was he likely to come to anything financially. Roaming about the drowsy, sun-baked realm, he had encountered Messner, an American and a fugitive, he guessed, and it was Messner who had outlined to him the very scheme by which he had been able, later, to amass his first quick fortune in New York. It was Messner who had told him of Torbey and how he had come up to London from Central Africa to offer shares in a bogus rubber enterprise based on immense forests which he was supposed to have found in the wilds of Africa yet which did not exist. And it was the immense though inaccessible rubber forests in Honduras that had inspired him to try the same

thing in New York. Why not? A new sucker was born
every minute, and he had all to gain and nothing to lose.
Messner said that Torbey had advertised for a widow with
some money to push his enterprise, whereupon he had proceeded to tell the London speculative public of his treasure
and to sell two pound shares for as low as ten shillings in
order to show tremendous rises in value—to issue two
million pounds' worth of absolutely worthless stock.

By these methods and by having the stock listed on the
London curb he was able to induce certain curb or "dog"
brokers to go short of this stock without having any of it
in their possession. Finally they began to sell so freely and
to pay so little attention to the amount that was being sold
that it was easy for Torbey to employ agents to buy from
all of them freely on margin. And then, as the law of the
curb and the state permitted, he had demanded (through
them, of course) the actual delivery of the shares, the full
curb value of the stock being offered. Of course the
brokers had none, although they had sold thousands; nor
had any one else except Torbey, who had seen to it that all
outstanding stock had been recalled to his safe. That meant
that they must come to Torbey to buy or face a jail sentence,
and accordingly they had flocked to his office, only to be
properly mulcted for the total face value of the shares when
they came.

Well, he had done that same thing in New York. Following the example of the good Torbey, he had picked up
a few unimportant options in Honduras, far from any railroad, and had come to New York to launch Calamita. Just
as Torbey had done, he had looked for a rich widow, a
piano manufacturer's wife in this case, and had persuaded
her that there were millions in it. From her he had gone
on to Wall Street and the curb and had done almost exactly
as Torbey had done. . . . Only that fellow De Malquit
had killed himself, and that was not so pleasant. He hadn't
anticipated that anything like that would happen! That
unfortunate wife of his. And those two children made

orphans. That was the darkest spot. He hadn't known, of course, that De Malquit himself was helping orphans— or— And from there he had gone on to the forests of Washington and Oregon, where he had bought immense tracts on which even yet he was realizing, more and more. And from there it had been an easy step to oil in southern California and Mexico— Ah, Greasadick, another sad case!— And from there to mines and government concessions in Peru and Ecuador, and the still greater ones in Argentina and Chile. Money came fast to those who had it. At last, having accumulated a fortune of at least nine millions, he had been able to interest Nadia, and through her the clever and well-to-do fashionable set who had backed his projects with their free capital. And by now his fortune had swollen to almost forty millions.

But what of it? Could he say he was really content? What was he getting out of it? Life was so deceptive; it used and then tossed one aside. At first it had seemed wonderful to be able to go, do, act, buy and sell as he chose, without considering anything save whether the thing he was doing was agreeable and profitable. He had thought that pleasure would never pall, but it had. There was this thing about age, that it stole over one so unrelentingly, fattening one up or thinning one down, hardening the arteries and weakening the muscles and blood, until it was all but useless to go on. And what was the import of his success, anyhow, especially to one who had no children and no friends worthy of the name? There was no such thing as true friendship in nature. It was each man for himself, everywhere, and the devil take the hindmost. It was life that used and tossed one aside, however great or powerful one might be. There was no staying life or the drift of time.

Of course there had been the pleasure of building two great houses for Nadia and living in them when he was not living in other parts of the world. But all that had come too late; he had been too old to enjoy them when they did come. She had been a great catch no doubt, but much too attractive to be really interested in him at his age. His wealth had been the point with her—any one could see that; he knew it at the time and would not now try to deceive himself as to that. At the time he had married her she had had social position whereas he had none. And after she married him all her social influence, to be sure, had been used to advance his cause. Still, that scheme of hers to get him to leave his great fortune to those two worthless sons of hers. Never! They were not worthy of it. Those dancing, loafing wasters! He would see to it that his fortune was put to some better use than that. He would leave it to orphans rather than to them, for after all orphans in his employ had proved more valuable to him than even they had, hadn't they?— That curious fellow, De Malquit!— So long ago. Besides wasn't it Nadia's two sons who had influenced their mother to interest herself in D'Eyraud, the architect who had built their two houses and had started Nadia off on that gallery idea. And not a picture in it that would interest a sensible person. And wasn't it because of her that he had never troubled to answer the letters of his sister Elvira asking him to educate her two boys for her. He had fancied at the time that taking her two children into his life would in some way affect his social relations with Nadia and her set. And now Elvira was dead and he did not know where the children were. He could charge that to her if he wanted to, couldn't he?

Well, life was like that. When he had built his two great houses he had thought they would prove an immense satisfaction to him, as they had for a time; but he would not be here much longer now to enjoy them. He wasn't nearly as active as he had been, and the sight of the large companies of people that came to pose and say silly things to each other was very wearying. They were always civil to him, of course, but little more. They wanted the influence of his name. And as long as he permitted it, his homes would be haunted by those who wished to sell him things—stocks, bonds, enterprises, tapestries, estates, horses. And those two boys of hers, along with Nadia herself where her so-called art objects were concerned, so busy encouraging them! Well, he was done with all that now. He would not be bothered. Even youth and beauty of a venal character had appeared on the scene and had attempted to set traps for him. But his day was over. All these fripperies and pleasures were for people younger than he. It required youth and energy to see beauty and romance in such things, and he hadn't a trace of either left. His day was over and he might as well die, really, for all the good he was, apart from his money, to any one.

V

The reminiscences of Byington Briggs, Esq., of Skeff, Briggs & Waterhouse, private legal advisers to the late J. H. Osterman, as developed in a private conversation at the Metropolitan Club in New York in December, 19—.

"You knew old Osterman, didn't you? I was his confidential adviser for the last eight years of his life, and a shrewder old hawk never sailed the air. He was a curious combination of speculator, financier and dreamer, with a high percentage of sharper thrown in for good measure. You'd never imagine that he was charitably inclined, now would you? It never occurred to me until about a year and a half before his death. I have never been able to explain it except that as a boy he had had a very hard time and in his old age resented seeing his two stepsons, Kester and Rand Benda, getting ready to make free use of his fortune once he was gone. And then I think he had come to believe that his wife was merely using him to feather her own nest. I wouldn't want it mentioned to a soul as coming from me, but three months before he died he had me draw up a will leaving his entire estate of something like forty millions, not to her, as the earlier will filed by her showed, but to the J. H. Osterman Foundation, a corporation whose sole purpose was to administer his fortune for the benefit of something like three hundred thousand orphans incarcerated in institutions in America. And but for the accident of his sudden death out there at Shell Cove two years ago, he would have left it that way.

"According to the terms of the will that I drew up, Mrs. Osterman and her two sons were to receive only the interest on certain bonds that were to be placed in trust for them for their lifetime only; after that the money was to revert to the fund. That would have netted them between forty and fifty thousand a year among them—nothing more. In the will I drew up he left $500,000 outright to that Gratiot Home for Orphans up here at 68th Street, and he intended his big country place at Shell Cove as the central unit in a chain of modern local asylums for orphans that was to have belted America. The income from the property managed by the foundation was to have been devoted to this work exclusively, and the Gratiot institution was to have been the New York branch of the system. His wife has leased the Shell Cove place to the Gerbermanns this year, I see, and a wonderful place it is too, solid marble throughout, a lake a mile long, a big sunken garden, a wonderful glassed-in conservatory, and as fine a view of the sea as you'll find anywhere. Yet she never knew until the very last hour of his life—the very last, for I was there—that he planned to cut her off with only forty or fifty thousand a year. If we weren't all such close friends I wouldn't think of mentioning it even now, although I understand that Klippert, who was his agent in the orphan project, has been telling the story. It was this way:

"You see, I was his lawyer, and had been ever since the K. B. & B. control fight in 1906, and the old man liked me —I don't know why unless it was because I drew up the right sort of 'waterproof contracts,' as he always called them. Anyway, I knew six or seven years before he died that he wasn't getting along so well with Mrs. Osterman.

She is still an attractive woman, with plenty of brain power and taste, but I think he had concluded that she was using him and that he wasn't as happy as he thought he would be. For one thing, as I gathered from one person and another, she was much too devoted to those two boys by her first husband, and in the next place I think he felt that she was letting that architect D'Eyraud lead her about too much and spend too much of his money. You know it was common rumor at the time that D'Eyraud and his friend Beseroe, another man the old captain disliked, were behind her in all her selections of pictures for the gallery she was bringing together up there in the Fifth Avenue place. Osterman, of course, knowing absolutely nothing about art, was completely out of it. He wouldn't have known a fine painting from a good lithograph, and I don't think he cared very much either. And yet it was a painting that was one of the causes of some feeling between them, as I will show you. At that time he looked mighty lonely and forlorn to me, as though he didn't have a friend in the world outside of those business associates and employés of his. He stayed principally in that big town house, and Mrs. Benda—I mean Mrs. Osterman—and her sons and their friends found a good many excuses for staying out at Shell Cove. There were always big doings out there. Still, she was clever enough to be around him sometimes so as to make it appear, to him at least, that she wasn't neglecting him. As for him, he just pottered around up there in that great house, showing his agents and employés, and the fellows who buzzed about him to sell him things, the pictures she was collecting —or, rather, D'Eyraud—and letting it appear that he was having something to do with it. For he was a vain old soldier, even if he did have one of the best business minds of his time. You'd think largeness of vision in some things might break a man of that, but it never does, apparently.

"Whenever I think of him I think of that big house, those heavily carved and gilded rooms, the enormous eighty-thousand dollar organ built into the reception-room, and

those tall stained-glass windows that gave the place the air
of a church. Beseroe once told me that if left to follow
her own taste Mrs. Osterman would never have built that
type of house, but that Osterman wanted something grand
and had got his idea of grandeur from churches. So there
was nothing to do but build him a house with tall Gothic
windows and a pipe-organ, and trust to other features to
make it homelike and livable. But before they were through
with it Mrs. Osterman and D'Eyraud had decided that the
best that could be done with it would be to build something
that later could be turned into an art gallery and either
sold or left as a memorial. But I think both D'Eyraud and
Mrs. Osterman were kidding the old man a little when they
had that self-playing attachment built in. It looked to me
as though they thought he was going to be alone a good
part of the time and might as well have something to amuse
himself with. And he did amuse himself with it, too. I
recall going up there one day and finding him alone, in so
far as the family was concerned, but entirely surrounded by
twenty-five or more of those hard, slick and yet nervous
(where social form was concerned) western and southern
business agents and managers of his, present there to hold a
conference. A luncheon was about to be served in the grand
dining-room adjoining the reception-room, and there were
all these fellows sitting about that big room like a lot of
blackbirds, and Osterman upon a raised dais at one end of
the room solemnly rendering *The Bluebells of Scotland,* one
of his favorites, from the self-player attachment! And
when he finished they all applauded!

"Well, what I wanted to tell you is this: One day while
I was there, some dealer dropped in with a small picture
which for some reason took his fancy. According to Beseroe,
it wasn't such a bad thing, painted by a Swedish realist by
the name of Dargson. It showed a rather worn-out woman
of about forty-three who had committed suicide and was
lying on a bed, one hand stretched out over the edge and a
glass or bottle from which she had taken the poison lying

on the floor beside her. Two young children and a man were standing near, commiserating themselves on their loss, I presume. It seemed to have a tremendous impression on Osterman for some reason or other. I could never understand why—it was not so much art as a comment on human suffering. Nevertheless, Osterman wanted it, but I think he wanted Nadia to buy it for her collection and so justify his opinion of it. But Nadia, according to Beseroe, was interested only in certain pictures as illustrations of the different schools and periods of art in different countries. And when the dealer approached her with the thing, at Osterman's suggestion, it was immediately rejected by her. At once Osterman bought it for himself, and to show that he was not very much concerned about her opinion he hung it in his bedroom. Thereafter he began to be quarrelsome in regard to the worthwhileness of the gallery idea as a whole and to object to so much money being squandered in that direction. But to this day no one seems to know just why he liked that particular picture so much.

"What I personally know is that it was just about this time that Osterman began to be interested in that fellow Klippert and his plan for improving the condition of the orphan. He finally turned him over to me with the request that I go into the idea thoroughly, not only in regard to the work done by the Gratiot Home but by orphan asylums in general in America. He told us that he wanted it all kept very quiet until he was ready to act, that if anything was said he would refuse to have anything further to do with it. That was a part of his plan to outwit Mrs. Osterman, of course. He told us that he wanted some scheme in connection with orphans that would be new and progressive, better than anything now being done, something that would do away with great barracks and crowd regulations and cheap ugly uniforms and would introduce a system of education and home life in cottages. I had no idea then that he was planning the immense thing that was really in his mind, and neither did Klippert. He thought he might be intending to furnish enough money to revive the Gratiot Home as an experiment, and he urged me to use my influence to this end if I had any. As it turned out, he wanted to establish an interstate affair, as wide as the nation, of which the place at Shell Cove was to be the centre or head —a kind of Eastern watering-place or resort for orphans from all over America. It was a colossal idea and would have taken all of his money and more.

"But since he wanted it I went into the idea thoroughly with this fellow Klippert. He was very clever, that man, honest and thorough and business-like and disinterested, in so far as I could see. I liked him, and so did Osterman, only Osterman wanted him to keep out of sight of his wife until he was ready to act. Klippert made a regular business of his problem and went all over the United States studying institutions of the kind. Finally he came back with figures on about fifty or sixty and a plan which was the same as that outlined to me by Osterman and which I incorporated in his will, and there it ended for the time being. He didn't want to sign it right away for some reason, and there it lay in my safe until—well, let me tell you how it was.

One Saturday morning—it was a beautiful day and I was thinking of going out to the club to play golf—I received a long distance call from Osterman asking me to get hold of Klippert and another fellow by the name of Moss and bring them out to Shell Cove, along with the will for him to sign. He had made up his mind, he said, and I have often wondered if he had a premonition of what was going to happen.

"I remember so well how excited Klippert was when I got him on the wire. He was just like a boy, that fellow, in his enthusiasm for the scheme, and apparently not interested in anything except the welfare of those orphans. We started for Shell Cove, and what do you think? Just as we got there—I remember it all as though it had happened yesterday. It was a bright, hot Saturday afternoon. There were some big doings on the grounds, white-and-green and white-and-red striped marque tents, and chairs and swings and tables everywhere. Some of the smartest people were there, sitting or walking or dancing on the balcony. And there was Osterman walking up and down the south verandah near the main motor entrance, waiting for us, I suppose. As we drove up he recognized us, for he waved his hand, and then just as we were getting out and he was walking towards us, I saw him reel and go down. It was just as though some one had struck him with something. I realized that it must be paralysis or a stroke of apoplexy and I chilled all over at the thought of what it might mean. Klippert went up the steps four at a time, and as we all ran down the verandah they carried him in and I telephoned for a doctor. Klippert was very still and white. All we could do was to stand around and wait and look at each other, for Mrs. Osterman and her sons were there and were taking charge. Finally word came out that Mr. Osterman was a little better and wanted to see us, so up we went. He had been carried into an airy, sunny room overlooking the sea and was lying in a big white canopied bed looking as pale and weak as he would if he had been ill for a month. He could scarcely speak and lay there and looked at us for a time, his mouth open and a kind of tremor passing over his lips from time to time. Then he seemed to gather a little strength and whispered: 'I want—I want—' and then he stopped and rested, unable to go on. The doctor arrived and gave him a little whisky, and then he began again, trying so hard to speak and not quite making it. At last he whispered: 'I want—I want—that—that—paper.' And then: 'Klippert—and you—' He stopped again, then added: 'Get all these others out of here—all but you three and the doctor.'

"The doctor urged Mrs. Osterman and her sons to leave, but I could see that she didn't like it. Even after she went out she kept returning on one excuse and another, and she was there when he died. When she was out of the room the first time I produced the will and he nodded his approval.

We called for a writing board, and they brought one—a Ouija board, by the way. We lifted him up, but he was too weak and fell back. When we finally got him up and spread the will before him he tried to grasp the pen but he couldn't close his fingers. He shook his head and half whispered: 'The——the——boys—th—the—boys.' Klippert was all excited, but Osterman could do nothing. Then his wife came into the room and asked: 'What is it that you are trying to make poor Johnnie sign? Don't you think you had better let it rest until he is stronger?' She tried to pick up the paper but I was too quick for her and lifted it to one side as though I hadn't noticed that she had reached for it. I could see that she was aware that something was being done that neither we nor Osterman wanted her to know about, and her eyes fairly snapped. Osterman must have realized that things were becoming a little shaky for he kept looking at first one and then another of us with a most unhappy look. He motioned for the pen and will. Klippert put down the board and I the paper, and he leaned forward and tried to grasp the pen. When he found he couldn't he actually groaned: 'The—the—I—I—I want to—to—do something—for—for—the—the—the—' Then he fell back, and the next moment was dead.

"But I wish you could have seen Klippert. It wasn't anything he said or did, but just something that passed over his face, the shadow of a great cause or idea dying, let us say. Something seemed to go out from or die in him, just as old Osterman had died. He turned and went out without a word. I would have gone too, only Mrs. Osterman intercepted me.

"You might think that at such a moment she would have been too wrought up to think of anything but her husband's death, but she wasn't. Far from it. Instead, as her husband was lying there, and right before the doctor, she came over to me and demanded to see the paper. I was folding it up to put into my pocket when she flicked it out of my hands. 'I am sure you can have no objection to my seeing this,' she said icily, and when I protested she added: 'I am sure that I have a right to see my own husband's will.' I had only been attempting to spare her feelings, but when I saw what her attitude was I let it go at that and let her read it.

"I wish you could have seen her face! Her eyes narrowed and she bent over the paper as though she were about to eat it. When she fully comprehended what it was all about she fairly gasped and shook—with rage, I think— though fear as to what might have happened except for her husband's weakness may have been a part of it. She looked at him, at his dead body, the only glance he got from her that day, I'm sure, then at me, and left the room. Since there was nothing more to do, I went too.

"And that's the reason Mrs. Osterman has never been friends with me since, though she was genial enough before. But it was a close shave for her, all the same, and don't you think it wasn't. Just an ounce or two more of strength in that old codger's system, and think what would have been done with those millions. She wouldn't have got even a million of it all told. And those little ragamuffins would have had it all. How's that for a stroke of chance?"

XIII

THE SHADOW

I

WHAT had given him his first hint that all might not be as well at home as he imagined was the incident of the automobile. Up to that time he had not had a troubled thought about her, not one. But after— Well, it was a year and a half now and although suspicion still lingered it was becoming weaker. But it had not been obliterated even though he could not help being fond of Beryl, especially since they had Tickles to look after between them. But anyhow, in spite of all his dark thoughts and subtle efforts to put two and two together, he had not been able to make anything of it. Perhaps he was being unjust to her to go on brooding about it. . . . But how was it possible that so many suspicious-looking things could happen in a given time, and one never be able to get the straight of them?

The main thing that had hampered him was his work. He was connected with the Tri-State Paper Company, at the City Order desk, and as a faithful employé he was not supposed to leave during working hours without permission, and it was not always easy to get permission. It was easy to count the times he had been off—once to go to the dentist, and two or three times to go home when Beryl was ill. Yet it just happened that on that particular afternoon his superior, Mr. Baggott, had suggested that he, in the place of Naigly who always attended to such matters but was away at the time, should run out to the Detts-Scanlon store and ask Mr. Pierce just what was wrong with that last order that had been shipped. There was a mix-up somewhere, and it had been impossible to get the thing straight over the telephone.

Well, just as he was returning to the office, seated in one of those comfortable cross seats of the Davenant Avenue line and looking at the jumble of traffic out near Blakely Avenue, and just as the car was nearing the entrance to Briscoe Park he saw a tan-and-chocolate-colored automobile driven by a biggish man in a light tan overcoat and cap swing into view, cross in front of the car, and enter the park. It was all over in a flash. But just as the car swung near him who should he see sitting beside the man but Beryl, or certainly a woman who was enough like her to be her twin sister. He would have sworn it was Beryl. And what was more, and worse, she was smiling up at this man as though they were on the best of terms and had known each other a long time! Of course he had only had a glimpse, and might have been mistaken. Beryl had told him that morning that she was going to spend the afternoon with her mother. She often did that, sometimes leaving Tickles there while she did her mother's marketing. Or, she and her mother, or she and her sister Alice, if she chanced to be there, would take the baby for a walk in the park. Of course he might have been mistaken.

But that hat with the bunch of bright green grapes on the side. . . . And that green-and-white striped coat. . . . And that peculiar way in which she always held her head when she was talking. Was it really Beryl? If it wasn't, why should he have had such a keen conviction that it was?

Up to that time there never had been anything of a doubtful character between them—that is, nothing except that business of the Raskoffsky picture, which didn't amount to much in itself. Anybody might become interested in a great violinist and write him for his photo, though even that couldn't be *proved* against Beryl. It was inscribed to Alice. But even if she had written him, that wasn't a patch compared to this last, her driving about in a car with a strange man. Certainly that would justify him in any steps that he chose to take, even to getting a divorce.

But what had he been able to prove so far? Nothing. He had tried to find her that afternoon, first at their own house, then at her mother's, and then at Winton & Marko's real estate office, where Alice sometimes helped out, but he couldn't find a trace of her. Still, did that prove anything once and for all? She might have been to the concert as she said, she and Alice. It must be dull to stay in the house all day long, anyhow, and he couldn't blame her for doing the few things she did within their means. Often he tried to get in touch with her of a morning or afternoon, and there was no answer, seeing that she was over to her mother's or out to market, as she said. And up to the afternoon of the automobile it had never occurred to him that there was anything queer about it. When he called up Beryl's mother she had said that Beryl and Alice had gone to a concert and it wasn't believable that Mrs. Dana would lie to him about anything. Maybe the two of them were doing something they shouldn't, or maybe Alice was helping Beryl to do something she shouldn't, without their mother knowing anything about it. Alice was like that, sly. It was quite certain that if there had been any correspondence between Beryl and that man Raskoffsky, that time he had found the picture inscribed to Alice, it had been Alice who had been the go-between. Alice had probably allowed her name and address to be used for Beryl's pleasure —that is, if there was anything to it at all. It wasn't likely that Beryl would have attempted anything like that without Alice's help.

But just the same he had never been able to prove that they had been in league, at that time or any other. If there was anything in it they were too clever to let him catch them. The day he thought he had seen her in the car he had first tried to get her by telephone and then had gone to the office, since it was on his way, to get permission to go home for a few minutes. But what had he gained by it? By the time he got there, Beryl and her mother were already there, having just walked over from Mrs. Dana's home, according to Beryl. And Beryl was not wearing the hat and coat he had seen in the car, and that was what he wanted to find out. But between the time he had called up her mother and the time he had managed to get home she had had time enough to return and change her clothes and go over to her mother's if there was any reason why she should. That was what had troubled him and caused him to doubt ever since. She would have known by then that he had been trying to get her on the telephone and would have had any answer ready for him. And that may have been exactly what happened, assuming that she had been in the car and gotten home ahead of him, and presuming her mother had lied for her, which she would not do—not Mrs. Dana. For when he had walked in, a little flushed and excited, Beryl had exclaimed: "Whatever is the matter, Gil?" And then: "What a crazy thing, to come hurrying home just to ask me about this! Of course I haven't been in any car. How ridiculous! Ask Mother. You wouldn't expect her to fib for me, would you?" And then to clinch the matter she had added: "Alice and I left Tickles with her and went to the concert after going into the park for a while. When we returned, Alice stopped home so Mother could walk over here with me. What are you so excited about." And for the life of him, he had not been able to say anything except that he had seen a woman going into Briscoe Park in a tan-and-chocolate car, seated beside a big man who looked like—well, he couldn't say exactly whom he did look like. But the woman beside him certainly looked like Beryl. And she had had on a hat with green grapes on one side and a white-and-green striped sports coat, just like the one she had. Taking all that into consideration, what would any one think? But she had laughed it off, and what was he to say? He certainly couldn't accuse Mrs. Dana of not knowing what she was talking about, or Beryl of lying, unless he was sure of what he was saying. She was too strong-minded and too strong-willed for that. She had only married him after a long period of begging on his part; and she wasn't any too anxious to live with him now unless they could get along comfortably together.

Yet taken along with that Raskoffsky business of only a few months before, and the incident of the Hotel Deming of only the day before (but of which he had thought nothing until he had seen her in the car), and the incident of the letters in the ashes, which followed on the morning after he had dashed home that day, and then that business of the closed car in Bergley Place, just three nights afterwards—well, by George! when one put such things together—

It was very hard to put these things in the order of their effect on him, though it was easy to put them in their actual order as to time. The Hotel Deming incident had occurred only the day before the automobile affair and taken alone, meant nothing, just a chance encounter with her on the part of Naigly, who had chosen to speak of it. But joined afterwards with the business of the partly burned letters and after seeing her in that car or thinking he had— Well— After that, naturally his mind had gone back to that Hotel Deming business, and to the car, too. Naigly, who had been interested in Beryl before her marriage (she had been Baggott's stenographer), came into the office about four—the day before he had seen Beryl, or thought he had, in the car, and had said to him casually: "I saw your wife just now, Stoddard." "That so? Where?" "She was coming out of the Deming ladies' entrance as I passed just now." Well, taken by itself, there was nothing much in that, was there? There was an arcade of shops which made the main entrance to the Deming, and it was easy to go through that and come out of one of the other entrances. He knew Beryl had done it before, so why should he have worried about it then? Only, for some reason, when he came home that evening Beryl didn't mention that she had been downtown that day until he asked her. "What were you doing about four to-day?" "Down-town, shopping. Why? Did you see me? I went for Mother." "Me? No. Who do you know in the Deming?" "No one"—this without a trace of self-consciousness, which was one of the things that made him doubt whether there had been anything wrong. "Oh, yes; I remember now. I walked through to look at the hats in Anna McCarty's window, and came out the ladies' entrance. Why?" "Oh, nothing. Naigly said he saw you, that's all. You're getting to be a regular gadabout these days." "Oh, what nonsense! Why shouldn't I go through the Deming Arcade? I would have stopped in to see you, only I know you don't like me to come bothering around there."

And so he had dismissed it from his mind—until the incident of the car.

And then the matter of the letters . . . and Raskoff-sky . . .

Beryl was crazy about music, although she couldn't play except a little by ear. Her mother had been too poor to give her anything more than a common school education, which was about all that he had had. But she was crazy about the violin and anybody who could play it, and when any of the great violinists came to town she always managed to afford to go. Raskoffsky was a big blond Russian who played wonderfully, so she said. She and Alice had gone to hear him, and for weeks afterward they had raved about him. They had even talked of writing to him, just to see if he would answer, but he had frowned on such a proceeding because he didn't want Beryl writing to any man. What good would it do her? A man like that wouldn't bother about answering her letter, especially if all the women were as crazy about him as the papers said. Yet later he had found Raskoffsky's picture in Beryl's room, only it was inscribed to Alice. . . . Still, Beryl might have put Alice up to it, might even have sent her own picture under Alice's name, just to see if he would answer. They had talked of sending a picture. Besides, if Alice had written and secured this picture, why wasn't it in her rather than Beryl's possession. He had asked about that. Yet the one flaw in that was that Alice wasn't really good-looking enough to send her picture and she knew it. Yet Beryl had sworn that she hadn't written. And Alice had insisted that it was she and not Beryl who had written. But there was no way of proving that she hadn't or that Beryl had.

Yet why all the secrecy? Neither of them had said anything more about writing Raskoffsky after that first time. And it was only because he had come across Raskoffsky's picture in one of Beryl's books that he had come to know anything about it at all. "To my fair little western admirer who likes my 'Dance Macabre' so much. The next time I play in your city you must come and see me." But Alice wasn't fair or good-looking. Beryl was. And it was Beryl and not Alice, who had first raved over that dance; Alice didn't care so much for music. And wasn't it Beryl, and not Alice, who had proposed writing him. Yet it was Alice who had received the answer. How was that? Very likely it was Beryl who had persuaded Alice to write for her, sending her own instead of Alice's picture, and getting Alice to receive Raskoffsky's picture for her when it came. Something in their manner the day he had found the picture indicated as much. Alice had been so quick to say: "Oh yes. I wrote him." But Beryl had looked a little queer when she caught him looking at her, had even flushed slightly, although she had kept her indifferent manner. At that time the incident of the car hadn't occurred. But afterwards,— after he had imagined he had seen Beryl in the car—it had occurred to him that maybe it was Raskoffsky with whom she was with that day. He was playing in Columbus, so the papers said, and he might have been passing through the city. He was a large man too, as he now recalled, by George! If only he could find a way to prove that!

Still, even so and when you come right down to it, was there anything so terrible about her writing a celebrity like that and asking for his picture, if that was all she had done.

But was it? Those long-enveloped gray letters he had found in the fireplace that morning, after that day in which he had seen her in the car (or thought he had)—or at least traces of them. And the queer way she had looked at him when he brought them up in connection with that closed car in Bergley Place. She had squinted her eyes as if to think, and had then laughed rather shakily when he charged her with receiving letters from Raskoffsky, and with his 'having come here to see her. His finding them had been entirely by accident. He always got up early to "start things," for Beryl was a sleepyhead, and he would start the fire in the grate and put on the water to boil in the kitchen. And this morning as he was bending over the grate to push away some scraps of burnt wood so as to start a new fire, he came across five or six letters, or the ashes of them, all close together as though they might have been tied with a ribbon or something. What was left of them looked as though they had been written on heavy stationery such as a man of means might use, the envelopes long and thick. The top one still showed the address—"Mrs. Beryl Stoddard, Care of ———" He was bending over to see the rest when a piece of wood toppled over and destroyed it. He rescued one little scrap, the half-charred corner of one page, and the writing on this seemed to be like that on Raskoffsky's picture, or so he thought, and he read: "to see you." Just that and nothing more, part of a sentence that ended the page and went to the next. And that page was gone, of course!

But it was funny wasn't it, that at sight of them the thought of Raskoffsky should have come to him? And that ride in the park. Come to think of it, the man in the car had looked a little like Raskoffsky's picture. And for all he knew, Raskoffsky might have then been in town—returned for this especial purpose,—and she might have been meeting him on the sly. Of course. At the Deming. That was it. He had never been quite able to believe her. All the circumstances at the time pointed to something of the kind, even if he had never been able to tie them together and make her confess to the truth of them.

But how he had suffered after that because of that thought! Things had seemed to go black before him. Beryl unfaithful? Beryl running around with a man like that, even if he was a great violinist? Everybody knew what kind of a man he was—all those men. The papers were always saying how crazy women were over him, and yet that he should come all the way to C—— to make trouble between him and Beryl! (If only he could prove that!) But why should she, with himself and Tickles to look after, and a life of her own which was all right—why should she be wanting to run around with a man like that, a man who would use her for a little while and then drop her. And when she had a home of her own? And her baby? And her mother and sister right here in C——? And him? And working as hard as he was and trying to make things come out right for them? That was the worst of it. That was the misery of it. And all for a little notice from a man who was so far above her or thought he was, anyhow, that he couldn't care for her or any one long. The papers had said so at the time. But that was the whole secret. She was so crazy about people who did anything in music or painting or anything like that, that she couldn't reason right about them. And she might have done a thing like that on that account. Personally he wouldn't give a snap of his finger for the whole outfit. They weren't ordinary, decent people anyhow. But making herself as common as that! And right here in C——, too, where they were both known. Oh, if only he had been able to prove that! If only he had been able to at that time!

When he had recovered himself a little that morning after he had found the traces of the letters in the ashes he had wanted to go into the bedroom where she was still asleep and drag her out by the hair and beat her and make her confess to these things. Yes, he had. There had been all but murder in his heart that morning. He would show her. She couldn't get away with any such raw stuff as that even if she did have her mother and sister to help her. (That sly little Alice, always putting her sister up to something and never liking him from the first, anyhow.) But then the thought had come to him that after all he might be wrong. Supposing the letters weren't from Raskoffsky? And supposing she had told the truth when she said she hadn't been in the car? He had nothing to go on except what he imagined, and up to then everything had been as wonderful as could be between them. Still . . .

Then another thought had come: if the letters weren't from Raskoffsky who were they from? He didn't know of anybody who would be writing her on any such paper as that. And if not Raskoffsky whom did she know? And why should she throw them in the fire, choosing a time when he wasn't about? That was strange, especially after the automobile incident of the day before. But when he taxed her with this the night of the Bergley Place car incident— she had denied everything and said they were from Claire Haggerty, an old chum who had moved to New York just about the time they were married and who had been writing her at her mother's because at that time he and she didn't have a home of their own and that was the only address she could give. She had been meaning to destroy them but had been putting it off. But only the night before she had come across them in a drawer and had tossed them in the fire, and that was all there was to that.

But was that all there was to it?

For even as he had been standing there in front of the grate wondering what to do the thought had come to him that he was not going about this in the right way. He had had the thought that he should hire a detective at once and have her shadowed and then if she were doing anything, it might be possible to find it out. That would have been better. That was really the way. Yet instead of doing that he had gone on quarreling with her, had burst in on her with everything that he suspected or saw, or thought he saw, and that it was, if anything, that had given her warning each time and had allowed her to get the upper hand of him, if she had got the upper hand of him. That was it. Yet he had gone on and quarreled with her that day just the same, only, after he had thought it all over, he had decided to consult the Sol Cohn Detective Service and have her watched. But that very night, coming back from the night conference with Mr. Harris Cohn, which was the only time he could get to give it, was the night he had seen the car in Bergley Place, and Beryl near it.

Bergley Place was a cross street two doors from where they lived on Winton. And just around the corner in Bergley, was an old vacant residence with a deal of shrubbery and four overarching trees in front. which made it very dark there at night. That night as he was coming home from Mr. Harris Cohn's—(he had told Beryl that he was going to the lodge, in order to throw her off and had come home earlier in order to see what he might see) and just as he was stepping off the Nutley Avenue car which turned into Marko Street, about half a block above where they lived whom should he see— But, no, let us put it this way. Just at that moment or a moment later as he turned toward his home an automobile that had been going the same way he was along Winton swung into Bergley Place and threw its exceptionally brilliant lights on a big closed automobile that was standing in front of the old house aforementioned. There were two vacant corner lots opposite the old house at Bergley and Winton and hence it was that he could see what was going on. Near the rear of the automobile, just as though she had stepped out of it and was about to leave, stood Beryl—or, he certainly thought it was Beryl, talking to some one in the car, just as one would before parting and returning into the house. She had on a hooded cape exactly like the one she wore at times though not often. She did not like hooded capes any more. They were out of style. Just the same so sure had he been that it was Beryl and that at last he had trapped her that he hurried on to the house or, rather, toward the car. But just as he neared the corner the lights of the car that had been standing there lightless flashed on for a second—then off and then sped away. Yet even with them on there had not been enough light to see whether it was Beryl, or who. Or what the number on the license plate was. It was gone and with it Beryl, presumably up the alley way and into the back door or so he had believed. So sure was he that she had gone that way that he himself had gone that way. Yet when he reached the rear door following her, as he chose to do, it was locked and the kitchen was dark. And he had to rap and pound even before she came to let him in. And when she did there she was looking as though she had not been out at all, undressed, ready for bed and wanting to know why he chose to come that way! And asking him not to make so much noise for fear of waking Tickles. . . .!

Think of it. Not a trace of excitement. No cape with a hood on. The light up in the dining-room and a book on the table as though she might have been reading—one of those novels by that fellow Barclay. And not a sign about anywhere that she might have been out—that was the puzzling thing. And denying that she had been out or that she had seen any car, or anything. Now what would you make of that!

Then it was, though, that he had burst forth in a fury of suspicion and anger and had dealt not only with this matter of the car in Bergley Place but the one in Briscoe Park, the letters in the ashes and the matter of Naigly seeing her come out of the Deming, to say nothing of her writing to Raskoffsky for his picture. For it was Raskoffsky, of course, if it was anybody. He was as positive as to that as any one could be. Who else could it have been? He had not even hesitated to insist that he knew who it was—Raskoffsky, of course—and that he had seen him and had been able to recognize him from his pictures. Yet she had denied that vehemently—even laughingly—or that he had seen any one, or that there had been a car there for her. And she did show him a clipping a week later which said that Raskoffsky was in Italy.

But if it wasn't Raskoffsky then who was it—if it was any one. "For goodness' sake, Gil," was all she would say at that or any other time, "I haven't been out with Raskoffsky or any one and I don't think you ought to come in here and act as you do. It seems to me you must be losing your mind. I haven't seen or heard of any old car. Do you think I could stand here and say that I hadn't if I had? And I don't like the way you have of rushing in here of late every little while and accusing me of something that I haven't done. What grounds have you for thinking that I have done anything wrong anyhow? That silly picture of Raskoffsky that Alice sent for. And that you think you saw me in an automobile. Not another thing. If you don't stop now and let me alone I will leave you I tell you and that is all there is to it. I won't be annoyed in this way and especially when you have nothing to go on." It was with that type of counter-argument that she had confronted him.

Besides, at that time—the night that he thought he saw her in Bergley Place—and as if to emphasize what she was saying, Tickles in the bedroom had waked up and begun to call "Mama, Mama." And she had gone in to him and brought him out even as she talked. And she had seemed very serious and defiant, then—very much more like her natural self and like a person who had been injured and was at bay. So he had become downright doubtful, again, and had gone back into the dining-room. And there was the light up and the book that she had been reading. And in the closet as he had seen when he had hung up his own coat was her hooded cape on the nail at the back where it always hung.

And yet how could he have been mistaken as to all of those things? Surely there must have been something to some of them. He could never quite feel, even now, that there hadn't been. Yet outside of just that brief period in which all of these things had occurred there had never been a thing that he could put his hands on, nothing that he could say looked even suspicious before or since. And the detective agency had not been able to find out anything about her either—not a thing. That had been money wasted: one hundred dollars. Now how was that?

II

The trouble with Gil was that he was so very suspicious by nature and not very clever. He was really a clerk, with a clerk's mind and a clerk's point of view. He would never rise to bigger things, because he couldn't, and yet she could not utterly dislike him either. He was always so very much in love with her, so generous—to her, at least—and he did the best he could to support her and Tickles which was something, of course. A lot of the trouble was that he was too affectionate and too clinging. He was always hanging around whenever he was not working. And with never a thought of going any place without her except to his lodge or on a business errand that he couldn't possibly escape. And if he did go he was always in such haste to get back! Before she had ever thought of marrying him, when he was shipping clerk at the Tri-State and she was Mr. Baggott's stenographer, she had seen that he was not very remarkable as a man. He hadn't the air or the force of Mr. Baggott, for whom she worked then and whose assistant Gil later became. Indeed, Mr. Baggott had once said: "Gilbert is all right, energetic and faithful enough, but he lacks a large grasp of things." And yet in spite of all that she had married him.

Why?

Well, it was hard to say. He was not bad-looking, rather handsome, in fact, and that had meant a lot to her then. He had fine, large black eyes and a pale forehead and pink cheeks, and such nice clean hands. And he always dressed so well for a young man in his position. He was so faithful and yearning, a very dog at her heels. But she shouldn't have married him, just the same. It was all a mistake. He was not the man for her. She knew that now. And, really, she had known it then, only she had not allowed her common sense to act. She was always too sentimental then—not practical enough as she was now. It was only after she was married and surrounded by the various problems that marriage includes that she had begun to wake up. But then it was too late.

Yes, she had married, and by the end of the first year and a half, during which the original glamour had had time to subside, she had Tickles, or Gilbert, Jr., to look after. And with him had come a new mood such as she had never dreamed of in connection with herself. Just as her interest in Gil had begun to wane a little her interest in Tickles had sprung into flame. And for all of three years now it had grown stronger rather than weaker. She fairly adored her boy and wouldn't think of doing anything to harm him. And yet she grew so weary at times of the humdrum life they were compelled to live. Gil only made forty-five dollars a week, even now. And on that they had to clothe and feed and house the three of them. It was no easy matter. She would rather go out and work. But it was not so easy with a three-year-old baby. And besides Gil would never hear of such a thing. He was just one of those young husbands who thought the wife's place was in the home, even when he couldn't provide a very good home for her to live in.

Still, during these last few years she had had a chance to read and think, two things which up to that time she had never seemed to have time for. Before that it had always been beaux and other girls. But most of the girls were married now and so there was an end to them. But reading and thinking had gradually taken up all of her spare time, and that had brought about such a change in her. She really wasn't the same girl now that Gil had married at all. She was wiser. And she knew so much more about life now than he did. And she thought so much more, and so differently. He was still at about the place mentally that he had been when she married him, interested in making a better place for himself in the Tri-State office and in playing golf or tennis out at the country club whenever he could afford the time to go out there. And he expected her to curry favor with Dr. and Mrs. Realk, and Mr. and Mrs. Stofft, because they had a car and because Mr. Stofft and Gil liked to play cards together. But beyond that he thought of nothing, not a thing.

But during all of this time she had more and more realized that Gil would never make anything much of himself. Alice had cautioned her against him before ever they had married. He was not a business man in any true sense. He couldn't think of a single thing at which he could make any money except in the paper business, and that required more capital than ever he would have. Everybody else they knew was prospering. And perhaps it was that realization that had thrown her back upon books and pictures and that sort of thing. People who did things in those days were so much more interesting than people who just made money, anyhow.

Yet she would never have entered upon that dangerous affair with Mr. Barclay if it hadn't been for the awful mental doldrums she found herself in about the time Tickles was two years old and Gil was so worried as to whether he would be able to keep his place at the Tri-State any longer. He had put all the money they had been able to save into that building and loan scheme, and when that had failed they were certainly up against it for a time. There was just nothing to do with, and there was no prospect of relief. To this day she had no clothes to speak of. And there wasn't much promise of getting them now. And she wasn't getting any younger. Still, there was Tickles, and she was brushing up on her shorthand again. If the worst came—

But she wouldn't have entered upon that adventure that

had come so near to ending disastrously for herself and Tickles—for certainly if Gil had ever found out he could have taken Tickles away from her—if it hadn't been for that book *Heyday* which Mr. Barclay wrote and which she came across just when she was feeling so out of sorts with life and Gil and everything. That had pictured her own life so keenly and truly; indeed, it seemed to set her own life before her just as it was and as though some one were telling her about herself. It was the story of a girl somewhat like herself who had dreamed her way through a rather pinched girlhood, having to work for a living from the age of fourteen. And then just as she was able to make her own way had made a foolish marriage with a man of no import in any way—a clerk, just like Gil. And he had led her through more years of meagre living, until at last, very tired of it all, she had been about to yield herself to another man who didn't care very much about her but who had money and could do the things for her that her husband couldn't. Then of a sudden in this story her husband chose to disappear and leave her to make her way as best she might. The one difference between that story and her own life was that there was no little Tickles to look after. And Gil would never disappear, of course. But the heroine of the story had returned to her work without compromising herself. And in the course of time had met an architect who had the good sense or the romance to fall in love with and marry her. And so the story, which was so much like hers, except for Tickles and the architect, had ended happily.

But hers—well—

But the chances she had taken at that time! The restless and yet dreamy mood in which she had been and moved and which eventually had prompted her to write Mr. Barclay, feeling very doubtful as to whether he would be interested in her and yet drawn to him because of the life he had pictured. Her thought had been that if he could take enough interest in a girl like the one in the book to describe her so truly he might be a little interested in her real life. Only her thought at first had been not to entice him; she had not believed that she could. Rather, it was more the feeling that if he would he might be of some help to her, since he had written so sympathetically of Lila, the heroine. She was faced by the problem of what to do with her life, as Lila had been, but at that she hadn't expected him to solve it for her—merely to advise her.

But afterwards, when he had written to thank her, she feared that she might not hear from him again and had thought of that picture of herself, the one Dr. Realk had taken of her laughing so heartily, the one that everybody liked so much. She had felt that that might entice him to further correspondence with her, since his letters were so different and interesting, and she had sent it and asked him if his heroine looked anything like her, just as an excuse for sending it. Then had come that kindly letter in which he had explained his point of view and advised her, unless she were very unhappy, to do nothing until she should be able to look after herself in the great world. Life was an economic problem. As for himself, he was too much the rover to be more than a passing word to any one. His work came first. Apart from that, he said he drifted up and down the world trying to make the best of a life that tended to bore him. However if ever he came that way he would be glad to look her up and advise her as best he might, but that she must not let him compromise her in any way. It was not advisable in her very difficult position.

Even then she had not been able to give him up, so interested had she been by all he had written. And besides, he had eventually come to U—— only a hundred and fifty miles away, and had written from there to know if he might come over to see her. She couldn't do other than invite him, although she had known at the time that it was a dangerous thing to do. There was no solution, and it had only caused trouble—and how much trouble! And yet in the face of her mood then, anything had been welcome as a relief. She had been feeling that unless something happened to break the monotony she would do something desperate. And then something did happen. He had come, and there was nothing but trouble, and very much trouble, until he had gone again.

You would have thought there was some secret unseen force attending her and Gil at that time and leading him to wherever she was at just the time she didn't want him to be there. Take for example, that matter of Gil finding Mr. Barclay's letters in the fire after she had taken such care to throw them on the live coals behind some burning wood. He had evidently been able to make out a part of the address, anyhow, for he had said they were addressed to her in care of somebody he couldn't make out. And yet he was all wrong, as to the writer, of course. He had the crazy notion, based on his having found that picture of Raskoffsky inscribed to Alice, some months before, that they must be from him, just because he thought she had used Alice to write and ask Raskoffsky for his picture—which she had. But that was before she had ever read any of Mr. Barclay's books. Yet if it hadn't been for Gil's crazy notion that it was Raskoffsky she was interested in she wouldn't have had the courage to face it out the way she had, the danger of losing Tickles, which had come to her the moment Gil had proved so suspicious and watchful, frightening her so. Those three terrible days! And imagine him finding those bits of letters in the ashes and making something out of them! The uncanniness of it all.

And then that time he saw her speeding through the gate into Briscoe Park. They couldn't have been more than a second passing there, anyhow, and yet he had been able to pick her out! Worse, Mr. Barclay hadn't even intended coming back that way; they had just made the mistake of turning down Ridgely instead of Warren. Yet, of course, Gil had to be there, of all places, when as a rule he was never out of the office at any time. Fortunately for her she was on her way home, so there was no chance of his getting there ahead of her as, plainly, he planned afterwards.

Still, if it hadn't been for her mother whom everybody believed, and who actually believed that she and Alice had been to the concert, she would never have had the courage to face him. She hadn't expected him home in the first place, but when he did come and she realized that unless she faced him out then and there in front of her mother who believed in her, that *she* as well as he would know, there was but one thing to do—brave it. Fortunately her mother hadn't seen her in that coat and hat which Gil insisted that she had on. For before going she and Alice had taken Tickles over to her mother's and then she had returned and changed her dress. And before Gil had arrived Alice had gone on home and told her mother to bring over the baby, which was the thing that had so confused Gil really. For he didn't know about the change and neither did her mother. And her mother did not believe that there had been any, which made her think that Gil was a little crazy, talking that way. And her mother didn't know to this day—she was so unsuspecting.

And then that terrible night on which he thought he had seen her in Bergley Place and came in to catch her. Would she ever forget that? Or that evening, two days before, when he had come home and said that Naigly had seen her coming out of the Deming. She could tell by his manner that time that he thought nothing of that then—he was so used to her going downtown in the daytime anyhow. But that Naigly should have seen her just then when of all times she would rather he would not have!

To be sure it had been a risky thing—going there to meet Mr. Barclay in that way, only from another point of view it had not seemed so. Every one went through the Deming Arcade for one reason or another and that made any one's being seen there rather meaningless. And in the great crowd that was always there it was the commonest thing for any one to meet any one else and stop and talk for a moment anyhow. That was all she was there for that day—to see Mr. Barclay on his arrival and make an appointment for the next day. She had done it because she knew she couldn't stay long and she knew Gil wouldn't be out at that time and that if any one else saw her she could say that it was almost any one they knew casually between them. Gil was like that, rather easy at times. But to think that Naigly should have been passing the Deming just as she was coming out—alone, fortunately—and should have run and told Gil. That was like him. It was pure malice. He had never liked her since she had turned him down for Gil. And he would like to make trouble for her if he could, that was all. That was the way people did who were disappointed in love.

But the worst and the most curious thing of all was that last evening in Bergley Place, the last time she ever saw Mr. Barclay anywhere. That *was* odd. She had known by then, of course, that Gil was suspicious and might be watching her and she hadn't intended to give him any further excuse for complaint. But that was his lodge night and he had never missed a meeting since they had been married— not one. Besides she had only intended to stay out about an hour and always within range of the house so that if Gil got off the car or any one else came she would know of it. She had not even turned out the light in the dining-room, intending to say if Gil came back unexpectedly or any one else called, that she had just run around the corner in the next block to see Mrs. Stofft. And in order that that state- ment might not be questioned, she had gone over there for just a little while before Mr. Barclay was due to arrive with his car. She had even asked Mr. Barclay to wait in the shadow of the old Dalrymple house in Bergley Place, under the trees, in order that the car might not be seen. So few people went up that street, anyhow. And it was always so dark in there. Besides it was near to raining which made it seem safer still. And yet he had seen her. And just as she was about to leave. And when she had concluded that everything had turned out so well.

But how could she have foreseen that a big car with such powerful lights as that would have turned in there just then. Or that Gil would step off the car and look up that way? Or that he would be coming home an hour earlier when he never did—not from lodge meeting. And besides she hadn't intended to go out that evening at all until Mr. Barclay called up and said he must leave the next day, for a few days anyhow, and wanted to see her before he went. She had thought that if they stayed somewhere in the neighborhood in a closed car, as he suggested, it would be all right. But, no. That big car had to turn in there just when it did, and Gil had to be getting off the car and looking up Bergley Place just when it did, and she had to be standing there saying good-bye, just as the lights flashed on that spot. Some people might be lucky, but certainly she was not one of them. The only thing that had saved her was the fact that she had been able to get in the house ahead of Gil, hang up her cape and go in to her room and undress and see if Tickles was still asleep. And yet when he did burst in she had felt that she could not face him—he was so desperate and angry. And yet, good luck, it had ended in his doubting whether he had really seen her or not, though even to this day he would never admit that he doubted.

But the real reason why she hadn't seen Mr. Barclay since (and that in the face of the fact that he had been here in the city once since, and that, as he wrote, he had taken such a fancy to her and wanted to see her and help her in any way she chose), was not that she was afraid of Gil or that she liked him more than she did Mr. Barclay (they were too different in all their thoughts and ways for that) or that she would have to give up her life here and do something else, if Gil really should have found out (she wouldn't have minded that at all)—but because only the day before Mr. Barclay's last letter she had found out that under the law Gil would have the power to take Tickles away from her and not let her see him any more if he caught her in any wrongdoing. That was the thing that had frightened her more than anything else could have and had decided her, then and there, that whatever it was she was thinking she might want to do, it could never repay her for the pain and agony that the loss of Tickles would bring her. She had not really stopped to think of that before. Besides on the night of that quarrel with Gil, that night he thought he saw her in Bergley Place and he had sworn that if ever he could prove anything he would take Tickles away from her, or, that he would kill her and Tickles and himself and Raskoffsky (Raskoffsky!), it was then really that she had realized that she couldn't do without Tickles—no, not for a time even. Her dream of a happier life would be nothing without him—she knew that. And so it was that she had fought there as she had to make Gil believe he was mistaken, even in the face of the fact that he actually knew he had seen her. It was the danger of the loss of Tickles that had given her the courage and humor and calmness, the thought of what the loss of him would mean, the feeling that life would be colorless and blank unless she could take him with her wherever she went, whenever that might be, if ever it was.

And so when Gil had burst in as he did she had taken up Tickles and faced him, after Gil's loud talk had waked him. And Tickles had put his arms about her neck and called "Mama! Mama!" even while she was wondering how she was ever to get out of that scrape. And then because he had fallen asleep again, lying close to her neck, even while Gil was quarreling, she had told herself then that if she came through that quarrel safely she would never do anything more to jeopardize her claim to Tickles, come what might. And with that resolution she had been able to talk to Gil so convincingly and defiantly that he had finally begun to doubt his own senses, as she could see. And so it was that she had managed to face him out and to win completely.

And then the very next day she had called up Mr. Barclay and told him that she couldn't go on with that affair, and why—that Tickles meant too much to her, that she would have to wait and see how her life would work out.

And he had been so nice about it then and had sympathized with her and had told her that, all things considered, he believed she was acting wisely and for her own happiness. And so she had been. Only since he had written her and she had had to say no to him again. And now he had gone for good. And she admired him so much. And she had never heard from him since, for she had asked him not to write to her unless she first wrote to him.

But with how much regret she had done that! And how commonplace and humdrum this world looked at times now, even with the possession of Tickles. Those few wonderful days. . . . And that dream that had mounted so high. Yet she had Tickles. And in the novel the husband had gone away and the architect had appeared.

XIV

THE "MERCY" OF GOD

"Once, one of his disciples, walking with him in the garden, said: 'Master, how may I know the Infinite, the Good, and attain to union with it, as thou hast?' And he replied: 'By desiring it utterly, with all thy heart and with all thy mind.' And the disciple replied: 'But that I do.' 'Nay, not utterly,' replied the Master, 'or thou wouldst not now ask how thou mayst attain to union with it. But come with me,' he added, 'and I will show thee.' And he led the way to a stream, and into the water, and there, by reason of his greater strength, he seized upon his disciple and immersed him completely, so that presently he could not breathe but must have suffocated and drowned had it not been his plan to bring him forth whole. Only when, by reason of this, the strength of the disciple began to wane and he would have drowned, the Master drew him forth and stretched him upon the bank and restored him. And when he was sufficiently restored and seeing that he was not dead but whole, he exclaimed: 'But, Master, why didst thou submerge me in the stream and hold me there until I was like to die?' And the Master replied: 'Didst thou not say that above all things thou desirest union with the Infinite?' 'Yea, true; but in life, not death.' 'That I know,' answered the Master. 'But now tell me: When thou wast thus held in the water what was it that thou didst most desire?' 'To be restored to breath, to life.' 'And how much didst thou desire it?' 'As thou sawest—with all my strength and with all my mind.' 'Verily. Then when in life thou desirest union with the All-Good, the Infinite, as passionately as thou didst life in the water, it will come. Thou wilt know it then, and not before.'"

Keshub Chunder Sen.

A FRIEND of mine, a quite celebrated neurologist, psychiatrist, and interpreter of Freud, and myself were met one night to discuss a very much talked-of book of his, a book of clinical studies relative to various obsessions, perversions and inhibitions which had afflicted various people in their day and which he, as a specialist in these matters, had investigated and attempted to alleviate. To begin with, I should say that he had filled many difficult and responsible positions in hospitals, asylums, and later, as a professor of these matters, occupied a chair in one of our principal universities. He was kindly, thoughtful, and intensely curious as to the workings of this formula we call life, but without lending himself to any—at least to very few—hard and fast dogmas. More interesting still life appeared to interest but never to discourage him. He really liked it. Pain, he said, he accepted as an incentive, an urge to life. Strife he liked because it hardened all to strength. And he believed in action as the antidote to too much thought, the way out of brooding and sorrow. Youth passes, strength passes, life forms pass; but action makes all bearable and even enjoyable. Also he wanted more labor, not less, more toil, more exertion, for humanity. And he insisted that through, not round or outside, life lay the way to happiness, if there was a way. But with action all the while. So much for his personal point of view.

On the other hand he was always saying of me that I had a touch of the Hindu in me, the Far East, the Brahmin. I emphasized too much indifference to life—or, if not that, I quarreled too much with pain, unhappiness, and did not impress strongly enough the need of action. I was forever saying that the strain was too great, that there had best be less of action, less of pain. . . . As to the need of less pain, I agreed, but never to the need of less action; in verification of which I pointed to my own life, the changes I had deliberately courted, the various activities I had entered upon, the results I had sought for. He was not to be routed from his contention entirely, nor I from mine.

Following this personal analysis we fell to discussing a third man, whom we both admired, an eminent physiologist, then connected with one of the great experimental laboratories of the world, who had made many deductions and discoveries in connection with the associative faculty of the brain and the mechanics of associative memory. This man was a mechanist, not an evolutionist, and of the most convinced type. To him nowhere in nature was there any serene and directive and thoughtful conception which brought about, and was still bringing about continually, all the marvels of structure and form and movement that so arrest and startle our intelligence at every turn. Nowhere any constructive or commanding force which had thought out, for instance, and brought to pass flowers, trees, animals, men—associative order and community life. On the contrary, the beauty of nature as well as the order of all living, such as it is, was an accident, and not even a necessary one, yet unescapable, a condition or link in an accidental chain. If you would believe him and his experiments, the greatest human beings that ever lived and the most perfect states of society that ever were have no more significance in nature than the most minute ephemera. The Macedonian Alexander is as much at the mercy of fate as the lowest infusoria. For every germ that shoots up into a tree thousands are either killed or stunted by unfavorable conditions; and although, beyond question, many of them—the most—bear within themselves the same power as the successful ones to be and to do, had they the opportunity, still they fail—a belief of my own in part, albeit a hard doctrine.

One would have thought, as I said to Professor Z—— at this meeting, that such a mental conviction would be dulling and destructive to initiative and force, and I asked him why he thought it had not operated to blunt and destroy this very great man. "For the very reasons I am always emphasizing," he replied. "Pain, necessity, life stung him into action and profound thought, hence success. He is the person he is by reason of enforced mental and physical action."

"But," I argued, "his philosophy makes him account it all as worthless, or, if not that, so fleeting and unstable as to make it scarcely worth the doing, even though he does it. As he sees it, happiness and tribulation, glory and obscurity, are all an accident. Science, industry, politics, like races and planets, are accidents. Trivial conditions cause great characters and geniuses like himself to rest or to remain inactive, and mediocre ones are occasionally permitted to execute great deeds or frustrate them in the absence of the chance that might have produced a master. Circumstances are stronger than personalities, and the impotence of individuals is the tragedy of everyday life."

"Quite so," agreed my friend, "and there are times when I am inclined to agree with him, but at most times not. I used to keep hanging in one of my offices, printed and framed, that famous quotation from Ecclesiastes: 'I returned, and saw under the sun that the race is not to the swift, nor the battle to the strong, neither yet bread to the wise, nor yet favor to men of skill; but time and chance happeneth to them all.' But I took it down because it was too discouraging. And yet," he added after a time, because we both fell silent at this point, "although I still think it is true, as time has gone on and I have experimented with life and with people I have come to believe that there is something else in nature, some not as yet understood impulse, which seeks to arrange and right and balance things at times. I know that this sounds unduly optimistic and vainly cheerful, especially from me, and many—you, for one, will disagree—but I have sometimes encountered things in my work which have caused me to feel that nature isn't altogether hard or cruel or careless, even though accidents appear to happen."

"Accidents?" I said; "holocausts, you mean." But he continued:

"Of course, I do not believe in absolute good or absolute

evil, although I do believe in relative good and relative
evil. Take tenderness and pity, in some of their results at
least. Our friend Z——, on the contrary, sees all as accident, or blind chance and without much if any real or
effective pity or amelioration, a state that I cannot reason
myself into. Quite adversely, I think there is something
that helps life along or out of its difficulties. I know that
you will not agree with me; still, I believe it, and while I
do not think there is any direct and immediate response,
such as the Christian Scientists and the New Thought
devotees would have us believe, I know there is a response
at times, or at least I think there is, and I think I can prove
it. Take dreams, for instance, which, as Freud has demon-
strated, are nature's way of permitting a man to sleep in the
presence of some mental worry that would tend to keep him
awake, or if he had fallen asleep, and stood in danger to
wake him."

I waived that as a point, but then he referred to medicine
and surgery and all the mechanical developments as well as
the ameliorative efforts of life, such as laws relating to child
labor, workingmen's compensation and hours, compulsory
safety devices and the like, as specific proofs of a desire on
the part of nature, working through man, to make life
easier for man, a wish on her part to provide him, slowly
and stumblingly, mayhap, with things helpful to him in
his condition here. Without interrupting him, I allowed
him to call to mind the Protestant Reformation, how it had
ended once and for all the iniquities of the Inquisition; the
rise of Christianity, and how, temporarily at least, it had
modified if not entirely ended the brutalities of Paganism.
Anesthetics, and how they had served to ameliorate pain.
I could have pointed out that life itself was living on life
and always had been, and that as yet no substitute for the
flesh of helpless animals had been furnished man as food.
(He could not hear my thoughts.) The automobile, he
went on, had already practically eliminated the long suffer-
ings of the horse; our anti-slavery rebellion and humane

opposition in other countries had once and for all put an end to human slavery; also he called to mind the growth of humane societies of one kind and another, that ministered to many tortured animals. And humane laws were being constantly passed and enforced to better if not entirely cure inhuman conditions.

I confess I was interested, if not convinced. In spite of life itself existing on life, there was too much in what he said to permit any one to pass over it indifferently. But there came to my mind just the same all the many instances of crass accident and brutish mischance which are neither prevented nor cured by anything—the thousands who are annually killed in railroad accidents and industrial plants, despite protective mechanisms and fortifying laws compelling their use; the thousands who die yearly from epidemics of influenza, smallpox, yellow fever, cholera and widespread dissemination of cancer, consumption and related ills. These I mentioned. He admitted the force of the point but insisted that man, impelled by nature, not only for his own immediate protection but by reason of a sympathy aroused through pain endured by him, was moved to kindly action. Besides if nature loved brutality and inhumanity and suffering why should any atom of it wish to escape pain, and why in those atoms should it generate sympathy and tears and rejoicing at escape from suffering by man, why sorrow and horror at the accidental or intentional infliction of disaster on man by nature or man?

After a time, he volunteered: "Let me give you a concrete instance. It has always interested me and it seems to prove that there is something to what I say. It concerns a girl I know, a very homely one, who lost her mind. At the beginning of her mental trouble her father called me in to see what, if anything, could be done. The parents of this girl were Catholics. He was a successful contractor and politician, the father of three children; he provided very well for them materially but could do little for them mentally. He was not the intellectual but the religious type.

The mother was a cheerful, good-natured and conventional woman, and had only the welfare of her children and her husband at heart. When I first came to know this family— I was a young medical man then—this girl was thirteen or fourteen, the youngest of the three children. Of these three children, and for that matter of the entire family, I saw that this girl was decidedly the most interesting psychically and emotionally. She was intense and receptive, but inclined to be morbid; and for a very good reason. She was not good-looking, not in any way attractive physically. Worse, she had too good a mind, too keen a perception, not to know how severe a deprivation that was likely to prove and to resent it. As I came to know through later investigations— all the little neglects and petty deprivations which, owing to her lack of looks and the exceeding and of course superior charms of her sister and brother, were throughout her infancy and youth thrust upon her. Her mouth was not sweet —too large; her eyes unsatisfactory as to setting, not as to wistfulness; her nose and chin were unfortunately large, and above her left eye was a birthmark, a livid scar as large as a penny. In addition her complexion was sallow and muddy, and she was not possessed of a truly graceful figure; far from it. After she had reached fifteen or sixteen, she walked, entirely by reason of mental depression, I am sure, with a slow and sagging and moody gait; something within, I suppose, always whispering to her that hope was useless, that there was no good in trying, that she had been mercilessly and irretrievably handicapped to begin with.

"On the other hand, as chance would have it, her sister and brother had been almost especially favored by nature, Celeste Ryan was bright, vivacious, colorful. She was possessed of a graceful body, a beautiful face, clear, large and blue eyes, light glossy hair, and a love for life. She could sing and dance. She was sought after and courted by all sorts of men and boys. I myself, as a young man, used to wish that I could interest her in myself, and often went to the house on her account. Her brother also was smart, well-

favored, careful as to his clothes, vain, and interested in and
fascinating to girls of a certain degree of mind. He and
his sister liked to dance, to attend parties, to play and dis-
port themselves wherever young people were gathered.

"And for the greater part of Marguerite's youth, or
until her sister and brother were married, this house was
a centre for all the casual and playful goings-on of youth.
Girls and boys, all interested in Celeste and her brother,
came and went—girls to see the good-looking brother, boys
to flirt with and dance attendance upon the really charming
Celeste. In winter there was skating; in summer auto-
mobiling, trips to the beach, camping even. In most of
these affairs, so long as it was humanly possible, the favor-
less sister was included; but, as we all know, especially where
thoughtless and aggressive youth is concerned, such little
courtesies are not always humanly possible. Youth will be
served. In the main it is too intent upon the sorting and
mating process, each for himself, to give the slightest heed
or care for another. Væ Victis.

"To make matters worse, and possibly because her several
deficiencies early acquainted her with the fact that all boys
and girls found her sister and brother so much more attractive, Marguerite grew reticent and recessive—so much
so that when I first saw her she was already slipping about
with the air of one who appeared to feel that she was not
as ingratiating and acceptable as she might be, even though,
as I saw, her mother and father sought to make her feel
that she was. Her father, a stodgy and silent man, too
involved in the absurdities of politics and religion and the
difficulties of his position to give very much attention to
the intricacies and subtleties of his children's personalities,
never did guess the real pain that was Marguerite's. He
was a narrow and determined religionist, one who saw in
religious abstention, a guarded and reserved life, the only
keys to peace and salvation. In fact before he died an altar
was built in his house and mass was read there for his
especial spiritual benefit every morning. What he thought

of the gayeties of his two eldest children at this time I do not know, but since these were harmless and in both cases led to happy and enduring marriages, he had nothing to quarrel with. As for his youngest child, I doubt if he ever sensed in any way the moods and torturous broodings that were hers, the horrors that attend the disappointed love life. He had not been disappointed in his love life, and was therefore not able to understand. He was not sensitive enough to have suffered greatly if he had been, I am sure. But his wife, a soft, pliable, affectionate, gracious woman, early sensed that her daughter must pay heavily for her looks, and in consequence sought in every way to woo her into an unruffled complacence with life and herself.

"But how little the arts of man can do toward making up for the niggardliness of nature! I am certain that always, from her earliest years, this ugly girl loved her considerate mother and was grateful to her; but she was a girl of insight, if not hard practical sense or fortitude, and loved life too much to be content with the love of her mother only. She realized all too keenly the crass, if accidental, injustice which had been done her by nature and was unhappy, terribly so. To be sure, she tried to interest herself in books, the theatre, going about with a homely girl or two like herself. But before her ever must have been the spectacle of the happiness of others, their dreams and their fulfilments. Indeed, for the greater part of these years, and for several years after, until both her sister and brother had married and gone away, she was very much alone, and, as I reasoned it out afterwards, imagining and dreaming about all the things she would like to be and do. But without any power to compel them. Finally she took to reading persistently, to attending theatres, lectures and what not— to establish some contact, I presume, with the gay life scenes she saw about her. But I fancy that these were not of much help, for life may not be lived by proxy. And besides, her father, if not her mother, resented a too liberal thought life. He believed that his faith and its teachings were the only proper solution to life.

"One of the things that interested me in connection with this case—and this I gathered as chief medical counsel of the family between Marguerite's fifteenth and twenty-fifth year—was that because of the lack of beauty that so tortured her in her youth she had come to take refuge in books, and then, because of these, the facts which they revealed in regard to a mere worthwhile life than she could have, to draw away from all religion as worthless, or at least not very important as a relief from pain. And yet there must have been many things in these books which tortured her quite as much as reality, for she selected, as her father once told me afterward—not her mother, who could read little or nothing—only such books as she should not read; books, I presume, that painted life as she wished it to be for herself. They were by Anatole France, George Moore, de Maupassant and Dostoyevsky. Also she went to plays her father disapproved of and brooded in libraries. And she followed, as she herself explained to me, one lecturer and another, one personality and another, more, I am sure, because by this method she hoped to contact, although she never seemed to, men who were interesting to her, than because she was interested in the things they themselves set forth.

"In connection with all this I can tell you of only one love incident which befell her. Somewhere around the time when she was twenty-one or-two she came in contact with a young teacher, himself not very attractive or promising and whose prospects, as her father saw them, were not very much. But since she was not pretty and rather lonely and he seemed to find companionship, and mayhap solace in her, no great objection was made to him. In fact as time went on, and she and the teacher became more and more intimate, both she and her parents assumed that in the course of time they would most certainly marry. For instance, at the end of his school-teaching year here in New York, and although he left the city he kept up a long correspondence with her. In addition, he spent at least some of his vacation near New York, at times returning and going about with her and seeming to feel that she was of some value to him in some way.

"How much of this was due to the fact that she was provided with spending money of her own and could take him here and there, to places to which he could not possibly have afforded to go alone I cannot say. None the less, it was assumed, because of their companionship and the fact that she would have some money of her own after marriage, that he would propose. But he did not. Instead, he came year after year, visited about with her, took up her time, as the family saw it (her worthless time!), and then departed for his duties elsewhere as free as when he had come. Finally this having irritated if not infuriated the several members of her family, they took her to task about it, saying that she was a fool for trifling with him. But she, although perhaps depressed by all this, was still not willing to give him up; he was her one hope. Her explanation to the family was that because he was poor he was too proud to marry until he had established himself. Thus several more years came and went, and he returned or wrote, but still he did not propose. And then of a sudden he stopped writing entirely for a time, and still later on wrote that he had fallen in love and was about to be married.

"This blow appeared to be the crowning one in her life. For in the face of the opposition, and to a certain degree contempt, of her father, who was a practical and fairly successful man, she had devoted herself to this man who was neither successful nor very attractive for almost seven years. And then after so long a period, in which apparently he had used her to make life a little easier for himself, even he had walked away and left her for another. She fell to brooding more and more to herself, reading not so much now, as I personally know, as just thinking. She walked a great deal, as her father told me, and then later began to interest herself, or so she pretended, in a course of history and philosophy at one of the great universities of the city. But as suddenly, thereafter, she appeared to swing between exaggerated periods of study or play or lecture-listening and a form of recessive despair, under the influence of which she retired to her room and stayed there for days, wishing neither to see nor hear from any one—not even to eat. On the other hand again, she turned abruptly to shopping, dress-making and the niceties which concerned her personal appearance; although even in this latter phase there were times when she did nothing at all, seemed to relax toward her old listlessness and sense of inconsequence and remained in her room to brood.

"About this time, as I was told afterwards, her mother died and, her sister and brother having married, she was left in charge of the house and of her father. It was soon evident that she had no particular qualifications for or interest in housekeeping, and a maiden sister of her father came to look after things. This did not necessarily darken the scene, but it did not seem to lighten it any. She liked this aunt well enough, although they had very little in common mentally. Marguerite went on as before. Parallel with all this, however, had run certain things which I have forgotten to mention. Her father had been growing more and more narrowly religious. As a matter of fact he had never had any sympathy for the shrewd mental development toward which her lack of beauty had driven her. Before she was twenty-three as I have already explained, her father had noted that she was indifferent to her church duties. She had to be urged to go to mass on Sunday, to confession and communion once a month. Also as he told me afterward, as something to be deplored, her reading had caused her to believe that her faith was by no means infallible, its ritual important; there were bigger and more interesting things in life. This had caused her father not only to mistrust but to detest the character of her reading, as well as her tendencies in general. From having some sympathy with her at first, as did her mother always, as the ugly duckling of the family, he had come to have a cold and stand-offish feeling. She was, as he saw it, an unnatural child. She did not obey him in respect to religion. He began, as I have hinted, to look into her books, those in the English tongue at least, and from a casual inspection came to feel that they were not fit books for any one to read. They were irreligious, immoral. They pictured life as it actually was, scenes and needs and gayeties and conflicts, which, whether they existed or not, were not supposed to exist; and most certainly they were not to be introduced into his home, her own starved disposition to the contrary notwithstanding. They conflicted with the natural chill and peace of his religion and temperament. He forbade her to read such stuff, to bring such books into his home. When he found some of them later he burned them. He also began to urge the claims of his religion more and more upon her.

"Reduced by this calamity and her financial dependence, which had always remained complete, she hid her books away and read them only outside or in the privacy of her locked room—but she read them. The subsequent discovery by him that she was still doing this, and his rage, caused her to think of leaving home. But she was without training, without any place to go, really. If she should go she would have to prepare herself for it by teaching, perhaps, and this she now decided to take up.

"About this time she began to develop those characteristics or aberrations which brought me into the case. As I have said, she began to manifest a most exaggerated and extraordinary interest in her facial appearance and physical well-being, an interest not at all borne out rationally by her looks. Much to her father's and his sister's astonishment, she began to paint and primp in front of her mirror nearly all day long. Lip sticks, rouge, eyebrow pencils, perfumes, rings, pins, combs, and what not else, were suddenly introduced—very expensive and disconcerting lingerie, for one thing.

"The family had always maintained a charge account at at least two of the larger stores of the city, and to these she had recently repaired, as it was discovered afterwards, and indulged herself, without a by-your-leave, in all these things. High-heeled slippers, bright-colored silk stockings, hats, blouses, gloves, furs, to say nothing of accentuated and even shocking street costumes, began to arrive in bundles. Since the father was out most of the day and the elderly aunt busy with household affairs, nothing much of all this was noted, until later she began to adorn herself in this finery and to walk the streets in it. And then the due bills, sixty days late; most disturbing but not to be avoided. And so came the storm.

"The father and aunt, who had been wondering where these things were coming from, became very active and opposed. For previous to this, especially in the period of her greatest depression, Marguerite had apparently dressed with no thought of anything, save a kind of resigned willingness to remain inconspicuous, as much as to say: 'What difference does it make. No one is interested in me.' Now, however, all this had gone—quite. She had supplied herself with hats so wide and 'fancy' or 'fixy,' as her father said, that they were a disgrace. And clothing so noticeable or 'loud'—I forget his exact word—that any one anywhere would be ashamed of her. There were, as I myself saw when I was eventually called in as specialist in the case, too many flowers, too much lace, too many rings, pins and belts and gewgaws connected with all this, which neither he nor his sister was ever quite able to persuade her to lay aside. And the colors! Unless she were almost forcibly restrained, these were likely to be terrifying, even laughter-provoking, especially to those accustomed to think of unobtrusiveness as the first criterion of taste—a green or red or light blue broad-trimmed hat, for instance, with no such color of costume to harmonize with it. And, whether it became her or not, a white or tan or green dress in summertime, or one with too much red or too many bright colors in winter. And very tight, worn with a dashing manner, mayhap. Even high-heeled slippers and thin lacy dresses in bitter windy weather. And the perfumes with which she saturated herself were, as her father said, impossible—of a high rate of velocity, I presume.

"So arrayed, then, she would go forth, whenever she could contrive it, to attend a theatre, a lecture, a moving picture, or to walk the streets. And yet, strangely enough, and this was as curious a phase of the case as any, she never appeared to wish to thrust her personal charms, such as they were, on any one. On the contrary, as it developed, there had generated in her the sudden hallucination that she possessed so powerful and self-troubling a fascination for men that she was in danger of bewildering them, enticing them against themselves to their moral destruction, as well as bringing untold annoyance upon herself. A single glance, one look at her lovely face, and presto! they were enslaved. She needed but to walk, and lo! beauty—her beauty, dazzling, searing, destroying—was implied by every motion, gesture. No man, be he what he might, could withstand it. He turned, he stared, he dreamed, he followed her and sought to force his attention on her. Her father explained to me that when he met her on the street one day he was shocked to the point of collapse. A daughter of his so dressed, and on the street! With the assistance of the maiden sister a number of modifications was at once brought about. All charge accounts were cancelled. Dealers were informed that no purchases of hers would be honored unless with the previous consent of her father. The worst of her sartorial offenses were unobtrusively removed from her room and burnt or given away, and plainer and more becoming things substituted.

"But now, suddenly, there developed a new and equally interesting stage of the case. Debarred from dressing as she would, she began to imagine, as these two discovered, that she was being followed and admired and addressed and annoyed by men, and that at her very door. Eager and dangerous admirers lurked about the place. As the maiden aunt once informed me, having wormed her way into Marguerite's confidence, she had been told that men 'were wild' about her and that go where she would, and conduct herself however modestly and inconspicuously, still they were inflamed.

"A little later both father and sister began to notice that on leaving the house or returning to it she would invariably pause, if going out, to look about first; if returning, to look back as though she were expecting to see some one outside whom she either did or did not wish to see. Not infrequently her comings-in were accompanied by something like flight, so great a need to escape some presumably dangerous or at least inpetuous pursuer as to cause astonishment and even fear for her. There would be a feverish, fumbled insertion of the key from without, after which she would fairly jump in, at the same time looking back with a nervous, perturbed glance. Once in she would almost invariably pause and look back as though, having succeeded in eluding her pursuer, she was still interested to see what he was like or what he was doing, often going to the curtained windows of the front room to peer out. And to her then confidante, this same aunt, she explained on several occasions that she had 'just been followed again' all the way from Broadway or Central Park West or somewhere, sometimes by a most wonderful-looking gentleman, sometimes by a most loathsome brute. He had seen her somewhere and had pursued her to her very room. Yet, brute or gentleman, she was always interested to look back.

"When her father and aunt first noted this manifestation they had troubled to inquire into it, looking into the street or even going so far as to go to the door and look for the man, but there was no one, or perchance some passing pedestrian or neighbor who most certainly did not answer to the description of either handsome gentleman or brute. Then sensibly they began to gather that this was an illusion. But by now the thing had reached a stage where they began to feel genuine alarm. Guests of the family were accused by her of attempting to flirt with her, of making appealing remarks to her as they entered, and neighbors of known polarity and conventional rigidity of presuming to waylay her and forcing her to listen to their pleas. Thus her father and aunt became convinced that it was no longer safe for her to be at large. The family's reputation was at stake; its record for freedom from insanity about to be questioned.

"In due time, therefore, I was sent for, and regardless of how much they dreaded a confession of hallucination here the confession was made to me. I was asked to say what if anything could be done for her, and if nothing, what was to be done with her. After that I was permitted to talk to Marguerite whom of course I had long known, but not as a specialist or as one called in for advice. Rather, I was presented to her as visiting again as of yore, having dropped in after a considerable absence. She seemed pleased to see me, only as I noticed on this, as on all subsequent occasions, she seemed to wish, first, not to stay long in my presence and more interesting still, as I soon noted, to wish to keep her face, and even her profile, averted from me, most especially her eyes and her glances. Anywhere, everywhere, save at me she looked, and always with the purpose, as I could see, of averting her glances.

"After she had left the room I found that this development was new to the family. They had not noticed it before, and then it struck me as odd. I suspected at once that there was some connections between this and her disappointed love life. The devastating effect of lack of success in love in youth had been too much for her. So this averted glance appeared to me to have something to do with that. Fearing to disturb or frighten her, and so alienate her, I chose to say nothing but instead came again and again in order to familiarize her with my presence, to cause her once more to take it as a matter of course. And to enlist her interest and sympathy, I pretended that there was a matter of taxes and some involved property that her father was helping me to solve.

"And in order to insure her presence I came as a rule just

before dinner, staying some little time and talking with her. To guarantee being alone with her I had her father and his sister remain out for a few minutes after I arrived, so as to permit me to seem to wait. And on these occasions I invented all sorts of excuses for coming into conversation with her. On all of these visits I noticed that she still kept her face from me. Having discussed various things with her, I finally observed: 'I notice, Marguerite, that whenever I come here now you never look at me. Don't you like me? You used to look at me, and now you keep your face turned away. Why is that?'

" 'Oh, of course I like you, doctor, of course,' she replied, 'only,' she paused, 'well, I'll tell you how it is: I don't want to have the same effect on you that I do on other men.' "

"She paused and I stared, much interested. 'I'm afraid I don't quite understand, Marguerite,' I said.

" 'Well, you see, it's this way,' she went on, 'it's my beauty. All you men are alike you see: you can't stand it. You would be just the same as the rest. You would be wanting to flirt with me, too, and it wouldn't be your fault, but mine. You can't help it. I know that now. But I don't want you to be following me like the rest of them, and you would be if I looked at you as I do at the others.' She had on at the time a large hat, which evidently she had been trying on before I came, and now she pulled it most coquettishly low over her face and then sidled, laughingly, out of the room.

"When I saw and heard this," he went on, "I was deeply moved instead of being amused as some might imagine, for I recognized that this was an instance of one of those kindly compensations in nature about which I have been talking, some deep inherent wish on the part of some overruling Providence perhaps to make life more reasonably endurable for all of us. Here was this girl, sensitive and seeking, who had been denied everything—or, rather, the one thing she most craved in life; love. For years she had been compelled to sit by and see others have all the attention and pleasures,

while she had nothing—no pleasures, no lovers. And because she had been denied them their import had been
exaggerated by her; their color and splendor intensified.
She had been crucified, after a fashion, until beauty and
attention were all that her mind cried for. And then, behold
the mercy of the forces about which we are talking! They
diverted her mind in order to save her from herself. They
appeared at last to preserve her from complete immolation,
or so I see it. Life does not wish to crucify people, of
that I am sure. It lives on itself—as we see,—is "red of
beak and claw" as the phrase has it—and yet, in the deep,
who knows there may be some satisfactory explanation for
that too—who can tell? At any rate, as I see it basically,
fundamentally, it is well-intentioned. Useless, pointless
torture had no real place in it; or at least so I think." He
paused and stared, as though he had clinched his argument.

"Just the same, as you say," I insisted, "it does live on
itself, the slaughter houses, the stockyards, the butcher shops,
the germs that live and fatten as people die. If you can get
much comfort out of these you are welcome."

He paid no attention to me. Instead, he went on: "This
is only a theory of mine, but we know, for instance, that
there is no such thing as absolute evil, any more than there
is absolute good. There is only relative evil and relative
good. What is good for or to me may be evil to you, and
vice versa, like a man who may be evil to you and good
to me.

"In the case of this girl I cannot believe that so vast a
thing as life, involving as it does, all the enormous forces and
complexities, would single out one little mite such as she
deliberately and specially for torture. On the contrary, I
have faith to believe that the thing is too wise and grand for
that. But, according to my theory, the machinery for creat-
ing things may not always run true. A spinner of plans or
fabrics wishes them to come forth perfect of course, arranges
a design and gathers all the colors and threads for a flawless
result. The machine may be well oiled. The engine per-

fectly geared. Every precaution taken, and yet in the spinning here and there a thread will snap, the strands become entangled, bits, sometimes whole segment spoiled by one accident and another, but not intentionally. On the other hand, there are these flaws, which come from where I know not, of course, but are accidental, I am sure, not intended by the spinner. At least I think so. They cause great pain. They cause the worst disasters. Yet our great mother, Nature, the greatest spinner of all, does what she can to right things—or so I wish to believe. Like the spinner himself, she stops the machine, unites the broken strands, uses all her ability to make things run smoothly once more. It is my wish to believe that in this case, where a homely girl could not be made into a beautiful one and youth could not be substituted for maturity, still nature brought about what I look upon as a beneficent illusion, a providential hallucination. Via insanity, Marguerite attained to all the lovely things she had ever longed for. In her unreason she had her beautiful face, her adoring cavaliers —they turned and followed her in the streets. She was beautiful to all, to herself, and must hide her loveliness in order to avert pain and disaster to others. How would you explain that? As reasoned and malicious cruelty on the part of nature Or as a kindly intervention, a change of heart, a wish on the part of nature or something to make amends to her for all that she suffered, not to treat her or any of us too brutally or too unfairly? Or just accident? How?"

He paused once more and gazed at me, as much as to say: "Explain that, if you can." I, in turn, stared, lost for the time being in thoughts of this girl, for I was greatly impressed. This picture of her, trying, in her deranged imaginings as to her beauty, to protect others from herself, turning her face away from those who might suffer because of her indifference, because she in her day had suffered from the indifference of others, finding in hallucination, in her jumbled fancies, the fulfilment of all her hopes, her dreams,

was too sad. I was too sad. I could not judge, and did not.
Truly, truly, I thought, I wish I might believe.

*   *   *   *   *   *   *

"Master, how may I know the Infinite, the Good, and attain
to union with it, as thou hast?" And the Master replied: "By
desiring it utterly."

XV

THE PRINCE WHO WAS A THIEF

An Improvisation on the Oldest Oriental Theme

THE doors of the mosque in Hodeidah stood wide and inviting after the blaze of an Arabian afternoon. And within, the hour of prayer having drawn nigh, were prostrated a few of the more faithful, their faces toward Mecca. Without, upon the platform of the great mosque and within the shadow of the high east wall, a dozen mendicants in their rags were already huddled or still arranging themselves, in anticipation of the departure of those of the faithful who might cast them a pice or an anna, so plain is the prescription of the Koran. For is it not written: "And forget not the poor, and the son of the road"? Even so, praise be to Allah, the good, the great.

Apart from them, oblivious of them and their woes, even of the import of the mosque itself, a score or more of Arabian children were at play, circling about like knats or bats. And passing among these or idling in groups for a word as to the affairs of the day, were excellent citizens of Hodeidah, fresh from their shops and errands—Bhori, the tin-seller, for one, making his way before going home to a comfortable mabraz, there to smoke a water-pipe and chew a bit of khat; and Ahmed, the carpet-weaver, stopping at the mosque to pray before going home; and Chudi, the baker, and Zad-el-Din, the seller of piece goods, whose shops were near together, both fathers, these, and discussing trade and the arrival of the camel train from Taif. And now came Azad Bakht, the barber, mopping his brow as was his wont. And Feruz, the water-carrier, to offer water for sale. And many others came and went, for this was the closing hour of the shops; soon all would be making for home or the mabrazes after a moment of prayer in the mosque, so near is the hereafter to the now.

But Gazzar-al-Din, a mendicant story-teller, fresh from the camel train out of Taif which within the hour had passed beyond the Chedar gate, was not one of these. Indeed he was a stranger in Hodeidah, one of those who make their way from city to city and village to village by their skill as tellers of tales, reciters of the glories of kings and princesses and princes and the doings of Jinn and magicians and fabled celebrities generally. Yet poor was he indeed. His tales he had gathered on many travels. And though nearing the age of eighty and none too prepossessing of mien, yet so artful was he in the manner of presenting his wares that he had not thus far died of want. His garb was no more than a loin-cloth, a turban and a cape as dirty as they were ragged. His beard and hair had not for years known any other comb than the sands of the desert and the dust of the streets. His face was parchment, his hands claws, one arm was withered.

Taking in at a glance the presence of a score of comrades in misery at or near the mosque door, Gazzar-al-Din betook himself to a respectful distance and surveyed the world in which he found himself. The cook-shop of Al Hadjaz being not far off and some inviting fragrance therefrom streaming to him on the wind, he made shift to think how he could best gather an audience of all who now came and went so briskly. For eat he must. No doubt there were many in Hodeidah who told tales, and by those about the mosque who sought alms certainly an additional seeker would not be welcomed. Indeed there had been times when open hostility had been manifested, as in Feruz where, after gathering many anna from an admiring throng, once he had been set upon and beaten, his purse taken, and, to crown it all, a pail of slops cast upon him by a savage she-wolf of their pack. It behooved him therefore to have a care.

Still, all things considered, it was not so poor a life. Many had their homes, to be sure, and their wives and shops, but were there not drawbacks? The best of them were as fixed as the palms and sands of the desert. Once in their lives perhaps they had journeyed to Mecca or Medina, to be preyed upon and swindled, in some instances even to be murdered, by the evil hawks that dwelt there. But in his case now. . . . The fragrances from the shop of Al Hadjaz renewed themselves. . . . There was nothing for it: he must find a comfortable doorway or the shaded side of a wall where he could spread his cape, belabor his tambour and so attract attention and secure as many anna as might be before he began to unfold such a tale of adventure and surprise as would retain the flagging interest of the most wearied and indifferent. And eventually secure him sufficient anna for his meal and lodging. But to do that, as he well knew, there must be in it somewhere, a beautiful princess and a handsome lover; also a noble and generous and magnificent caliph. And much talk to be sure of gold and power where so little existed in real life. In addition there should be cruel robbers and thieves, and, also, a righteous man too—though in real life, how few. Sometimes as the faces of those addressed showed a wane of interest it was wise to take apart and recombine many tales, borrow from one to bolster up another.

As he walked, looking at the windows and doors of all the shops and residences about him, he eventually spied a deep recess giving into the closed market a score of feet from the public square. Here he seated himself and began softly to thump his tambour, lest those religiously minded should take offense. Also it was no part of his desire to attract the mendicants, who were still before the door of the mosque. Soon they might depart, and then he would feel safer, for in them, especially for such as he—a fellow craftsman, as it were—was nothing but jibes and rivalry. He drummed softly, looking briskly about the while, now at the windows, now toward the mosque, now along the winding street.

Seeing two urchins, then a third, pause and gaze, he reasoned that his art was beginning to lure. For where children paused, their elders were sure to follow. And so it proved. Drawing nearer and nearer these first children were joined by a fourth, a fifth, a sixth. Presently Haifa, the tobacco vendor, limping toward the mosque to sell his wares, paused and joined the children. He was curious as to what was to fellow—whether Gazzar would secure an audience. Next came Waidi, the water-seller, fresh from a sale; then Ajeeb, ne'er-do-well cleaner of market stalls for the merchants, and full of curiosity ever. And after him came Soudi and Parfi, carriers, an appetite for wonders besetting them; and then El-Jed, the vendor of kindling.

As they gathered about him Gazzar-al-Din ventured to thrum louder and louder, exclaiming: "A marvelous tale, O Company of the Faithful! A marvelous tale! Hearken! A tale such as has never yet been told in all Hodeidah—no, not in all Yemen! 'A Prince Who was a Thief.' A Prince Who Was a Thief! For a score of anna—yea, the fourth part of a rupee—I begin. And ah, the sweetness of it! As jasmine, it is fragrant; as khat, soothing. A marvelous tale!"

"Ay-ee, but how is one to know that," observed Ahmed, the carpet-weaver, to Chudi, the tailor, with whom he had drawn near. "There are many who promise excellent tales but how few who tell them."

"It is even as thou sayst, O Ahmed. Often have I hearkened and given anna in plenty, yet few there are whose tales are worth the hearing."

"Why not begin thy tale, O Kowasji?" inquired Soudi, the carrier. "Then if, as thou sayst, it is so excellent, will not anna enough be thine? There are tellers of tales, and tellers of tales—"

"Yea, and that I would," replied the mendicant artfully, "were all as honest as thou lookest and as kind. Yet have I traveled far without food, and I know not where I may rest this night. . . . A tale of the great caliph and the Princess

Yanee and the noble Yussuf, stolen and found again. And the great treasury sealed and guarded, yet entered and robbed by one who was not found. Anna—but a score of anna, and I begin! What? Are all in Hodeidah so poor that a tale of love and pleasure and danger and great palaces and great princes and caliphs and thieves can remain untold for the want of a few anna—for so many as ten dropped into my tambour? A marvelous tale! A marvelous tale!"

He paused and gazed speculatively about, holding out his tambour. His audience looked dubiously and curiously at him; who now was this latest teller of wonders, and from whence had he come? An anna was not much, to be sure, and a tale well told—well—yet there had been tellers of such whose tales were as dull as the yawn of a camel.

"An excellent tale, sayst thou?" queried Parfi cautiously. "Then, if it be so marvelous, why not begin? For a handful of anna one may promise anything."

"A great promiser there was here once," commented Ajeeb, the gossip, sententiously, "and he sat himself in this self-same door. I remember him well. He wore a green turban, but a greater liar there never was. He promised wonders and terrors enough, but it came to nothing—not a demon or Jinn in it."

"Is it of demons and Jinns only that thou thinkest, donkey?" demanded Haifa. "Verily, there are wonders and mysteries everywhere, without having them in tales."

"Yea, but a tale need not be for profit, either," said Waidi, the water-seller. "It is for one's leisure, at the end of a day. I like such as end happily, with evil punished and the good rewarded."

"Come, O friends," insisted Gazzar-al-Din, seeing that one or two were interested, "for a score of anna I begin. Of Yemen it is, this very Yemen, and Baghdad, once a greater city than any to-day—"

"Begin then," said Azad Bakht, the barber. "Here is an anna for thee," and he tossed a coin in the tambour.

"And here is another for thee," observed Haifa, fishing in his purse. "I do not mind risking it."

"And here is another," called Soudi condescendingly. "Begin."

"And here is yet another," added Parfi grandiosely. "Now, then, thy tale, and look thee that it is as thou sayst, marvelous." And they squatted about him on the ground.

But Gazzar, determined not to begin until he had at least ten anna, the price of a bowl of curds and a cup of kishr, waited until he had accumulated so many, as well as various "Dogs!" and "Pigs!" and "Wilt thou begin, miser, or wilt thou fill thy tambour?" into the bargain. He then crouched upon his rags, lifted his hand for silence, and began:

"Know then, O excellent citizens of Hodeidah, that once, many years since, there lived in this very Yemen where now is Taif, then a much more resplendent city, a sultan by the name of Kar-Shem, who had great cities and palaces and an army, and was beloved of all over whom he ruled. When he—wilt thou be seated, O friend? And silence!—when he was but newly married and ruling happily a son was born to him, Hussein, an infant of so great charm and beauty that he decided he should be carefully reared and wisely trained and so made into a fit ruler for so great a country. But, as it chanced, there was a rival or claimant to this same throne by another line, a branch long since deposed by the ancestors of this same king, and he it was, Bab-el-Bar by name, who was determined that the young Prince Hussein should be stolen and disposed of in some way so that he should never return and claim the throne. One day, when the prince was only four years of age, the summer palace was attacked and the princeling captured. From thence he was carried over great wastes of sand to Baghdad, where he was duly sold as a slave to a man who was looking for such, for he was a great and successful thief, one who trained thieves from their infancy up so that they should never know what virtue was."

"Ay-ee, there are such," interrupted Ahmed, the carpet-weaver, loudly, for his place had only recently been robbed. "I know of the vileness of thieves."

"Peace! Peace!" insisted Waidi and Haifa sourly.

Gazzar-al-Din paused until quiet should be restored, then resumed:

"Once the Prince Hussein was in the hands of this thief, he was at once housed with those who stole, who in turn taught him. One of the tricks which Yussuf, the master thief, employed was to take each of his neophytes in turn at the age of seven, dress him in a yarn jacket, lower him into a dry cistern from which there was no means of escape, place a large ring-cake upon a beam across the top and tell him to obtain the cake or starve. Many starved for days and were eventually dismissed as unworthy of his skill. But when the young Prince Hussein was lowered he meditated upon his state. At last he unraveled a part of his yarn jacket, tied a pebble to it and threw it so that it fell through the hole of the cake, and thus he was able to pull it down. At this Yussuf was so pleased that he had him drawn up and given a rare meal.

"One day Yussuf, hearing good reports from those who were training Hussein in thieving, took him to the top of a hill traversed by a road, where, seeing a peasant carrying a sheep on his back approaching, Yussuf Ben Ali asked of Hussein, now renamed Abou so that he might not be found: 'How shall we get the sheep without the peasant learning that we have taken it?' Trained by fear of punishment to use his wits, Abou, after some thought replied: 'When thou seest the sheep alone, take it!' Stealing from the thicket, he placed one of his shoes in the road and then hid. The peasant came and saw the shoe, but left it lying there because there was but one. Abou ran out and picked up the shoe, reappearing from the wood far ahead of the peasant where he put down the mate to the first shoe and then hid again. The peasant came and examined the shoe, then tied his sheep to a stake and ran back for the first one. Yussuf, seeing the sheep alone, now came out and hurried off with it, while Abou followed, picking up the last shoe."

"He was a donkey to leave his sheep in the road," interpolated Parfi, the carrier, solemnly.

"But more of a donkey not to have taken up the first shoe," added Soudi.

"Anna! Anna!" insisted Gazzar-al-Din, seizing upon this occasion to collect from those who had newly arrived. " 'Tis a marvellous tale! Remember the teller of good tales, whose gift it is to sweeten the saddest of days. He lightens the cares of those who are a-weary. Anna! Anna!" And with a clawy hand he held out the tambour to Zad-el-Din and Azad Bakht, who began to regret their interest.

"Cannot a man speak without thou demandest anna?" grumbled Zad-el-Din, fishing in his purse and depositing an anna, as did Azad Bakht and several more? Whereupon, the others beginning to grumble, Gazzar continued:

"The peasant coming back to where he had seen the first shoe and not finding it, was dazed and ran back to his sheep, to find that that and the second shoe were gone. Yussuf was much pleased and rewarded Abou with a new coat later, but for the present he was not done. Judging by long experience that the peasant had either bought the sheep and was taking it home or that he was carrying it to market to sell, he said to Abou: 'Let us wait. It may be that he will return with another.' "

"Ah, shrewd," muttered Ajeeb, nodding his head gravely. "Accordingly," went on Gazzar-al-Din, "they waited and soon the peasant returned carrying another sheep. Yussuf asked Abou if he could take this one also, and Abou told him that when he saw the sheep alone to take it."

"Dunce!" declared Chudi, the baker. "Will he put another sheep down after just losing one? This is a thin tale!" But Gazzar was not to be disconcerted.

"Now Yussuf was a great thief," he went on, "but this wit of Abou's puzzled him. Of all the thieves he had trained few could solve the various problems which he put before them, and in Abou he saw the makings of a great thief. As the peasant approached, Abou motioned to Yussuf to conceal himself in a crevice in the nearby rocks, while he hid in the woods. When the peasant drew near Abou placed his hands to his lips and imitated a sheep bleating, whereupon the peasant, thinking it must be his lost sheep, put down behind a stone the one he was carrying, for its feet were tied, and went into the woods to seek the lost one. Yussuf, watching from his cave, then ran forth and made off with the sheep. When the peasant approached, Abou climbed a tree and smiled down on him as he sought his sheep, for he had been taught that to steal was clever and wise, and the one from whom he could steal was a fool."

"And so he is," thought Waidi, who had stolen much in his time.

"When the peasant had gone his way lamenting, Abou came down and joined Yussuf. They returned to the city and the home of Yussuf, where the latter, much pleased, decided to adopt Abou as his son." Gazzar now paused upon seeing the interest of his hearers and held out his tambour. "Anna, O friends, anna! Is not the teller of tales, the sweetener of weariness, worthy of his hire? I have less than a score of anna, and ten will buy no more than a bowl of curds or a cup of kishr, and the road I have traveled has been long. So much as the right to sleep in a stall with the camels is held at ten anna, and I am no longer young." He moved the tambour about appealingly.

"Dog!" growled Soudi. "Must thy tambour be filled before we hear more?"

"Bismillah! This is no story-teller but a robber," declared Parfi.

"Peace, friends," said Gazzar, who was afraid to irritate his hearers in this strange city. "The best of the tale comes but now—the marvelous beauty of the Princess Yanee and the story of the caliph's treasury and the master thief. But, for the love of Allah, yield me but ten more anna and I pause no more. It is late. A cup of kishr, a camel's stall—" He waved the tambour. Some three of his hearers who had not yet contributed anything dropped each an anna into his tambour.

"Now," continued Gazzar somewhat gloomily, seeing how small were his earnings for all his art, "aside from stealing and plundering caravans upon the great desert, and the murdering of men for their treasure, the great Yussuf conducted a rug bazaar as a blind for more thievery and murder. This bazaar was in the principal street of the merchants, and at times he was to be seen there, his legs crossed upon his pillows. But let a merchant of wealth appear, a stranger, and although he might wish only to ask prices Yussuf would offer some rug or cloth so low that even a beggar would wish to take it. When the stranger, astonished at its price, would draw his purse a hand-clap from Yussuf would bring forth slaves from behind hangings who would fall upon and bind him, take his purse and clothes and throw his body into the river."

"An excellent robber indeed!" approved Soudi.

"Yussuf, once he had adopted Abou as his son, admitted him to his own home, where were many chambers and a garden, a court with a pool, and many servants and cushions and low divans in arcades and chambers; then he dressed him in silks and took him to his false rug market, where he introduced him with a great flourish as one who would continue his affairs after he, Yussuf, was no more. He called his slaves and said: 'Behold thy master after myself. When I am not here, or by chance am no more—praise be to Allah, the good, the great!—see that thou obey him, for I have found him very wise.' Soon Yussuf disguised himself as a dervish and departed upon a new venture. As for Abou, being left in charge of the rug market, he busied himself with examining its treasures and their values and thinking on how the cruel trade of robbery, and, if necessary, murder, which had been taught him, and how best it was to be conducted.

"For although Abou was good and kind of heart, still

being taken so young and sharply trained in theft and all things evil, and having been taught from day to day that not only were murder and robbery commendable but that softness or error in their pursuit was wrong and to be severely punished, he believed all this and yet innocently enough at times sorrowed for those whom he injured. Yet also he knew that he durst not show his sorrow in the presence of Yussuf, for the latter, though kind to him, was savage to all who showed the least mercy or failed to do his bidding, even going so far as to slay them when they sought to cross or betray him."

"Ay-ee, a savage one was that," muttered Al Hadjaz, the cook.

"And I doubt not there are such in Yemen to this day," added Ajeeb, the cleaner of stalls. "Was not Osman Hassan, the spice-seller, robbed and slain?"

"Soon after Yussuf had left on the secret adventure, there happened to Abou a great thing. For it should be known that at this time there ruled in Baghdad the great and wise Yianko I., Caliph of the Faithful in the valleys of the Euphrates and the Tigris and master of provinces and principalities, and the possessor of an enormous treasury of gold, which was in a great building of stone. Also he possessed a palace of such beauty that travelers came from many parts and far countries to see. It was built of many-colored stones and rare woods, and possessed walks and corridors and gardens and flowers and pools and balconies and latticed chambers into which the sun never burst, but where were always cool airs and sweet. Here were myrtle and jasmine and the palm and the cedar, and birds of many colors, and the tall ibis and the bright flamingo. It was here, with his many wives and concubines and slaves and courtiers, and many wise men come from far parts of the world to advise with him and bring him wisdom, that he ruled and was beloved and admired.

"Now by his favorite wife, Atrisha, there had been born to him some thirteen years before the beautiful and tender and delicate and loving and much-beloved Yanee, the sweetest and fairest of all his daughters, whom from the very first he designed should be the wife of some great prince, the mother of beautiful and wise children, and the heir, through her husband, whoever he should be, to all the greatness and power which the same must possess to be worthy of her. And also, because he had decided that whoever should be wise and great and deserving enough to be worthy of Yanee should also be worthy of him and all that he possessed—the great Caliphate of Baghdad. To this end, therefore, he called to Baghdad instructors of the greatest wisdom and learning of all kinds, the art of the lute and the tambour and the dance. And from among his wives and concubines he had chosen those who knew most of the art of dress and deportment and the care of the face and the body; so that now, having come to the age of the ripest perfection, thirteen, she was the most beautiful of all the maidens that had appeared in Arabia or any of the countries beyond it. Her hair was as spun gold, her teeth as pearls of the greatest price, lustrous and delicate; her skin as the bright moon when it rises in the east, and her hands and feet as petals in full bloom. Her lips were as the pomegranate when it is newly cut, and her eyes as those deep pools into which the moon looks when it is night."

"Yea, I have heard of such, in fairy-tales," sighed Chudi, the baker, whose wife was as parchment that has cracked with age.

"And I, behind the walls of palaces and in far cities, but never here," added Zad-el-Din, for neither his wife nor his daughters was any too fair to look upon. "They come not to Hodeidah."

"Ay-ee, were any so beautiful," sighed Al Tadjaz, "there would be no man worthy. But there are none."

"Peace!" cried Ahmed. "Let us have the tale."

"Yea, before he thinks him to plead for more anna," muttered Hadjaz, the sweeper, softly.

But Gazzar, not to be robbed of this evidence of interest,

was already astir. Even as they talked he held out the tambour, crying: "Anna, anna, anna!" But so great was the opposition that he dared not persist.

"Dog!" cried Waidi. "Wilt thou never be satisfied? There is another for thee, but come no more."

"Thou miser!" said Haifa, still greatly interested, "tell thy tale and be done!"

"The thief has rupees and to spare, I warrant," added Scudi, contributing yet another anna.

And Zad-el-Din and Ahmed, because they were lustful of the great beauty of Yanee, each added an anna to his takings.

"Berate me not, O friends," pleaded Gazzar tactfully, hiding his anna in his cloak, "for I am as poor as thou seest —a son of the road, a beggar, a wanderer, with nowhere to lay my head. Other than my tales I have nothing." But seeing scant sympathy in the faces of his hearers, he resumed.

"Now at the time that Abou was in charge of the dark bazaar it chanced that the caliph, who annually arranged for the departure of his daughter for the mountains which are beyond Azol in Bactria, where he maintained a summer palace of great beauty, sent forth a vast company mounted upon elephants and camels out of Ullar and Cerf and horses of the rarest blood from Taif. This company was caparisoned and swathed in silks and thin wool and the braided and spun cloth of Esher and Bar with their knitted threads of gold. And it made a glorious spectacle indeed, and all paused to behold. But it also chanced that as this cavalcade passed through the streets of Baghdad, Abou, hearing a great tumult and the cries of the multitude and the drivers and the tramp of the horses' feet and the pad of the camels', came to the door of his bazaar, his robes of silk about him, a turban of rare cloth knitted with silver threads upon his head. He had now grown to be a youth of eighteen summers. His hair was as black as the wing of the uck, his eyes large and dark and sad from many thoughts as is the pool into which the moon falls. His face and hands were tinted as with henna when it is spread very thin, and his manners were graceful and languorous. As he paused within his doorway he looked wonderingly at the great company as it moved and disappeared about the curves of the long street. And it could not but occur to him, trained as he was, how rich would be the prize could one but seize upon such a company and take all the wealth that was here and the men and women as slaves.

"Yet, even as he gazed and so thought, so strange are the ways of Allah, there passed a camel, its houdah heavy with rich silks, and ornaments of the rarest within, but without disguised as humble, so that none might guess. And within was the beautiful Princess Yanee, hidden darkly behind folds of fluttering silk, her face and forehead covered to her starry eyes, as is prescribed, and even these veiled. Yet so strange are the ways of life and of Allah that, being young and full of the wonder which is youth and the curiosity and awe which that which is unknown or strange begets in us all, she was at this very moment engaged in peeping out from behind her veils, the while the bright panorama of the world was passing. And as she looked, behold, there was Abou, gazing wonderingly upon her fine accoutrements. So lithe was his form and so deep his eyes and so fair his face that, transfixed as by a beam, her heart melted and without thought she threw back her veil and parted the curtains of the houdah the better to see, and the better that he might see. And Abou, seeing the curtains put to one side and the vision of eyes that were as pools and the cheeks as the leaf of the rose shine upon him, was transfixed and could no longer move or think.

"So gazing, he stood until her camel and those of many others had passed and turned beyond a curve of the street. Then bethinking himself that he might never more see her, he awoke and ran after, throwing one citizen and another to the right and the left. When at last he came up to the camel of his fair one, guarded by eunuchs and slaves, he drew one aside and said softly: 'Friend, be not wrathful and I will give thee a hundred dinars in gold do thou, within such time as thou canst, report to me at the bazaar of Yussuf, the rug-merchant, who it is that rides within this houdah. Ask thou only for Abou. No more will I ask.' The slave, noting his fine robes and the green-and-silver turban, thought him to be no less than a noble, and replied: 'Young master, be not overcurious. Remember the vengeance of the caliph. . . . 'Yet dinars have I to give.' . . . 'I will yet come to thee.'

"Abou was enraptured by even so little as this, and yet dejected also by the swift approach and departure of joy. 'For what am I now?' he asked himself. 'But a moment since, I was whole and one who could find delight in all things that were given me to do; but now I am as one who is lost and knows not his way.' "

"Ay-ee," sighed Azad Bakht, the barber, "I have had that same feeling more than once. It is something that one may not overcome."

"Al Tzoud, in the desert—" began Parfi, but he was interrupted by cries of "Peace—Peace!"

"Thereafter, for all of a moon," went on Gazzar, "Abou was as one in a dream, wandering here and there drearily, bethinking him how he was ever to know more of the face that had appeared to him through the curtains of the houdah. And whether the driver of the camel would ever return. As day after day passed and there was no word, he grew thin and began to despair and to grow weary of life. At last there came to his shop an aged man, long of beard and dusty of garb, who inquired for Abou. And being shown him said: 'I would speak with thee alone. And when Abou drew him aside he said: 'Dost thou recall the procession of the caliph's daughter to Ish-Pari in the mountains beyond Azol?' And Abou answered, 'Ay, by Allah!' 'And dost thou recall one of whom thou madest inquiry?' 'Aye,' replied Abou, vastly stirred. 'I asked who it was that was being borne aloft in state.' 'And what was the price for that knowledge?' 'A hundred dinars.' 'Keep thy dinars—or, better yet, give them to me that I may give them to the poor, for

I bring thee news. She who was in the houdah was none other than the Princess Yanee, daughter of the caliph and heir to all his realm. But keep thou thy counsel and all thought of this visit and let no one know of thy inquiry. There are many who watch, and death may yet be thy portion and mine. Yet, since thou art as thou art, young and without knowledge of life, here is a spray of the myrtles of Ish-Pari—but thou art to think no further on anything thou hast seen or heard. And thou dost not—death!' He made the sign of three fingers to the forehead and the neck and gave Abou the spray, receiving in return the gold."

"Marhallah!" cried Soudi. "How pleasant it is to think of so much gold!"

"Yea," added Haifa, "there is that about great wealth and beauty and comfort that is soothing to the heart of every man."

"Yet for ten more anna," began Gazzar, "the price of a bed in the stall of a camel, how much more glorious could I make it—the sweetness of the love that might be, the wonder of the skill of Abou—anna, anna—but five more, that I may take up this thread with great heart."

"Jackal!" screamed Ajeeb fiercely. "Thou barkst for but one thing—anna. But now thou saidst if thou hadst but ten more, and by now thou hast a hundred. On with thy tale!"

"Reremouse!" said Chudi. "Thou art worse than thy Yussuf himself!" And none gave an anna more.

"Knowing that the myrtle was from the princess," went on Gazzar wearily, "and that henceforth he might seek but durst not even so much as breathe of what he thought or knew, he sighed and returned to his place in the bazaar.

"But now, Yussuf, returning not long after from a far journey, came to Abou with a bold thought. For it related to no other thing than the great treasury of the caliph, which stood in the heart of the city before the public market, and was sealed and guarded and built of stone and carried the wealth of an hundred provinces. Besides, it was now the time of the taking of tithes throughout the caliphate, as

Yussuf knew, and the great treasury was filled to the roof, or so it was said, with golden dinars. It was a four-square building of heavy stone, with lesser squares superimposed one above the other after the fashion of pyramids. On each level was a parapet, and upon each side of every parapet as well as on the ground below there walked two guards, each first away from the centre of their side to the end and then back, meeting at the centre to reverse and return. And on each side and on each level were two other guards. No two of these, of any level or side, were permitted to arrive at the centre or the ends of their parapet at the same time, as those of the parapets above or below, lest any portion of the treasury be left unguarded. There was but one entrance, which was upon the ground and facing the market. And through this no one save the caliph or the caliph's treasurer or his delegated aides might enter. The guards ascended and descended via a guarded stair. Anna, O friends," pleaded Gazzar once more, "for now comes the wonder of the robbing of the great treasury—the wit and subtlety of Abou—and craft and yet confusion of the treasurer and the Caliph—anna!—A few miserable anna!"

"Jackal!" shouted Azad Bakht, getting up. "Thou robbest worse than any robber! Hast thou a treasury of thine own that thou hopest to fill?"

"Give him no more anna," called Feruz stoutly. "There is not an anna's worth in all his maunderings."

"Be not unkind, O friends," pleaded Gazzar soothingly. "As thou seest, I have but twenty annas—not the price of a meal, let alone of a bed. But ten—but—five—and I proceed."

"Come, then, here they are," cried Al Hadjaz, casting down four; and Zad-el-Din and Haifa and Chudi each likewise added one, and Gazzar swiftly gathered them up and continued:

"Yussuf, who had long contemplated this wondrous storehouse, had also long racked his wits as to how it might be entered and a portion of the gold taken. Also he had counseled with many of his pupils, but in vain. No one had solved the riddle for him. Yet one day as he and Abou passed the treasury on their way to the mosque for the look of honor, Yussuf said to Abou: 'Bethink thee, my son; here is a marvelous building, carefully constructed and guarded. How wouldst thou come to the store of gold within?' Abou, whose thoughts were not upon the building but upon Yanee, betrayed no look of surprise at the request, so accustomed was he to having difficult and fearsome matters put before him, but gazed upon it so calmly that Yussuf exclaimed: 'How now? Hast thou a plan?' 'Never have I given it a thought, O Yussuf,' replied Abou; 'but if it is thy wish, let us go and look more closely.'

"Accordingly, through the crowds of merchants and strangers and donkeys and the veiled daughters of the harem and the idlers generally, they approached and surveyed it. At once Abou observed the movement of the guards, saw that as the guards of one tier were walking away from each other those of the tiers above or below were walking toward each other. And although the one entrance to the treasury was well guarded still there was a vulnerable spot, which was the crowning cupola, also four-square and flat, where none walked or looked. 'It is difficult,' he said after a time, 'but it can be done. Let me think.'

"Accordingly, after due meditation and without consulting Yussuf, he disguised himself as a dispenser of fodder for camels, secured a rope of silk, four bags and an iron hook. Returning to his home he caused the hook to be covered with soft cloth so that its fall would make no sound, then fastened it to one end of the silken cord and said to Yussuf: 'Come now and let us try this.' Yussuf, curious as to what Abou could mean, went with him and together they tried their weight upon it to see if it would hold. Then Abou, learning by observation the hour at night wherein the guards were changed, and choosing a night without moon or stars, disguised himself and Yussuf as watchmen of the city and went to the treasury. Though it was as well guarded as ever they stationed themselves in an alley nearby. And Abou, seeing a muleteer approaching and wishing to test his disguise, ordered him away and he went. Then Abou, watching the guards who were upon the ground meet and turn, and seeing those upon the first tier still in the distance but pacing toward the centre, gave a word to Yussuf and they ran forward, threw the hook over the rim of the first tier and then drew themselves up quickly, hanging there above the lower guards until those of the first tier met and turned. Then they climbed over the wall and repeated this trick upon the guards of the second tier, the third and fourth, until at last they were upon the roof of the cupola where they lay flat. Then Abou, who was prepared, unscrewed one of the plates of the dome, hooked the cord over the side and whispered: 'Now, master, which?' Yussuf, ever cautious in his life, replied: 'Go thou and report.'

"Slipping down the rope, Abou at last came upon a great store of gold and loose jewels piled in heaps, from which he filled the bags he had brought. These he fastened to the rope and ascended. Yussuf, astounded by the sight of so much wealth, was for making many trips, but Abou, detecting a rift where shone a star, urged that they cease for the night. Accordingly, after having fastened these at their waists and the plate to the roof as it had been, they descended as they had come."

"A rare trick," commented Zad-el-Din.

"A treasury after mine own heart," supplied Al Hadjaz.

"Thus for three nights," continued Gazzar, fearing to cry for more anna, "they succeeded in robbing the treasury, taking from it many thousands of dinars and jewels. On the fourth night, however, a guard saw them hurrying away and gave the alarm. At that, Abou and Yussuf turned here and there in strange ways, Yussuf betaking himself to his home, while Abou fled to his master's shop. Once there he threw off the disguise of a guard and reappeared as an aged vendor of rugs and was asked by the pursuing guards if he had seen anybody enter his shop. Abou motioned them to the rear of the shop, where they were bound and removed by Yussuf's robber slaves. Others of the guards, however, had betaken themselves to their captain and reported, who immediately informed the treasurer. Torches were brought and a search made, and then he repaired to the caliph. The latter, much astonished that no trace of the entrance or departure of the thieves could be found, sent for a master thief recently taken in crime and sentenced to be gibbeted, and said to him:

" 'Wouldst thou have thy life?'

" 'Aye, if thy grace will yield it.'

" 'Look you,' said the caliph. 'Our treasury has but now been robbed and there is no trace. Solve me this mystery within the moon, and thy life, though not thy freedom, is thine.'

" 'O Protector of the Faithful,' said the thief, 'do thou but let me see within the treasury.'

"And so, chained and in care of the treasurer himself and the caliph, he was taken to the treasury. Looking about him he at length saw a faint ray penetrating through the plate that had been loosed in the dome.

" 'O Guardian of the Faithful,' said the thief wisely and hopefully, 'do thou place a cauldron of hot pitch under this dome and then see if the thief is not taken.'

"Thereupon the caliph did as advised, the while the treasury was resealed and fresh guards set to watch and daily the pitch was renewed, only Abou and Yussuf came not. Yet in due time, the avarice of Yussuf growing, they chose another night in the dark of the second moon and repaired once more to the treasury, where, so lax already had become the watch, they mounted to the dome. Abou, upon removing the plate, at once detected the odor of pitch and advised Yussuf not to descend, but he would none of this. The thought of the gold and jewels into which on previous nights he had dipped urged him, and he descended. However, when he neared the gold he reached for it, but instead of gold he seized the scalding pitch, which when it burned, caused him to loose his hold and fall. He cried to Abou: I burn in hot pitch. Help me!' Abou descended and took the hand but felt it waver and grow slack. Knowing that death was at hand and that should Yussuf's body be found not only himself but Yussuf's wife and slaves would all suffer, he drew his scimiter, which was ever at his belt, and struck off the head. Fastening this to his belt, he re-ascended the rope, replaced the plate and carefully made his way from the treasury. He then went to the house of Yussuf and gave the head to Yussuf's wife, cautioning her to secrecy.

"But the caliph, coming now every day with his treasurer to look at the treasury, was amazed to find it sealed and yet the headless body within. Knowing not how to solve the mystery of this body, he ordered the thief before him, who advised him to hang the body in the market-place and set guards to watch any who might come to mourn or spy. Accordingly, the headless body was gibbeted and set up in the market-place where Abou, passing afar, recognized it. Fearing that Mirza, the wife of Yussuf, who was of the tribe of the Veddi, upon whom it is obligatory that they mourn in the presence of the dead, should come to mourn here, he hastened to caution her. 'Go thou not thither,' he said; 'or, if thou must, fill two bowls with milk and go as a seller of it. If thou must weep drop one of the bowls as if by accident and make as if thou wept over that.' Mirza accordingly filled two bowls and passing near the gibbet in the public square dropped one and thereupon began weeping as her faith demanded. The guards, noting her, thought nothing—'for here is one,' said they, 'so poor that she cries because of her misfortune.' But the caliph, calling for the guards at the end of the day to report to himself and the master thief, inquired as to what they had seen. 'We saw none,' said the chief of the guard, 'save an old woman so poor that she wept for the breaking of a bowl!' 'Dolts!' cried the master thief. 'Pigs! Did I not say take any who came to mourn? She is the widow of the thief. Try again.

Scatter gold pieces under the gibbet and take any that touch them.'

"The guards scattered gold, as was commanded, and took their positions. Abou, pleased that the widow had been able to mourn and yet not be taken, came now to see what more might be done by the caliph. Seeing the gold he said: 'It is with that he wishes to tempt.' At once his pride in his skill was aroused and he determined to take some of the gold and yet not be taken. To this end he disguised himself as a ragged young beggar and one weak of wit, and with the aid of an urchin younger than himself and as wretched he began to play about the square, running here and there as if in some game. But before doing this he had fastened to the sole of his shoes a thick gum so that the gold might stick. The guards, deceived by the seeming youth and foolishness of Abou and his friend, said: 'These are but a child and a fool. They take no gold.' But by night, coming to count the gold, there were many pieces missing and they were sore afraid. When they reported to the caliph that night he had them flogged and new guards placed in their stead. Yet again he consulted with the master thief, who advised him to load a camel with enticing riches and have it led through the streets of the city by seeming strangers who were the worse for wine. 'This thief who eludes thee will be tempted by these riches and seek to rob them.'

"Soon after it was Abou, who, prowling about the market-place, noticed this camel laden with great wealth and led by seeming strangers. But because it was led to no particular market he thought that it must be of the caliph. He decided to take this also, for there was in his blood that which sought contest, and by now he wished the caliph, because of Yanee, to fix his thought upon him. He filled a skin with the best of wine, into which he placed a drug of the dead Yussuf's devising, and dressing himself as a shabby vendor, set forth. When he came to the street in which was the camel and saw how the drivers idled and gaped, he began to cry, 'Wine for

a para! A drink of wine for a para!' The drivers drank
and found it good, following Abou as he walked, drinking
and chaffering with him and laughing at his dumbness, until
they were within a door of the house of Mirza, the wife of
the dead Yussuf, where was a gate giving into a secret court.
Pausing before this until the wine should take effect, he
suddenly began to gaze upward and then to point. The
drivers looked but saw nothing. And the drug taking effect
they fell down; whereupon Abou quickly led the camel into
the court and closed the gate. When he returned and
found the drivers still asleep he shaved off half the hair of
their heads and their beards, then disappeared and changed
his dress and joined those who were now laughing at the
strangers in their plight, for they had awakened and were
running here and there in search of a camel and its load and
unaware of their grotesque appearance. Mirza, in order to
remove all traces, had the camel killed and the goods distributed. A careful woman and housewifely, she had caused
all the fat to be boiled from the meat and preserved in jars,
it having a medicinal value. The caliph, having learned
how it had gone with his camel, now meditated anew on
how this great thief, who mocked him and who was of great
wit, might be taken. Calling the master thief and others in
council he recited the entire tale and asked how this prince
of thieves might be caught. 'Try but one more ruse, O
master,' said the master thief, who was now greatly shaken
and feared for his life. 'Do thou send an old woman from
house to house asking for camel's grease. Let her plead that
it is for one who is ill. It may be that, fearing detection,
the camel has been slain and the fat preserved. If any is
found, mark the door of that house with grease and take all
within.'

"Accordingly an old woman was sent forth chaffering of
pain. In due time she came to the house of Mirza, who gave
her of the grease, and when she left she made a cross upon
the door. When she returned to the caliph he called his
officers and guards and all proceeded toward the marked

door. In the meantime Abou, having returned and seen the mark, inquired of Mirza as to what it meant. When told of the old woman's visit he called for a bowl of the camel's grease and marked the doors in all the nearest streets. The caliph, coming into the street and seeing the marks, was both enraged and filled with awe and admiration for of such wisdom he had never known. 'I give thee thy life,' he said to the master thief, 'for now I see that thou art as nothing to this one. He is shrewd beyond the wisdom of caliphs and thieves. Let us return,' and he retraced his steps to the palace, curious as to the nature and soul of this one who could so easily outwit him.

"Time went on and the caliph one day said to his vizier: 'I have been thinking of the one who robbed the treasury and my camel and the gold from under the gibbet. Such an one is wise above his day and generation and worthy of a better task. What think you? Shall I offer him a full pardon so that he may appear and be taken—or think you he will appear?' 'Do but try it, O Commander of the Faithful,' said the vizier. A proclamation was prepared and given to the criers, who announced that it was commanded by the caliph that, should the great thief appear on the market-place at a given hour and yield himself up, a pardon full and free would be granted him and gifts of rare value heaped upon him. Yet it was not thus that the caliph intended to do.

"Now, Abou, hearing of this and being despondent over his life and the loss of Yanee and the death of Yussuf and wishing to advantage himself in some way other than by thievery, bethought him how he might accept this offer of the caliph and declare himself and yet, supposing it were a trap to seize him, escape. Accordingly he awaited the time prescribed, and when the public square was filled with guards instructed to seize him if he appeared he donned the costume of a guard and appeared among the soldiers dressed as all the others. The caliph was present to witness the taking, and when the criers surrounding him begged the thief to appear and be pardoned, Abou called out from

the thick of the throng: 'Here I am, O Caliph! Amnesty!'
Whereupon the caliph, thinking that now surely he would
be taken, cried: 'Seize him! Seize him!' But Abou, mingling with the others, also cried: 'Seize him! Seize him!'
and looked here and there as did the others. The guards,
thinking him a guard, allowed him to escape, and the caliph,
once more enraged and chagrined, retired. Once within
his chambers he called to him his chief advisers and had
prepared the following proclamation:

" 'BE IT KNOWN TO ALL

" 'Since within the boundaries of our realm there
exists one so wise that despite our commands and best
efforts he is still able to work his will against ours and
to elude our every effort to detect him, be it known that
from having been amazed and disturbed we are now
pleased and gratified that one so skilful of wit and
resourceful should exist in our realm. To make plain
that our appreciation is now sincere and our anger
allayed it is hereby covenant with him and with all
our people, to whom he may appeal if we fail in our
word, that if he will now present himself in person and
recount to one whom we shall appoint his various adventures, it will be our pleasure to signally distinguish
him above others. Upon corroboration by us of that
which he tells, he shall be given riches, our royal
friendship and a councillor's place in our council. I
have said it.

" 'YIANKO I.'

"This was signed by the caliph and cried in the public
places. Abou heard all but because of the previous treachery
of the caliph he was now unwilling to believe that this was
true. At the same time he was pleased to know that he was
now held in great consideration, either for good or ill, by
the caliph and his advisers, and bethought him that if it were
for ill perhaps by continuing to outwit the caliph he might
still succeed in winning his favor and so to a further knowl-

edge of Yanee. To this end he prepared a reply which he posted in the public square, reading:

" 'PROCLAMATION BY THE ONE WHOM THE CALIPH SEEKS

" 'Know, O Commander of the Faithful, that the one whom the caliph seeks is here among his people free from harm. He respects the will of the caliph and his good intentions, but is restrained by fear. He therefore requests that instead of being commanded to reveal himself the caliph devise a way and appoint a time where in darkness and without danger to himself he may behold the face of the one to whom he is to reveal himself. It must be that none are present to seize him.

" 'THE ONE WHOM THE CALIPH SEEKS.'

"Notice of this reply being brought to the caliph he forthwith took counsel with his advisers and decided that since it was plain the thief might not otherwise be taken, recourse must be had to a device that might be depended upon to lure him. Behind a certain window in the palace wall known as 'The Whispering Window,' and constantly used by all who were in distress or had suffered a wrong which owing to the craft of others there was no hope of righting, sat at stated times and always at night, the caliph's own daughter Yanee, whose tender heart and unseeking soul were counted upon to see to it that the saddest of stories came to the ears of the caliph. It was by this means that the caliph now hoped to capture the thief. To insure that the thief should come it was publicly announced that should any one that came be able to tell how the treasury had been entered and the gold pieces taken from under the gibbet or the camel stolen and killed, he was to be handed a bag of many dinars and a pardon in writing; later, should he present himself, he would be made a councillor of state.

"Struck by this new proclamation and the possibility of once more beholding the princess, Abou decided to match his skill against that of the caliph. He disguised himself as a vendor of tobacco and approached the window, peered through the lattice which screened it and said: 'O daughter of the great caliph, behold one who is in distress. I am he whom the caliph seeks, either to honor or slay, I know not which. Also I am he who, on one of thy journeys to the mountain of Azol and thy palace at Ish-Pari thou beheldest while passing the door of my father's rug-market, for thou didst lift the curtains of thy houdah and also thy veil and didst deign to smile at me. And I have here,' and he touched his heart, 'a faded spray of the myrtles of Ish-Pari, or so it has been told me, over which I weep.'

"Yanee, shocked that she should be confronted with the great thief whom her father sought and that he should claim to be the beautiful youth she so well remembered, and yet fearing this to be some new device of the vizier or of the women of the harem, who might have heard of her strange love and who ever prayed evil against all who were younger or more beautiful than they, she was at a loss how to proceed. Feeling the need of wisdom and charity, she said: 'How sayst thou? Thou are the great thief whom my father seeks and yet the son of a rug-merchant on whom I smiled? Had I ever smiled on a thief, which Allah forbid, would I not remember it and thee? Therefore, if it be as thou sayst, permit it that I should have a light brought that I may behold thee. And if thou art the rug-merchant's son or the great thief, or both, and wishest thy pardon and the bag of dinars which here awaits thee, thou must relate to me how it was the treasury was entered, how the gold was taken from under the gibbet and my father's camel from its drivers.' 'Readily enough, O Princess,' replied Abou, 'only if I am thus to reveal myself to thee must I not know first that thou art the maiden whom I saw? For she was kind as she was fair and would do no man an ill. Therefore if thou wilt lower they veil, as thou didst on the day of thy departure, so that I may see, I will lift my hood so that thou mayst know that I lie not.'

"The princess, troubled to think that the one whom she had so much admired might indeed be the great thief whose life her father sought, and yet wavering between duty to her father and loyalty to her ideal, replied: 'So will I, but upon one condition: should it be that thou art he upon whom thou sayst I looked with favor and yet he who also has committed these great crimes in my father's kingdom, know that thou mayst take thy pardon and thy gold and depart; but only upon the condition that never more wilt thou trouble either me or my father. For I cannot bear to think that I have looked with favor upon one who, however fair, is yet a thief.'

"At this Abou shrank inwardly and a great sorrow fell upon him; for now, as at the death of Yussuf, he saw again the horror of his way. Yet feeling the justice of that which was said, he answered: 'Yea, O Princess, so will I, for I have long since resolved to be done with evil, which was not of my own making, and will trouble thee no more. Should this one glance show me that beloved face over which I have dreamed, I will pass hence, never more to return, for I will not dwell in a realm where another may dwell with thee in love. I am, alas, the great thief and will tell thee how I came by the gold under the gibbet and in thy father's treasury; but I will not take his gold. Only will I accept his pardon sure and true. For though born a thief I am no longer one.' The princess, struck by the nobility of these words as well as by his manner, said sadly, fearing the light would reveal the end of her dreams: 'Be it so. But if thou art indeed he thou wilt tell me how thou camest to be a thief, for I cannot believe that one of whom I thought so well can do so ill.'

"Abou, sadly punished for his deeds, promised, and when the torch was brought the princess lifted her veil. Then it was that Abou again saw the face upon which his soul had dwelt and which had caused him so much unrest. He was now so moved that he could not speak. He drew from his face its disguise and confronted her. And Yanee, seeing for the second time the face of the youth upon whom her memory had dwelt these many days, her heart misgave her and she dared not speak. Instead she lowered her veil and sat in silence, the while Abou recounted the history of his troubled life and early youth, how he could recall nothing of it save that he had been beaten and trained in evil ways until he knew naught else; also of how he came to rob the treasury, and how the deeds since of which the caliph complained had been in part due to his wish to protect the widow of Yussuf and to defeat the skill of the caliph. The princess, admiring his skill and beauty in spite of his deeds, was at a loss how to do. For despite his promise and his proclamation, the caliph had exacted of her that in case Abou appeared she was to aid in his capture, and this she could not do. At last she said: 'Go, and come no more, for I dare not look upon thee, and the caliph wishes thee only ill. Yet let me tell my father that thou wilt trouble him no more,' to which Abou replied: 'Know, O Princess, thus will I do.' Then opening the lattice, Yanee handed him the false pardon and the gold, which Abou would not take. Instead he seized and kissed her hand tenderly and then departed.

"Yanee returned to her father and recounted to him the story of the robbery of the treasury and all that followed, but added that she had not been able to obtain his hand in order to have him seized because he refused to reach for the gold. The caliph, once more chagrined by Abou's cleverness in obtaining his written pardon without being taken, now meditated anew on how he might be trapped. His daughter having described Abou as both young and handsome, the caliph thought that perhaps the bait of his daughter might win him to capture and now prepared the following and last pronunciamento, to wit:

" 'TO THE PEOPLE OF BAGHDAD

" 'Having been defeated in all our contests with the one who signs himself *The One Whom the Caliph Seeks,* and yet having extended to him a full pardon

signed by our own hand and to which has been affixed
the caliphate seal, we now deign to declare that if this
wisest of lawbreakers will now present himself in person before us and accept of us our homage and good
will, we will, assuming him to be young and of agreeable manners, accept him as the affiant of our daughter
and prepare him by education and training for her
hand; or, failing that, and he being a man of mature
years, we will publicly accept him as councillor of state
and chiefest of our advisers. To this end, that he may
have full confidence in our word, we have ordered that
the third day of the seventh moon be observed as a
holiday, that a public feast be prepared and that our
people assemble before us in our great court. Should
this wisest of fugitives appear and declare himself we
will there publicly reaffirm and do as is here written
and accept him into our life and confidence. I have
said it.

" 'YIANKO I.'

"The caliph showed this to his daughter and she sighed,
for full well she knew that the caliph's plan would prove
vain—for had not Abou said that he would return no more?
But the caliph proceeded, thinking this would surely bring
about Abou's capture.

"In the meantime in the land of Yemen, of which Abou
was the rightful heir, many things had transpired. His
father, Kar-Shem, having died and the wretched pretender,
Bab-el-Bar, having failed after a revolution to attain to
Kar-Shem's seat, confessed to the adherents of Kar-Shem
the story of the Prince Hussein's abduction and sale into
slavery to a rug-merchant in Baghdad. In consequence,
heralds and a royal party were at once sent forth to discover
Hussein. They came to Baghdad and found the widow of
Yussuf, who told them of the many slaves Yussuf had
owned, among them a child named Hussein to whom they
had given the name of Abou.

"And so, upon Abou's return from 'The Whispering Window,' there were awaiting him at the house of Mirza the representatives of his own kingdom, who, finding him young and handsome and talented, and being convinced by close questioning that he was really Hussein, he was apprised of his dignity and worth and honored as the successor of Kar-Shem in the name of the people of Yemen.

"And now Hussein (once Abou), finding himself thus ennobled, bethought him of the beautiful Yanee and her love for him and his undying love for her. Also he felt a desire to outwit the caliph in one more contest. To this end he ordered his present entourage to address the caliph as an embassy fresh from Yemen, saying that having long been in search of their prince they had now found him, and to request of him the courtesy of his good-will and present consideration for their lord. The caliph, who wished always to be at peace with all people, and especially those of Yemen, who were great and powerful, was most pleased at this and sent a company of courtiers to Hussein, who now dwelt with his entourage at one of the great caravanseries of the city, requesting that he come forthwith to the palace that he might be suitably entertained. And now Abou, visiting the caliph in his true figure, was received by him in great state, and many and long were the public celebrations ordered in his honor.

"Among these was the holiday proclaimed by Yianko in order to entrap Abou. And Yianko, wishing to amuse and entertain his guest, told him the full history of the great thief and of his bootless efforts thus far to take him. He admitted to Hussein his profound admiration for Abou's skill and ended by saying that should any one know how Abou might be taken he would be willing to give to that one a place in his council, or, supposing he were young and noble, the hand of his daughter. At this Hussein, enticed by the thought of so winning Yanee, declared that he himself would attempt to solve the mystery and now prepared to appear as a fierce robber, the while he ordered one of his followers to impersonate himself as prince for that day.

"The great day of the feast having arrived and criers having gone through the streets of the city announcing the feast and the offer of the caliph to Abou, there was much rejoicing. Long tables were set in the public square, and flags and banners were strung. The beautiful Yanee was told of her father's vow to Hussein, but she trusted in Abou and his word and his skill and so feared naught. At last, the multitude having gathered and the caliph and his courtiers and the false Hussein having taken their places at the head of the feast, the caliph raised his hand for silence. The treasurer taking his place upon one of the steps leading to the royal board, reread the proclamation and called upon Abou to appear and before all the multitude receive the favor of the caliph or be forever banned. Abou, or Hussein, who in the guise of a fierce mountain outlaw had mingled with the crowd, now came forward and holding aloft the pardon of the caliph announced that he was indeed the thief and could prove it. Also, that as written he would exact of the caliph his daughter's hand. The caliph, astounded that one so uncouth and fierce-seeming should be so wise as the thief had proved or should ask of him his daughter's hand, was puzzled and anxious for a pretext on which he might be restrained. Yet with all the multitude before him and his word given, he scarce knew how to proceed or what to say. Then it was that Yanee, concealed behind a lattice, sent word to her father that this fierce soul was not the one who had come to her but an impostor. The caliph, now suspecting treachery and more mischief, ordered this seeming false Abou seized and bound, whereupon the fictitious Hussein, masquerading in Hussein's clothes, came forward and asked for the bandit's release for the reason that he was not a true bandit at all but the true prince, whom they had sought far and wide.

"Then the true Hussein, tiring of the jest and laying aside his bandit garb, took his place at the foot of the throne and proceeded to relate to Yianko the story of his life. At this the caliph, remembering his word and seeing in Abou, now that he was the Prince of Yemen, an entirely satisfactory husband for Yanee, had her brought forward. Yanee, astonished and confused at being thus confronted with her lost love, now become a Prince, displayed so much trepidation and coquetry that the caliph, interested and amused and puzzled, was anxious to know the cause. Whereupon Hussein told how he had seen her passing his robber father's bazaar on her way to Ish-Pari and that he had ever since bemoaned him that he was so low in the scale of life as not to be able to aspire to her hand yet now rejoiced that he might make his plea. The caliph, realizing how true a romance was here, now asked his daughter what might be her will, to which she coyly replied that she had never been able to forget Abou. Hussein at once reiterated his undying passion, saying that if Yanee would accept him for her husband and the caliph as his son he would there and then accept her as his queen and that their nuptials should be celebrated before his return to his kingdom. Whereupon the caliph, not to be outdone in gallantry, declared that he would gladly accept so wise a prince, not only as his son by marriage but as his heir, and that at his death both he and Yanee were jointly to rule over his kingdom and their own. There followed scenes of great rejoicing among the people, and Hussein and Yanee rode together before them.

"And now, O my hearers," continued Gazzar most artfully, although his tale was done, "ye have heard how it was with Abou the unfortunate, who came through cleverness to nothing but good—a beautiful love, honor and wealth and the rule of two realms—whereas I, poor wanderer that I am—"

But the company, judging that he was about to plead for more anna, and feeling, and rightly, that for so thin a tale he had been paid enough and to spare, arose and as one man walked away. Soudi and Parfi denounced him as a thief and a usurer; and Gazzar, counting his small store of anna and looking betimes at the shop of Al Hadjaz, from which still came the odors of food, and then in the direction of the caravan where lay the camels among which he must sleep, sighed. For he saw that for all his pains he had not more than the half of a meal and a bed and that for the morrow there was nothing.

"By Allah," he sighed, "what avails it if one travel the world over to gather many strange tales and keep them fresh and add to them as if by myrrh and incense and the color of the rose and the dawn, if by so doing one may not come by so much as a meal or a bed? Bismillah! Were it not for my withered arm no more would I trouble to tell a tale!" And tucking his tambour into his rags he turned his steps wearily toward the mosque, where before eating it was, as the Koran commanded, that he must pray.

THE END